RETURN TO THE GARDEN CITY

By the same author

The Colonial Gentleman's Son, Book Guild Publishing, 2010

RETURN TO THE GARDEN CITY

John Powell

Book Guild Publishing
Sussex, England

First published in Great Britain in 2013 by
The Book Guild Ltd
The Werks
45 Church Road
Hove, BN3 2BE

Copyright © John Powell 2013

The right of John Powell to be identified as the author
of this work has been asserted by him in accordance with the
Copyright, Designs and Patents Act 1988.

Typesetting in Garamond by
Keyboard Services, Luton, Bedfordshire

Printed and bound in Great Britain by
CPI Antony Rowe

A catalogue record for this book is available from
The British Library

ISBN 978 1 84624 949 5

BURKINA FASO

Bolgatanga

G H A N A

Wa

Tamale
Yendi

TOGO

CÔTE
D'IVOIRE

Lake
Volta

Wenchi

Sunyani

Techiman

Kumasi

Konongo

Obuasi

Ho

Oda

Koforidua

Akosombo

Tarkwa

Tema
Accra

Cape Coast

Takoradi

| 0 | Kilometres | 200 |

| 0 | | 150 |

Contents

1

A Rough Landing

Kwame couldn't believe what Akosua had told him. How could Comfort have been so thoughtless as to put live snails in their daughter's luggage? 'Are you sure your mother packed live snails for Auntie Akos?' he asked.

'Yes, Dad; she said Auntie Akos Mary would be very happy to have them.'

'Does Afriyie know they are there?'

'No, you're the only one I've told.'

'Perhaps Mummy told Afriyie.'

'I don't think so; she told me not to tell anybody until we met Auntie Akos.'

'But you told me.'

'Yes Dad, but Mummy knows I tell you everything.'

Kwame wasn't so sure.

The snails in question were African forest snails, as large as tennis balls but with pointed conical shells. They were a delicacy much enjoyed in the soups eaten with fufu in the villages of southern Ghana. According to Akosua they were being sent to Akos Mary, the Ghanaian wife of Kwame's friend, Dr Tom Arthur. It seemed that since she had been living in England Akos Mary had missed eating snails and had taken the opportunity of their trip to have some brought to her. If that was all, it would be innocent enough, and Kwame's only worry would concern the legality of bringing live snails into the UK. Would he need to declare them on arrival at Customs, and would he be allowed to carry them through?

It was that last conversation with Comfort in Kumasi that now cast a dark shadow on his mind. She had told him that the drugs traffickers were now concealing cocaine inside the shells of live snails. He could not believe that Comfort was involved with the drugs cartel. It was she who had prevented him from inadvertently becoming a courier on his first

1

trip to the UK in 1985, and she had repeatedly expressed her disapproval of the cartel's activities. So he found it hard to believe that the snails intended for Akos Mary were anything but wholesome food. At the same time he wondered why Comfort had not told him about the snails. Was it just a joke to be enjoyed when Akos Mary served up the snails in a steaming bowl of fufu?

Then another thought came to him: what if the cartel had found a way to insert the contraband snails into Akosua's luggage, perhaps by substituting Comfort's innocent package? Or had they found some way to coerce Comfort, either by threats to Akosua at school in Kumasi or some other way? Comfort had borrowed money from Lebanese businessmen to fund her shoe importation; could she have unwittingly indebted herself to the cartel? Could Comfort ever have done anything unwittingly? It was hard to believe. This woman whom he had loved and admired, as much for her brain as for her beauty, was an idol he could never imagine falling from her pedestal.

Every minute as he pondered his dilemma the airliner was carrying Kwame fifteen kilometres closer to his destination. He must make up his mind about what to do on arrival. He couldn't consult his fourteen-year-old daughter but it might be worth rousing Afriyie from her slumbers. Noticing that Akosua had once again fallen asleep, he gently roused his sleeping partner. Afriyie woke slowly and reluctantly with a series of deep yawns. 'Not there already,' she complained.

'No, but I want to ask you something.'

'What is it?'

'Do you know what Comfort is sending to Akos Mary?'

'Some shoes?'

'No, I mean Ghanaian food.'

'Yams and plantain – that sort of thing?'

'Yes, do you know about it?'

'No, what is she sending?'

'Akosua told me she is sending live snails.'

'Akos Mary loves snails.'

'That's not the point; will we be allowed to take them through customs?'

'What's wrong with snails?'

'The *abrofo* probably don't allow in live animals.'

'Then we either don't tell them or we leave them at the airport.'

Kwame realised that Afriyie was unaware of the possible illegal uses of the monster molluscs. 'Comfort told me that the drugs smugglers are using live snails to carry cocaine to London,' he said.

'How do they do that?'

'They have a way of cutting the shells and putting the drugs inside.'

'Do they glue them closed again?'

'I suppose so.'

'Well, Comfort wouldn't do that.'

'That's what I think, but I can't be sure.'

'I'm sure.'

Kwame wanted to follow Afriyie in believing that his only problem was the live condition of the snails. He felt that there would be no problem if the snails were dead. He wasn't sure, but he thought that meat for private consumption could be imported, while live animals needed a special licence and health certificate. Would the snails be alive? Comfort's remarks seemed to imply that the snails usually survived the journey but it seemed likely that there would be some fatalities. Here was a Schrödinger's cat situation: the condition of the snails couldn't be known until the suitcase was opened. Until then they must be considered both alive and dead. If alive they should be declared to customs; if dead, perhaps not.

Remembering how he had reluctantly been recruited into helping the UK Customs break up a Kumasi-based drugs cartel operating in Britain, Kwame felt that he had established a sound reputation that he wanted to keep. He believed that if he was open in declaring the live snails, whatever the outcome, he would be believed by the officials and would not get himself or his family into serious trouble. So, he concluded, that would be his decided policy, but he found it difficult to sleep through the remainder of the journey.

After disembarking they made their way through immigration control to the baggage hall. Fourteen-year-old Akosua insisted on finding the carousel and standing guard on a luggage trolley until the bags began to arrive. Two of their suitcases arrived early but there was a long delay before the third and last bag reached Kwame's outstretched hand. With it came the moment of truth. Now, for the first time, on arrival in Britain Kwame led his family past the red 'Something to Declare' sign.

He handed the three passports to the uniformed official and lifted the offending case onto the table, asking Akosua for the key. 'Where are you coming from?' was the first question.

'Accra, Ghana.'

'What do you want to declare?'

'I believe that there are live snails in this case.'

'What do you mean by *you believe*? Don't you know what you put in the case?'

'My ex-wife packed the case for our daughter – it's her case.'

'It's your responsibility to know what's in the case.'

'I appreciate that; it was an oversight.'

'Please open it.'

Kwame opened the case prepared for a surprise and was relieved at first to see the usual collection of balls of kenke, jars of shito and packets of gari, filling the spaces between yams, coco-yams and hands of green plantain. Then he noticed the string of snails, still lashed together with the coarse dried-grass cord. Most appeared to be dormant inside their shells but a few of the more adventurous creatures were extending long grey feelers, a sure indication of invertebrate life. 'They're alive all right!' exclaimed the official, signalling to a superior officer that he needed help.

The two officials consulted, moving away out of earshot. Kwame guessed that they were considering the possibility of the snails, and perhaps other commodities, concealing more sinister cargo. He remembered how a decade earlier balls of kenke had been used to smuggle cannabis and how, but for the vigilance of Comfort, he might himself have been drawn into the trade. Now he was hoping that he would be able to escape from Heathrow with his reputation untarnished.

The junior official returned to the table and it was clear from his expression that he was not the bringer of good tidings. 'I'm afraid that we must search all your bags and you will be detained while tests are carried out,' he said. Then the officer was joined by two other colleagues for a thorough rummage through all three suitcases and their hand baggage. Kwame sensed the concern of Akosua and Afriyie as they drew closer to him on each side. 'Don't worry, it will be all right,' he told them quietly in Twi.

After the bag search was completed the three Ghanaians were conducted to a small lounge where they were asked to wait.

'Why are we here Dad? I want to see Auntie Akos and Uncle Tom.'

'I'm sure they will wait for us; it won't be long.'

It was longer than Kwame had hoped, and when the official came back Kwame could feel his heart pounding. 'I'm afraid that we cannot allow you to take the snails with you but otherwise you are free to proceed,' said the man. 'But if you can spare a few minutes more we have someone who would like to see you.' Kwame was about to complain that they were already very late meeting their friends when he saw a familiar face with a broad welcoming grin. It was Leon Thornet, the senior customs officer who had recruited Kwame as an interpreter when he was a student at Warwick University in 1987. He greeted Kwame with, 'It's good to see you again, Mr Mainu. Are you back for more studies?'

'It's good to see you. How are Jack and David?'

'They're fine thanks; Jack's still here, but David has been transferred to Edinburgh.'

'Do you remember Afriyie and Akosua?'

'How could I forget the lady who left the kenke on the plane? As for Akosua, she has grown a lot but I still recognise her father's smile.'

'I'm sorry about the snails. Did they present a problem?'

'Look! Why don't we let the ladies go on to meet their friends while you and I have a little chat?'

Leon Thornet called a female official and asked her to take Afriyie and Akosua through to the arrivals hall where Tom and Akos Mary had been waiting patiently. 'Don't be long, Dad,' Akosua called back as they hurried away. Leon led Kwame to a small office and they sat down. 'You were right to declare the snails. I'm sorry that we couldn't let them in, but next time, bring a health certificate and an import licence.'

'I hope there won't be a next time. It was Comfort who packed them without telling me.'

'Ah yes, Comfort, I'm sorry you split up.'

'It was the arrests in Ghana that did it I'm afraid.'

'But they're letting them out now, aren't they?'

'Yes, one man died in prison and then they released the others.'

'That's a worry for us.'

'Do you expect them to start again?'

'It's not a matter of expectation, they already have. It's a constant battle against heroin and cocaine smugglers these days.'

'Well, I came to England hoping to work for a few years but I'm not looking for another job with HM Customs.'

'That's a shame because I still need a reliable Twi translator.'

'Please, not me this time.'

'Here's my card; give me a call if you change your mind.'

Kwame followed his family out into the arrivals hall and joined in the reunion with Tom and Akos Mary. 'We're going to stay with Uncle Tom and Auntie Akos, Dad,' said Akosua excitedly.

Over their handshake Kwame asked, 'Are you sure that's OK, Tom?' but any doubts he might have had were swept away by a chorus of approval from the other four. 'Well, just until we get ourselves settled,' he ended in surrender.

In Tom's Range Rover on the M25 Kwame experienced a real time

5

déjà vu. The scene recalled the drive on the motorway from Accra to Tema on Tom's last visit to Ghana. The two men, sitting in front, were updating each other in English; the two women in the back chatted in Twi, and Akosua did her best to monitor both conversations and ensure that all her contributions were heard. Kwame again reflected with pride on the bilingual skills of his daughter, but the teenager's English dried up when Akos Mary told Afriyie that she was pregnant. This was a topic that demanded total attention.

'I hope you'll be able to help me,' said Akos Mary to Afriyie.

'Don't worry, I'll be there,' replied Afriyie, and Akosua added, 'I will also do whatever you need.' Then switching to English she said, 'I will be your babysitter-in-chief.' Kwame, catching the gist of the back seat conversation, said to Tom, 'So you've managed it at last! Congratulations! What's your ETA?'

'He should be here in time for Christmas.'

'He! Are you sure?'

'These days they can tell you from an ultrasound scan.'

'There's always something new in England!'

Kwame also congratulated Akos Mary. He knew how proud she must be to be bearing a son. 'Have you told your father?' he asked in Twi.

'No, I haven't seen him since you chased him away. Please don't say anything to Tom. He thinks that Papa went back to Ghana after the wedding.' Kwame assured her that the secret was still safe with him. Akosua seemed about to say something but a sharp look from her father conveyed the curse of the *mmoatia*, forest spirits that are believed to strike people dumb.

In spite of much traffic on the motorway the happy conversation sped the miles away and they soon reached Tom and Akos Mary's pleasant residence in the Warwickshire countryside. 'You have a nice place here,' remarked Kwame.

'Yes, thanks to Dad.'

'How are Dr Arthur Senior and his good lady?'

'They're fine, and looking forward to seeing you again.'

'Are they happy to become grandparents?'

'They can't wait.'

Later that evening, when the girls were looking at catalogues of baby goods, Kwame and Tom had a chance for a serious discussion. First Tom wanted to know what had caused their precipitous departure from Ghana, and so Kwame told him how Uncle George had died in prison and Mama Kate and the Lebanese cartel members had been set free. Comfort had

6

warned him that a revitalised cartel might again try to recruit him and might threaten Akosua to achieve that end. He could no longer leave Akosua alone at boarding school in Kumasi. He also suspected that corrupt elements in the Ghana Regional Industrial Development Project (GRID) were connected to the drug traffickers and enjoyed a similar level of political protection.

'So you ran out of options for continuing your good work,' said Tom.

'That's the situation until we get a government that will make a greater effort to oppose crime and corruption.'

'When can the government be changed?'

'Elections must be held at the end of 1999; if we can trust Rawlings to stick to the Constitution.'

'In the meantime, how do you see our link with the Technology Consultancy Centre?'

'You have no problem with the TCC.'

'That's a relief!'

Tom now turned to Kwame's personal situation. 'What are you planning to do while you're in the UK?'

'I'm hoping to get an academic job. Is there any chance here at Warwick?'

'That's what I've been wondering about. Would you like to join my team liaising with the TCC?'

'That would be ideal, but would I need to go to Ghana?'

'We could keep you here for some time – maybe a year – but I think that some short trips would be essential after that.'

'I hadn't planned on going back until there was a change of government, but with my family safe I might risk short trips, hoping I won't be noticed.'

'Give it more thought; talk it over with Afriyie.'

'Right, I will.'

Kwame was delighted at the prospect of a job arising so quickly, especially a job working with Tom, but he had a feeling of being rushed into making a decision. There was also the problem of trips back to Ghana. Could he really slip in and out without being noticed by the cartel? How keenly would they be on the lookout for him? Could they again pose a threat to his people in the UK? He didn't want to create once more a situation in which his family needed to be hidden away in a safe house. He pondered these issues for a few days before taking Tom's advice to talk it over with Afriyie.

The girls were planning yet another shopping expedition but Kwame asked Afriyie to stay behind. 'You like it here, don't you?' he began.

'I like being near Akos Mary and Tom.'

'Would you like me to work here with Tom?'

'Where would we live?'

'We would have to look for our own place: a house or a flat.'

'Near here?'

'As near as possible; it would depend on what's available.'

'I would like to be near here.'

'If I work with Tom it will involve some short trips to Ghana; would you mind that?'

'Not if you promise not to take any new girl.'

Afriyie wasn't being much help, but Kwame realised that he had always shielded her from fully appreciating the potential danger of his situation. He decided to be more blunt. 'You do realise that Peter Sarpong's people might want to take revenge on me for helping the UK customs put them in prison?'

'Do you think they will be waiting for you to go back to Ghana?'

'I'm not sure, but it's possible.'

'You could wait before going; they will grow tired.'

'Tom says I could wait for one year.'

'That's good.'

Kwame still wasn't sure that Afriyie had fully grasped the situation but at least she would mount no strong opposition. Sometimes he missed Comfort's quick wits and sharp intuition. Maybe he should write to ask her how she saw the prospect of short visits. It needn't prevent him starting the work; he had plenty of time to get feedback before the first trip would be scheduled. He decided to tell Tom that he was interested in the position on offer.

The next day Tom drove them to the university. They went first to the faculty office where Kwame filled in an application form and handed in a copy of his CV. Then Tom suggested that they could go to his office for a more detailed discussion of what the new job would involve. Kwame thought he knew the way, but Tom led him in a different direction. 'Isn't this where the professors have their offices?' Kwame asked.

'That's right,' said Tom with a wide grin, and then Kwame saw the name on the door before him. 'Congratulations! Why didn't you tell me?' he cried, seizing his friend's hand and then enveloping him in a bear hug.

'I wanted it to be a surprise,' gasped the new professor, 'but I think I'll break my news more gently in future.'

Once they were settled in his office Tom said, 'You'll have to come for an interview in the usual way. There are two other candidates for the post. It will be appointed at the grade of research fellow, that's equivalent to lecturer, but a person judged to have more experience might be appointed senior research fellow.'

'How do you rate my chances?'

'I can't see anyone having more relevant experience. You probably qualify for the senior position.'

'Will you be on the appointments board?'

'Nominally yes, but if I write a reference for you, as I will of course, I feel that I should withdraw from the interview and leave the final decision to my colleagues.'

'I understand.'

'You'll need two references. Who else will give you one?'

'The best person would be Dr Jones but he's in Ghana.'

'Why not ring him and ask him to fax his reference? You have time for that.'

'Good idea, I'll do it today.'

Kwame wanted to know what his duties might entail.

'Initially I feel that we would ask you to advise on which Kumasi people should come here to train or research,' said Tom, 'and then you would help in arranging the appropriate programmes and monitoring progress.' He handed Kwame a printed copy of the job description.

'Will I be able to do my own research?'

'Of course, I was only outlining the administrative part.'

'I would like to do more towards making diesel engines in Ghana.'

'That will be ideal – be sure to mention it at your interview.'

'I'll do more than that; I'll show them my paper.'

'Good man!'

'I'm looking forward to this.'

'Don't count your *akoko* before they're hatched! There, I've remembered some Twi.'

'Don't worry, I'll prepare well for the interview – in English!'

Back at home, Tom and Kwame were relaxing when the three ladies returned with more bulging bags of neonatal necessities. 'Do you know who we saw in Marks and Spencer?' cried Akosua, rushing to her father.

'Mrs Chichester?'

'Oh Dad, how did you guess?'

'I couldn't think of anyone else who would get you so excited.'

'She says I can go there tomorrow to bake a cake. Can I go?'

'Perhaps Uncle Tom could drop us there on his way to work. Shall we ask him?'

'No problem, Miss Sunday,' said Tom.

Kwame was nearly as pleased to see his old landlady as Akosua, and they all had much news to share in bringing each other up to date. However, the cake baking could not be too long delayed, so Kwame left the experts searching for the big bowl and walked the short distance to the foundry school where he hoped to see his old instructor, employer and friend, Fred Brown. This time he was out of luck. 'Fred took early retirement and moved to Spain with his family,' explained his successor Martin Hutchinson, 'but there are several of us still here who remember you, especially the talk you gave about your work in Ghana.'

'Well, I've come back here to work for a few years.'

'Here, at the foundry school?'

'No, I didn't mean that, but somewhere around Coventry.'

'With Professor Arthur at the university?'

'That's a possibility.'

Kwame explained how he hoped to do some research into the manufacture of diesel engines. He might want to experiment with some of the processes at the foundry school; would that be possible?

'I'm sure we could help you,' said Martin, 'as long as you have funds to cover material and labour costs. The experience will be very good for our students. They will be interested to know that what we do here is to be reproduced in Africa.'

'Then I'll be back to discuss the details if I get the position at Warwick,' said Kwame.

'When will the cake be ready?' he asked when he got back to the Chichester residence. 'Not until teatime, Dad,' said the junior chef with a reproving look, 'but Mrs Chichester has made us some lunch to keep us going.'

'For a long time, if I remember Mrs Chichester's lunches,' said Kwame.

'Just a snack,' called a voice from the kitchen.

After lunch, Kwame relaxed with a newspaper and the TV until it was deemed to be time for tea and the welcoming cake was consumed with due ceremony. 'You must take the rest home for the professor and the ladies,' said Mrs Chichester. 'Be sure to come again soon and bring the others.'

Kwame asked about the ladies club. His one-time landlady replied that it was still functioning but not like when he was barman.

'Is the new barman supplying all Ethel's needs?' he joked, but immediately felt he had said the wrong thing.

'I'm afraid Ethel's heavy drinking caught up with her. She passed away just a few months ago.'

'Oh, I'm very sorry,' said Kwame, surprised that he felt a real sense of loss. He had admired the older woman's determined hedonism, at the same time as fearing its likely outcome.

Within a few days Kwame realised that he had reconnected with his old life in Coventry. It was as if he had never been away. The cares that had brought him from Ghana had receded to the back of his mind. He was glad that Peter Sarpong was still detained at Her Majesty's Pleasure and was not around to complicate his life. At the same time he wondered who had taken Peter's place as cartel coordinator and self-appointed leader of the local Kumasi community. He decided that life would be more peaceful if he remained in ignorance but feared that Peter's successor might find him out.

The day of the interviews soon arrived. Tom drove Kwame to the campus and then they went their separate ways. Kwame reported to the secretary of the head of department and was asked to wait in an outer office. He was joined by two others. The man appeared to be native British and the woman seemed to be of Asian origin. It was clear that they knew one another, and in the course of conversation Kwame learned that they were both junior members of Tom's team hoping for promotion to a more senior position.

Kwame always had difficulty in judging the age of different races but he had the impression that the other two were his juniors. This gave him no reassurance, as he knew that most people in Britain gained their qualifications at an early age. He could only hope that his years of practical experience, both pre- and post-graduation, would be given due weight.

The lady was first to be called. It seemed that she was soon out again. Looking glum and saying nothing, she hurried out of the office. Much to his surprise Kwame was called next. He looked in vain for Tom's friendly face but recognised two of the four members of the interview board. Wishing them all 'Good morning', he took the lonely seat and faced his fate. The chairman introduced himself and his colleagues, two men and a woman. He asked Kwame to confirm his identity and say a few words about his background. Then he was asked to say why he wanted the position.

'I have devoted my career to date to trying to assist the economic development of my country by promoting grassroots and small-scale industries,' he began. 'I came to Warwick to study for my first degree and I had the opportunity to assist Professor Arthur in negotiating the agreement between this university and my university in Kumasi. Having studied here, and having worked for five years at the TCC, your partner in Ghana, I feel I have the right background to nurture an effective collaboration that will yield benefits for my country and for Warwick University.'

'You have work experience outside the university, don't you?' interjected one of the panel.

'Yes, I worked for the GRID Project for more than four years and then I spent about eighteen months with an NGO, Appropriate Technology Ghana.'

'Why did GRID choose Cranfield for your post-graduate studies?'

'My director, Dr Jones, liked the MSc in Production Management programme with its strong links to industry. He sent three or four of us there.'

'Were you satisfied with the programme?'

'Yes, very satisfied.'

'Mr Mainu, what do you see as the next challenge to the small-scale engineering industry in Ghana?' It was the chairman who was speaking.

'My own idea is that we should start producing a small diesel engine for water pumping, corn milling and electricity generation in remote areas.'

'What is needed to achieve this objective?'

'We already have most of the basic technologies. I would like to show you this paper in which I have listed what we already have, what we can easily add, and where we still need some technical help from Warwick to complete the competency.'

Kwame passed to the chairman four copies of his paper, which was based on the drawings that Fred Brown had given him. The board took a few moments to study the document. 'Would this paper form the basis of your own personal research if you gained this position?' the chairman asked.

'That's my plan.'

'And you would seek collaboration from the foundry school, Cranfield University and the Ford Motor Company?'

'Yes, they all have something to contribute.'

'You certainly believe in networking!'

'Now Mr Mainu, hitherto you have worked in Ghana and only come to the UK for training and education,' said the lady from human resources. 'Why have you now left your country to seek work in the UK?' This was the question that Kwame had hoped to avoid. How frank should he be in answering? Then he remembered that he had been forced to be very frank on a previous occasion at Warwick, when he had been asked to advise on the negotiations with Kumasi. It had been the best policy then, and was probably the best policy now.

'I would not have left Ghana if my family had not been in danger,' he began. 'While I was studying at Warwick I assisted the British authorities in breaking up a Kumasi-based drugs cartel. Some people were also arrested in Ghana and this made me potential enemies. Recently some prisoners were released and my ex-wife pointed out that our daughter at boarding school in Kumasi seemed to be very vulnerable to any revenge directed against me. So I decided to leave for a few years in the hope that the situation might improve, perhaps with a change of government in 2000. However, I want very much to continue to help my country through my work, and this position at Warwick is the ideal opportunity.'

'Thank you for being so frank with us,' said the chairman. He turned to his colleagues. 'Do you have any more questions?'

'We have heard about a drugs cartel in Kumasi and there are rumours of corruption and nepotism at GRID,' said one professor whom Kwame did not know. 'Can Mr Mainu comment on the integrity of the people at the TCC? We're not twinned with a den of thieves are we?' The chairman frowned and asked Kwame to ignore the last remark.

'I must emphasise that the TCC is a quite exceptional organisation,' said Kwame, trying to subdue his anger and follow the chairman's advice. 'In Ghana many professionals join an organisation to gain a few years' experience and then move on, often overseas. At the TCC, however, people find the work so interesting that they stay on indefinitely. Both the director and deputy director have served for more than twenty years, and several other senior members have been at post for more than ten years. The team in Kumasi not only maintained their local work programme but recently implemented a three-year project in Malawi for the World Bank, on a contract won in open international competition.

'As for integrity, several of the senior people have gained international recognition for publications in Europe and the USA and short assignments for UN agencies, yet they have stayed based in Ghana and accepted the deprivation that that entails. They suffer the ridicule of those who ran away for driving an old car and not having built a house, but thousands of poor men and women sing their praises for having provided them with their livelihoods.'

The chairman turned to his outspoken colleague. 'Well, that answers your question, Professor Thomas. We must be grateful that Mr Mainu has chosen to serve as an engineer when he could so easily have become a politician or a lawyer.' Then turning back to Kwame he added, 'That will be all for now. Please wait outside; we may need you again.'

After exchanging places with the other candidate, Kwame wondered if he had spoken too long and too strongly. Professor Thomas's remark had angered him and he had felt it a matter of national honour to give a firm repost. Yet he had said nothing that he could not fully justify. He was not allowed much time to lower his chest, however, as a rather crestfallen young man told him that the chairman wanted him to return to the interview room.

This time the panel had been joined by Tom Arthur. They were all grinning, even Professor Thomas. The chairman held out his hand. 'Congratulations, Mr Mainu, we are appointing you Senior Research Fellow attached to Professor Arthur's Kumasi liaison group on a three-year contract. Your appointment letter with full details of pay and conditions will follow shortly. May I say how happy I am to have you on our team. I hope that you and your family will have a happy stay.'

'Let's go back and tell the girls to get ready for a celebratory dinner out,' said Tom, as soon as they met up in the car park.

'You weren't at the interview, Tom, but you must have worked hard behind the scenes.'

'Don't undervalue yourself, my friend; you impressed them all, even Professor Thomas.'

'Well he made me angry, asking if the TCC was a den of thieves.'

'They told me you answered with passion! I would have expected nothing less.'

'I hope I didn't say too much.'

'Not at all. The chairman said that, if you were typical of the TCC people, we had found ourselves excellent partners.'

It was Kwame's happiest evening for a long time. Not only was he feeling safe in England but he had secured himself good employment for the next three years. Best of all, he would still be working to help his people home in Ghana. He still had much to do: find a house to please Afriyie, a school to suit Akosua and a car to join them together, but he was charged with energy to face these tasks. The dinner wasn't fufu and Star beer, but it tasted almost as good!

2

Settling In

Kwame asked Tom for two weeks to sort out his domestic arrangements before taking up his regular duties. 'Maybe if I help we can speed things up,' said Tom, and Kwame explained that he needed somewhere to live and a school for Akosua.

'Let's take them one at a time. First a place to stay; what's wrong with here?' Tom said.

'You won't want us here all the time, but we'd like to be near.'

'Well the university has been buying up properties around here with a view to establishing a satellite campus. The project is several years away and in the meantime they're letting the houses to staff. Some of them are very nice.'

'The houses or the staff?'

'Both, but it's a house you need.'

'Do you think I could get one?'

'We can put your name on the list right away. Let's call at the office this afternoon. We might even be given keys to look at one or two places.'

'Then we'd better take Afriyie and Akosua.'

'We'll all go.'

'Even Dr Tom Arthur the third?'

'Even he!'

When considering the women in his life there were two topics that Kwame always disliked discussing: funerals and houses. So it was with some trepidation that he broached the latter topic with Afriyie. 'Tom says that we can rent a nice house from the university.'

'Why will you rent and not buy?'

'We don't know how long we will stay here. Renting is better for short periods.'

'Will it be near here?'

'That's what Tom says.'

'Tom has a car; what about walking?'

'We may be able to see for ourselves this afternoon.'

Tom led them to the estates office and Kwame filled in the application form. Then armed with two sets of keys they set out to see what might become available. They had been warned that the houses were empty and unfurnished, although they had been redecorated. Kwame worried that they would not look attractive to Afriyie, and he was grateful to Akos Mary for offering to lend them some furniture and to help them find whatever else they needed to make the chosen place homely. 'It shouldn't take a seamstress long to run up some attractive curtains and furniture covers,' she'd added, but Afriyie warned her that it would mean less time for making baby clothes.

Much to Kwame's relief, Afriyie agreed that the houses were within reasonable walking distance of Tom's house. One, a fairly modern three-bedroom detached house, was deemed to be acceptable, and Tom said they could register their preference when returning the keys. They were told that the house was scheduled for allocation at the end of the month. 'You will stay with us while you wait,' said Akos Mary to Afriyie, and Kwame was happy that his partner had raised no unreasonable difficulties.

Next morning Akos Mary was dressing Afriyie's hair and Akosua claimed to be helping. This gave Kwame the opportunity to broach the matter of a school for Akosua. 'She was going to a girls' secondary school in Ghana,' he told Tom.

'Do you want a girls' school here?'

'That's what I'd prefer.'

'According to Yellow Pages there's only one state school for girls around here and you're not in the catchment area.'

'What's the alternative?'

'There are two independent schools: one in Leamington and one in Warwick.'

'You pay fees for those, don't you?'

'That's right.'

'Well, I was paying fees in Ghana.'

'Here the fees will be much higher.'

'I don't mind if the education is good.'

'Then I'll ring them and get them to send prospectuses.'

The prospectuses arrived next day and Kwame called Akosua to come and read them carefully. 'Tell me which school you prefer and we will go there and see how it is,' he said.

'Like when we went to St Louis?'

'Just like that, Little One.'

'Will I do another test?'

'I expect so, but we can't be sure.'

Akosua came back to announce that she wanted to go to The King's High School for Girls in Warwick. 'It's more than a hundred years old,' she announced, 'founded in 1879!' Kwame agreed that would also be his preference and telephoned to arrange an appointment to visit. He was told that it could be scheduled during the following week and in the meantime he would be posted an application form to fill in and bring with him.

That afternoon, Kwame wrote to Comfort.

Coventry
10th August 1994

Dear Comfort,

This is to let you know that we arrived safely and are all well. You will be pleased to hear that Akos Mary is expecting a son before Xmas. Yes, in England they can tell you in advance! Afriyie and Akosua are very excited and involved in all the preparations. Tom and Akos Mary have a nice house but not perhaps quite up to your standards. They have given me a job working with Tom at the university and we are hoping to get a university house.

I hope that all is well at your end but I am cross with you about one thing. Why didn't you tell me about the snails in Akosua's bag? I found out by accident and was lucky to declare them – otherwise I might have been in trouble. They don't allow in live animals without the proper papers. At least they didn't have cocaine inside!

My job with Tom might involve short trips to Ghana. They won't start for a year but I rely on you to warn me of any possible threat from the cartel. Please let me know of any hint of danger you pick up from your business friends. Apart from Akos Mary, I haven't met any Ghanaians in Coventry and I'm not looking for them. I'm hoping that Peter Sarpong hasn't been replaced and they won't try to involve me again.

I hope we will keep in touch.

Greetings from us all,

Kwame

PS Lots of love from Akosua xxx

'Can we take the letter to the post office right way?' asked Akosua. Kwame fancied a stroll in the gentle August sunshine and readily agreed. It was about a kilometre to the village high street and they were already familiar with the route. 'I like the summer weather in England,' said Akosua. 'It's not hot like in Ghana.'

'You're not so keen on the winter though, are you?'

'Will we see real snow this time, Dad?'

'I hope so; you've waited a long time for it.'

'Will the uniform suit me?'

'What are the colours?'

'Jade green and navy blue.'

'I'm fairly sure about the green. Let's hope there's not too much navy blue.'

'That's what I think.'

'You've not been given a place yet.'

'No, but I want to get ready.'

Kwame had become accustomed to the towns in England where most passers-by appeared to be sleepwalking, and it was Akosua who returned the first greeting. He rebuked himself silently for forgetting his Akan manners and promised his father to do better.

'Why does everybody tell us that it's nice weather, Dad?'

'Probably because they don't get enough of it.'

'It's funny but I like it.'

'Our greetings are also funny, aren't they?'

'Yes, we say: sorry for the morning cold; sorry for the afternoon sun; sorry for the evening cool.'

'It's even funnier when you say it in English.'

'I like it when I make you laugh, Dad.'

Kwame realised that he hadn't been laughing enough for some time. Now that he had much to be happy about he resolved to try to adopt a brighter outlook. He began by turning into the newsagents.

'This isn't the post office, Dad.'

'No, but they don't sell ice cream in the post office, do they?'

'You can always lick the stamps.'

'Not all of them, these days. What are you going to have?'

They found a seat in the market square and sat down to enjoy their ices. The elderly gentleman on the next bench agreed that it was lovely weather, and his large fluffy dog yawned and stretched out on the ground at his feet. 'What's your dog's name?' asked Akosua.

'I call him Takoradi.'

'Takoradi!' exclaimed Kwame, 'That's a town in Ghana. Why do you call him that?'

'I was stationed there during the war.'

'We're from Ghana.'

'I thought you might be. *Akwaaba!*

'*Ya agya.* So you even remember some Twi!'

'It's a bit rusty now but I'd really like to hear it again – brings back fond memories.'

'I'll talk to your dog in Twi and you can answer for him,' said Akosua. '*Wo den de sen?*'

'*Me den de Takoradi.*'

'*W'adi mfie sen?*'

'Oh, he must be about ten years old now.'

'Well, that's not bad after all these years,' said Kwame. 'I'm really impressed.'

'I'm really impressed with your daughter. She speaks English with no accent!'

'She spent two years at school in England while still young enough to get it right.'

'It's all coming back to me,' mused the old man. 'Fufu and groundnut soup, red-red, dokono, gari.'

'Look,' said Kwame, 'We've still got plenty of yams and plantain that we brought with us. Why don't you come for a meal one day soon, before we finish it all?'

'Oh that's very kind, but I couldn't impose on you.'

'No trouble at all; you're a friend of Ghana, and we'd love to hear what happened during the war.'

'Please bring Takoradi,' added Akosua.

Later, over their evening meal, Kwame said to Tom and Akos Mary, 'I hope you don't mind, but I've invited a guest to dinner tomorrow evening. Akosua and I met the old gentleman in the village this afternoon. He was in Ghana during the war and even remembers some Twi. He was missing Ghanaian food so much that I couldn't resist the urge to help him relive the pleasures of his youth.'

'That's OK,' said Tom. 'Akos Mary and Afriyie can prepare us something special. It should be an interesting evening. But who is he? What's his name?'

Kwame rummaged through his pockets. 'I've got his card here somewhere. Yes, here it is.' He passed a rather crumpled slip to Tom.

'What's this? Tam Gordon DFC, Squadron Leader RAF (ret); this should be even more interesting than I thought!'

The next morning Afriyie decided to spend her time making baby clothes. In the afternoon she would help Akos Mary prepare the evening meal. Akosua said that she would buy some treats for Takoradi and take him for a walk while the men were chatting. Kwame accepted Tom's invitation to accompany him to the university to meet his new colleagues but he went with mixed feelings. 'I hope my rival candidates won't blame me for their disappointment,' he said.

'If there's any problem, the sooner you meet them the better,' advised Tom.

'This is our general office,' said Tom, 'and you will have that office over there as soon as we've cleared out all the gear. We'll put in a desk and chair and a PC, filing cabinets, etc. It's only a view over the car park, I'm afraid, but that's all any of us get!' Kwame recognised his two rivals talking to another young person. 'Let me introduce our assistant research fellows,' said Tom, 'Here is Sandra Garg, Greg Anderson and Mick Gould; I think you've met two of them already; and this is Mr Kwame Mainu who's from Ghana and worked for five years at the TCC.' All three voiced their welcome and Kwame returned their greetings with his famous grin.

Tom suggested that each of the young people spend some time with Kwame, briefing him on their work in turn, and then they would all meet up for lunch in the senior common room for a more social chat. Kwame learned that Sandra was a metallurgist and her family came from India. Greg was from Australia and a production engineer with a special interest in computer-controlled machining centres.

In the course of conversation, Kwame asked his third new colleague, Mick Gould, why he had not joined his work mates in applying for the research fellow post. Was it just the natural modesty of the English? Mick laughed and said that in his view all three of them lacked the necessary experience. 'None of us comes anywhere near your practical field experience, and we look forward to working with you in Ghana and making up the deficit.' Kwame assured him that he would do all he could to find them relevant experience and he was sure that they would enjoy working in Ghana.

Over lunch they relaxed and the conversation came around to the interviews. 'I was in and out so quickly that I knew I had no chance,' said Sandra.

'Same here,' muttered Greg. 'I was just a messenger boy for Kwame, but now we've had a chance to cool down we realise that we can learn a lot from you, especially about working in developing countries.'

Kwame thanked them for their kind remarks and said that he was happy to be joining such a friendly international team. Tom said very little but was satisfied that his aim had been accomplished.

That evening the squadron leader came to dinner. Kwame introduced him to Tom, Akos Mary and Afriyie, and Akosua took Takoradi into the garden to play with a ball. 'He'll soon get tired,' Tam warned, but neither girl nor dog took any notice. Tom suggested a drink before dinner and the three men sat down together.

'What will you have?' asked Tom.

'It's a bit early for *akpeteshie*, do you have any *pito*? You know, the beer made from Guinea corn?' enquired Tam.

'The best we can do is Star beer, but at least it's brewed in Ghana,' laughed Kwame, again surprised at the visitor's familiarity with his homeland.

Another surprise awaited them when the fufu was served. Although a spoon was provided, Tam washed his hand in the finger bowl and plunged it into the food in the traditional Ghanaian way. This made Tom feel the odd man out in his own home as he shyly worked with his mechanical aid.

'My, that brings back a few memories,' said the squadron leader, 'and today I haven't been fixing a fuel pump to a Beaufighter engine so the soup tastes just as it should. You know, I never could get used to high octane seasoning!'

'Tell us a bit about your time in Takoradi,' said Tom when they were relaxing after the meal.

'I went out early in '41, just commissioned as a pilot officer. The planes were brought to us by sea packed in crates; we had to set up workshops to assemble them and get them ready for service in Egypt. Then the ferry pilots took them across to Kenya and up to the Delta.'

'You must have done well to advance to squadron leader,' prompted Tom.

'Promotion came fast in those days if you worked hard and kept your nose clean. I didn't make squadron leader until later in the war, but I ended up at Takoradi running the workshop where we installed the engines.'

'Now what engines would those have been?' Tom wondered aloud as he tried to remember what his father had told him.

'Bristol Hercules in the Beaufighters, big twin-row radial jobs.'

'How many cylinders?'

'Two rows of nine, eighteen in all.'

Kwame had felt rather left out of this review of British military history but the visitor brought him back into the conversation with a question about his present employment.

'I'm taking up a post in Tom's department at the university,' Kwame said.

'Are there many other Ghanaians in your department?'

'I've not met any others yet.'

'Nigerians, maybe?'

'Again, I've not met any.'

'Won't you want to meet up with more of your people?'

'I've got my people with me here; that's enough.'

Kwame was saved from more questions by Akosua coming back from an after-dinner stroll with Takoradi. 'Shall we play the game again?' she asked Tam.

'What game was that?' he replied.

'You know, where I talk to Takoradi in Twi and you reply for him.'

'Won't the others be rather bored?'

Akosua turned to the dog and hugged him round his shaggy neck. '*Takoradi dea, wo ho ye fe.*'

'*Wo dea nso saa ara.*'

All the Ghanaians were startled at this fluent reply. 'It seems that your enjoyment of Ghana wasn't restricted to purely gastronomic pleasures,' said Kwame, and thought he saw the visitor's ruddy complexion deepen one shade. Was it because of his remark, or had the old man remembered more than he previously realised?

'I was young and hot blooded and the girls were very beautiful,' he reflected almost inaudibly.

'I can confirm that that is still true,' said Tom, smiling across at his wife.

The squadron leader departed with profuse thanks for an enjoyable evening. Akosua was sad to see Takoradi go. Tom sat quiet for a while. 'I'm trying to remember something,' he told Kwame. He decided to telephone his father. After the usual exchange of pleasantries and enquiries about Mum's health, he asked, 'Dad, you remember a lot about World War Two aircraft don't you? The Bristol Hercules engine had how many cylinders?' He put down the phone and turned to Kwame. 'Dad confirms that they had fourteen cylinders, two rows of seven, not eighteen as Tam said.'

'It was a long time ago; the old man's memory may not be as sharp as it used to be.'

'But he remembered the Twi, didn't he?'

'Yes he did, but what are you implying?'

'Oh nothing, I guess he mixed it up with a later Bristol engine, the Centaurus. Dad said that had eighteen cylinders.'

The weekend passed quietly, punctuated by Akosua's repeated requests to have a dog of her own. 'I'll consider your request when I think that you're mature enough to look after it properly and take it for a walk every day,' was her father's stock reply. He suspected that once the novelty wore off, it would be left to him to provide the daily exercise, as well as feeding, bathing and other routine maintenance. He drew his daughter's attention to the notice in the rear window of some cars: 'A puppy is for life not just for Christmas.'

'Well, can we at least go to the village square to see Takoradi sometimes?' she pleaded, but the next time they strolled to the village shops the old man and his dog were not there.

Akosua had been looking forward to visiting the girls' school but when the day came she was nervous. 'I'm worried about the test,' she told Kwame.

'They say it's good to be nervous before you start, but once you get under way you'll soon forget to worry and concentrate on answering the questions,' he assured her. 'Remember how well you did at St Louis.'

They went with Tom to the university and then Kwame borrowed the Range Rover to drive on to Warwick. Akosua was excited to see the castle towering over the town and she was very pleased that the school was so close. Kwame was concerned that he had driven about 25 kilometres, which would mean driving 100 kilometres every day to support his daughter's education. He would have to find a better means for Akosua's commuting. Maybe there was a bus service or perhaps a car pool; but first they must secure a place.

'Your daughter was fourteen in February.' It didn't sound like a question to Kwame but he hastened to assure the headmistress that the statement was correct. 'Our standard entry to the secondary school is year 7, at age 11. Akosua – is that how you pronounce her name? – should be entering the GCSE course in year 10. We do admit a few girls at that age but she will need to be up to standard.'

'We understand,' said Kwame. 'She has come prepared to do the test.'

'Then Akosua may go with Miss Honess, and while they are busy Mrs Murphy will show you around the school. I'm sorry that there's not much happening during the summer vacation but a few things are going on. I suggest that we all meet up in the dining room for lunch.'

Kwame went off with Mrs Murphy, crossing his fingers and hoping that the year at St Louis in Kumasi had kept Akosua abreast of her age group. 'Our average class size is 16,' said his guide, 'and we have more than 500 girls here.'

'What about school uniform?'

'Uniform must be worn up to year 11 but not in years 12 and 13.'

'Where do we get the uniform?'

'There is a local shop and the parents' association organises the sale of second-hand uniform. You will be given all the details in writing before the beginning of term in September.'

There is something about schools, thought Kwame, that makes them all look the same, especially during the vacations when little is going on. Here the facilities were good, and there were some splendid views of the castle, but Kwame regretted that no classes were in progress to allow him to sample the atmosphere. 'Would you say the girls are happy here?' he asked Mrs Murphy.

'Oh yes, we work closely with the parents' association to ensure a family atmosphere.'

'What about food?'

'All meals are freshly prepared on the premises daily and we have a lunch committee comprising girls of all ages that meets regularly to ensure standards are maintained and improved.'

Kwame remembered the comments about school food made by the student at St Louis. Here in Warwick, he reflected, the girls won't be bringing red pepper to add to their meals. No fear of stomach ulcers! 'Do you have a nurse here during term time?' he asked.

'Yes, Matron is always in attendance during the school day.'

They reached the dining room but Akosua had not finished her test, so Mrs Murphy gave Kwame a cup of coffee and her copy of the *Independent*. 'Please excuse me for a few minutes while I attend to some routine matters. I'll join you shortly when your daughter is finished.' Kwame settled back for a good read but Mainu's law ensured that the wait was short. Akosua and the headmistress arrived together in time for lunch.

'The teachers need a little time to assess Akosua's performance but you'll receive a letter from us in the next two or three days,' the headmistress assured Kwame. 'Now let's sample the school's cooking.'

* * *

Back in the Range Rover, as they set out on the return journey, Kwame knew that Akosua was bursting to tell him something. 'Do you know the school is haunted?' she shouted as soon as they drove off.

'Please don't shout, you're only a few centimetres from my ear.'

'Not just one ghost but two!'

'Then calm down and tell me about it.'

'I met a sixth-former here on a summer school. She said one of the old buildings, called Landor House, is haunted by two ghosts, and one is a boy who killed himself riding downstairs on a bicycle!'

'Why did he do that?'

'The other boys dared him, of course!'

'Does he ring his bell?'

'Oh Dad, be serious. Some girls doing a physics experiment actually recorded bumps and bangs in the night.'

'Probably just the old heating system.'

'I knew you'd say that, Dad.'

'Do you still want to go to the school?'

'Oh yes, It's really exciting.'

'Well, at least you won't be boarding. I guess you wouldn't want to sleep in Landor House, would you?'

'Perhaps not.'

Kwame asked about the tests and was assured that all went well. 'I liked the physics test best, Dad. It was a practical experiment.'

'What did you do?'

'They gave me a big bowl of water, a ball of Plasticine and some weights.'

'Then what?'

'I was told to make a boat to carry as many weights as possible.'

'How did you get on?'

'I made the biggest boat I could with very thin walls and the physics teacher said I had done very well.'

'Archimedes' principle, eh?'

'That's right; I called the boat *Miss Eureka*.'

Kwame drove to the university to ensure that Tom had transport home. He was grateful for the loan of the car but realised that he must get his own vehicle if he was to take Akosua to Warwick every day.

Later that evening he broached the subject with Tom. 'I really enjoyed driving your Range Rover, today,' he began. 'It made me realise that I must get my own wheels if I'm to take Akosua to school in Warwick.'

'What do you have in mind?'

'Most Ghanaians choose BMW or Mercedes Benz cars but I've always driven Land Rovers in Ghana and I like your one here.'

'Well, you have three models to choose from: the Range Rover like mine, the traditional Land Rover you drove in Ghana, and the Discovery.'

'I'd like something a bit more comfortable than my car in Ghana, and your car may be too expensive; what's the Discovery like?'

'Why don't we go and look tomorrow?'

The salesman at the Land Rover dealership remembered Tom, and Kwame was soon test driving a new Discovery. Akosua and Afriyie were both urging him to buy it but Kwame was wary of spending too much of his scarce reserves. Tom said that they could negotiate with the dealer, and there were credit terms available, so the two men went into the office to discuss details.

Akosua, Akos Mary and Afriyie stayed sitting in the Discovery, admiring its many novel features and enjoying the new car smell, but the teenager soon grew restless and started to roam about the forecourt, casually appraising the other cars. She felt that her father was not very good with colours and she didn't want him to make a bad choice just because the right one wasn't immediately available. The colour would have to complement her school uniform.

Akosua had some interest in cars but much more in dogs, so she was quick to spot any sniffing nose or wagging tail. The interest redoubled when she realised that the tail she saw wagging was a tail she recognised. 'Takoradi!' she shouted and ran behind Tom's big maroon Range Rover. Ignoring the threat to her jeans, she was on her knees with her arms around the big dog's fluffy neck, asking him in Twi what he was doing there.

Kwame and Tom left the office and walked back to where Afriyie and Akos Mary were still sitting in the Discovery. 'Have you bought it?' they asked.

'We have,' said Kwame proudly. 'We can collect it in a few days, after it's registered, taxed and insured.' Then, noticing how quietly this news was received, he asked where Akosua had gone.

'She shouted "Takoradi" and ran off over there,' said Afriyie.

'She must have seen the dog,' Kwame said, but before he could go to investigate Akosua came back holding the big dog by his collar.

'It's strange that he should be here on his own,' said Tom. 'I wonder where the squadron leader is?'

'I haven't seen him,' said Akosua, 'and Takoradi doesn't seem to know.'

'Can we take the dog back to Tam's place?' asked Kwame. 'Is the address on his card?'

'It's on Takoradi's collar,' said Akosua, in a voice that implied pained tolerance of people who didn't know about dogs.

They called at the squadron leader's cottage on the way back home. Akosua jumped down from the car and ran to the front door, with Takoradi bounding at her side. The girl knocked and the dog scratched but there was no response. Then the girl shouted and the dog barked. 'It seems that nobody's at home,' said Tom.

'Maybe Tam's out looking for Takoradi,' suggested Kwame.

'Can we take him home to keep him safe?' pleaded Akosua.

'We haven't reached that stage yet,' said Tom. 'Look, here he comes now.'

The wobbly figure on the bicycle came down the hill, growing steadily larger until he half-fell off his machine outside the garden gate. Takoradi's enthusiastic greeting did little to restore his stability. Struggling to regain his breath, as well as his military bearing, Tam apologised for having lost contact with his canine companion, and invited his visitors to take tea. 'As for the young lady,' he added, 'I have some ice cream in the fridge.'

'I suppose that I should walk with him,' said the squadron leader, over the clinking of the tea cups, 'but these days I find it easier on the bike. It's all right in the countryside but difficult in town where the cycle tracks are not continuous.'

'Such a big dog needs a lot of exercise,' said Tom sympathetically. 'It must be quite a challenge, keeping him fit.'

'It certainly is,' agreed Tam. 'He's an old dog now, but his energy isn't decreasing as fast as mine.'

Back in the car Tom said, 'I forgot to tell you, Kwame, I called in at the estates office and they told me that you have been allocated the house you liked. You can pick up the keys tomorrow.'

'Oh good,' said Akos Mary to Afriyie, 'now we can sort out some furniture and get you started on moving in.'

'Yes, and we can go to town to buy the rest,' said Afriyie happily.

Later that evening when the girls were watching television Kwame and Tom returned to the incident of the lost dog. 'I can't help wondering about your friend the squadron leader,' he said, 'he must have been somewhere around the car dealer's; I'm wondering why we didn't see him or he didn't see us.'

'The dog could have run far away from Tam, couldn't he?'

'Yes, but Takoradi is an old dog and quite calm natured; I don't think he would go far away from Tam, even if he slipped his leash.'

'What are you suggesting?'

'Maybe Takoradi was let off his leash.'

'For what reason?'

'That's what puzzles me.'

Kwame sensed that Tom's problem with Tam Gordon ran deeper than concern about the lost dog, so he prompted, 'It seems that you don't like Tam.'

'Oh, I like him all right; he has a pleasant personality.'

'Then what's the problem?'

'I'm not sure he's telling us the truth.'

'How do you mean?'

'Well, there's his war record for a start. Was he really in Takoradi assembling Beaufighters in 1941?'

'He certainly knows some Twi.'

'Yes, but did he really pick it up during his war service?'

'That's what he says.'

'There are people we call confidence tricksters who often claim false military rank and a war record.'

'So what do you advise?'

'Maintain a friendly relationship but be very wary if he tries to draw us into any investment or business scheme.'

When a few days later a letter arrived from the school confirming a place for Akosua, Kwame felt that he had established the basis of their new life in England. With a job, a home, a car and a school for his daughter he could look forward to a lengthy period of peaceful development in close association with old friends, plenty of opportunity to make new friends, and interesting and rewarding work. It was still exile from his motherland, but exile that was as pleasant as exile can be. He wished that the ghosts from his past could be dismissed as easily as the ghosts at Landor House, but he also knew that living ghosts were more to be feared than the ghosts of the long since dead.

Kwame's life gradually merged into a dull routine. It was exactly what he wanted. For the time being he had a nine-to-five job, with much opportunity to pursue his personal research, and supportive and stimulating colleagues. Akosua settled into school in Warwick, and by joining a car pool Kwame reduced his chauffeuring support to one day a week.

Furnishing her new home and helping Akos Mary prepare for the arrival of her son kept Afriyie busy for several weeks. Then she decided to revive the work she had been doing so successfully at Cranfield: adjusting today's fashions to suit yesterday's dimensions, and introducing Ghanaian styles to those ladies who had given up the struggle. This was work she could do at home, but with ample opportunity to display her creations at various social gatherings at the university. She was soon getting enough commissions to fully occupy her nimble fingers. Inevitably her thoughts turned to employing an apprentice.

There was no economic necessity for Akos Mary to work, but she found it difficult to adapt to a life without perms, plaits and ladies' chats. There was a demand for hairdressers skilled in the ways of African hair and the salon where she worked was reluctant to let her go. So she continued to indulge her artistic and social interests while adjusting her hours in inverse proportion to her expanding waistline. As the days shortened she was compelled to restrict her services to a small group of long-term clients who had now become old friends. One of these was Auntie Rose.

Belonging to a sub-set of Ghanaian women in whom middle-age spread is negative, Auntie Rose seemed to have grown ever smaller. Akos Mary found herself having to resist the temptation to lift her client into the chair before starting to unravel her tightly woven greying plaits. The hairstyle was always the same and only one pair of hands was ever permitted to participate in its renovation. Long before her birth certificate would have provided confirmation, Auntie Rose manifested the persona of the innocent old lady. Yet Akos Mary knew Auntie Rose as the most successful of the drugs mules commuting between Accra and London in the 1980s, and one of the few employed by the Kumasi cartel to have escaped arrest in 1988.

Auntie Rose had told Akos Mary that she had been deeply shocked by the arrests. It wasn't her employers' sudden disappearance that impacted her as much as the realisation of the fate she had so narrowly avoided. She had vowed that she would never run such risks again. Akos Mary had served a prison sentence for her involvement in the drugs smuggling, and since her release and marriage to Tom she had encouraged Auntie Rose to stick to her vow and avoid all contact with her former paymasters. They supported each other in their resolve to live a life free of crime. This had not been difficult as long as the leaders of the cartel remained incarcerated.

None of the drugs bosses imprisoned in Britain was likely to be released for a number of years. In Ghana, however, following the death of Uncle George, all the leaders had been freed, and it was this that had led to Kwame's exile. Now it seemed efforts were being made to revive the business in the UK. Auntie Rose said that she had been approached with a view to resuming her former illicit activities. 'I hope you didn't agree,' said Akos Mary.

'Of course I don't want to, but what can I do?'

'How do you mean?'

'They say they will report me for the old work if I don't start again.'

'That's a big problem.'

'What can I do?'

'I don't know, but I think I know someone who might be able to help – can I ask him?'

'Can he be trusted?'

'I guarantee it.'

3

Auntie Rose

Kwame was enjoying his work at the university. Tom gave him the freedom to run his project in his own way, offering advice when asked but otherwise staying in the background. Kwame had assessed the strengths and weaknesses of his three assistants and had decided that they were strong on theory but lacking in the practical hands-on skills that he judged to be essential to the work in Ghana. He could begin by arranging for them to have some training at the foundry school where he had himself learned so much. So he rang Martin Hutchinson, the new manager, and negotiated for his people to spend one day a week on a course tailored to their needs. Later he would arrange practical training on a similar basis in a precision machine shop.

He already suspected that Mick Gould had rather more practical technical skills than Greg Anderson or Sandra Garg, but felt it best to treat all three the same for the time being. It would be embarrassing, as well as unproductive, to give the impression that he was biased against his two rivals for the research fellow post. He would know more when Martin Hutchinson sent in his progress reports on the three trainees.

When Akos Mary found an opportunity to tell him about Auntie Rose, Kwame was dismayed. This was the sort of situation that he had been determined to avoid. It had ruined his life once, and once was enough. He had been so intent on avoiding contact with any potential drugs traders that he had denied himself all social interaction with West Africans. He tried to marshal every argument to convince Akos Mary that there was nothing he could do to help Auntie Rose. At the same time he appreciated the plight of his countrywoman. Akos Mary could not discuss this problem with her husband and there was nobody else to whom she could turn. She was obviously a lady in distress and Kwame was ever a knight in shining armour. He had been able to solve Akos Mary's problem when her father overstayed his visa after her wedding; maybe he could find an equally quick and effective solution in this case. He guessed that

after an hour's driving in heavy traffic, half of it filled with loudly animated schoolgirl chatter. Tonight hadn't been too bad with its discussion of elephants. Why hadn't he taken Akosua to see them in the wild? He was ashamed to recall that the one in Kumasi zoo was from India. He must put a visit to the north on the list of things to do when they had a chance to go home.

That weekend Akosua asked if they could call at Tam's to take Takoradi for a walk. Tam was happy to agree, it relieved him of the need to provide the day's exercise and gave him a chance to watch a rugby match on television. 'You're very fond of this big dog, aren't you?' said Kwame.

'I love him, Dad, I wish he was mine.'

'He's an old dog and might not live much longer. Wouldn't you rather have a puppy?'

'I would still like Takoradi best, even if he died after a short time. I would give him a proper funeral and put flowers on his grave.'

'Let's think of happier things.'

'Yes, let's go on the common and play with the ball.'

After a vigorous game with dog and daughter, Kwame was first to flag and looked for a suitable resting place. He found an old wooden bench under a big oak tree to complete his metamorphosis from player to spectator. Some boys were playing football, and Kwame became concerned when Takoradi decided that he liked chasing the big ball better than his small one, but a few words from Akosua seemed to resolve the issue. She brought Takoradi over to sit with Kwame and ran off to join in the soccer match. The old dog lay panting at his feet so Kwame released his grip on the dog collar and idly watched as his daughter shoulder-charged her way through the opposing team. He wondered how long it would be before the boys protested at her rough play

Takoradi revived, and started to look around. Something had caught his attention. His nose was twitching rapidly. Then he plunged his head under the bench. It was fortunate that the combination of a large head and a sunken bench prevented the dog from reaching his target, because behind the bench Kwame saw to his horror that the object of interest was a hypodermic syringe.

Kwame didn't want Takoradi to touch the syringe, nor did he intend to touch it himself. Above all he wanted to avoid Akosua seeing it. So he put the big dog back on his leash and called to his daughter to release the boys from their torment. He resolved to report the dangerous litter when an opportunity arose.

'Where did you learn to play football like that?' he asked Akosua.

'I played at St Louis and we play at King's High,' she replied.

'Don't you think you played rather roughly?'

'Boys like it rough!'

When they reached the squadron leader's house Akosua stayed playing with Takoradi in the garden while the two men went inside for a cup of tea. 'Can I use your telephone?' Kwame asked Tam. Responding to a military nod, Kwame made a call to the local police station reporting the syringe left behind the bench on the common. Noticing Tam's interest, he explained. 'The dog sniffed it out.'

'That's not surprising; that's what he's trained to do,' said Tam. 'The dogs' home told me he's retired from the police.'

'So Akosua was right,' exclaimed Kwame. 'It seems she's inherited her mother's power of intuition!'

That evening Kwame related the incident to Tom. 'The common must be used by heroin addicts,' Tom said.

'So does that mean the dog has been trained to sniff out heroin?' asked Kwame.

'It's possible; you said Tam confirmed that Takoradi used to be a police dog. On the other hand, dogs are interested in smells generally, and it might have been some other scent that attracted his attention.'

'Do you think Takoradi might be able to sniff out other drugs as well as heroin?'

'Yes, I believe so. The drugs sniffers are trained to detect a range of different substances.'

'Was Takoradi looking for drugs when we found him at the car dealers?'

'If he was, it's likely he was freelancing – like today.'

Kwame had not been looking forward to meeting Auntie Rose, but the day came, and at the close of work he made his way to the hairdressing salon. Nobody was in the partners' room so he settled down to wait. He anticipated a long delay, and the only available reading material was a tabloid newspaper. Even the attractions of a page three girl quickly evaporated and after half an hour he began to pace about the room, trying to think of a good excuse in anticipation of a late return home. Through a glass panel in the door he could see Akos Mary still busy with a client. She was the only one left at work.

When Akos Mary eventually came to release him it was to explain that Auntie Rose felt the partners' room was too exposed to outside view. They had waited until the proprietor went home so that they could use an inside office. Now all was ready. Kwame followed Akos Mary into what seemed to be a converted storeroom with no windows. When he saw the small figure of Auntie Rose he couldn't help blurting out, 'You're name's not Akomwa, is it?'

'Yes, how do you know?'

'I know a young woman in Kumasi, a welder, who looks very much like you.'

'Not my niece, Akosua?'

'It must be – well it's a small world!'

Auntie Rose told her story. Essentially it was what Kwame already knew. The little woman didn't want to go back to her old ways but thought that she would face a long gaol sentence if she refused to cooperate with the cartel. 'You will certainly get a long sentence if you resume activities and then get caught,' said Kwame. 'I think your best course is to confess to the authorities, take your punishment, like Akos Mary, and then walk free.'

'I don't want to go to prison.'

'Nobody does, but if you're willing to tell the authorities all you know about the cartel they may well reduce your sentence. You will certainly get a much shorter sentence than if the cartel carries out its threat to report you.'

'I'm still not sure I could do it.'

Kwame wanted to ask Auntie Rose if he could talk to someone he knew, without mentioning her name, to determine her likely fate if she did confess to the British authorities. However, he didn't want to say anything in the presence of Akos Mary that might confirm her suspicion of his role in *her* imprisonment. He knew that one day soon he must tell Akos Mary and beg her forgiveness, but all he could do today was to repeat his advice to Auntie Rose and promise to meet her again in two weeks. In the meantime he intended to discuss the case with Leon Thornet, without mentioning names and, if possible, completely off the record.

'Why were you so late coming home this evening?' asked Afriyie, as they settled down for the night.

'I went to the hairdressing salon to meet a friend of Akos Mary who's being asked to carry drugs from Ghana,' he said, having decided that a story close to the truth was the best policy.

'Oh please don't get involved in that again,' pleaded Afriyie.

'No, I only advised the lady to keep out of trouble, like you did.'

Kwame realised that, apart from in the matters of the house and the car, he had rather neglected seeking Afriyie's thoughts and feelings. She was such a compliant person in most respects that it was easy to assume she would happily go along with whatever he decided. Now, swayed by strong feelings of gratitude and guilt he asked her if she was happy with their new life.

'I miss Ghana, but I would miss you and Akosua more if I wasn't here,' she confided, 'and I wish that we could make more Ghanaian friends here in England.'

'I know what you mean,' said Kwame, 'but I'm afraid of getting involved with the cartel again. It's difficult to know who's involved and who isn't. So it's safer to avoid all contacts.'

'Could I have an apprentice to work with me; someone to help with the work and keep me company while you and Akosua are away?'

'To chat with all day in Twi?'

'I would love that.'

'Well, it's not as easy as in Ghana; getting a visa to bring the girl in would be the first problem.'

'Could we bring my sister's daughter from Koforidua?'

'We can try. I'll talk it over with Tom.'

'What again?'

'Well, here you would have to pay the girl a proper salary, not just chop money.'

'The business is good; I could afford that.'

'And we must treat her very well, make her one of the family, or she might run away and become an illegal immigrant.'

'She wouldn't do that.'

'Many young people do.'

'Can we try?'

'Yes.'

Afriyie lay silent for some time but Kwame sensed that she had more on her mind. 'Can I learn to drive?' she asked at last.

'That's a good idea,' replied Kwame. 'Why haven't we thought of it before?'

'Will you teach me?'

'This isn't Ghana; you have to drive well here and observe all the regulations. I'll arrange for you to have lessons with the British School of Motoring.'

'Won't it be expensive?'

'We can afford it.'

'You're a kind man, Kwame Mainu.'

'Not only kind. I'm thinking you'll be able to do some of the school runs.'

Next morning, in his office at the university, Kwame used the number from Leon Thornet's latest business card to telephone the senior customs official at Heathrow airport and ask for a meeting. After explaining his daily routine he was told that the next time he drove his daughter to school in Warwick he should report to the police station. Kwame groaned as he put down the telephone. He hoped that the meeting would be a one-off event, not the first in a long series of clandestine trysts like last time.

So Auntie Rose was Akosua Akomwa's real aunt! The little welder's small stature was genetic after all. He recalled Akosua asking him why Akomwa was so small at dinner in the senior staff club at the university on the day they met her in Kumasi. His daughter would be pleased to know that the little welder had not necessarily suffered an undernourished childhood. He wondered if and when Akosua might meet Auntie Rose and be told of the family connection. He wasn't sure why, but he hoped that it might be soon.

Mick Gould came in from the general office. 'Prof is saying you will send one of us to Ghana soon to start selecting the engineering firms that will help build the diesel engine.'

'That's what we are planning,' said Kwame.

'I would like to be the one who goes.'

Kwame had got used to this blunt way of speaking and had not allowed it to influence his assessment of Mick's knowledge and practical skills. His companions, Sandra Garg and Greg Anderson, had showed themselves to be more ambitious and they had good academic qualifications, but they lacked Mick's ability to improvise; a skill essential to engineering in the Third World. In his approach to the work Mick reminded Kwame of Frank Johnson, the black Texan appropriate technologist who had taught him so much during his service in Tamale.

Kwame had already decided that Mick would be the best qualified of his assistants to undertake the assignment in Ghana. In our vernacular, he reflected, many of us Asantes are equally blunt-spoken. Mick's manner of speech would go largely unnoticed, but his practical skills would be greatly appreciated.

'Can you tell me why I should send you?'

'We'll be working with practical people solving hands-on manufacturing problems. I believe that I have more experience of this work than the others.'

'Then you will be pleased to know that I am of the same opinion and my written recommendation has already been sent to Professor Arthur.'

'That's great!'

* * *

'Today we went on a tour of Warwick Castle,' cried Akosua, as soon as her father came in. 'It's more than six hundred years old. Some parts were built in 1383, that's nearly a hundred years before the Portuguese came to Ghana!'

'What did you like best?' asked Kwame.

'The doll museum – seeing the beautiful dolls girls played with hundreds of years ago,' was the eager reply.

'So that's what you do at your school: sight-seeing trips?'

'Oh Dad, you know we have a history assignment on mediaeval castles.'

'You're going to write about dolls?'

'About everything: the historic tableaux, state rooms, dungeons and torture chambers, the hospital, the market hall, everything!'

'Then you have a lot to do.'

The telephone rang and Akosua dashed to pick it up. After a few minutes of cheerful banter she called to her father, 'It's Uncle Tom; he wants to talk to you.'

'Sorry to disturb your evening Kwame, but I was tied up in meetings today. It's your note about sending Gould to Kumasi; he's not going to tread on any toes is he?'

'I've given that some thought and I think he'll be all right. I'll give him a good briefing on local customs and how to behave.'

'What about his technical ability?'

'He's the best we have; highly adaptable and resourceful. I'm confident that he will solve any problems he meets that can be solved at that end.'

'So any problem he brings back really will need to be tackled here?'

'Exactly.'

'Then I'll start the paperwork in the morning.'

'While you're on, can I remind you that it's my day on the school run tomorrow and I may be back a little later than usual.'

'That's fine, we'll talk later.'

After dropping his boisterous cargo at school, Kwame reported to the police station in Warwick and was conducted into an interview room. Much to his surprise, Leon Thornet was already there. Kwame noticed that a glass of water had already been provided, and after the usual greetings he was asked if he would like some tea or coffee. Leon sipped his black coffee and looked directly at his visitor, 'So you've changed your mind about doing some translating for us.'

'I'm afraid not,' Kwame replied, 'I have a well paid job at the university these days and I'm not looking to earn more money.'

'Then do it purely out of interest and for the good of the community.'

'I can't risk putting my family in more danger.'

'So why did you want to see me?'

'Can I put a problem to you for advice, off the record?'

'Normally I would say no, but as you've helped us in the past I will grant you this one favour.'

Kwame began by recalling that when the leaders of the Kumasi cartel were arrested in 1988, several couriers or mules were also arrested in the UK and in Ghana. Now that the top people had been released from prison in Ghana, they might be attempting to restart the business by recruiting more couriers. What would be the position of a courier who had escaped arrest in 1988 but was threatened with exposure if they didn't join the new venture? Wouldn't it be better for such a person to confess to the authorities, collaborate fully, and take whatever prison sentence might be handed down, rather than get in deeper and risk imprisonment later for a more serious offence?'

'So you've come to ask me about Auntie Rose,' said Leon Thornet with obvious relief. 'Good man! I told my bosses that we could trust you but they insisted on the test.'

Kwame was surprised, confused and angry all at once. 'Why should I need to be tested?' he protested. 'I've come here to live peacefully and do honest work to keep my family safe. I came here today of my own free will. I can't see that I've done anything to justify being put to a test and I must protest most strongly at the way I've been treated.'

'We found cocaine in the live snails,' said Leon quietly.

Now there were so many questions teeming in Kwame's head that he didn't know where to begin. The silence extended for what seemed like a long time. At last Leon took pity on his victim and began an explanation. 'Our people were very surprised to find cocaine in live snails that had been freely declared. It seemed obvious to me that you did not know the drugs were there. Knowing your background I was sure that you had been tricked in some way, but for what purpose? Did some remnant of the Kumasi cartel really think that you would deliver the drugs, or were they seeking revenge for your efforts against them in the past? Either way, it seemed that they had failed. What was certain was that we needed to know more about what was going on if we were to frustrate a new Kumasi-based effort in drug importation. It was decided not to tell you about the cocaine in the snails and to keep track of you all.'

Seeing Kwame still sitting in stunned silence Leon continued, 'My bosses decided that we needed to be sure you weren't involved in the revival movement, so we called upon Auntie Rose to be the cheese in the mousetrap. Just as I expected, you brought the matter back to us in your characteristically diffident manner that we have come to respect and admire.'

'*Okisi mpow adjwe*, the rat doesn't refuse palm nuts,' muttered Kwame to himself.

'What was that?' enquired Leon.

'Oh, I was just wondering if it was true that refusing the cheese proves you're not a mouse. Seems to smell of Hempel's paradox.'

'My bosses may not be well read in philosophy,' Leon went on, 'but they are prepared to accept your reporting here today as a good indication that you want nothing to do with the narcotics trade and will do what you can to keep your people out of it.'

Kwame's head was beginning to clear. A number of things were starting to fall into place. 'I may be able to forgive you for the Auntie Rose test,' he said, 'but was it really necessary to put the squadron leader and his bloodhound on my trail as well?'

It was with a broad smile that Leon Thornet replied, 'I don't think Takoradi would like to be called a bloodhound. Let's join some friends in a more comfortable setting, have some more coffee and biscuits and go over these issues in a more relaxed manner.' He led the way into an adjacent room where one and half of the easy chairs were already occupied. Kwame was greeted by his old interlocutor, Jack Preece, and his new acquaintance, Auntie Rose Akomwa, both with broad smiles that he wasn't quite ready to reciprocate.

'It's all come as a bit of a shock, eh?' said Jack Preece sympathetically.

'It pains me that I tricked you; I beg you let your chest down,' added Auntie Rose in Twi, putting her tiny hand on his forearm.

'Oh, don't worry, I'm sure I'll be able to forgive you all – one day,' replied Kwame. 'I guess in your business you don't trust anybody.'

Leon let the small talk linger on. He wanted Kwame to relax before exchanging more detailed explanations, reviewing what had happened and defining future objectives. So he sat listening to the others and watching for signs of returning cardiac normality. He noticed that Auntie Rose was very effective in calming Kwame and he congratulated himself on having included her in the welcoming committee.

'I would like to review what has happened from the beginning,' he said at last, 'but if you have any urgent questions, Kwame, we will deal with them first.'

'No, you go ahead,' said Kwame. 'I will ask questions as we go along.'

So Leon began to relate recent events in the context of concern over drug imports to the UK. It was the release of Ghanaian and Lebanese drugs traders in Ghana that alerted the British authorities to a possible renewal of Kumasi-based activity. So they were on the lookout for signs of revival, and when Kwame handed in a consignment of live snails with cocaine cargos the alarm bells rang. Had Kwame been recruited, perhaps under threat, or was it a form of revenge to try to incriminate him? The first question that arose, said Leon, was, 'If you, Kwame, didn't insert the cocaine into the snails, who did?'

'I really don't know,' replied Kwame. 'My ex-wife, Comfort, said she packed Akosua's case but I'm sure she did not put in the cocaine, and I can think of nobody else who might have had access to the case.'

'Then there is the matter of the consignee,' Leon continued. 'I believe your daughter was told to hand over the case to Akos Mary, Professor Arthur's wife?'

'That's right,' said Kwame, 'but I'm sure she didn't know she was to receive anything more than edible snails.'

'Well, we included her in Auntie Rose's trial and she made an acceptable response in advising Auntie Rose to keep out of trouble and reporting the matter to you. This would seem to suggest that Akos Mary wasn't involved in a new smuggling scheme and that the plot was designed only to embarrass you.'

'Well, it's certainly succeeded in doing that,' said Kwame glumly. He was beginning to revive, however. 'Can I ask a question now?'

'Go ahead.'

'Why was it necessary to put the sniffer dog on our trail?'

'My bosses wanted to be sure that no contraband had come through undetected by our people or by you. The snails might have been a decoy.'

'So you checked out Professor Arthur's house and car?'

'You all have a clean bill of health – Takoradi detected nothing untoward.'

'At least Akosua made a friend.'

'Every cloud has a silver lining,' added Jack Preece.

'Then what about Tam Gordon?' Kwame asked. 'I suppose that's not his real name.

'It is, actually,' Leon replied, 'and he really is a squadron leader retired from the RAF.'

'But Professor Arthur doubts that he's an engineer.'

'No, he was in intelligence, and we had to invent his war service in the Gold Coast in 1941, he's not really quite old enough for that.'

'He's been in Ghana, though, his Twi isn't bad.'

'I'd rather not elaborate on that.'

'Now,' said Leon, 'we come to the important issue: where do we go from here?'

'I'm going back to Coventry to get on with my work.'

'It's not quite as simple as that – we need your help again.'

'I told you before – no thanks!'

'We need to find out what's happening in Kumasi.'

'Then send your aunt and uncle.'

Leon looked across at Auntie Rose, pleading for help.

'Kwame, let me tell you why I'm helping the *abrofo*,' she said quietly.

'I'm listening.'

'When our people and the Kumasi Lebanese were bringing drugs here, they were not trying to sell the drugs in Ghana. They used to say that if the *abrofo* are foolish enough to buy the drugs they would take the opportunity to supply them.'

'So what has changed?'

'The cocaine comes from South America, from Brazil, Venezuela and other places. Now traders from these countries are coming to Ghana, trying to cut out the middlemen. There's a war developing to capture the trade with the UK.'

'How does that affect us?'

'The South American traders don't care who they sell to. So while they are waiting to take over the trade to the UK they are busy developing a local market in Ghana.'

'You mean our people are becoming cocaine addicts?'

'Not only cocaine but heroin and other hard drugs.'

'So far,' cut in Leon, 'the Ghanaian authorities have been lukewarm in cooperating with us. You saw how the drugs traders were released early. Now we feel that we have an opportunity to convince them to work more closely with us because they will be helping to protect both countries against the scourge.'

'I wish you well,' said Kwame, 'but I don't see how I can help.'

'First you can help us to find out what's happening in Kumasi; second, you can help us here like you did before with translation and interpretation; and third, you can help us convince your government of the value of cooperation.'

'The present government in Ghana is protecting the drugs traders,' said Kwame. 'Media reports from the USA and UK quoting evidence given in drugs trials suggest that people in the government are even directly involved. I don't think that you will get any effective agreement before the general election in late 1999, and then only if there's a change of regime.'

'We are well aware of what you say, but we feel that we can do much preparatory work to be ready at the opportune time.'

Kwame was still not convinced. 'I'm an engineer, not a detective, and I'm working in the best interest of my country in trying to accelerate industrialisation. I did not choose to get involved with the drugs trade and past involvement has made my life very difficult. I want to live quietly, doing my work and looking after my family.' He turned to Auntie Rose. 'I'm as concerned as you are about drugs being pushed on our children in Ghana, as I am also concerned about the children here, but surely the work should be left to professionals like you?'

Auntie Rose said it was true that she had chosen to devote her life to this cause and was prepared to accept the risks, and she had no dependents to worry about. She understood Kwame's position, especially the risk of danger to his family, but it was sometimes necessary to answer the call of duty, irrespective of the risks. The *abrofo* would do all they could to protect his family, as they had before. She had taken a liking to him from their first meeting and admired his integrity. It would be a pleasure to work with him and she would be sad if the opportunity never came about.

Kwame was impressed that his tiny countrywoman was prepared to take a stand against the evil of the drugs trade, but even a strong feeling of guilt couldn't push him into changing his mind. 'You know I'm always slow to arrive at a decision,' he said. 'Please give me some time to think through all I have learned today.'

Accepting this plea, Leon Thornet drew the meeting to a close. Auntie Rose promised to keep in touch.

Kwame drove carefully back to Coventry. He knew that there was so much circulating in his head that he needed to drive with more than usual care. He also knew that he could never settle down to work, he needed more answers; so instead of driving to the university he drove to Tom's house.

Akos Mary opened the door with some surprise. She had been expecting a private hairdressing client. 'What brings you here at this time, Kwame?'

'I suppose that I could say Auntie Rose,' he replied, 'but it's rather more than that.' She brought him a glass of water and asked if he would like some coffee but he replied that he had already consumed a year's supply in one morning.

'When we came from Ghana,' he began, 'we brought you some edible snails from Comfort but they were taken away from us at the airport.'

'Yes, I remember.'

'Well, I have now been told that they found cocaine in the snails; do you know anything about that?'

He immediately regretted making such a blunt statement because the heavily pregnant woman before him broke down in tears. 'Oh Kwame, what have I done? Am I in trouble?'

He hastened to reassure her. 'No immediate trouble as far as I know. The *abrofo* sent Auntie Rose as a sort of test for both of us and we seem to have passed.'

The sobbing persisted, 'Oh Kwame, it's my father again, he will never leave me in peace. I wish Dr Arthur hadn't invited him to the wedding.'

'What's he up to now?'

'The old business: demanding money.'

'Did you give him any?'

'I gave him what I could but he said it wasn't enough.'

'What then?'

'He said I must hand over to him the snails that you were bringing from Ghana.'

'So he must have known about the cocaine.'

'Do you think he's joined the cartel?'

'It sounds as though he might have done.'

Kwame sat in silence while his friend fought to recover her composure. He remembered Mr Konadu only too well: an absent father, restless failed trader and opportunist who had seized his one big chance in life as an illegal immigrant in the UK. He wondered if Konadu had legalised his status. If not, Kwame resolved, he would carry out his threat to report him to the police. 'Where is he staying now?' he asked, 'do you have any contact details?'

Akos Mary passed him a slip of paper with what looked like a telephone number. 'What are you going to do?'

'I threatened to take action if he troubled you again, and I will.'

'What action?'

'I'll not tell you, so nobody can say you were involved.'

The doorbell rang and Akos Mary quickly started to repair her face. 'Kwame, would you like to open the door, show Mrs Richards into the other room and say that I'll be right along?' It wasn't really a question, and Kwame didn't *like* it, but he carried out her instructions to the letter. Mrs Richards later complimented Akos Mary on her husband's impeccable manners.

4

New Arrivals

Kwame still wasn't in the right frame of mind for work, and he needed more time to think so he made his way home. Afriyie hadn't expected him for lunch but she was happy to see him. It wasn't long before she had prepared something and they were sitting at table. 'You're quiet today, is anything wrong?' she asked.

'I've learned a lot this morning,' he replied, 'and it will take me some time to digest it all.'

Kwame wasn't sure how much he should tell Afriyie; he certainly didn't want to worry her unnecessarily. So he said, 'I really need a quiet time to think things through. I'll tell you about it later.'

After lunch Afriyie went back to her sewing machine and Kwame sat in his favourite armchair in the lounge. Now he was free for two or three hours calm before Akosua burst into his life again like a vivid flash of lightning followed by a deafening clap of thunder. He wanted his mind to be well composed before that storm broke.

Mr Konadu had popped up unexpectedly in the conversation with Akos Mary and his involvement had raised fresh doubts about the purpose of the snails. Leon Thornet had concluded that the purpose was directed against Kwame, but if Konadu was expecting to collect the snails the possibility of a smuggling attempt could not be ruled out. Should he report Konadu's involvement to Thornet? Or should he just try to get Konadu removed as an illegal immigrant? Either way, he risked getting into trouble for not reporting Konadu earlier; he must be resolved to face that risk.

Kwame was forced to admit that the tests instigated by Leon Thornet had been both sensitive and effective. They had resulted in suspicion being lifted from all of them, even though they had landed in the country with a consignment of cocaine. Tom had almost seen through Tam Gordon's pretence, through his slip over the aero engine and the temporary loss of his dog, but Tam had effectively established that no trace of the drug remained with them. Yet the full truth had not been uncovered. Mr Konadu's involvement still needed to be fitted into the narrative as understood by Leon Thornet and his associates.

After turning these thoughts over in his mind for some time, and trying to see them from various points of view, Kwame decided that he should tell Leon Thornet about Mr Konadu. He would ask for Konadu's relationship to Akos Mary to be handled with sensitivity and for the outcome, whatever it might be, to shield his friend's wife from further harassment. Above all, he wanted to establish a regimen in which none of his close associates had any links to the drugs traders. This was something he had sought for a long time but which seemed to be constantly eluding him.

Akosua burst in with, 'I need more on elephants, Dad!'

'How can I help you?'

'You said that the elephant is part of our culture and so must have been very familiar to our ancestors.'

'That's right.'

'Well, I need some references to elephants, say from the proverbs.'

'One very well-known proverb in several African countries is "When elephants fight the grass is trampled".'

'What does that mean?'

'When big men fight for power many little people get hurt.'

'Of course! Tell me another one.'

'What about *Wodi esono akyi bosu nkawo.*'

'How would you say that in English, Dad?'

'If you walk behind an elephant the dew won't wet you.'

'How would you interpret it?'

'Why don't you think about it?'

The problem, mused Kwame, as Akosua went off to attend to her homework, is finding the right pachyderm to follow, then making sure you're not around when the fight comes. Was Leon Thornet the elephant of choice? Was he powerful enough to defeat the next terrible *sasabonsam* to emerge from the West African jungle? Would an Asante party government in Ghana, whose logo was the elephant, join in the fight against the drugs traders? There were no elephants in South America; was that a good omen or bad? Kwame knew that churning these thoughts any longer would only curdle the output, so he let them dissolve into fantasy as he drifted off to sleep. It wasn't his usual time for a nap, but this wasn't a usual day.

* * *

The next morning he was in trouble with Tom. 'Where were you all day yesterday, Kwame? You missed the meeting on the Ghana trip.'

'Oh, I'm really sorry, Tom, something important came up.'

'You could have telephoned to postpone the meeting.'

'You're right, I should have done that.'

'In the end, we discussed Gould's arrangements without you.'

'I understand.'

'Look, check it all out with Gould; you can tell me the rest over lunch.'

'Yes Prof.'

Kwame was anxious that his assistant's first trip to Kumasi should be successful so he went over the details with care. He knew that Mick Gould would do a good job technically but he needed to be well briefed on customs and protocol. He decided to write a letter to the TCC director warning him not to be put off by Gould's abrupt manner but to take time to get to know him and appreciate his good qualities. He was also wondering if he should take advantage of the visit to send a confidential letter to Comfort asking for her ideas about how the drugged snails got into Akosua's luggage. This decision depended upon whether he wanted to get involved again in helping Leon Thornet's people.

Kwame also needed to think about just how much he should tell Tom. He certainly didn't want to mention Akos Mary's problem with her father. On the other hand, Tom's support and advice had been much appreciated during his previous effort at sleuthing, as Tom liked to call it. So over lunch Kwame launched into an almost full account of what had transpired on the previous day.

'You must be unique in landing in this country with a detected consignment of cocaine and not being detained,' said Tom. 'It's no wonder they wanted to keep a check on us! Thank goodness we all came through with a clean bill of health.'

'You nearly saw through the squadron leader.'

'Not to mention Takoradi.'

'That can't be the dog's real name, can it?'

'I doubt it; but he will always be Takoradi to Akosua.'

'She'll miss the old dog.'

'I'm afraid so.'

That afternoon, Kwame telephoned Leon Thornet to tell him he had some information that might be useful to him. He was told that Jack Preece would be contacting him. Having spent the morning with Mick Gould, Kwame called his other assistants together to review their progress and ensure that all the work was going forward in a coordinated manner. Sandra and Greg had both voiced their disappointment at not being chosen to go on the first mission to Ghana so Kwame took pains to assure them that their turns would come as the project went forward.

The following Sunday morning there was a knock on Kwame's front door. Akosua dashed to open it and then fell on her knees, her arms around the big dog's neck. 'Takoradi's come to see us,' she called out. Kwame hurried to welcome his visitors and invite them inside. Tam followed him into the lounge and accepted a seat. Soon Afriyie was there with water, tea and the few biscuits that remained after Akosua had taken a generous share for Takoradi.

'I thought the young lady would like to take Takoradi for a walk,' said Tam.

'Oh yes please, can I Dad?'

'You can, but I would keep off the common; go to the town square or the park.'

'Thanks Dad.'

After their departure the squadron leader turned to Kwame. 'Now I've finished with Takoradi his future must be decided. I told you he was retired but this was really his last working assignment. Now he really has come to the end of his service and will go to a new home. However, as your daughter has grown so fond of him I wondered if you would let her have him, as a Christmas present perhaps.'

'Please say yes,' said Afriyie.

Kwame usually took his time in reaching a decision but he had already changed his mind about Akosua having a dog. He felt that she could now be trusted to maintain an exercise regime and take a major share in caring for Takoradi. He also admitted that Takoradi would provide a good incentive for himself taking more exercise. So he agreed to take advantage of Tam's kind offer. 'Let's not tell Akosua until you are leaving,' he said.

Tam was persuaded to stay for lunch and afterwards the men relaxed in conversation. Kwame opened with, 'So you weren't in Ghana during the war.'

'No, I'm afraid not; I'm not quite ancient enough for that.'

'But you have spent time in Ghana.'

'Yes, but I'm not supposed to talk about it.'

'Will you be going again?'

'Sorry, I'm not cleared to discuss this issue.'

There was a period of silence while both men tried to find a new topic of conversation. At length Tam said, 'I believe both you and Professor Arthur became suspicious of my role.'

'More Tom than I, I'm afraid.'

'Where did I slip up?'

'First of all there was a problem with the aero engines – the wrong number of cylinders.'

'What then?'

'He wondered where you were when we found Takoradi sniffing around at the Land Rover dealers.'

'What did he conclude?'

'He warned me that you might be a confidence trickster.'

'Well at least that was what I hoped would be your first guess if you had any doubts. Our problem was to get in fast before any traces of cocaine could be lost.'

Akosua and Takoradi came in from the garden. 'Is it four o'clock already, I must be off,' said the squadron leader.

'Oh, must Takoradi leave already,' pleaded Akosua. 'We are having a great game of hunt the slipper.'

'I must go,' said Tam, 'but your father has agreed that Takoradi can stay. Please take good care of him.'

'Is he really staying, is he really?'

'If you promise to exercise him properly.'

'Oh I will, I will! Thank you Uncle Tam.'

'Can I come to see him sometimes?'

'Of course you can; we will always be pleased to see you; won't we Takoradi?'

'Then I'll slip away,' said Tam to Kwame. 'Many thanks for your hospitality. I'll leave the playfellows to continue their game.'

'Goodbye,' said Kwame, 'and be sure to come back any time you want to see Takoradi.'

Kwame closed the door softly, thinking as he turned away that he had not seen the last of the squadron leader.

Christmas was approaching and Kwame was discussing with Mick Gould if he wanted to travel before the holiday or afterwards. 'Mum and Dad want me around over the holiday,' Mick said, 'so would it be OK if I leave early in the New Year?'

50

'That's fine with me,' said Kwame, 'but as Prof is here we'll ask him as well.'

Tom said that he would endorse their decision. After Mick had gone, he asked Kwame if he had any plans for Christmas. 'We've made no firm plans yet,' said Kwame, 'but we were rather hoping to get together with you and your new son.'

'If he arrives in time.'

'I'm sure he will; *abrofo* are good at time management.'

'But his mum is *abibini* so he could still come late!'

'Look,' said Tom, 'Mum and Dad want to do another of their big Christmases and they are inviting you and Afriyie and Akosua.'

'That's wonderful,' said Kwame, remembering the last time that he had spent the festive season with the Arthurs in 1986, during his second year as an undergraduate. Then, remembering the arrow of time, he added, 'Are you sure your parents can cope with so many of us?'

'Oh, we'll all pitch in; I'm sure that you and Afriyie will do your bit. Akos Mary might not be able to do much but I'm sure the rest of us will manage.'

Tom saw Kwame frown and asked if he had thought of a problem. 'I forgot to tell you,' Kwame said, 'but the squadron leader has given Takoradi to Akosua; what will he do while we're away?'

'That's wonderful news, I'm sure she's really happy. Bring them both along; Mum and Dad are serious dog lovers. They will be fascinated to hear the story – the part we can tell them, of course.'

After Tom had gone, Kwame sat thinking of the letter he might send to Comfort with Mick Gould. He decided that whether or not he agreed to help Leon Thornet, he wanted to know who had put the cocaine into Akosua's luggage. Comfort had replied to his first letter apologising for not telling him about the live snails. She also hinted that the remaining cartel members seemed to be intent on reviving their business but she had detected no direct threat to him or Akosua. He decided to send a letter but to keep it short.

Coventry
19th December 1994

Dear Comfort,

    I am sending this letter by hand of Mick Gould because I don't want to risk it going astray in the post. Please send a reply back through Mick.

Thank you for your reply to my first letter and for your apology about the live snails. The creatures didn't cause too much embarrassment at first but they are causing more now. The *abrofo* found cocaine in the shells after all! They didn't tell us at the airport because they were hoping we might lead them to the big people but of course we didn't lead them anywhere. So they called me to a meeting and told me about the cocaine. They want me to help them again but I haven't agreed.

Who do you think could have tampered with Akosua's case and put in the snails with cocaine, and why did they do it? Was it just another attempt at smuggling or was it intended to get me in trouble? Please let me have your thoughts.

By the way, do you know an Auntie Rose? Akos Mary remembers her as one of Mama Kate's girls carrying drugs to London. She is a very small lady – this might jog your memory.

We all wish you a Merry Christmas and a Happy New Year.

Kwame

Kwame put the letter in an envelope and gave it to Mick Gould with instructions on how to find Comfort in Kumasi. It was likely to be more than two months before he would receive a reply but he was content to wait.

Leon Thornet and his people were much less willing to go slowly with their investigations. So that afternoon when Kwame called at the foundry school Jack Preece was waiting in Martin Hutchinson's office. Jack asked to be allowed to talk to Kwame in private for a few minutes and Martin withdrew with rather less grace than Fred Brown used to do. Kwame found himself missing his old friend's conspiratorial wink.

'Leon said that you had some information for us,' said Jack.

'It's a long story for a small piece of information,' said Kwame, 'but it might give you a new lead.' Kwame hoped that he could impart the information without putting Akos Mary or himself under suspicion of aiding and abetting an illegal immigrant. He told Jack about Tom and Akos Mary's wedding and how Dr Arthur Senior had brought Akos Mary's father from Ghana to give her away. The father, Mr Konadu, had disappeared after the wedding and must have remained in the UK as an illegal immigrant. He had recently reappeared in his daughter's life, demanding money and favours. One favour was for Akos Mary to hand over to him the live snails that Kwame was expected to bring from Ghana.

'So it seems that somebody at this end was interested in the live snails, presumably because they were expecting drugs to be hidden inside,' mused Jack. 'Yes, that is interesting, and it does give us a new lead.' Jack was busy making copious notes and Kwame waited for the detailed questioning to begin.

'Do you have any contact details for this Mr Konadu?'

'Only this piece of paper with a telephone number.'

'When did you last see him?'

'Shortly after the wedding in 1990.'

'He's on the wedding photographs, right?'

'Yes, I have one here from Afriyie's album; I thought you might need it.'

'Can Akos Mary provide any more information on his whereabouts?'

'I'd rather you didn't ask her in her present condition.'

'I understand, but it seems that her father has broken the law and tried to force her to do the same. The matter could be too serious to wait.'

Jack Preece copied the telephone number into his notebook, put the slip inside and closed it with a resolute snap. 'I'll pass this on to Leon and await instructions,' he said. 'I don't know how he will want to play it. I'll pass on your plea about the lady's condition and hopefully we can delay any contact until after the delivery.'

'Thank you.'

'And thank you, Kwame. Any more tips like this will be much appreciated.'

When Kwame got back to the office, Tom wasn't there. Seeing Kwame come in, Sandra came over and told him that the professor had received a telephone call and left in a hurry. 'I think his wife is nearly ready,' she said. Kwame decided to go home and collect his family and then follow his friends to the hospital. He knew that was what Afriyie would want to do and Akosua wouldn't want to be left out. Regrettably, this was one occasion when his daughter would have to leave her new pet at home.

Kwame was happy that Akos Mary had been left in peace to bring forth her firstborn son, Thomas Arthur III, the centrepiece of Christmas celebrations for the Arthurs and the Mainus in 1994. Trials lay in wait with the potential to diminish the happiness of the New Year, but everything was perfectly in place for a Merry Christmas.

Akosua had wanted to experience a white Christmas but she was disappointed once again. Mrs Arthur senior recalled seeing a few snowflakes falling the previous year but the snow had not settled. She had done all she could to construct an Old English Christmas but there were some factors that even a professor's wife, and a professor's mother, could not control. So Akosua had to be content to hand out the presents from under the festive tree, making sure that each package was checked for contraband by a good sniff from Takoradi.

When Akosua was not doting over Takoradi she was trying to take a turn tending Thomas Arthur III, but in this she was in keen competition with Akos Mary, Afriyie and Mrs Arthur Senior. Tom would also have liked to get more involved with his son but he told Kwame that he was content to wait until the novelty wore off. He guessed that getting up for the two a.m. and six a.m. feeds would not remain popular for long and he was ready to step in when needed. Dr Arthur Senior contented himself with recalling the trials and tribulations he experienced with Tom as a baby.

The grandparents remembered Afriyie staying with them for a few days on her first visit to England in 1986, and asked what had happened to that handsome and polite Ghanaian gentleman, Peter Sarpong, who had called to take her home. Neither Tom nor Kwame wanted to report that Peter was now a long-term resident of one of Her Majesty's penal institutions, but Tom managed to mumble something through a minced pie about losing track of students after they leave university. Afriyie recalled that she had met the Arthurs again at Tom and Akos Mary's wedding and the conversation quickly reverted to the new baby.

When the baby was sleeping, and the adults and Akosua were gathered around a real log fire and a dormant dog, Akosua's account of the ghosts of Landor House at her school in Warwick provoked a general discussion of the occult. Everyone agreed that if there were ghosts anywhere in those parts it would be in or around Warwick Castle, where so many unfortunates had been tortured and done to death.

'What about ghosts in Ghana?' asked Dr Arthur Senior.

Seeing that the ladies were shy to contribute, Kwame took up the challenge. 'Traditionally in Ghana almost everything is seen as inhabited by spirits,' he began, 'trees and rocks and streams, animals and people. It is generally believed that the spirits of our ancestors are everywhere around us, sometimes manifested as what you call ghosts, but more often speaking through fetish priests. Life is seen by many as a war between good and bad spirits and people seek favours from the one and protection from the other.'

'Don't some people seek the help of evil spirits to harm people they don't like?' asked Dr Arthur, puffing on an annual Christmas cigar which

Mrs Arthur Senior certainly regarded as evidence of possession by an evil spirit.

Kwame, hastening to preserve the peace, answered, 'Those who achieve great wealth or political power quickly are usually suspected of employing occult forces. Many people think that the successful trader, politician or rich person has been helped by black magic, cannibalism or Satan. Our popular press often reports witchcraft accusations and stories about *sika duro*, or money medicine, rituals in which vampires suck the blood of innocent relatives in order to get rich.'

'Oh please stop Dad, you're making my flesh creep,' cried Akosua, and Akos Mary supported her plea, but Dr Arthur was curious to know Kwame's own view of these beliefs.

'I was lucky that my father was a serious rationalist,' he said. 'He told me very little about animistic beliefs and I really only came across them seriously after I started work at the TCC and I was forced to investigate a case of possession by the *mmoatia*.'

'*Mmoatia*? What are *mmoatia*?'

'They are small creatures of human form who are invisible to most people. They live in the forest and have backward pointing feet.'

'How do they possess people?'

'They are said to be employed by fetish priests to capture people who break the fetish law, like working on the *dabone*, the day of evil.'

'Is that like a Sabbath?'

'Exactly.'

'How do people escape from the *mmoatia*?' asked Dr Arthur.

'They must make sacrifices of goats, chickens, eggs, yams and so on, and pour libations of strong spirits.'

'Does it work?'

'As far as I'm aware: it did in the case I encountered.'

'So the fetish priests eat and drink very well!'

'In Ghana all priests are assumed to be rich.'

'But you, personally, Kwame, how do you perceive these fetish beliefs?' Dr Arthur persisted.

'How do you perceive Father Christmas?'

'I get your point.'

'These concepts are as real as we want to make them and they can serve a useful purpose. The problem comes when people lose the power of judgement and become open to exploitation by those intent on gaining money and dominance.'

'The opium of the people, eh?'

'Full Marx!' laughed Tom.

As he made his way to bed, Kwame reflected happily on this conversation. The drugs traders who so afflicted his life were just like the purveyors of religion in exploiting human gullibility. He recalled how he had once told Peter Sarpong, when he spoke of introducing his wares to schoolchildren, that he sounded like a Jesuit priest. Once again he thanked his father for preserving him from such irrationallity.

The ancient bed with its soft springs groaned and sagged even deeper as Afriyie climbed in beside him. 'Kwame, do you remember how you sometimes say good things and bad things come in threes?'

'Yes, I remember.'

'Well, I've asked you for two things.'

'And now you want a baby, to go with the apprentice and the driving lessons.'

'How did you guess?'

'OK, but we must be as quiet as possible!'

Universities have long breaks between the teaching terms but for the researchers the work continues throughout most of the vacation. So, early in the New Year, Kwame was back in the office helping Mick Gould prepare for his imminent departure. Within another few days Mick had flown out, and Kwame was concentrating on giving more attention to the work of his remaining two associates. Both Greg and Sandra were making good progress, but the task was more complex than Kwame had imagined and there were a number of problems to be overcome. Tom had made some useful suggestions and the team had consulted other specialists in the department.

Tom had other concerns. 'We shall soon have to plan for the arrival of the first two academics from Kumasi,' he said. 'One is involved in the solar energy project and the other in electric motor rewinding. We must contact our research teams in these areas to see how best they can fit in an extra pair of hands for a few weeks. Here are the written requests from your people in Kumasi; they're rather brief but it seems the lady, Peggy Osei-Wusu, is mostly interested in solar battery charging and the gentleman, Kwaku Darko, is interested in the small motors used in electronic equipment. The overall aim seems to be to support the use of modern electronic devices in remote areas.'

'When are they coming?' asked Kwame.

'It's not quite settled but we're hoping they can fly back with Mick Gould,' Tom replied.

Kwame realised that he did not have much time in which to prepare, and his research work would need to slow down while he attended to these administrative duties. He began telephoning the people who he believed could help with the programme, and arranged to visit them in their offices, workshops and laboratories. While on the telephone, he rang a local driving school and booked some driving lessons for Afriyie.

Over lunch Kwame asked Tom's advice about Afriyie's first request. 'You had one of Akos Mary's relatives come to stay for some time, didn't you?'

'We did; Celestine stayed for a gap year before starting at the University of Ghana, Legon.'

'Was it difficult to get her papers?'

'Not too bad; we applied for a six-month visitor's visa and later for an extension. Why do you ask?'

'Afriyie wants to bring an apprentice for her dressmaking business.'

'You'll need to provide an air ticket and guarantee her upkeep throughout her stay but that's about it.'

'She will need to stay for longer than one year.'

'Once she's here you can begin applying for a work permit and a residence permit. It's best to hire a specialist lawyer to take care of everything.'

'That's what I was thinking.'

Kwame knew that Afriyie would be happy with the progress he had made on her first two requests, and it would all help with the accomplishment of the third. With that happy thought in mind he went back to his office and his regular duties.

The next few weeks passed uneventfully but with steady progress on all fronts. Afriyie began her driving lessons and an application was made at the British High Commission in Accra for her apprentice to come to the UK. Arrangements went forward for the visits of the Kumasi academics to coincide with the return of Mick Gould. According to his expectations over Christmas, Tom took over the two a.m. bottle feed, and when that ended, the six a.m. feed. Akos Mary, in spite of her undisturbed nights, wrestled with post-partum depression, but her recovery was helped by some fashionable new dresses prepared in advance by Afriyie.

On the appointed day, Kwame drove to Heathrow to meet Mick Gould and the two Ghanaian academics. He met them all together and was pleased that they had got to know one another. This made his administrative task a little easier as Mick might be willing to take over some of the routine activities in support of the visitors.

Driving back to Coventry Kwame asked the visitors if it was their first time in Britain. The man nodded but the woman, Peggy Osei-Wusu, replied that she had relatives in London and had visited before. They were both interested in doing evening and weekend work and they wanted to know if they could get on to post-graduate programmes to stay longer in the UK. Neither asked about the work they had come to do or showed any particular interest in what had been prepared for them. Kwame was disappointed. He knew that Warwick expected people to come from Ghana with his level of enthusiasm for helping in the development of his country, but he also realised that such people were hard to find. He consoled himself with the thought that when they met Tom they would show different faces.

It wasn't until they reached the university that Mick Gould handed Kwame Comfort's letter. He related how he had gone to collect it the day before he left Kumasi. 'Such a beautiful house!' he said. 'The men must be queuing up to get their hands on it.'

Kwame asked Mick to introduce the visitors to their colleagues and hurried to his office. He was anxious to read Comfort's reply that he had anticipated for so long.

Kumasi
8 February 1995

Dear Kwame,
    Thanks for yours of 19 December and for Xmas greetings.
    I was shocked to read that cocaine was found in the snails. I don't know how it got there. I sent my maid to Kejetia market to buy the snails at the same time as yams, plantain, etc. Then I put everything in the case and locked it. Somebody must have changed the snails at some time before I went to St Louis for Akosua but I can't think who. The only person I know who handled the case, apart from me, was my driver and old friend, Kofi Adjare, who you know is quite trustworthy.
    Yours,
    Comfort

This letter didn't tell him anything new, Kwame thought. The only possible suspect seemed to be Kofi Adjare, Comfort's albino driver. Kofi had been Oboroni's driver in Kumasi at the time when Oboroni was Comfort's boyfriend and benefactor. Kofi was wise in the traditional culture of the Akans and an *okyeame* or chief's linguist. Later he had been recruited to be Oboroni's driver in England and had been central to the communications network of the Kumasi drugs cartel, passing on messages in classical Twi. He had been arrested with the other cartel members in the UK in the summer of 1988 but had been released early and repatriated to Ghana on the grounds that he was not fully aware of the activities of the cartel and had been tricked into playing his part. He did not appear to have benefited materially from his involvement.

Comfort had taken pity on Kofi Adjare when he returned from the UK, and given him employment as her driver. She had managed to retain his services even though Mama Kate, a market queen and another former employer, had been released from prison in Ghana and reassumed her former dominant position in the shoe trade.

Kwame reprocessed this history repeatedly but it yielded no clear-cut explanation. Had the reviving cartel found some way to coerce the old *okyeame* into changing the snails in Akosua's case? He had paid his debt for his past crimes and so was immune to threat of exposure; he appeared to seek no material advantage and so was immune to cash inducement. Only threats of actual physical harm remained as a credible possibility.

Kwame felt that he had no reason to tell Leon Thornet about Comfort's letter, as he had learned nothing new that was relevant to the drugs trade in the UK. So he made no attempt to contact his one-time employer. However, Leon's people were leaving no stone unturned in pursuit of their own goals.

On reaching home that evening he found Akos Mary talking to Afriyie. Both women were upset. 'Kwame, some customs officials have called on Akos Mary asking about her dad,' said Afriyie.

'What did they want to know?' asked Kwame.

'They wanted to know where they could find him,' said Akos Mary, 'but I only knew the telephone number that I gave to you, Kwame.'

'Then don't worry; you can't be held responsible for your father's activities.'

'What will happen to him?'

'If he has committed no other offence he will be deported back to Ghana.'

'What if he has already been working with the cartel?'

'Then they will either arrest him and charge him with an offence, or follow him in the hope of catching his bosses.'

'Oh, I hope they just deport him.'

'So do I.'

As Kwame had expected, Peggy Osei-Wusu and Kwaku Darko expressed a keen interest in their designated tasks when they met Professor Tom Arthur, and they were soon settled into the departments where the bigger part of their assignments would be undertaken. After all the initial arrangements had been completed, Kwame was free to discuss his research project with Mick Gould.

'How did you find the workshops in Kumasi and Tema?' he asked.

'Technically they are very good and they have most of the manufacturing capabilities we need but we'll have trouble getting them to work from drawings. They work mostly from memory and by copying imported products or standard products made by competitors. If we want several workshops to collaborate, we must get them working from drawings.'

'What do you suggest?'

'The university in Kumasi could run some short courses on working from engineering drawings.'

'Did you consult anyone at the School of Engineering?'

'Yes, Professor Akuffo, Professor Kwami and Mr Dodoo are all keen to help.'

'Did you get a cost estimate?'

'They gave me the cost of tuition fees and use of technical facilities and I checked the cost of board and accommodation with your TCC colleagues.'

'How many students can they take on each course?'

'They said twenty-five, thirty maximum.'

'So you have a total cost for one course?'

'We can run a two week residential course for thirty artisans for a round figure of four thousand pounds.'

Kwame had been expecting this outcome but he felt that it was good for it to be confirmed by one of his colleagues. Now he set his team to plan a course to be run at the School of Engineering, liaising with the people in Kumasi. The timing would have to be during a university vacation, the engineers would deliver the instruction and the TCC would arrange board and accommodation in a hall of residence on campus. They should also arrange at least one field trip to a modern manufacturing enterprise, like the Neoplan bus assembly plant in Kumasi, to see how engineering drawings were used in practice.

One of the most difficult issues was whether to charge a fee for attendance and, if so, how much. Not charging a fee could result in a large number of applicants, many of whom were not seriously interested in the course content. Too high a fee, on the other hand, could mean that serious candidates were prevented from attending. He decided to ask the people in Kumasi to suggest a low fee that would deter free-riders, but hopefully not keen young engineers anxious to improve their skills.

The people in Kumasi would also be charged with recruitment once the timing of the course had been set. Kwame asked Mick if he felt that they could be ready in time to schedule the event during the Easter vacation. Mick thought that in view of slow communications with Kumasi it was safer to aim for July, at the beginning of the summer vacation. Kwame agreed that it was sensible to take more time and do a better job.

One issue that Kwame knew would soon need his attention was which of his associates should travel to Kumasi to help with the final preparations and delivery of the course. They would all want to go, but it was likely that funding would be approved for only one. Ideally, he would like Mick to follow up on his groundwork but that might be viewed by the others as unfair. He thought that he could satisfy Greg with the promise of a computer-aided drawing course to follow sometime after the basic course had been run once or twice. Sandra posed a more difficult problem; her opportunity seemed much more remote. Yet it would be good to have all his people familiar with conditions in Kumasi as early as possible. Maybe he should ask Tom to approve both Mick and Sandra travelling to Ghana in July. He would take time to think about whether such expenditure could be justified.

5

Echoes From the Past

Akosua's fifteenth birthday on the sixteenth of February was quickly followed by Kwame's thirty-eighth on the second of March. Preparations for the course in Kumasi progressed slowly. Mick had been right; it would have been too much of a rush to try to mount it in March or April, so they confirmed the date in July.

Kwame was surprised that Leon Thornet's people had allowed him such a respite, but that was coming to an end. He was asked to meet Auntie Rose once more at the hairdresser's at the close of work.

This time the little woman was waiting for him in the same office they had used before. Akos Mary was not around and Kwame wondered how Auntie Rose had arranged the one-to-one meeting. After the usual greetings, Kwame sat in the only chair and Auntie Rose perched herself on the desk with her tiny feet swinging to and fro in an arc that bisected the space between desk top and floor. He noted with relief that her feet really did point forwards.

'Leon wants you to help him with just one more thing,' she said.

'You all know I want nothing more to do with it,' Kwame replied, annoyed that the sleuths wouldn't leave him in peace.

'But this is connected to your old assignment.'

'How can it be, they're all in prison?'

'That's what puzzled us, but the messages have resumed.'

'What messages?'

'The telephoned instructions in Twi to the drugs sellers.'

'You can tell Leon what's being said.'

'Yes, but I don't know the old Twi like you do, and I didn't hear the messages that you interpreted last time.'

Kwame couldn't see any problem that necessarily involved him. It was obvious that some new people had taken over the drugs trade and had adopted a similar means of communication.

'Why does Leon want me to get involved again?'

62

'Because, as far as we can tell, it's the same voice.'

'You mean the voice of Kofi Adjare?'

'Yes.'

When Kwame recovered from the shock of this revelation he realised that the information gleaned from Comfort's letter was relevant to Leon's quest after all. So he told Auntie Rose about the possibility that Kofi Adjare, the albino *okyeame*, might have put the cocaine snails in Akosua's suitcase. 'If it is Kofi Adjare sending the messages,' he said, 'he's sending them from Ghana. He must be using a mobile phone like I was using before I came here. He can use it anywhere around Accra, Tema and Kumasi and soon the coverage will be extended more widely.'

'Leon is interested in who's giving him his instructions.'

'That could be any one of the recently released drugs bosses.'

'Will you listen to some of the new messages?'

'OK. Shall I come to the police station in Warwick?'

'Yes please.'

Akos Mary came in, saying that if they had finished she would close the salon. Auntie Rose thanked her for her cooperation and slipped away almost unnoticed, saying that she had her own transport. Kwame asked Akos Mary to wait a moment. 'I need to get something off my chest,' he said. 'I've been trying to tell you for a long time. I must beg your forgiveness for having been indirectly involved in your arrest. Can you forgive me?'

'I forgave you long ago, Kwame Mainu. Tom explained it all to me.'

'I was only interpreting some messages for the *abrofo*. I didn't realise how many people would be arrested.'

'It's OK Kwame, you both tried to help me to stop, like Afriyie did. It was my own fault that I kept on working with Peter Sarpong.'

'Well, it's important that we understand each other because the *abrofo* want me to give them more help and this time your father could be involved.'

'I still hope my father will be deported before he does anything more serious.'

'I hope so too, but they haven't found him yet.'

'Is Auntie Rose helping them?'

'Yes, she brought the message to me from the *abrofo*.'

'Oh Kwame, do be careful.'

When Kwame reached home, Afriyie had some good news. 'My sister's girl, Elsie Ntim, has got her visa,' she told him. 'She'll be coming before the end of April.'

'Then we must get her room ready.'

'Can we buy a few new things?'

'Of course, how old is she?'

'About eighteen, I think.'

'Then she'll be good company for you and Akosua.'

'Who will be good company for me?' asked Akosua, coming in from the garden with Takoradi.

'Afriyie's niece, Elsie, is coming to help her with the dressmaking,' said Kwame, 'and we must all help to get her room ready and give her a warm welcome. We must treat her like a member of the family, not as a house girl.'

'That's fine with me Dad; we never had a house girl in Ghana and we won't have one here, will we Takoradi?'

Takoradi said nothing.

'How much schooling has Elsie had?' asked Kwame.

'According to my sister she finished middle school,' replied Afriyie.

Kwame frowned, 'Then she won't speak much English and will probably have problems with reading and writing. We must give some thought to helping her continue her education by distance learning or evening classes.'

'I'll help her with all that,' said Akosua.

Next time it was Kwame's turn to take the girls to school he made his way dutifully to the police station in Warwick. He was surprised to meet the full reception committee of Leon, Jack and Auntie Rose. He had not realised that the matter was accorded that degree of importance. 'Tam couldn't make it then,' he observed in greeting but without provoking any response. Leon invited them all to sit down and make themselves comfortable. Then he turned to the tape recorder on the central coffee table.

'I want to begin by playing some of the tapes we kept of old messages that Kwame interpreted back in 1987,' he said. 'This will freshen our memories of the sound of Adjare's voice. For those of us who speak no Twi, here are copies of Kwame's translations. However, I want us to concentrate on the sound of the voice rather than on the content of the messages.'

The sound of the tapes took Kwame back nearly eight years and revived memories of those fraught times. It was difficult to concentrate on the job in hand when threatened by a flood of freshly thawed emotions. Leon sensed something of Kwame's turmoil and patiently played several tapes, pausing between recordings to allow comments and discussion. Only when he was sure Kwame was restored to equilibrium did he suggest moving on to some of the current material.

As soon as the new recordings started Kwame was convinced that it was the old familiar voice of the albino *okyeame*. Quite apart from the sound of the voice, there was the use of classical language and quotations from the oral literature of the Akans that had presented Kwame with so much difficulty in 1987. The old master had lost none of his skill; in fact, returning to Ghana seemed to have helped him to reach an even higher level.

'Do you really understand all that stuff?' asked Auntie Rose.

'Only if I listen to it several times over,' Kwame replied.

'So we can conclude that the Kumasi cartel is still using the same person to communicate information and instructions,' said Leon, 'and as that person is now in Ghana, we can assume that the control is being exercised from Ghana.' Nods all round signified unanimous agreement. Leon continued, 'Kwame thinks that this has been made possible by the use of mobile telephones, which have recently become available in Ghana.'

Kwame added, 'When I left last year the service only embraced Accra, Tema and Kumasi, but that would be enough for a start.'

Leon continued, grim faced, 'This development concerns us because the cartel no longer needs to expose one of its leaders to our attention here in the UK. They don't need to send another Crispin Russell, alias Charles Richards, for us to arrest and put out of circulation. Auntie Rose can confirm that they don't take much care of the foot soldiers, and they will probably take even more risks now all the leaders are safe in Ghana. They only need a proportion of their couriers to get through to maintain a highly profitable operation.'

Leon turned to Kwame. 'I know you've only listened to the new tapes once, but can you tell us anything interesting?'

Kwame asked to hear the recordings again and then he listened to one a third time. 'Most of it is straightforward instructions,' he said, 'but there are a few remarks that indicate new developments that we already know something about. The cartel is worried about the South Americans coming to Ghana. What concerns them most is first that their experienced local managers in the UK are being head-hunted and they are pleading with them to stay loyal to their own people. Second, they are worried about the sale of drugs in Ghana. They feel that as people see the bad effects on the local youth they will lose their tacit support.'

'How do you mean?'

'Well, most Ghanaians are reluctant to get involved in other people's business and so they are unlikely to risk taking any action to expose the drug traders as long as the bad effects are limited to foreigners.'

'Can you give us an example of this attitude?'

'You can see it in the national press, which sees the drugs trade as a contest of wits between the smugglers and the British customs. If anything, the journalists side with the smugglers.'

'Anything else?'

'The cartel leaders also fear that the changing attitude of the people will put pressure on the Ghana government to take stronger action against the drugs trade.'

Kwame turned to Auntie Rose. 'You said that you had difficulty understanding the recordings, how did you get on when you were an active courier?'

'The messages are intended for local managers like Peter Sarpong,' Auntie Rose replied, 'and these people are given a small code book which is changed from time to time. They are told to memorise it and then destroy it.'

'So the couriers don't hear the messages directly.'

'No, they are told what to do by the managers. In any case, many of the couriers are illiterates.'

After an exchange of signals with Leon, Jack Preece said, 'We have some good news for you, Kwame, or rather for the professor's wife. Mr Konadu has been arrested as an illegal immigrant.'

'How did that happen?'

'Someone telephoned to the police giving his current address.'

'Do you know who that someone might be?'

'We think that the informer was acting for the Kumasi cartel.'

'Why should he do that?'

'We suspect that Mr Konadu had gone over to the South Americans.'

'Was he trying to divert the cocaine in my snails?'

'It's possible.'

As soon as Kwame got back to his office he telephoned Akos Mary to tell her that her father had been arrested. She received the news with relief and concern. 'Will he be deported back to Ghana?' she asked.

'That's the most likely outcome,' said Kwame, 'but they will want to interrogate him about his other activities before sending him home.'

'How will they treat him?'

'You should know.'

'I guess he won't be hurt.'
'I'm sure he won't.'

Tom had given provisional approval for a budget of £12,000 to fund three courses in Kumasi. The first two would be on the use of engineering drawings in manufacturing and the third on computer-aided drawing. Kwame held a meeting with his team to review progress. The content of the first course had been agreed with the professors in Kumasi and the TCC had made all arrangements for board and lodging for thirty people. A detailed costing could now be done. The one issue to be resolved was the fee to be charged to participants. Opinions were divided, both in Kumasi and in Coventry. Eventually, it was agreed to keep the fee very low but to vet the applicants to try to eliminate time-wasters. The fee level could be raised for future courses as long as it was found that the serious applicants were not deterred.

It was with a feeling of having accomplished some useful work that Kwame set out once more for Warwick. The school trip shortened his working day, and this morning's meeting in Warwick had eaten up more time, but it had answered some questions and cleared up some concerns. So he was in a cheerful mood when he met Akosua and her four classmates. He was even more cheerful when he was told, 'Thank you, Mr Mainu, for helping us with the assignment on endangered species. Our report on the West African elephant was given an A. The teacher particularly commended what we did on the local cultural background.' Kwame checked in the rear view mirror to see a beaming Akosua, lit up in her father's reflected glory.

Next day, on the drive down to Heathrow to meet Afriyie's new apprentice, Kwame tried to remember what an eighteen-year-old girl would be like. Some eighteen-year-olds projected the persona of women in their twenties, while others could still be mistaken for middle school leavers in their mid-teens. Village girls tended to be somewhat retarded in their development, and so Kwame hoped to meet someone who looked and behaved like Akosua and whom he could regard as another daughter or niece. He had invested much time and effort into establishing his monogamous relationship with Afriyie and he would prefer to avoid any destabilising influence invading his presently peaceful home.

They waited patiently for the passengers to emerge into the arrivals hall, Afriyie holding a large card with ELSIE NTIM written in bold letters. They were assuming that even a middle school leaver would be able to read her own name. In the end, however, literacy was irrelevant because Afriyie recognised her sister's daughter and called the bewildered teenager to push her trolley in their direction.

Kwame noted with relief that Elsie could easily pass for Akosua's younger sister. Her relief at seeing the welcoming party was openly expressed and Afriyie and Akosua immediately engulfed her in a torrent of Twi.

On the journey back to Coventry not a word of English was spoken. Kwame realised that this was an essential part of making Elsie feel at home but it could not be allowed to develop into a permanent condition. He must ensure that the use of English was gradually restored, to support Elsie's adaptation to English life and to avoid any impediment to Akosua's progress. At the same time he reassured himself that Akosua would not tolerate any restriction of her freedom to express herself fully in whichever language she pleased.

That evening Afriyie thanked Kwame for bringing her an apprentice. 'How are the driving lessons going?' he asked.

'Oh fine, I can now do three-point turns but backing around a corner is difficult.'

'Do you have a test scheduled?'

'Mrs Parker will book it when I'm ready.'

'And your third request; any news about that?'

'None so far, I'm afraid.'

'Then we must try harder.'

Tom called Kwame to a meeting in his office. 'A most unusual situation has arisen,' he began, 'and I'm wondering how it could have come about.'

'How do you mean?'

'It concerns your engineering drawing course in Kumasi.'

'What about it?'

'We agreed to send Mick back there with Sandra, didn't we?'

'That's right. Mick will ensure continuity and Sandra needs the experience.'

'Well, I had a Jack Preece in here yesterday offering to fund the cost of sending you as well.'

'Oh no!'

'What's going on, Kwame? Why should Her Majesty's Customs want to fund part of your research project? If you're working for the sleuths again, shouldn't I know about it?'

'You're right, but as far as I'm aware I'm not working for the sleuths again and I have no plans to go to Ghana in July.'

Kwame told Tom about his recent meetings with Leon Thornet and how it was now believed that the revived drugs trade was being directed from Ghana with the same person involved in communications. 'Do you mean that albino fellow you exposed is now back on the telephone?' Tom asked.

'Yes, but they don't know who's directing operations.'

'Does it matter? I mean, if they're not in the UK there's not much they can do about it, is there?'

'They seem to want to know what's going on. They suspect that some Venezuelans or Brazilians are trying to cut out the Kumasi middle men and take over the trade through Ghana to the UK.'

'Is that relevant to what's happening here?'

'Yes, the South Americans are selling drugs in Ghana and this could turn the people and government against the traders.'

'How does that help the UK?'

'The British feel that it will make it possible to negotiate an international agreement to collaborate in stopping the trade.

'An Anglo-Ghanaian treaty, eh? Now that's something worth striving for.'

'So you would support my involvement?'

'If you want to do it, I won't object.'

Kwame realised that Leon Thornet had been very clever in devising a way of using Tom to help persuade him to resume his collaboration with the British customs. 'So Jack Preece succeeded in recruiting your support for Leon's scheme,' he said.

'Oh no, he only asked me to send you to Ghana with your two colleagues at Her Majesty's expense,' replied Tom with a knowing smile.

The four weeks of the study tour for the two Ghanaian academics had passed and Kwame prepared to drive them back to the airport. Progress reports had been sent from the departments to which they had been attached and these were generally satisfactory. Kwame was relieved that they had not disgraced themselves by poor attendance or overt lack of interest. Nevertheless, on the journey to Heathrow he was forced to listen to complaints about poor pay and lack of opportunity to buy all the things they needed to return home without loss of face. He wondered what he and Tom could do in future to select better-motivated people. Perhaps, if he took up the offer to go to Ghana in July, he could take a closer hand in the selection of the next group.

In spite of their complaints about lack of funds, both Peggy and Kwaku had filled their cases well beyond the airline's weight allowance. When this was pointed out by Kwame, efforts were made at the airport to transfer as much as possible to hand bags. In this exercise much advice was gained from other Ghanaians travelling on the same flight, many of whom seemed to be in the same plight. Large reinforced woven plastic bags with red or blue stripes seemed to be much in favour for hand baggage. Kwame felt sorry for the airline officials who had to deal with this situation on every flight. He had seen on his own journeys how extra personnel were stationed at the door of the aircraft to remove large hand bags from struggling passengers for safer transport in the baggage hold.

The repacking was almost complete and Kwame was looking forward to seeing his charges safely checked in and through passport control when a well-dressed Ghanaian gentleman with carefully parted hair and horn-rimmed spectacles came up to them and introduced himself as Peggy's senior brother, Yaw. 'You don't need to go through yet, your flight's not for another hour,' he said. 'Come for a coffee and a chat.' Kwame, assuming that all were invited, turned to follow. 'It's OK, I'll look after her from here,' said big brother airily, as he walked off, one arm around his sister's shoulders and the other pushing her baggage trolley. They made a handsome couple but left Kwame in a quandary.

A good general does not divide his forces and for Kwame, being alone, division of forces was impossible. So he watched helplessly as one of his charges escaped. Then he focused his attention on Kwaku, gazing wistfully at the back of his departing colleague. No, thought Kwame, you're not going to abscond as well, and he marched Kwaku over to the check-in desk and from there to passport control. He waited until the young man was lost from view in the departures lounge, then turned quickly away and headed for the coffee shop. As he had expected, the brother and sister were not there, nor in any of the other refreshment areas. As he walked slowly back to the car park he wondered if Kwaku, too, would find a way to avoid travelling, even though his checked-in baggage was probably already loaded on the aircraft.

On the drive back to Coventry Kwame tried to convince himself that he had done all he could. There was a good chance that he had scored fifty per cent. It was a pass, but well short of a distinction. He reflected with pride that during his period of service, both the TCC and GRID had succeeded in recovering one hundred per cent of their people sent overseas for training and work experience. Why were people from other departments and institutions so much less likely to return home? What was wrong with his country? It was little consolation that people from other developing countries behaved in a similar way. He couldn't help wondering if he would ever see Afriyie's new apprentice return to Ghana.

'How's Elsie getting on?' he asked Afriyie on his return.

'As far as learning the sewing,' Afriyie replied, 'she's doing very well, but she won't go out to meet people.'

'Is she shy of speaking English?'

'I think that's part of the problem.'

'And the rest?'

'Well, she's a village girl, a *kuraseni*; it's too big a step for her to take.'

'She should start English lessons. That will give her more confidence.'

'I hope you're right.'

After making enquiries, Kwame found that there were many English courses on offer at schools and libraries in all parts of Coventry. Basic English for foreigners was offered at part-time day classes extending over thirty-six weeks. He enrolled Elsie on one such course at a school within walking distance of his house. Afriyie accompanied Elsie on her first day and was relieved to find other African men and women attending the class. She told Kwame that she hoped Elsie would make one or two friends to encourage her to keep up attendance and study seriously.

Kwame asked Afriyie how she would feel about him travelling to Ghana in July. 'Will it be safe for you to go?' she asked. 'You said that you wouldn't go back for at least a year.'

'It will be almost a year since we came and it will be a short trip.'

'How long?'

'About three weeks, perhaps four, the training course is for two weeks but we must go early to help with the preparations.'

'Well, I will have Elsie for company, as well as Akosua and Akos Mary.'

'Not to mention Tom Arthur the Third.'

'Oh yes, and Takoradi!'

With no strong objection from Afriyie, and with Tom's support, Kwame decided to accept Leon's offer of a trip back to Ghana. He had been slow in reaching his decision but now it was made he had to admit to a feeling of excitement. He was curious to know what was going on in Kumasi, and now that the work could be seen as helping Ghana he was more strongly motivated to do what he could to defeat the drug traders. The thought of monetary reward had not featured in reaching his decision but he now reflected happily that a little extra cash would facilitate the expansion of his family.

Kwame called Mick and Sandra to his office to review progress in preparing the Kumasi course. 'It's much as we imagined,' said Mick, 'The first course is oversubscribed and we are already taking bookings for a repeat course in January.'

'Our friends in Kumasi have been working hard,' said Kwame, 'but it also seems that we pitched the fee too low.'

'It's too late to change the fee now, but we could charge more for the repeat course and for Greg's computer drawing course,' said Sandra.

Kwame asked to see the list of companies applying to attend, 'We need to ensure a balance between foundries and machine shops.' Mick passed him a copy of the latest note from Kumasi and Kwame scanned a column of familiar names. 'It's very encouraging that so many Tema firms are coming,' he told his colleagues. 'It keeps open the option of building the prototype engine in Kumasi or Tema, or perhaps working with two teams in parallel.

'Which team would you expect to do the better job?' asked Mick. 'That's a good question,' said Kwame. 'The Kumasi workshops have a wider range of relevant technologies and make a wider range of products but the Tema companies have more modern managements and tend to work to higher standards. I would expect the Tema firms to work with us more smoothly but they might have to send to Kumasi for specialist operations like crankshaft grinding and cylinder boring.'

'I'm really looking forward to seeing what's going on down there,' said Sandra, 'especially the foundries.'

'Then we'd better arrange for you to spend a few days in Tema,' said Kwame.

The next time that Kwame saw Tom, he asked him if anything had been agreed with Jack Preece about dividing his time between Leon's work and the engineering drawing course. 'Nothing definite was agreed but we assumed a roughly even division of time,' said Tom. 'I felt that you would be much involved in preparations for the course but you would have time to spare for your sleuthing while classes were in progress.'

'That's roughly how I see it too,' said Kwame, 'but I will need to take some time early on to set up meetings or I might not achieve anything useful in the time available.'

'That's fine with me.'

With GCSE examinations approaching, Akosua's evenings were filled with homework and revision. So it was Kwame who often found himself walking the dog on fine May evenings. Takoradi usually showed his advanced years and good training in his willingness to advance at the pace of whoever was holding the other end of his lead, but this evening he showed an uncharacteristic enthusiasm for a higher rate of progression. By the time they reached the common Kwame was speculating about the ultimate tensile strength of dog leads, as Takoradi towed him straight towards the old bench under the big oak tree.

It wasn't the memory of a heroin syringe that attracted the big dog but the sight or scent of the old man sitting on the bench. He didn't look like the squadron leader but Kwame knew that it must be Tam Gordon. He immediately recognised the familiar voice and clipped military pronunciation that greeted Takoradi, 'Hello old chap, so you remember your old master.' Then looking up at Kwame, '*Y'ahyiahyia.*'

'*Ya agya.*'

'*Okraman ani agyie!*'

'Yes, it makes him happy to see you.'

'It seems you look after him well.'

'We try, but I'm afraid that we spoil him.'

'Who will look after him while you're in Ghana?'

'My wife and daughter.'

'Afriyie and Akosua, how are they?'

'By God's grace, they are well.'

So far, apart from greeting the dog, the old man had said nothing in English and Kwame realised that Tam seemed to be more fluent in Twi every time he met him. He speculated on the level of the asymptote. Sitting down on the bench, he waited for the serious business to begin while Tam continued to make a fuss of his former canine conspirator.

'Here are your instructions from Leon,' Tam began. 'Commit them to memory but make no written notes. In Kumasi you will talk to your contacts that are close to the cartel and try to find out who is giving instructions to the linguist. You must try to move and act as though you are carrying out your university duties or making social calls, and you are not expected to take any unnecessary risks. You will carry this mobile phone and dial this number if you need urgent help. Don't try to report to the UK until you return, when you will be debriefed by Leon. Do you have any questions?'

'Can I come back early if I get into difficulty?'

'Yes, you will be given priority if you change your air travel arrangements; just ring the airline on this number.'

'Can I delay coming back if I need more time?'

'Yes, but use the mobile phone to give warning of the delay. You should also have a covering reason related to your university work.'

'Can I send letters home?'

'Yes, provided that they are purely personal or relate only to your regular work.'

'Will I have any support?'

'Auntie Rose will be there but your paths might not cross.'

'What about you?'

'That's up to Leon.'

At his office in the university the post had just arrived, and Kwame had begun to sort the urgent matters from the routine, when Sandra came to say that Prof needed him. As soon as he saw Tom's face he knew what had happened. The letter in Tom's hand bore the logo of Kumasi university and the discarded envelope on the desk displayed a general's chest-spread of brightly coloured Ghanaian postage stamps. 'So the young lady didn't make it back to Ghana,' Kwame said.

'You suspected this, didn't you?' said Tom grimly.

'Yes, I lost control of the situation when her big brother took her away at the airport. I couldn't be with them both at the same time.'

'No one is blaming you, Kwame; you did your best.'

'Will you write back and explain what happened?'

'Yes, but I suppose we could give the lady a little more time before writing her off for good.'

'We could, but I suspect she will stay in the UK on a more or less permanent basis.'

'And we have no way of tracing her?'

'None that I can think of.'

'At least Darko returned to Kumasi on schedule.'

'That's a relief! I thought he might find a way to escape.'

'No big brother, eh?'

'We must try to find a way to stop this happening,' said Tom, 'otherwise our training programme loses much of its purpose.'

'It's very difficult,' replied Kwame. 'You really have to know people very well before you can be sure that they are dedicated to their work back home and want to return to it more than they want to run away to greener pastures.'

'Are there any practical steps that we can take?'

'We must find a way to select the people more carefully.'

'Would that mean you getting involved in Kumasi in every case?'

'That might help.'

'Anything else?'

'Could we think of some incentives?'

'Like what?'

'Payments collectable only after return to Ghana, opportunities to publish books and articles, that sort of thing; just something to help tip the scales.'

'Could you write a short paper on this; something I can use when the sponsors start asking questions about the output benefits, or lack of them?'

'OK.'

'Kwame, don't these people have families to return to?' asked Tom earnestly.

'It's the families that cause the trouble,' Kwame replied. 'They want a family member to succeed in *aborokyiri* and send money home.'

'Yes, but I mean wives and children, not extended family members.'

'The married ones are just as keen to escape overseas; I was. They expect to be able to send for their nuclear family in due course.'

'So it's only dedication to their work in Ghana, or some counterbalancing financial benefit, that can guarantee return.'

'In general, yes.'

Kwame felt distinctly uncomfortable discussing this issue with Tom. He had done his best to ensure the return of the two academics but had known in advance that he was likely to fail. He felt that Tom understood the issue in his personal capacity as a friend but was compelled to question it rigorously in his official capacity of project leader. Each absconder would be viewed by Tom's superiors and the project sponsors as a lost output; a trained professional who would not apply his new knowledge and skills in Ghana. A multiplicity of absconders would be seen to render the programme non-cost-effective, and funding might be curtailed.

The next time Kwame was summoned to Tom's office it was to be confronted by an immigration official. 'It seems that a spot check has revealed that Miss Peggy Osei-Wusu did not board her return flight to Accra,' said Tom, 'The immigration officials are trying to trace her whereabouts.'

Kwame retold the story of what happened at the airport. 'Can you describe the brother who seems to have prevented her departure?' asked the official.

'He looked like a typical businessman: in a smart suit, collar and tie, parted hair in the way some Africans copy traditional European hairstyle, horn-rimmed glasses.

'Did he give a name?'

'Only Yaw, meaning born on Thursday, it's very common in Ghana.'

'Would he have the same surname or family name as his sister?'

'It's possible but by no means certain; they might not be true siblings, and even if they were, their names could be different.'

The official turned to Tom. 'Please provide us with copies of whatever documents you have related to Miss Osei-Wusu. If she attempts to contact you, or if you hear anything of her whereabouts, you should tell us.'

'We will certainly do that,' said Tom.

When the official had gone, Tom said that this was another reason for tightening up on their selection procedures. 'We don't want immigration officials calling here every time we take some trainees from Kumasi,' he said. 'It will bring the university into disrepute and further damage the project. We must suspend recruitment until you've had a chance to interview the next batch of candidates. In the meantime, is there anything we can do to trace Peggy from here?'

'I could make some enquiries in the department where she worked but I doubt if she left any contact details in the UK.'

'You do that, but don't waste too much time on it.'

Kwame decided to start straight away; so that afternoon he walked over to the solar energy research laboratory where Peggy had worked during her stay at the university. He was known to the laboratory staff so his visit excited no special interest. 'Your lady has left,' called a research assistant from down the corridor but a door slammed before Kwame could make a reply. He found two lab technicians dismantling an experimental rig, 'Is this Peggy's experiment?' he asked.

'Yes, she didn't have time to take it down before she left,' replied one. 'Too busy shopping,' added the other.

'Did she leave any notes?' asked Kwame.

'Not here, but you could check her office. She shared with Doctor Leggit-Brown.'

Kwame knew Sam Leggit-Brown, a post-doctoral research fellow who had supervised Peggy's research. Sam was one of those keen young researchers who never seemed to go home so Kwame was not surprised to find him hard at work on a personal computer. 'I'm sorry to disturb you,' he said, 'but we need to clear up Peggy's assignment. Did she leave any notes with you?'

'That's the desk she used,' replied Sam. 'See what you can find.'

Kwame rummaged through some pamphlets on the desk and looked inside the drawers. He found a notebook but it contained very few notes and no contact details of any kind. A mail order catalogue for ladies' clothes had some items circled and some notes on colour combinations and price calculations, but nothing relevant to the current quest. So

Kwame turned back to the earnest researcher. 'Did she leave any contact details?'

'We only have her official address in Kumasi.'

'Nothing here in the UK?'

'No, even when she went away for the weekend she forgot to leave a contact telephone number.'

'Did she leave you her final report on her research assignment?' asked Kwame.

'No, she did not. She said something about sending it later,' Sam replied.

'What about your report; when will we get it?'

'Oh, you'll have my report by next Friday but it won't be very long.'

'How's that?'

'She didn't do very much.'

'So how would you summarise her visit?'

'To be frank; it was a waste of time.'

Sam had returned to his computer screen and remained silent for some time. Kwame waited patiently expecting more to come. 'We've all been impressed with your work, Kwame, and we were keen to help you and Professor Arthur with your project, but if Peggy is typical of the people you are bringing here we will have to reconsider our involvement. We do serious work in this laboratory and can't afford to waste resources carrying passengers. We expect to have to teach them a few new tricks, but we assume that they have a good basic understanding and a keen interest in the work. If Peggy has any technical knowledge she concealed it effectively, and as for interest, that seemed to be limited to nail polish and hair styles.'

Kwame was taken aback by this frank outburst. He had always regarded Sam as a quiet intellectual who avoided confrontation. If Peggy's attitude had upset him to this extent something could be seriously wrong with the selection procedures. Tom was justified in stopping recruitment until he, Kwame, could interview the next batch of hopefuls in Kumasi. He thanked Sam for his plain speaking and said that he looked forward to reading his official report.

He was now convinced that Peggy had planned to abscond from the outset. He remembered how such thoughts had circulated in his own mind on his first visit to England. However, in his case he had taken a serious interest in his work and studies, and eventually this interest had steered him onto his present course. He couldn't bring himself to condemn Peggy, but he wished she had done more for the programme, and for her colleagues, by showing more enthusiasm for the opportunity she had been given.

Although he seemed to have drawn a blank, he picked up Peggy's notebook and the mail order catalogue. It was a remote possibility, but the lady might have ordered something to be delivered after she left Coventry, in which case she must have provided a delivery address. Although the marketing company was unlikely to supply such information to a private person, the immigration authorities or the police could gain access to it.

The next day Kwame decided to visit the laboratory where Kwaku Darko had undertaken his assignment. Here he was relieved to find that his compatriot had left a good impression. Doctor Thomas Wright reported that Kwaku had shown keen interest, put in sufficient time and effort and produced good results. He handed Kwame a copy of Darko's final report and promised to send his own report within the next few days. 'Will we be getting any more of your Kumasi people?' asked Dr Wright.

'It's possible,' replied Kwame. 'It depends on who's selected and where their technical interest lies.'

'So maybe next time we'll get the dolly bird!'

Kwame was puzzled by this remark, 'Are you referring to Peggy Osei-Wusu?' he asked.

'Is that what Sam's girl is called? Well she certainly caused a stir amongst the single chaps.'

'How do you mean?'

'It seems they were all after her, but Sam claimed proprietary rights.'

'Did he succeed?'

'I guess not; she seemed to be playing the field.'

These remarks did little to redeem Peggy's reputation but they might shed some light on Sam Leggit-Brown's stern condemnation. This was the sort of problem he used to like to discuss with Comfort but she was no longer available. He doubted if Afriyie would be much help. Then Kwame remembered that a decade ago Akos Mary had created much the same reaction amongst the male members of the West African club. He decided to make a social call on the Arthurs that evening.

'You will be interested to hear about this, Tom, but I'm really here to ask Akos Mary for her views,' Kwame said by way of introduction. He then explained what he had learned from the two supervisors.

'Peggy came in twice to have her hair done,' said Akos Mary. 'I got the impression that she was looking for a way to extend her stay, but then we all do it, don't we?'

'That's why I'm asking,' said Kwame. 'You captured Tom; did she show any interest in following a similar path?'

'She did ask one time which hairstyles the *abrofo* liked.'

'Do you think that her presence provoked exceptional male interest, perhaps even jealousy? Yours certainly did!'

'Yes, I would say it could easily have done that. She took much care over her appearance. What do you think, Tom?'

'Well, I only met her once on a one-to-one basis but she could certainly turn on the charm.'

Tom turned to Kwame, 'You think that Dr Leggit-Brown's comments might have been sharpened by jealousy?'

'Yes, it seems possible, but it doesn't tell us anything about the lady's whereabouts or do much to change our perception of her performance. Whatever she focused her energy on it wasn't her work and her studies.'

'What I don't understand,' said Tom, 'was why you didn't pick up the problem sooner.'

'Well, she wasn't here for long, and I guess the interim reports from the department allowed some scope for settling in. Unfortunately, she never settled.'

'Or settled too well!'

Kwame gave Tom Peggy's notebook and the mail order catalogue. 'You could pass these on to your official friends,' he said. 'It's just possible they might get an address from the mail order company. The items she ringed and annotated might help to identify an order, if she made one.'

'I'll do that,' agreed Tom. 'It's a long shot but at least it shows that we tried to help the authorities in their enquiries.'

'Oh, please let me have a look at the catalogue first,' said Akos Mary.

6

Sustainability

Overseas trips, like birthdays, always arrive before one is ready, and that was how Kwame found himself flying to Accra on a Monday afternoon in July 1995. Mick Gould had gone in advance and so Kwame was accompanying Sandra Garg on her first visit to Africa. He tried to prepare her for what lay ahead. 'You'll find it rather hot and humid although this is usually the coolest time of the year. We'll spend one night in Accra at the university guest house and in the morning we will travel to Kumasi in a TCC vehicle.'

'Will it be cooler in Kumasi?'

'It is usually less humid so you will feel a little cooler.'

'How do you cope with the heat?'

'It's OK indoors, most rooms have fans or air conditioners.'

'And outdoors?'

'You won't be outdoors too much, but try to run your errands in the early morning or the evening.'

Sandra found the drive to Kumasi long, rough, hot and dusty. The old Land Rover was suited to the frequent off-road conditions but was cooled only by wind through the open front vents and half-opening sliding glass windows that never seemed to slide far enough. Kwame noticed Sandra's discomfort but could do little about it. He had given her the only fully upholstered seat in front beside the driver, and his own ride, sitting behind on a few centimetres of soft foam cushioning, was much less comfortable. After more than four hours of this state of purgatory the lady's mind was firmly focused on a cold drink and a cold shower. So Kwame directed the driver to go straight to the university guest house where he gave his assistant two hours to recuperate.

After sending his bag to his own chalet, Kwame went straight to the TCC office for a reunion with his old colleagues. There he was warmly greeted and assured that all preparations for the engineering drawing course were well advanced. He went through his own check list and was satisfied that everything was under control. Mick Gould had gone to Suame with Sam Sanders and they were expected back later. When Sandra's two hours respite had expired Kwame sent the driver to bring her to the office where he introduced her to her new colleagues. He was relieved to find that she had fully recovered her composure.

Sam and Mick returned from Suame, and Kwame went with them to the School of Engineering, as it was now called, to meet the professors who were in charge of the training. Here he dealt with the usual requests for additional expenditures and was again satisfied that all seemed to be going ahead on schedule. Mick and Sam confirmed that this was so.

Mick suggested looking in on Kwaku Darko, recently returned from Coventry, and Kwame agreed that was a good idea. They found him in his laboratory still fixing some of the new test equipment he had learned to use at Warwick. He was pleased to see them and said that he had learned a good deal that would be useful but he complained that he hadn't been given enough money to return with a car and asked if he would be accorded a second chance. Kwame answered that he was sure there were others who should be given a turn before repeat visits could be considered.

Sandra had not been very satisfied with lunch on the road of bananas and groundnuts so Kwame decided on an early supper at the senior staff club. He invited Mick and Sam to join them. It was good to be back home and to talk about the work with colleagues who shared his enthusiasm, but he couldn't entirely erase his other mission from the back of his mind. He decided to make an early start on his non-academic duties by telephoning Comfort as soon as the team dispersed to their various places of rest.

'Kwame, welcome back,' said the familiar voice. 'When did you arrive?'

'Just today in Kumasi,' he replied. 'I need to see you but I don't want to come to your house. Where can you suggest?'

'How about the seamstresses' kiosk where Afriyie used to work, near the lorry park at Tek junction? I need to collect a dress there tomorrow.'

'That's good for me; how about one pm?'

'One pm it is then.'

'Will you drive yourself?'

'Of course.'

In his guest chalet Kwame lay spread-eagled on his bed in the downdraught of the ceiling fan. He had put on a stoical performance for the benefit of Sandra but he too had been afflicted by the savage heat of his homeland. Shouldn't it be rather cooler at this time of year? He was happy that both his missions had made a good start. The team he had assembled could be relied on to do a good job and his own role could recede to one of monitoring and dealing with emergencies. This would leave ample time for other matters. He looked forward to seeing Comfort and was pleased with the arrangements they had made. He wondered what Comfort would tell her albino driver to ensure that he had no knowledge of the meeting.

Next morning, Kwame persuaded the TCC director to chair an informal meeting to discuss the level of fees that should be charged for future short courses. This issue was important for the long-term sustainability of the programme. The present level of fees would recover only a small fraction of the cost of mounting the course. This was acceptable while an overseas sponsor was involved but only in the initial phase. If the university were to continue the programme on a permanent basis, cost recovery would have to rise to one hundred per cent.

The problem was always the same. The small industrialists and artisans could afford to pay only a modest fee in local currency. The university professors, for their part, required fees at international rates paid in foreign currency. For them it was work extra to their regular academic duties, which they would undertake only for what they considered a worthwhile reward. The result was a gap between potential income and expected expenditure that seemed impossible to bridge.

A policy of gradually increasing the attendance fee had been agreed, but this only improved the cost recovery by a few percentage points. Nobody expected that the professors would accept lower fees for teaching, and Kwame had already been warned that the present fees were seen as inadequate and more would be demanded for future courses. So with increasing expenditure and only small increases expected in income the long-term sustainability of the programme looked very doubtful.

A lengthy discussion rehearsed all the old issues. Only one ray of hope was perceived. Foreign funding was regarded as essential to initiating the programme, but it was also part of the problem. The instructors knew that a foreign donor was sponsoring the course and that was what prompted them to demand high fees in foreign currency. It was hoped that the courses would be successful and generate a strong demand from local industry for more of the same. However, with the foreign donor withdrawn, it would be apparent that no foreign funding was available and there was a slight chance that some instructors might settle for fees that the market could bear; this being the only income enhancing option then available.

It could be said that little or nothing new was achieved by the meeting but Kwame was intent on keeping the problem of long-term sustainability in focus. Even if the problem was very difficult, he wanted everyone concerned to be aware of the real issues and to hold the long-term objective in mind. He didn't want only a temporary programme while outside support was available, but a permanent programme sustained locally for as long as the need persisted.

After the meeting Kwame walked to the junction to keep his appointment with Comfort. He was pleased to see the shiny BMW draw up in the lorry park beside the yellow-winged taxis and decrepit trotros. She was only a few minutes late. He walked to the driver's door and Comfort lowered the window of her air-conditioned cubicle, spilling cold air over the damp fabric of his shirtfront. Reluctantly he lowered his face into the icy draught but was recompensed by the warmth of her greeting. He responded in kind and she said, 'We can't talk here; there are too many people around. Get in and wait while I collect my dress. Then you can show me a suitably quiet spot.'

Kwame complied with these instructions, and after she had returned with her package, he guided his ex-wife onto the campus and to a secluded corner of the extensive oil palm plantation where he knew they were unlikely to be disturbed. In the shade of the palm fronds they each tried to assess the changes that time had wrought. It was only just a year since the fateful conversation that had spurred his emigration, but to Kwame it seemed much longer. 'You haven't changed,' he told her.

'How much change do you expect in one year?' she laughed, but he thought that she was pleased by the compliment.

'So you managed to leave your *okyeame* driver behind,' Kwame began.

'If you mean Kofi Adjare, he's gone back to Mama Kate,' she replied.

'That's a relief!'

'Why?'

'It makes our meetings easier.'

'How many meetings do you need, Kwame Mainu?'

She smiled as she spoke and Kwame was happy that his full name had been used only in jest. She seemed to retain none of the hostility that had led to their separation and none of the coolness of their last meeting. 'I'll meet you as many times as you allow, Comfort Opokua,' he replied in the same vein. 'That is, during the three weeks or so that I will be in Kumasi.'

'Won't Afriyie be jealous?'

'I'm not sure; she still seems to regard you as senior wife.'

Kwame had come with a definite objective but, as always, it was Comfort who was setting the agenda. It was tempting to try to rekindle the old flame and Comfort seemed willing to help fan the embers. It was with an effort that he forced himself to steer the conversation back towards the business of the day. 'It seemed from your letter there was a possibility of Kofi being still involved with the drugs cartel,' he said, rather abruptly changing the drift of their banter. 'With Kofi around at your house, and driving you everywhere, I felt that it would be difficult for us to meet, but if he's not there, the problem is removed.'

'Do you really think that he put the cocaine snails in Akosua's suitcase?'

'Can you suggest anyone else?'

'No, I can't'

'You say he's gone back to Mama Kate; isn't that also suspicious?'

'Yes I suppose so, but I guess he felt loyalty to his old employer.'

'You always want to think the best of him.'

'That's true, but why did you need to see me?'

Kwame wasn't quite sure how to answer this question. He felt that it would be unwise to divulge his full mission at this point although it might become necessary later. Comfort had never been happy with him helping the British authorities and he must wait until he had a full justification to offer her. He decided to fall back on the reason that had led him to consult her a year before, and to write his first letter to her from Coventry. 'I will be making short visits to Kumasi in my new job,' he explained, 'but I'm still worried that the cartel might seek to take revenge on me in some way. I rely on you to warn me of any threat.'

'Do you think I know everything the cartel is up to?'

'No, of course not, but you're in touch with the Lebanese and trading communities. What's going on?'

'These days it's hard to say. There are tensions between the Ghanaians and the Lebanese.'

'You say Ghanaians, who's siding with Mama Kate?'

'There's Bra Yaw, he's been released from prison since you left, Kofi Boateng and a few of her other boys and girls.'

'Was Oboroni the glue between the two groups?'

'Yes, he and Uncle George.'

'And now they're out of action, there's a split?'

'That's part of it, but I suspect there's more.'

Kwame tried another approach, 'How's your shoe trading now that Mama Kate is back in action?'

'Oh, she's old now and losing her grip.'

'So you've held on to your share of the market?'

'You could say that.'

'What do you say?'

'I think Mama Kate's preoccupied with her other business.'

'With help from Kofi Adjare?'

'It's possible, but I always hoped Kofi would keep out of it.'

Kwame decided he had gone far enough at this stage and thanked Comfort for agreeing to see him. He asked her to keep eyes and ears open for any possible threat and to keep him informed. He hoped they would be able to keep in touch by telephone and would be able to meet a few more times during his visit.

Comfort drove back to the junction and stopped briefly for him to alight. As he stepped out of the refrigerator the afternoon sun wrapped him in its familiar warm blanket. It was such a pleasant sensation that it was hard to imagine he would soon be feeling much too hot. With a mild dizziness he took care crossing the busy road, wondering idly what other damage such sharp temperature changes could inflict on the human constitution. It was only a short walk past the university hospital back to the TCC office, but by the time he rejoined his colleagues the cold of Comfort's car was forgotten.

Edward Opare and Mick Gould were waiting with the old Land Rover to take him to Suame Magazine where they planned to visit some of the workshops sending artisans on the engineering drawing course. Kwame enjoyed meeting old friends and making new ones, as he updated his knowledge of what was being achieved in some long-established machine shops and some newly created foundries.

They stumbled through the Magazine on broken, rutted, orange-pink dirt tracks, braving the heat, the dust and the fumes of passing traffic and charcoal-burning cupola furnaces. He congratulated Edward Opare on being the prime mover behind the rapid multiplication of iron foundries. Edward proudly showed him the work of his own private foundry and Kwame was happy to tell him, 'Now I have seen in Suame the good work that inspired me when I first met Fred Brown at the foundry school in Coventry in 1984.'

'Wait until you see what we can do in another eleven years!' replied Edward.

The team was also impressed by the work of Abu Musah at Stone Foundry. This young man from Tamale, a protégé of the Texan sailor, Frank Johnson, had been sent to Kumasi for training on Frank's recommendation. After completing an apprenticeship in iron casting at the Suame ITTU, he had opted to stay in the Magazine and run his own foundry.

85

Abu Musah had achieved remarkable progress. Doing everything by the book, and taking much pride in his work, he had maintained the quality standards he had been taught at the ITTU. Now he was in process of expanding his business of producing corn mill grinding plates to include casting the bronze bearing bushings that were also needed to keep corn mills in operation. 'I have bought a centre lathe and I want to machine the bushings in-house,' Abu Musah told Kwame. 'When I come on the course, can I learn how to design a suitable holding fixture?' Kwame assured him that if he asked one of the instructors he would be shown how to do it.

It had been a long, hot and tiring day and Kwame was glad to get back to his guest house. After a light supper he stretched out under the ceiling fan to review what he had learned in the shade of the oil palms. He had been asked to try to find out who was giving instructions to the *okyeame*, Kofi Adjare, and through him to the local distributors in the UK. He had learned that the albino linguist had returned to work for his old employer, Mama Kate, who had recently served a term of imprisonment for her involvement in the drugs trade. So the obvious conclusion was that Kofi Adjare was now receiving his instructions from Mama Kate.

Was Kwame's task already accomplished? Could he return to tell Leon that Mama Kate was now running what was left of the cartel? It was a neat and easy solution, too neat and too easy. Kwame had serious doubts. Comfort had hinted that Mama Kate was a spent force, not as active in business as in the past. Did she really have the authority and energy to direct operations after spending several years in a local prison at an age when most people are retiring? Surely there were younger, more vigorous, people with ambitions to take over: Bra Yaw for instance, what was he doing? Then there were the Lebanese, what role were they playing in the revived enterprise? Comfort had hinted at a split; were the Lebanese still partners in the enterprise? He decided to keep an open mind and hope that he could learn more before his visit was over.

The next few days were taken up in last-minute preparations for the training course. Kwame and Mick gave what support they could on technical issues and Sandra helped the TCC people with the domestic arrangements. Kwame had control of expenditure and was constantly faced with demands for cash to buy items that had been overlooked. He wondered why people only thought of essential inputs when faced with the immediate requirement. He was compelled to hand out rather more cash than budgeted and was glad that Tom had backed him in insisting on a generous allowance for contingencies.

On Sunday afternoon the team stood ready to greet their students. The participants had been asked to come to the TCC office from where they would be conducted to Unity Hall, a students' accommodation where each had been allotted a room. Even those living in Kumasi had been encouraged to lodge on campus during the course because activities were expected to go on into the evenings.

The participants began to arrive in ones, twos and threes and then a car arrived from Tema with six of Kwame's old associates. By the early evening all thirty-five participants were on campus and Kwame, Mick and Sandra joined them in Unity Hall dining room for their first meal together. It was a happy gathering at which Kwame knew almost every person. The course had been over-subscribed; the organisers had not been able to keep to their limit of thirty, but Kwame felt that with such a fund of goodwill all difficulties would be overcome.

One participant had been especially pleased to see him, rushing forward to hug him around the waist like his daughter, Akosua Mainu, used to do. He told Akosua Akomwa that he had met her Auntie Rose in England. 'She's back in Ghana,' she replied. 'She told me she would see me in Kumasi this week.' It was then that Kwame realised that Comfort had not answered the question in his letter and he had forgotten to ask her again if she knew Auntie Rose. It didn't seem important until Akomwa told him her aunt was in Kumasi. If Auntie Rose met Comfort he could not know what might pass between them concerning his clandestine mission.

When the course got under way Kwame could see that everything was moving smoothly and there was little for him to do, apart from hand out cash when it was needed. He had ample time to write letters to Afriyie and Akosua and post them at the university post office. At first he wrote every few days, but the frequency dropped as he realised that the slowness of the postal service would result in him getting very few letters back before his visit came to an end. He also tried telephoning Afriyie but soon became frustrated by the delays and faults in the service. He managed to get through to Tom to tell him that the course had started on time with no serious problems. After that, he hoped that the professor would assume that no news was good news.

He made a routine of taking lunch and dinner with the participants so that they had easy access to him and he could assess their level of satisfaction. Some students were making rapid progress. With help from Mick Gould, Abu Musah had drawn the work-piece holder he needed for the corn mill bearing sleeve. Others, like Akosua Akomwa, were finding the going more difficult, largely because they lacked the necessary basic education. Kwame told Mick to monitor the progress of the students and keep accurate records so that they would know the technical capabilities of each workshop.

Sandra Garg had become friendly with Ophelia Darko, a metal products designer spending her national service year with the TCC, as Kwame had done fifteen years earlier. Ophelia was planning a trip to Tema to study the aluminium spinning industry so Kwame arranged for Sandra to go with her. Sandra had taken the opportunity to see much of the foundries at Suame Magazine and now she had a chance to see their counterparts in Tema, as Kwame had promised she would. He advised the two women to travel early in the morning to avoid the heat that had afflicted Sandra on the drive from Accra. They would be back within a week and before the end of the engineering drawing course.

Mick told Kwame that some of the participants had said that they were disappointed that they would not be able to actually produce engineering drawings by the end of the course. Kwame said that obviously it takes much longer to train to become a draughtsman. The objective of the short course was to teach how drawings are used in modern manufacturing and to equip the participants with the basic knowledge to interpret them. This should be made clear to all participants. It was hoped that eventually the workshops could be supplied with drawings and they would be able to produce parts to order.

Kwame told Mick to emphasise to the instructors that participants should be encouraged to undergo further training, by attending more of the short courses or taking evening courses at the polytechnics. It was hoped that some of these informal sector industrialists would become aware of the value of technical knowledge and develop an appetite for more training. If some workshops went on to train and employ draughtsmen and produce their own drawings, so much the better.

On Friday evening, at the end of the first week of training, a group of workshop owners asked for a meeting with Kwame and so he stayed behind at Unity Hall after dinner. These men were all experienced artisans who had built up substantial businesses employing between fifteen and thirty technicians and apprentices. Included were Kofi Asiamah, Isaac Anfom and Samuel Quaye from Tema and Frank Awuah, Nana Abrefa and Solomon Djokoto from Kumasi. These were much respected elders of their informal sector communities and Kwame was happy to listen to their views and valued their advice. It intrigued him that they seemed to have constituted themselves into an unofficial advisory committee.

The group had chosen as its spokesman Mr Samuel Quaye of ENTESEL Ltd of Tema. This quiet-spoken man of commanding presence and natural authority began by praising the organisers for mounting the course, which they were sure would do much to strengthen the industry. They were learning things that they knew they needed to know, as well as things that they didn't realise they needed to know. They hoped that there would be more such courses in the future but what concerned them was sustainability. They were anxious that the courses should continue long after the foreign support ended, and they warned the organisers not to set expectations too high.

'Take the example of the food you have provided,' said Mr Quaye. 'It is much better than most of the participants are used to eating. The food alone must have cost more than the entire attendance fee. The same could be said of the accommodation. When word gets out about the catering and accommodation on these courses, people will rush to enjoy a cheap holiday in Kumasi. You will attract people who have no interest in improving their technical knowledge.'

Kwame had not expected to be told that the arrangements for the course were too good, but he was pleased that these responsible people had recognised his essential dilemma. 'I understand what you are saying,' he told them, 'but can you suggest some solutions?'

It was Sam Quaye who again spoke for his peers, 'We believe that you could save a lot of money by asking participants to find their own accommodation in Kumasi. Catering costs could be reduced to providing only a light lunch to minimise loss of teaching time at midday. Mid-morning and mid-afternoon snacks are certainly unnecessary. At the same time you could increase the fee which would then contribute to offsetting the cost of technical instruction.'

Kwame thanked the group for offering this advice and being long-sighted enough to look beyond immediate benefits. He explained that he shared their concerns about sustainability and wanted to move gradually in the direction they had indicated. It was generally believed that fees should increase but there must be a way to help bright young people who couldn't raise the money. He felt that it would help the two universities to move in this direction if the authorities knew of the support of the artisans. Sam Quaye said that he would write to the two universities, Kumasi and Warwick, expressing the views of the group.

On the matter of campus accommodation, Kwame believed that it conferred a number of advantages, like the opportunity for this meeting, and he had observed several people going back to the drawing office after dinner to complete their assignments. It also gave people who never had the opportunity to study at university a feeling that they had experienced university life, including part of the on-campus social dimension.

In conclusion Kwame asked them to accept a compromise. 'These courses can only succeed with your support,' he told them. 'You pay for yourselves and, in many cases, for your technicians and apprentices to attend the training. Can I take it that you would accept higher fees and a reduced level of on-campus catering and accommodation as a step towards long-term sustainability? To save on catering, for example, we could cut out the snacks, cut down a little on lunch and dinner and charge for soft drinks if they are wanted. As for accommodation, the regular students sleep two to a room; could we ask you to do the same?'

Nods all round signified agreement and Kwame thanked them again for offering their advice in such an unselfish and public-spirited way. He hoped that they would continue to bring their concerns to him, either collectively or when he met them one by one. He was glad to hear that they were benefiting from the course and he hoped that the new technical knowledge would improve the operations of all their workshops.

Later, back in his chalet, Kwame reflected on the meeting with much satisfaction. If what he was doing was so well understood and supported by these leaders of the industry, it was sure to be right. Working together in this way, using their own resources, they could succeed in building a strong industrial community upwards from the grass roots. This was what Fritz Schumacher had written about in *Small is Beautiful* and Prime Minister Kofi Busia had tried to put into effect during his short administration. Even though governments and institutions had since been diverted by short-term self-interest, there were still many men and women who were dedicated to continuing the crusade. These were his people, this was where he belonged! Tonight he could rest with pride in his heart. The cicadas were in full voice and the frogs had started their nightly chant, but this was the lullaby he loved and it presaged the soundest sleep.

On Saturday morning, Kwame lay in bed thinking that he should get up but enjoying the feeling that there was no urgent need, when there was a knock on his chalet door. Wrapping a cloth over his shoulder and around his boxer shorts he hastened to greet the visitor. Much to his surprise, Kwaku Darko stood at the door. 'Come in Kwaku,' he said, 'I wasn't expecting a visitor this early in the day.'

'I thought I might catch you before you went out.'

'You certainly did that, you got me out of bed.'

'Oh, I'm sorry.'

'It's nothing, I needed to get up.'

Kwame offered his visitor the customary water and then asked if he had taken breakfast. They remained silent as they ate sugar bread and margarine and drank large mugs of cocoa. When the pangs of hunger had abated Kwame asked what had brought Kwaku on his early morning mission.

'It's a delicate matter,' he said, 'but I feel that it might get your training programme into trouble.'

'Which programme are you referring to?' asked Kwame. 'The one at Warwick or the one here in Kumasi?'

'The one at Warwick; the one that I was involved in.'

'Right.'

'Before I left for the UK a guy calling himself Bra Yaw came to see me.'

'Go on.'

'He offered me money to take a package to London, to be given to someone at the airport on arrival.'

'Did you agree?'

'No, I suspected that it might involve drugs or some other contraband.'

'You made a wise decision.'

'But I suspect that Peggy might have agreed.'

'Why do you say that?'

'Well, she seemed to have much more money to spend in Coventry.'

'Anything else?'

'She went off alone at the airport and Mick and I spent some time looking for her.'

'You were all together when I met you.'

'Yes, but we had only just joined up again.'

Although this news did not surprise him, Kwame could see the damage the matter might do to his project. In the past, Mama Kate, Bra Yaw, and Peter Sarpong in Coventry, had asked about movements to the UK generated by the universities' activities. Kwame, and even Tom Arthur, had been asked several times to provide information but they had always avoided saying anything specific. Once the actual programme got under way, however, it was almost inevitable that the cartel would get wind of the academic movements.

In talking to Kwaku Darko, Kwame did not want to reveal that he already knew of the drugs smuggling scheme, so he tried to be very careful about what he said. At the same time it would be useful to gain more information, as much for the benefit of his university work as for reporting to Leon. 'Did Bra Yaw say who would meet you at London airport?' he asked. 'He said that I would be told after I agreed to help them,' replied Kwaku.

'And you don't know who met Peggy at the airport?'

'No, she said nothing to me about it.'

'So all we know for sure is that there are people who know about our movements and want to take the opportunity to send packages to London.'

'That's all I'm sure of, the rest is conjecture.'

After Kwaku departed, Kwame decided to check what happened on arrival at London airport with Mick Gould so he walked down the line of guest chalets to his assistant's temporary residence. He met Mick at his door on the way out.

'You're lucky to catch me; I'm just off to Suame to help Musah get his fixture made.'

'I won't delay you. I just wanted to ask you a quick question.'

'Fire away.'

'When you arrived at London airport with Kwaku and Peggy, did you all stay together until I met you?'

'Well, Peggy went off for a while. I assumed she had gone to the ladies'.'

'How long was she gone?'

'I can't be sure; she came back just before we met you.'

'Thanks Mick; that's all. Good luck at the Magazine!'

Kwame walked slowly back towards his chalet, deep in thought about what he had learned. Peggy had behaved much as Akos Mary had done a decade before. Both women showed a determination to seek their fortune overseas and to take whatever personal risks were involved in seizing opportunities that arose. It could be said that Akos Mary had succeeded, but only after being convicted of a crime and spending time in prison. What would the future hold for Peggy? The cartel would want her to go to and fro between Accra and London, while her brother in London, if he was her real brother, would want her to stay in the UK. Her fate seemed to rest in the hands of the suave gentleman who had met her at the airport. It could be determined by whether or not he was really a blood relation. A further factor, however, was the immigration and customs authorities. At any time, one or other might provide a shock awakening and put all of her dreams on hold.

As with Akos Mary, Kwame felt sympathy for Peggy's plight. He had been prepared to help the immigration service to trace her, partly to restore the good record of his academic programme and partly for the lady's own sake. As a qualified professional she could find a legitimate way to stay in the UK and need not hide from the authorities like an illiterate illegal immigrant. Now he had been told she might be a drugs mule. How did that affect his position? Should he report this possibility to Leon? He knew that Afriyie, Comfort and Akos Mary would all say no. They would not want him to add to their countrywoman's problems. On the other hand, if she had decided to work for the cartel, the earlier she was caught the lighter her sentence might be.

He should also consider his own position. Having agreed to help Leon, was it wise to withhold anything? Leon had shown that he had numerous sources of intelligence. Peggy may have already appeared on his radar. If Kwame withheld what he had learned from Kwaku, Leon might soon be aware, and a bond of trust would be broken. Reluctantly, he decided that he had better pass on his suspicions in his end-of-mission report.

7

Convergence

Thoughts of Peggy and her absconding oppressed Kwame and he had a strong desire to return to his professional duties. Mick had taken the Land Rover so he hailed a passing taxi and told the driver to head for Suame Magazine. He would join Mick on his quest to help Abu Musah solve his corn mill bearing production problem. As he expected, he found the two engineers at the ITTU, not in the main workshop but in the workshop of a client who rented space.

Frank Awuah described himself as an automobile engine repair machinist who had served an apprenticeship in Britain. He was one of the best lathe turners known to the TCC and one of the most mature and experienced businessmen. In the early days of the GRID project, when Dr Francis Acquah was still Minister for Industries, Science and Technology, Frank Awuah had been appointed a member of the GRID Project Board. Frank had been one of the mature workshop proprietors who had expressed their concern about the sustainability of the short courses. Kwame was not surprised that Mick and Musah had chosen to place the manufacture of their new jig in Frank's skilful hands.

Frank studied the drawing that Musah had made of his bearing sleeve holder. 'What's the most critical feature of your bearing sleeve?' he asked. Abu looked puzzled and Mick also appeared lost for an answer. Kwame waited patiently for his people to come up with a response. At length it was Frank who spoke again, 'Surely, it's the concentricity of the cylindrical exterior location to the internal bore?' Smiles broke out all around.

'I'm glad you've come to the right place,' said Kwame.

Frank then suggested a minor change to the holder to ensure the highest possible degree of concentricity and then turned to his much envied Colchester Mascot lathe, the biggest and newest used machine yet supplied by the TCC. It wasn't long before Abu was holding the jig that opened up new vistas of production at Stone Foundry. He pulled out his wallet but Frank stopped him. 'We can never repay the help we have had from the TCC,' he said, 'but we can try to help each other in the same spirit.' Kwame turned quickly away hoping no one had noticed the glistening in his eyes.

After a few seconds with his handkerchief, Kwame observed the stack of finished products awaiting collection on a bench near the door. To an engineer they were objects of beauty. Among them was a batch of shining aluminium engine pistons. Kwame was aware that centre lathe turners were occasionally called upon to make replacement pistons for motorcycle engines but these were usually made only in ones or twos. Frank's pistons were larger and could be for a car or a light truck.

This was an interesting development and directly related to Kwame's project to manufacture a diesel engine. 'Could you produce these in cast iron for a diesel engine?' he asked.

'If you can supply the right grade of material,' Frank replied. Then he added, 'These pistons can't be for use in an engine though; the material isn't specified and the machining limits are too broad.'

This remark immediately rang an alarm bell for Kwame. If the pistons were not for use in an engine what was their purpose? He knew of engineers who used an old piston as an ash tray but it seemed unlikely that they could become widely popular in this role. Then, with thoughts of drugs trafficking at the back of his mind, Kwame recalled reading a newspaper report about consignments sent to Europe hidden in engine parts. He decided to ask a few more questions while trying to decide whether he should warn Frank about the possible irregular use of his products. 'What type of vehicle are the pistons supposed to be for?' he asked.

'They vary from order to order, but they're usually said to be for one of the popular Japanese models used as taxis: Toyota or Nissan,' Frank replied.

'Are they for local use?'

'That's what they tell me, but I've never seen them being fitted to an engine around the Magazine. They wouldn't be any good anyway.'

Kwame suspected that the customer was not interested in the quality of the pistons, only that they looked like the genuine article. He couldn't be sure on what pretext they could be sent to the UK, but there could be a niche market for cheap spare parts. It seemed unlikely that anyone intended the pistons to be used in an engine but their hollow interior offered scope for concealing contraband. 'Who comes to collect the pistons?' he asked Frank.

'An apprentice from *Sika Ye Na* enterprise.'

'What do they do?'

'I believe they're a spare parts store.'

'Where is their shop?'

'I don't know.'

'Are they in the Magazine?'

'They might be, it's very big as you know, but they could be anywhere.'

The more Kwame learned, the more he was convinced that the pistons were wanted for the drugs trade. He decided that he should warn Frank that he might at some stage be held to be complicit in this illegal activity. So he let Mick and Musah go ahead to Stone Foundry to try their new fixture while he stayed behind for a private chat. They went into Frank's small office.

'What I have to say is strictly confidential,' said Kwame, 'but do you know that three directors of a Kumasi company have been sentenced to prison terms for sending cocaine and heroin to the UK?'

'I believe I did read something about it in the newspaper some years ago.'

'One was imprisoned in the UK; he's still behind bars. The other two were imprisoned here in Ghana and they were released last year.'

'So you think that my pistons might be used for smuggling drugs?'

'That's what I'm afraid of.'

'If they're caught again, could I be in trouble?'

'I'm not a lawyer but you might be wise to refuse any more orders.'

'I'll take your advice.'

Kwame had come to Suame to pursue his professional duties but his other mission had become his shadow. He felt that he was gathering information without expending any effort, like a magnet attracts iron filings. It would be useful for Leon to be warned about consignments of engine pistons and he could pass on this valuable information without mentioning Frank Awuah. As he hurried to catch up with his friends at Stone Foundry he wondered if he should try to find out more about *Sika Ye Na* enterprise.

Mick and Musah were wrapped up in trying their new toy and it was some time before they were free to chat. Musah was happy with the results of the early trials and Mick was happy that he had succeeded with his first technical input to Suame Magazine. Kwame congratulated his friends and waited patiently for the euphoria to subside. Then he asked if anyone knew the whereabouts of *Sika Ye Na* enterprise.

'*Sika ye na*, money is scarce, that could be a popular name around here,' said Mick, who had been busy learning Twi in his spare time.

'He's right,' said Musah, 'I think there are several workshops with that name. Let's ask around and see what we can find.'

The three men walked some distance along the broken dirt roads, hailing the artisans and posing their question. This seemed to raise no suspicion, as verbal questioning was the universal method of locating workshops. The vast Magazine sprawled over several square kilometres and encompassed some nine or ten thousand independent enterprises. With no road names or sign posts it was inevitable that the residents should meet a steady stream of strangers seeking directions to a location where their needs might be supplied. Kwame knew that most craftsmen and apprentices would be happy to help, but at the same time, most would be ignorant of all but their immediate surroundings. As Musah had suggested, *Sika Ye Na* was a popular name for businesses, but the two or three they found were fitting shops or parts stores that didn't deal in pistons. After an unproductive hour or so in the midday sun the team was wilting and craving refreshment.

They found some shade in which to rest under a forlorn mango tree and Musah sent a boy to fetch soft drinks, plantain chips and groundnuts. 'This isn't working,' said Kwame. 'We must ask at the office of the Suame Mechanical Association and hope that their records are up to date.' He asked Musah if he knew the location of the office and was told that the association had recently moved to new premises. Mick and Kwame walked back to the ITTU and drove in their Land Rover to what turned out to be a smart new building on the Techiman road.

'What does the mechanical association do?' asked Mick.

'It's a funeral society set up to help its members bear the high cost of bereavement,' Kwame replied.

'Do all the enterprises belong to it?'

'Almost all.'

They found the office locked and deserted. It was, after all, Saturday, the day for attending funerals. He remembered from his years in the Magazine that many of the self-employed artisans worked through all the daylight hours on Saturdays, unless they had a funeral in their own family. Those with a salaried office job, however, worked business hours, Monday to Friday, and were free to enjoy all of Saturday's entertainment. Kwame realised that he might have to return at a more favourable time.

There was little more that they could do, and Kwame wanted Mick to have some time to rest over the weekend, so they drove back to the campus and their guest chalets.

Kwame had plenty to think about. If he had entertained any doubts about the Kumasi cartel reviving its activities, these were now dispelled. The cartel had attempted to recruit Kwaku Darko, may have succeeded in recruiting Peggy Osei-Wusu, and might have opened a new channel for exporting contraband using engine pistons as packaging. However, Kwame could not be sure that the cartel was still a combined Ghanaian-Lebanese operation.

On the evidence available, the recruitment of couriers was handled by Bra Yaw, one of Mama Kate's associates, whereas the order for pistons had come from a spare parts store, *Sika Ye Na*. Did this store have any connection with the Lebanese company Hanabis? In the absence of Oboroni and Uncle George it was reasonable to believe the rumour that there was a split developing between the Ghanaians and the Lebanese. Hitherto, Kwame had only come into direct contact with the Ghanaian operation, which involved using air passengers to carry drugs to the UK. Now, for the first time, he might have made contact with the Lebanese operation: exporting drugs concealed in otherwise legitimate merchandise. Should he explore this side further, or restrict his enquiries to Mama Kate's activities?

Kwame's instructions from Leon, conveyed through Tam Gordon, had only mentioned trying to identify who was directing the UK distribution system. Previously this might well have handled drugs supplied through both channels, as the Ghanaian diaspora in the UK was the one great asset that Mama Kate's side could bring to the partnership. If a split developed, however, the existing distribution system might be fed only by the courier stream, and the Lebanese would be faced with the need to establish a parallel UK distribution system to retail their export trade.

Next morning, Sunday, Kwame had two more visitors. Akosua Akomwa came with her aunt, but he was surprised to find that it was not just a courtesy call. Akosua had brought Auntie Rose to support her plea to be allowed to repeat the engineering drawing course. It was a feature of Akan social custom to ask an older relative or friend to plead on one's behalf but Kwame had not expected to see Auntie Rose in quite this situation. 'Is there a problem?' he asked Akosua in Twi.

'I'm trying to understand everything but it is very hard.'

'Have you asked the lecturers to help you?'

'Yes, and I've stayed in class when they have closed, but it won't reach.'

'So you want to come back when we repeat it in January.'

'I beg you, yes.'

Auntie Rose vigorously supported her niece, expanding in English what Akosua had said. She pointed out that Akosua had not enjoyed much schooling and had worked very hard to get into Kumasi Technical Institute and become the first female welder in Kumasi. After listening politely to all they had to say, Kwame said that he had no objection to Akosua repeating the course but it wasn't up to him alone. The course was run by the School of Engineering and it was the course director, Professor Kwami, who would decide if Akosua had shown sufficient achievement and potential to benefit from the repeat. She should ask Professor Kwami for his permission, mentioning that he, Kwame Mainu, had no objection to committing the necessary resources. He promised to confirm this to Professor Kwami when he next saw him.

Kwame wondered if he should talk to Auntie Rose alone but he wasn't sure how to arrange it. The tiny matron must have read his thoughts because she reminded Akosua that she would be late for church if she delayed any longer. Akosua took her leave saying that she would speak to Professor Kwami next morning. The two elders were left in silence, each wondering what the other knew and what it was safe to tell.

At length Kwame opened the conversation, 'Were we supposed to meet?'

'No, I suppose not, but Akosua provided a valid excuse.'

'Tam told me you would be here but that we might not meet.'

'Well, we've met now.'

'Should we discuss our missions or part in ignorance?'

'I can't tell you anything, but if you've found something useful you can pass it on through me or wait until you see Leon.'

'Tam told me to report to Leon.'

'That's OK by me.'

He decided to change the subject. 'Akosua is the only woman on our course; it's a shame she's finding it so difficult.'

'She told me that you helped her a lot.'

'Yes, we had a "women in engineering" programme and we appreciated her involvement.'

'She benefited from it.'

'She also helped to make it a success.'

'That's good!'

Kwame was beginning to wish that Auntie Rose was also a churchgoer. The conversation was obviously an embarrassment to them both, but in Ghana the host can never ask a guest to leave or even when they intended to leave. The lady was perched awkwardly on her chair, with her characteristic leg swing, and Kwame wondered idly if she borrowed furniture from an infants' school for her own accommodation. Where was she staying? What was she doing in Kumasi? The lady wouldn't say, so maybe he would never know. He felt a strong desire to talk to someone with empathy, someone with whom he could freely discuss his problems and share his ideas. He decided that as soon as Auntie Rose had gone he would telephone Comfort and arrange a second meeting.

Comfort invited him to call that evening. He drove to Nhyiasu after dark, left his vehicle some distance from the house and groped his way around to the back door to avoid passing under the glare of the front security lights. It might be paranoid, but he felt that if anyone was trying to track his movements it was wise to take a few precautions. 'So you remembered where I live,' Comfort joked, as she closed the door quickly behind him.

'Are you sure there's nobody here with links to the cartel?' he asked.

'Not since Kofi left,' she replied, 'There's only my maid and she's out with her boyfriend.'

They sat sipping soft drinks and Kwame asked if Comfort had heard anything that he should know. 'I met Bra Yaw in the market the other day,' she said, 'and he mentioned your new project. He seemed very interested in your programme to send people to England on training courses.'

'He still has kenke to send, eh?'

'If he has, I think he's upgraded the stuffing!'

'Does he ever travel himself?'

'I don't think so. Since they let him out he seems to have limited his activities to recruiting other people.'

'Even before his second term in prison, his code name was "the one who fears the worm". I guess he won't risk a third term.'

'That name doesn't show much respect.'

'No, I wonder where he stands in the organisation.'

'Judging by the size of the house he's building, he's very ambitious. Maybe he wants to step into Uncle George's shoes.'

'That won't please Peter Sarpong.'

'No, but Peter is under lock and key, five thousand kilometres away.'

Kwame told Comfort that he suspected that one of the trainees sent to Warwick had already been recruited as a courier and another had told him that he had been approached by Bra Yaw. 'Was the one who carried the kenke called Peggy Osei-Wusu?' asked Comfort.

'Yes, do you know her?'

'She used to buy shoes, always the most expensive and fashionable ones.'

'Do you know if she has a brother in London?'

'She never mentioned one, why do you ask?'

'A man took her off at the airport and prevented her return to Ghana. She's now an illegal immigrant in the UK. I've been wondering if the man was a real brother or a member of the cartel.'

'I'm sorry, I can't help you there.'

'By the way,' said Kwame, 'you never replied to the question in my letter about Auntie Rose Akomwa.'

'Oh, didn't I? I'm sorry.'

'Do you know her?'

'Wait a moment, I'll see if she's in.'

So Comfort didn't just know Auntie Rose, the little lady was her houseguest. Before Kwame had time to savour his surprise the two women were back. Auntie Rose was smiling, 'So we meet for the second time in one day!' she said. He sensed at once that this was a different woman from the one who had visited him earlier. One of his questions had been answered: he now knew where she was staying. Hopefully he would also get an answer to his second question: what was she doing in Kumasi?

'Comfort has been kind enough to let me stay with her in her lovely home,' said Auntie Rose. 'It has changed a routine assignment into a pleasant holiday.'

'It must be a big improvement on the City Hotel,' said Kwame.

'Or even on a campus guest chalet,' she replied with a matching smile.

'Oh, don't worry about Kwame,' said Comfort. 'He's used to the simple life.'

They settled back into their well-upholstered easy chairs and Comfort brought Star beer for herself and Auntie Rose and a soft drink for Kwame. There was an uneasy silence while they sat sipping and wondering who would be first to speak. It was Auntie Rose who opened the proceedings with, 'I felt bad about leaving you in the dark, Kwame, and after talking things over with Comfort we've decided to share our information. We feel that we can achieve more working together and that the gain will offset the greater risk.'

Kwame, still struggling to recover his balance of mind, responded with a slow nod that encouraged the little lady to continue. 'Officially, I'm a representative of a British shoe manufacturer, here to negotiate a new contract with our accredited agents in Ghana. At the same time, like you, I'm collecting information on the drugs cartel, especially with regard to who's in charge of UK distribution.'

'Then it seems a shame that we both have the same contact,' said Kwame, looking at Comfort. 'It might have been more useful if we were tapping different sources.'

'Oh, Comfort isn't my only source of information, just my best friend.'

'So you're also selling shoes to Mama Kate?'

'And you also have other sources, don't you?'

'Yes I do, but how do you know?'

'Aren't you looking for *Sika Ye Na* enterprise?'

'How do you know about that?'

'You were asking all over Suame Magazine.'

Kwame realised that he had not been very discreet in his enquiries at Suame but he was still surprised that Auntie Rose knew about them so quickly. She must have a network of informers in Suame, as well as among the trading community and beyond. He decided to tell her what he had discovered so far.

'This is what I know,' he began. 'We recently had two academics from the School of Engineering visiting Warwick on short assignments. One of them, Kwaku Darko, told me that Bra Yaw tried to persuade him to carry a package to London but he refused. He suspects that his colleague, Peggy Osei-Wusu, accepted the offer because she went off alone on arrival at London Airport and seemed to have plenty of spending money during her stay in Coventry.'

'This is the lady who stayed in Britain,' prompted Auntie Rose. 'What do you know about that?'

'When I took her to the airport she was met by a man who said he was her brother and they went off together. Later, the immigration authorities came to tell my boss, Prof Arthur, that she had overstayed her visa and asked for help in tracing her. I found a clothes catalogue she had left behind with some items annotated, and handed this over to the authorities as a possible means to tracing her.'

Auntie Rose's syncopated nodding had hurried Kwame through his account and he guessed that she had heard most of it before. 'In summary,' she said, 'you have evidence that Bra Yaw is active again in recruiting couriers, that some drugs have been sent to London in your snails, and perhaps by Peggy, and the cartel has revived its activities. What else can you tell us?'

Kwame was still not sure of the role Comfort played in Auntie Rose's team and he wanted to know more before reporting on what he had learned at Suame, so he asked if Comfort was now actively aiding the investigation. Comfort said that Auntie Rose had persuaded her to help because she now saw the drugs trade as a threat to Ghanaians as well as to foreigners. She had found a few of Mama Kate's former boys and girls had become addicts and she wanted to do all she could to prevent the use of hard drugs spreading more widely.

Kwame was curious to know more about this surprising change of heart but for the moment he was ready to continue with his report. He told the two women how he had found a machine shop at Suame making engine pistons that could not be used in a real engine. He had been told that they were collected by an apprentice from *Sika Ye Na* enterprise. As far as his informants knew, the pistons were not used locally for repairing vehicle engines and neither were they suitable for that purpose. Kwame suspected they were being used to conceal cocaine or heroin in export consignments. He recalled that Comfort had told him how drugs were being hidden inside traditional wood carvings and it seemed a natural progression to use metal products.

'Yes, but there's one big difference,' said Auntie Rose, 'wood carvings are usually carried by tourists travelling as air passengers but engine parts would be sent by air or sea cargo.'

'You mean the wood carvings would be used by Mama Kate's people, who handle the courier traffic,' said Kwame, 'but the engine parts would be used by the Lebanese, who organise the export trade.'

'Exactly, and we don't know if the two groups are still working together or separately.'

'I've thought a lot about that. Can the Lebanese afford to lose Mama Kate's UK distribution system?'

'They might consider that in the absence of Oboroni, Peter Sarpong and other regional managers, it's no longer effective; that there's a need for a new system.'

'So Mama Kate and Bra Yaw are struggling to keep going?'

'To keep going and to retain the confidence of their partners.'

'Is Mama Kate in charge, giving instructions through Kofi Adjare?' asked Kwame.

'Comfort and I are both doubtful,' replied Auntie Rose. 'We can see that her prison sentence sapped her energy. She lost some weight, which was probably a good thing, but she's about sixty-five years old and looks ready for retirement.'

'Then who's running the business?'

'That's what we are trying to find out.'

Kwame turned to Comfort and asked, 'What about Kofi Adjare? Have you seen him lately?'

'That's strange, he was asking the same question about you.'

'Are you sure that's what he asked you?'

'He calls you "the heir of the tripping stone". I don't think I made a mistake.'

'So Dad was the tripping stone?'

'He was for the Lebanese sawmill owners, wasn't he?'

'Yes he was, but what did you tell Kofi?'

'At that time I hadn't seen you, so I had nothing to tell.'

Auntie Rose slid down from her chair and said she would leave Kwame and Comfort to discuss their private business. Kwame had told Auntie Rose everything he knew but he was sure that she had not fully reciprocated. He felt that it had not been a fair exchange. As usual, he had been outwitted by a lady. Nevertheless, he welcomed the opportunity of a one-to-one chat with Comfort. 'So you've joined us in helping the *abrofo*,' he joked.

'I'm doing it for my people.'

'Do you see they are in danger?'

'Yes I do. Many of them used to take "wee" but it didn't seem to harm them, at least not permanently. Now they are beginning to take the hard drugs and the effects are very bad.'

'Who's selling the drugs in Ghana?'

'I'm not sure, but Uncle George and Mama Kate didn't sell them here. It must be some new people.'

'The Lebanese?'

'I'm not sure.'

Kwame remembered Comfort telling him about the Lebanese parties she used to attend in her teens. These celebrations of wine, women and song were just the sort of venues for introducing drugs. 'Those parties you used to go to,' he said. 'Did they give you drugs?'

'There were a few people taking wee, and a lot of heavy drinking, but no hard drugs.'

'Do you think they use hard drugs these days?'

'I don't know.'

'If they are selling drugs in Ghana, wouldn't they also use them at their parties?'

'Probably.'

'Could you find out?'

'Don't you think I'm too old?'

'For the Lebanese men, maybe.'

For the second time Comfort seemed pleased at something he had said, and for a second time he drew back from blowing on the embers. 'I wasn't thinking of a personal investigation,' he said, 'but you know some young shoe traders who have recently escaped, don't you?'

'Yes I do. I'll ask a few questions.'

Kwame was curious about Auntie Rose's background, so he asked, 'How long have you known Auntie Rose?'

'Oh, many years; she was one of Mama Kate's girls, going to and from London.'

'Until she was caught?'

'That's right.'

'But she was never imprisoned?'

'No, it seems the *abrofo* thought she would be more use as a spy.'

'Posing as an agent of a British shoe manufacturer?'

'Mama Kate's people think that is her cover for her courier activities.'

'Then she's a sort of double agent!'

'Her life is very complicated.'

'Can we trust her?'

'I think so.'

Kwame wondered why, if Auntie Rose had been involved with the cartel for so long, she seemed to know so little about it. When he asked Comfort she replied that couriers were not told very much. They already knew this from Afriyie and Akos Mary. The mention of Afriyie revived a twinge of conscience and he decided it was time to return to the simple life of his on-campus guest chalet. So with a brief excuse, and a light peck on the cheek of a rather startled Comfort, he took his leave.

He had regarded the weekend as a brief respite between the two busy weeks of the engineering drawing course, when he might pursue his extra mural investigations at leisure, but the two days had been packed with unforeseen activity and he had learned much more than had been expected. Now he needed another weekend to reflect on his new knowledge, but that was unlikely to be available. He would have to be content with a good night's sleep and the hope of awaking with his mind switched back to its technical agenda.

The second week of a two-week course is always more hectic than the first. Not only is there realisation of the approaching end, with the loss of half a day on a formal closing ceremony, but there are also all those interesting issues swept forward from the first week. Abu Musah needed help to upgrade his drawings in line with Frank Awuah's suggestions and Akosua Akomwa was trying to catch the course director with her request to repeat the course in January. Several of the other students had individual requirements that kept Mick and the course instructors busy throughout the lunch breaks and after-hours sessions. Fortunately, few of these needed to be filtered through to Kwame and he was free to concentrate on other matters.

On Tuesday there was a visit to the Neoplan bus assembly plant. It was located close enough to Suame to have made it possible a decade earlier for the TCC to install an underground cable to enable the Magazine to share the same electricity sub-station. Kwame was keen to accompany the students and take advantage of the opportunity to see what a large modern industry was able to do within the constraints of a Third World economy. The visit was intended to bring home to the artisans the necessity of using engineering drawings in such complex operations. They would be shown how the work of every manufacturing section was guided by a set of drawings from Germany.

Kwame had always assumed that most of the parts of the buses were imported but it depressed him to see the reality in practice. 'Have any local parts or materials been substituted?' he asked the general manager.

'Just a few,' the German replied. 'We use local plywood for interior panelling in place of imported plastic.'

'No engineering parts?' prompted Kwame.

The frown he received in reply seemed to reflect doubt of his sanity. There's no chance of Frank Awuah selling his pistons here, he thought. He reflected once again that such assembly plants achieved very little in terms of technology transfer or the development of local manufacturing industry. The present visit by the artisans was probably the foreign company's first direct contact with the informal and small-scale sector.

In the university bus on the way back to the campus the students expressed much delight with the visit. 'It's the only chance we will ever get to see how work is done in a big modern factory,' said Isaac Anfom, an old Suame hand recently moved to Tema. Several others voiced their agreement. Their thanks as they shook Kwame's hand on descending from the bus informed him that this visit alone had justified the course. The same thanks and thoughts were repeatedly expressed throughout a buoyant evening meal in Unity Hall.

The next day Ophelia Darko and Sandra Garg returned from their visit to Tema. Kwame had not expected to see Sandra directly on her return, as she had not found long-distance travelling easy in the heat and dust of the tropics. So he was surprised that she came looking for him as the class trooped back to lunch. 'We made an early start as you advised and covered most of the way before it got hot,' she said. 'I had a quick shower, and feeling hungry, hurried to join you for lunch.'

'Welcome back, where's Ophelia?'

'She's gone to lunch with her TCC people.'

'You stayed a little longer than planned, was it interesting?'

'Oh, very interesting! Dan Nyarko is a mine of useful information. We saw everything from the government's Tema Steelworks to grassroots aluminium pot casters in Ashiaman, and every ferrous and non-ferrous foundry in between.'

'I look forward to reading your report.'

Kwame had noticed how several of the younger men on the course had taken an interest in Sandra, perhaps sensing an escape route, so he made no attempt to continue their conversation over lunch. Some of the artisans were complaining that Neoplan did not do enough to purchase parts and materials locally. They pointed out that the bus assembly plant was next door to Suame Magazine but, as far as they knew, no Neoplan engineer or manager had ever come into the magazine to find out what could be done there. Kwame suggested that the Suame Mechanical Association should make formal contact with the Neoplan management and suggest a programme of reciprocal visits. By this means, some areas of cooperation might become apparent to both parties.

Frank Awuah recalled that in the 1980s his neighbour at the Suame ITTU, GAMATCO, had produced gear wheels and chain sprocket wheels for the Yugoslavian Tomos motorcycle assembly plant. This was the first opportunity for a Suame workshop to sub-contract for a foreign manufacturer. Everyone hoped that it would be the beginning of more international cooperation but Tomos had closed after the break-up of Yugoslavia and nothing else had started. Kwame pointed out that before you can work for an international manufacturer you must be able to work from engineering drawings, so the present course was essential to achieving this long-term objective.

8

Ladies' Tales

After lunch Kwame asked Sandra if they could review her Tema visit together with Ophelia, so they walked across to the TCC office. They found the young metal products designer reporting to her director, Sosthenes Battah, and were invited to join them. 'Ophelia is telling me about the phenomenal rise of the aluminium spinning industry in Tema,' Sosthenes told them. 'There are already dozens of small firms employing hundreds of workers.'

'I think it will grow much bigger,' said Kwame. 'Traders come from all over Ghana and from neighbouring countries to buy the products; the metal spinners find it hard to keep up with demand.'

'What made this spectacular growth possible?' asked Sosthenes.

'Let's see if the ladies have found out,' Kwame replied.

The two young women looked at one another, wondering who would tell the tale. 'How far do you want to go back?' asked Ophelia.

'To the beginning,' instructed her director.

'Then I'd better take the lead,' Ophelia said. 'As we all know, one of the projects of Kwame Nkrumah was to invite the American company, Kaiser Aluminium, to establish an aluminium smelting plant at Tema using the electrical power generated at the newly constructed Akosombo dam on the Volta River. For many years all the aluminium produced at Tema was exported. However, after years of complaints from industrialists the government was persuaded to renegotiate the contract so that some of the aluminium was made available in Ghana. A new company, Aluworks Ltd, was set up to produce aluminium roofing sheets and these quickly became popular on the local market.

'The industrial community was still not satisfied and lobbied the government to allow Aluworks to produce flat sheets of aluminium for other industrial uses. When this was done one company, Ayigya Metal Products, with help from the TCC here, began producing spun aluminium pots and pans using an old metal spinning lathe imported from Switzerland by you, Sir,' Ophelia said nodding towards her director. 'Now you tell the rest,' she said turning to Sandra.

'From what we were told in Tema by Dan Nyarko,' Sandra began, 'Kofi Asiamah of Redeemer, with some help from Tema ITTU, began manufacturing a copy of the Swiss metal spinning lathe. People rushed to buy the lathes to engage in the new activity and a rapid expansion got under way that is still in progress.'

'You went to Tema to study foundries,' Kwame reminded them, 'What has aluminium spinning got to do with metal casting?'

'The pots and pans are all spun on metal formers,' Sandra continued. 'These are specially shaped to produce each type of product. The aluminium spinners all need many different formers, one for each product they produce, from cups and dishes to huge bowls used by market traders. Most of the formers are produced from brass or bronze and must be cast in a non-ferrous foundry before final shaping and polishing on a metal turning lathe. Some firms are experimenting with cast iron formers for small products, and aluminium formers for the largest products. This activity creates a lot of work for foundries.'

'Well done!' said Kwame. 'You certainly didn't waste your time in Tema. Now tell us about the foundry industry generally.'

'In Kumasi here,' Ophelia said, 'all the operating foundries are established by clients of the ITTU in the informal sector, and they all use either crucible lift-out furnaces or cupola furnaces. In Tema, however, the situation is much more diverse.'

'Yes,' said Sandra, 'there is the government-owned Tema Steelworks, recycling scrap steel into reinforcing rods for concrete construction; a long-established large private foundry, Mankoadze Ltd, now gone into liquidation; several private non-ferrous foundries; ferrous foundries recently promoted by the Tema ITTU and many grassroots aluminium casters at Ashiaman. It was because of this greater diversity, as well as interest in the metal spinning industry, that our study took longer than expected.'

'What did you learn in Tema that would be useful here in Kumasi?' asked Sosthenes.

'Well, the best foundries in Tema operate tilting furnaces using large crucibles. There are none of these furnaces in use in Kumasi.'

'No, but the foundry-men here like the cupola furnace because it doesn't need a crucible, which is imported, expensive and hard to find,' said the TCC director. 'What advantage does the tilting furnace offer?'

'The main advantage is a better quality product made possible by better control of the carbon content of the iron.'

Sosthenes looked at Kwame, 'I guess we can wait for their written report for full technical details.' Kwame was happy to concur. He again congratulated the two young women on their good work as they gathered up their papers and left to put the finishing touches to their report.

Kwame took the opportunity to consult his former boss on one of his biggest problems. He remembered how it was Sosthenes who had first recommended his attachment to the TCC in 1980 and started him on his professional career. The past fifteen years had increased his respect for the senior man who had pursued his whole life's work in Kumasi, doing so much to promote the grassroots industrial development of his country. There was no man whose advice he valued more highly.

'We have a problem that I would like to discuss with you,' he said to Sosthenes when they were alone.

'I'll help if I can.'

'It's about the people who are coming to Warwick on short assignments.'

'From the School of Engineering?'

'Yes. One of them stayed on in England illegally, and I suspect that the other one would have done the same if I hadn't prevented him.'

'You want to find people who are keen to return and apply their new skills here in Ghana.'

'That's what we want, but how do we find them?'

'Look for people who are deeply involved and committed to a long-term project of their own choosing – like our people here at the TCC.'

'Will you help us identify them?'

'Yes, of course, but if other faculties are involved we must move diplomatically.'

'I understand that, but we can build it into our selection protocols.'

Kwame felt that with Sosthenes vetting future candidates he would be much more confident of their returning to Ghana on schedule. However, he was still not sure how this could be arranged. The School of Engineering would insist on having some say over which of their people should visit Warwick. He could insist on Sosthenes being a member of a vetting committee; he was the TCC director and the Warwick contract was with the TCC, but how could he ensure a majority of reliable people? Then Sosthenes offered a solution. 'Why don't *you* chair the selection committee, representing Warwick, with me representing the TCC, together with the dean of the School of Engineering. The school can nominate its candidates but you and I will be able to control the final selection.'

Kwame breathed a sigh of relief, 'That's a good suggestion. I knew you'd come up with something useful.'

Tom had suspended the visits to Warwick pending a better vetting system being put in place. Kwame was anxious to restart the visits as soon as possible and so he asked Sosthenes if the first meeting of the new vetting committee could be held at the TCC during the following week. Assuming that they could obtain the agreement of the School of Engineering, he would delay his return to the UK in order to chair the meeting. Sosthenes agreed to arrange the meeting and also to talk to the dean of engineering. Kwame said that he would telephone Professor Arthur to obtain his approval of the new arrangements.

Kwame had only just finished talking to Tom when his telephone rang again. Much to his surprise, it was Comfort reporting that she had made some enquiries about the Lebanese parties. 'One of the young traders who buys my shoes has been attending the parties,' she said. 'I have helped her a lot in the past and she is prepared to help us now. I have asked her to call on you this evening.'

Kwame wondered why Comfort had sent the girl to him rather than question her herself. Then he remembered that Comfort lived permanently with this community and would not wish to be seen to be connected to any investigation.

He ate supper at Unity Hall with the students on the engineering drawing course and afterwards sat chatting with some of his old friends. He was happy that the course was going well and the morale of the attendees was high. He had come to realise that for many of them attending the course was a welcome break from a routine that had continued unbroken for several years. For a community that never experienced a holiday it was a very acceptable substitute. He appreciated more and more the warning he had been given about not pitching the fee too low. He wanted the students to enjoy the experience but it was also essential that they gained knowledge that would help promote their businesses.

These thoughts were still circulating pleasantly in his head as he walked back to his chalet, carefully navigating in the shadows between widely spaced street lights dimmed by clouds of circling insects. She was waiting for him at his door and he had forgotten that she was expected. Transported back twenty years, he was confronted by the dark silhouette of a teenage Comfort. He fumbled to unlock the door and groped for the light switch. In the half-hearted glow that rewarded his haste, the spell was broken. 'I'm Janet Dery,' she said. 'Comfort Opokua sent me.'

'I'm sorry you were kept waiting,' said Kwame. 'Comfort didn't tell me the time you would come.' Then he realised how foolish this must sound in a world where time is seldom specified and waiting is not a burden. It was, after all, his world and he was ashamed to feel alien to it.

'It's nothing,' she replied brightly. 'Comfort told me you're a busy man.'

'What else did Comfort tell you?' he asked, after they were settled with water and soft drinks.

'She said you wanted to talk to someone who had been to parties with the Lebanese men.'

'Have you been to these parties?'

'Yes, but I've stopped now I have enough money.'

'For shoe trading?'

'That's right.'

'Has Comfort been helping you?'

'Oh yes, but for her help I couldn't have stopped.'

Kwame realised that Janet had come as a favour to Comfort but he wanted to know what Comfort had said. 'Did Comfort tell you what I wanted to ask you?'

'She said you wanted to know about the parties.'

'Tell me about them.'

'Well, there's a lot of food and drink and loud music.'

'And plenty of girls?'

'Of course!'

'Anything else?'

'Some things I don't want to talk about.'

'That's OK, but I guess some people smoked wee.'

'Yes.'

'Were there any other drugs apart from wee?'

'How do you mean?'

'Did they mix anything with the wee before smoking?'

'Some were adding a powder.'

'Did you see people sniffing powder or pricking themselves with a needle?'

'No.'

Kwame was not sure what drugs like cocaine and heroin might be called locally. He knew that popular names varied widely between youth cultures in different parts of the world. 'Did you hear anyone talking about dope, coke or smack?' he prompted, but she didn't recognise these names. He feared that he was unlikely to get anything more definite than this but he tried one last time, 'Did any of the girls like wee too much?'

'Only Obaa Yaa, she would do anything to get it, even steal money from her mother.'

'You don't need much money to buy wee?'

'No, it's the powder that's costly.'

'Where does she go to buy the powder?'

'I think one of the Lebanese men sells it to her.'

'Does she still go to the parties?'

'No, they sacked her when she became ill.'

That sounds like hard drug use promoted by the Lebanese, thought Kwame, but the addiction of poor Obaa Yaa might have come about unintentionally. Nevertheless, such an accident might have initiated a split between the Lebanese and Ghanaian wings of the cartel. He thanked Janet for her help and they sipped their drinks in silence. The interlude gave Kwame a chance to appraise his visitor.

Janet Dery was certainly an attractive young woman, well up to the selection standards set by the Lebanese in past generations. He could be excused for having mistaken her in the shadows of the street for a youthful Comfort. Now he saw her in the light, however, Kwame had to admit that he still preferred the original. This thought surprised him, and he wondered how Comfort would feel about it if she knew. She would probably say something about him growing old, he reflected ruefully.

'Do you want me to stay the night?' The question roused Kwame from his reverie. Did he? Should he? Was Comfort playing a joke on him? Was she testing him? Or was Janet taking a chance to augment her income? That was it; she wanted some money.

'It's kind of you to offer,' he said, 'but I'll telephone for a taxi to take you home.' Then he told her that the information she had given him was valuable and pressed a twenty-pound note into her hand. He knew she would prefer the hard currency, and that exchanged into Ghanaian cedis at a forex bureau it would be regarded as a large sum. He added a few cedis to pay for the taxi.

It seemed to Kwame that Janet departed happy and a little confused. I guess she doesn't get turned down very often, he mused. Had he made the right decision? He knew that whichever way he had turned he would regret it for years to come. Why were women sent to inflict such torture? At the same time that he agonised over Janet, however, he knew that Comfort posed a much bigger challenge to his peace of mind. That night, there were many more beats of the ceiling fan before sleep released him from his torment.

*   *   *

Kwame had decided to stay on for a week after the close of the course in order to interview candidates for visits to Warwick.

Sosthenes had told him that the dean of the School of Engineering had agreed to the idea of a selection committee with Kwame, representing Warwick, in the chair. The dean was as keen as Kwame that his staff should return to post. The first meeting was scheduled for Wednesday afternoon. Mick and Sandra were scheduled to fly back on Wednesday night but would still be working in Kumasi on Monday and Tuesday.

On Saturday morning Kwame gave Mick the names of four people applying to come to Warwick and asked him to work with Sandra to provide assessments of each person and their projects. Some they might know already, and the others they should try to see on their remaining two working days. Mick had lived up to Kwame's expectations and had made a valuable contribution to the preparation and execution of the engineering drawing course. His practical approach was much appreciated by the artisans and his help for Musah had facilitated a minor innovation. On this his second visit to Kumasi, Mick had demonstrated the familiarity of a resident and interacted well with all his campus colleagues. Sandra, too, had fulfilled Kwame's expectations, especially on her visit to metal foundries in Tema. Mick and Sandra's assessments of the candidates would enhance confidence in the work of the selection committee, especially in Warwick.

Last weekend had been busy and Kwame had looked forward to a more restful break now the course was over. At the same time, he was anxious not to waste any opportunity to gather information on the cartel. What could he do that might yield dividends? He had a strong inclination to visit Comfort one more time but that could be tomorrow. What could he do today? Everything about the drugs cartel seemed to hinge upon what was happening at Mama Kate's. Could he summon up the courage to visit his old benefactor in her house? She had invited him last year but he had not gone. Could he find plausible excuses for his omission last year and his delay this year?

Kwame knew that he was inclined to vacillate and delay making decisions but on this occasion he pushed himself into the Land Rover and set out towards Manhyia where both the King of Ashanti and the market queen had their palaces. He parked outside the gates and announced himself to the gatekeeper. Even though it was several years since his last visit he was recognised and allowed to enter the compound. Still pressed forward by an invisible hand, he strode boldly up the long drive towards the big lady's residence. He wished that Comfort was by his side as in the old days.

At the door of the mansion a maid informed him that her mistress was in an important meeting that would take some time. He could wait if he wished and he was brought some water, so he settled himself in a plush armchair in opulent surroundings that had faded only slightly since his last visit. Unfortunately Mainu's law dictated that the only reading materials to hand were three local newspapers, the *Daily Graphic*, the *Ghanaian Times* and the *Pioneer*, which together provided less than thirty minutes' diversion for a thorough reader. Soon he grew restless and decided to stretch his legs in the garden.

Remembering that Mama Kate usually kept three or four vehicles ready for any eventuality, he wondered idly what the market queen was riding in these days. He strolled around to the rear of the building to where he remembered the cars were parked. Half expecting to meet Kofi Adjare, the albino driver-linguist, he was surprised to find Kofi Boateng polishing a new Alfa Romero. It was Kofi who had brought Mama Kate's last invitation to him in Tema, just before his abrupt emigration a year before. Resolved to continue as he had started, Kwame greeted Kofi with, 'It took me a while, but I've made it!' Then, realising that his English joke would not be appreciated, he switched immediately to '*Y'ahyiahyia*', and received the response, '*Ya enua.*' They shook hands with standard current elaborations.

Kwame expressed his surprise at their chance meeting, 'So you're still working here!'

'These days, only at the weekends.'

'You're not flying to the UK?'

'Sometimes, during the vacations.'

'Have you gone back to school?'

'I'm a mature student at Tek.'

At this pronouncement, alarm bells rang in Kwame's head. If Kofi Boateng was studying at Tek, the popular name for the University of Science and Technology, he might well provide the channel by which the cartel learned about the people travelling to the UK under the Warwick cooperation agreement. Kwame felt that his bold step had already been rewarded with useful information. He wondered why Kofi, usually guarded in his statements, had been so open. Perhaps he was proud to announce that he was a university student, or maybe he thought Kwame was somehow involved in Mama Kate's activities. He might not know that Kwame had not followed up earlier on last year's invitation.

Kwame pursued his unexpected advantage, 'That's an expensive car; the big lady's business must be doing well.'

'It's a beauty isn't it; too good for our roads.'

'Do you get a chance to drive it?'

'I drive Mama Kate sometimes when Kofi is off duty.'

'Kofi Adjare?'

'Of course!'

'Is he around?'

'No, that's why I'm here.'

'No funerals today?'

'Oh, she has plenty to attend after the meeting.'

'Seems like an important meeting; I've been waiting for ages.'

'Shoe business, she's with Madam Akomwa from England.'

More useful information, thought Kwame, glad of the warning. He decided that it would be better not to recognise the little lady if their paths crossed. He needn't have worried; however, as a maid came to tell him that her mistress was free and would like to see him now. By the time that he had taken leave of Kofi and followed the maid around to the front door, Madam Akomwa had made her departure.

Kwame entered the royal presence in some trepidation. He was not sure how he would be received after so long an interval, extending over the period of Mama Kate's imprisonment as well as his own year of exile. He was expecting a shock but not this high on the Richter scale. The market queen was still sitting on her throne, surrounded by courtiers, but in place of that shining black corpulent presence that threatened to burst its textile bonds he found a dull pale shrunken form enveloped in loose folds of redundant drapery. Immediately he understood why Comfort and Auntie Rose doubted if Mama Kate was directing the operations of the cartel. He had a strange feeling of role reversal as he not only took her hand but leaned forward to kiss her cheek in a vain effort to donate a modicum of his own health and vitality.

Perhaps in response to this intimate gesture, Mama Kate waved away her retinue and invited Kwame to draw his chair closer. He relaxed as he realised that all formality was being abandoned and he was invited to an intimate one-to-one conversation. After the usual exchange of greetings he apologised for not having been able to answer her invitation of the previous year. He explained that he had been offered an academic post in England that had kept him away until this visit. Even now he was engaged on official duty in collaboration with Kumasi University and must return to *aborokyiri* within a few days. However, he could not

116

leave Kumasi without paying a courtesy call on his old benefactor.

Mama Kate said that she was happy to see him and he should call on her any time that he was in town. She was sorry to hear that he had broken up with Comfort but she wished him well with his new life in England. When Kwame asked how she was, she admitted that she had lost much weight, which many people viewed as a good thing, but she felt much weaker. She made no mention of her spell in prison but Kwame saw that her year of freedom had done little to repair the damage. He expressed his sympathy and the wish for a speedy return to full health.

Kwame formed the strong impression that Mama Kate's affliction had persuaded her of the frailty of human life. He could not imagine the woman before him as the ruthless entrepreneur he once knew: subordinating everything to the accumulation of money and rejoicing in its power. Here, rather, was an old friend, even a lover, who welcomed companionship and the opportunity to recall happier days. She was not a person to be feared, and if he had cause still to fear the cartel, Mama Kate could not be its source. For her sake as much as for his own, he was very glad that he had forced himself to make this visit. As he took his leave with a fond embrace, he wondered if he would ever kiss that faded cheek again.

It wasn't until he was walking down the gravel path to the great iron gates that Kwame remembered that Mama Kate's previous meeting had been reported to him as a business one. Could this enfeebled woman have spent such a long period in fierce negotiations, or had Auntie Rose's visit been for another purpose. Were they, perhaps, old friends, reminiscing about old times. Auntie Rose had admitted being a courier for several years so she might have come to know Mama Kate very well. Then he remembered Comfort hinting that Auntie Rose was regarded by the cartel as a kind of double agent. The two older women's conversation must have covered a wide range of topics. No doubt, Auntie Rose would report in due course on what was relevant to the investigation.

Kwame still didn't know who was directing operations for the drugs cartel in the UK but he was convinced that it wasn't Mama Kate. He also doubted if the Lebanese partners would want to continue to work with Mama Kate in her present condition, and he knew of no other senior Ghanaian left to take over. So the splitting of the cartel along national lines now seemed more credible.

Kwame thought that he had discovered who was reporting to the cartel about academics being sent to Warwick. He could ask the dean to severely restrict who was in the know. As an undergraduate, Kofi Boateng would not normally have access to information on senior members and restricting the circulation of documents to a few members of the school board should block his sources.

As he drove back towards the campus, Kwame had good reason to be happy with his morning's work. He decided to relax for the rest of the weekend, but he would ring Comfort to arrange to meet her in her house again on Sunday evening. Auntie Rose would probably be there and it might be their last chance to pool and summarise what they had learned before his return to England.

Feeling that he deserved a reward, Kwame stopped at the swimming pool restaurant and treated himself to one of Mrs Dodoo's lunches. He toyed with the idea of taking one of the nubile waitresses back to his chalet for an enhanced siesta, but decided not to spoil his record. In spite of the heightened sexuality of his homeland, he had rejected Janet's offer and denied himself a rekindled affair with Comfort, so he resolved to maintain his celibacy until he was home again with Afriyie. Back in his room, shaded from the afternoon sun, lying prone and alone in the downward draught of the ceiling fan, he reflected ruefully that he didn't need Comfort to remind him of his advancing years.

His waking thoughts were also of Comfort. He must telephone to check that she would be home on Sunday evening. After that, he turned on the television. Kwame didn't spend much time watching in Ghana as he had grown used to the high quality of programmes in England. On this occasion, however, he thought that the closing ceremony of his course might be featured in the news. Cameras had been present, but he knew from experience that this did not guarantee inclusion in the broadcast. Over the years the projects and activities of the TCC had been well covered in the media: TV, radio and the national newspapers, and if there was no mention in the television news, he could still expect an article in the Monday or Tuesday editions of the *Daily Graphic* or the *Ghanaian Times*. He hoped that he would have at least a newspaper cutting to include in his report for Warwick.

The TV was playing a popular comedy called *Osofo Dadzie*, recounting the trials and tribulations of a church minister in modern Ghana. Kwame found himself laughing at the antics portrayed on the small glass screen. During much time spent in Britain he had made a big effort to understand British humour, and he was relieved not to have lost his own sense of humour in the process. The programme was in the vernacular of present day Ghana, Akan dialects with many key phrases and words expressed in English. This was not the pure Twi of the *okyeame* and Kwame wondered what Kofi Adjare would think of it. It was not the classical Twi that Kofi used in communicating on behalf of the cartel. This reminded Kwame that he still did not know who was giving Kofi his instructions, so he was glad of a distraction when he heard a knock on the door of his chalet.

Mick and Sandra had come to thank him for the opportunity he had given them to come to Ghana on their present assignment. Kwame was forced in a very un-Ghanaian way to hasten his visitors to easy chairs with a warning that they might see themselves on TV. The news was just beginning but it seemed a long time before the international and national news was finished and some local items flickered on the small screen for a few moments. Sure enough, a brief feature on the engineering drawing course was included and, as usual, the cameras panned the whole gathering at the closing ceremony. Mick and Sandra were as surprised as they were gratified. They couldn't imagine an opportunity to appear on the TV news in the UK.

Sandra was particularly delighted. 'That's amazing,' she cried. 'I had no idea that the course would create that level of interest.'

'The TCC has always invited the media to its special functions,' explained Kwame, 'and after twenty-three years the reporters and cameras still keep coming. There is widespread interest in activities leading to national economic development. We can expect to read something about ourselves in the newspapers on Monday or Tuesday.'

Mick was also pleased, saying, 'It certainly helps to make us feel that our efforts are worthwhile and appreciated. Which brings us to our reason for coming here,' Mick continued. 'We really can't thank you enough for this chance to work here and see what you have all been doing over so many years. What you and your colleagues have achieved in Suame and Tema is most impressive and we are very pleased to have the opportunity to join the team and be part of the programme. We hope that we can make an important contribution and continue to come here from time to time.'

Kwame assured his visitors that their efforts were much appreciated, not least by the local academics they had come to support. Even if he had no definite plans to bring them back he was sure that he would get requests from these friends. They were less than a year into a three-year programme and there would be plenty of further opportunities to get involved in activities here in Ghana. He was sure that Professor Arthur would want to take full advantage of their growing skills and experience.

Sandra took her leave, saying that she had an invitation to dinner and must get ready. Mick, however, said that he had something to report that would be of interest to Kwame. 'One of the TCC vehicles broke down the other day,' he began, 'and I went with the driver to look for spare parts. It was a chance to see more of the markets and back streets of the town. Do you know there are dozens of small auto parts stores on the narrow road running behind Prempeh II Street?'

'I know it, it's very congested, so I try to avoid it.'

'Yes, we had trouble parking. The police have recently put in new restrictions.'

'Did you get the parts you wanted?'

'We did, but only after calling at many of the stores.'

'So is there another problem?'

'No problem, but I found *Sika Ye Na* enterprise!'

'Are you sure it's the one we were looking for in Suame?'

'Well, they sell auto parts, including pistons.'

Kwame had a strong feeling that Mick had found the right place. Hanabis had their main department store on Prempeh II Street, with offices above, and he wondered if this *Sika Ye Na* enterprise might back onto Hanabis or even occupy part of the same building. He could easily check this for himself tomorrow morning when the Sunday traffic would be light. He thanked Mick for this help and complimented him on his good memory and powers of observation. 'Did you see any of Frank Awuah's pistons for sale?' he asked.

'There were none visible from outside, only boxes of imported ones,' said Mick, 'and I couldn't think of a good excuse to go inside.' Kwame was glad of this; a foreigner enquiring about these particular auto parts might have aroused suspicion.

Kwame had brought Mick to Kumasi to help with his university work. Now he had also helped him with his extramural duties, although he had not been told why there was a special interest in *Sika Ye Na* enterprise. Kwame was happy that he had backed his own judgement to bring Mick here in spite of his rough manners. As he had hoped, the roughness had hardly been noticed, and Mick's manners had smoothed as he came to realise how much his practical skills were appreciated.

The next day Kwame drove into town. The light Sunday morning traffic allowed him to park in the small space still free of police restrictions. He marvelled at how different the scene looked almost devoid of motor vehicles; how wide the road looked without lines of parked cars on both sides. The contrast with the other six days of the week was almost unbelievable. He walked down the sidewalk past the closed and shuttered auto parts stores feeling rather exposed in the absence of other pedestrians. Counting his paces, he estimated how far it was from the end of the street to *Sika Ye Na* enterprise. Then, sauntering around to Prempeh II Street, casually looking through the iron grilles of closed department stores, he repeated the exercise, past the enticing display of imported goods in the expansive windows of Hanabis Ghana Ltd.

He had been right. *Sika Ye Na* enterprise might or might not be an independent business, but it could easily serve as the back door of Hanabis. Kwame now felt sure that Frank Awuah's pistons were not intended for sale as spare parts in the local market but came straight to Hanabis to be used for a quite different purpose. He was confident that Leon could be advised to instruct his people to watch out for this new drug-smuggling device. Frank Awuah had been warned to stop making the pistons and this might delay the trade temporarily. The Lebanese would find another manufacturer but Kwame was sure the pistons would then be of inferior quality and more easily identified as fakes. He had done what he could to expose and delay the trade at this end; the rest would be up to Leon.

That evening he drove once more up the hill to Nhyiasu for his meeting with Comfort. He also expected to see Auntie Rose but not to be cross-examined on his visit to Mama Kate. The little lady told him that she had been sitting in her meeting with the market queen when a housemaid had come to announce that Mr Kwame Mainu was waiting for an audience. She had been immediately concerned that his presence there raised the possibility of their connection being recognised. His visit was unnecessary duplication in information gathering. It was fortunate that he was not in the waiting room when she left the meeting. Kwame tried to defend himself on the grounds that Mama Kate was an old friend and benefactor whom custom required should be visited whenever he was in town. He added that, as their paths had not crossed, no harm had been done, but Auntie Rose replied that security could not be left to chance.

Kwame was forced to admit to himself that he had not originally intended to see Mama Kate. Quite uncharacteristically, he had responded to impulse. He did not regret his impromptu visit, however, as it had yielded both emotional and intelligence benefits. It was also accidental that Auntie Rose's visit had coincided with his own. If she was so concerned about this security issue she could have informed him of her intended visit in advance. The discussion had left them both smarting and it took some time for Comfort's cold drinks to cool them down.

At length Comfort managed to draw her guests to summarising the important issues. Now they all agreed that Mama Kate was unlikely to be directing the cartel's activities in the UK. According to Auntie Rose, even the shoe business was being conducted by long practised routine rather than any semblance of entrepreneurial initiative. 'Your competition is fast fading,' Auntie Rose quipped to Comfort. 'You will soon be sitting on the stool again.'

Kwame mentioned his meeting with Kofi Boateng who had been standing in for Kofi Adjare as Mama Kate's driver. He told the ladies that Kofi Boateng was now a student at Tek and was probably the person reporting the movement of academics to Warwick. Fortunately, steps had now been taken to restrict knowledge of the movements to a small group of senior members. This should frustrate the cartel in recruiting couriers from the university. He had also taken action to select candidates more carefully, to try to guarantee their return to Ghana. One way or another he was doing all he could to prevent another Peggy Osei-Wusu slipping through to a life of international crime.

'Have you found where Money is Scarce?' asked Auntie Rose with a broad smile as she used the English translation of the store's name. Kwame relaxed, now he felt that the little lady had forgiven or forgotten and he must respond in the same vein. 'Money is scarce where money is plentiful,' he replied, 'at the back door to the Hanabis department store on Prempeh II Street.'

Kwame told the tale of how Mick Gould had gone in search of spare parts for a TCC vehicle and had stumbled upon *Sika Ye Na* enterprise. He had himself verified its exact location.

'Well done!' said Auntie Rose. 'Now we can assume that your made-in-Suame car parts are likely to be used for exporting drugs to the UK.'

'Yes,' said Kwame, 'but by the Lebanese faction. We still don't know if we have one cartel or two. We suspect that the Ghanaian side is very weak; are the Lebanese still working with them?'

'If they're not,' said Auntie Rose, 'they must be active building up a rival distribution network in the UK. Leon's people should be able to detect something of that activity.'

Kwame had hoped that he might have more time one-to-one with Comfort but Auntie Rose did not offer nor Comfort suggest. Later he felt that it was probably just as well. What did he want it for anyway? He had decided against blowing on a dying ember; but was it dying? Comfort had left him, not the other way round. Had he succeeded in healing the wound? He couldn't be sure. Now as he lurched over countless potholes, back to the campus in the ancient but trusty Land Rover, he looked forward to the last stage of his mission and the return to his reconstructed family in Coventry.

application through his head of department to the dean. 'The selection committee will meet in two days, on Wednesday afternoon, and the papers must be ready.'

'Who's on the committee?'

'The dean, the TCC director and me.'

'What are my chances?'

'Very good. You're an old client of the TCC and the director will support you. You will get my vote, so all you need to do is have a chat with your dean.'

Kwame was very happy as he said goodbye to Stephen. At least he had one suitable candidate for the cooperation programme. If only he could find one or two more his quota would be complete for the year. He wondered how Mick and Sandra were faring as he made his way under the blazing midday sun to where his vehicle was parked in a patch of shade. Instinctively he turned towards the swimming pool restaurant. Once again he had something to celebrate.

On Tuesday afternoon Kwame met with Mick and Sandra to discuss the candidates. They met in Kwame's chalet where they had watched the brief TV news report of the engineering drawing course. Now, all had copies of Monday's *Daily Graphic* to show each other the printed report of the event. They laughed as they realised their common intention. 'Paste it into your reports to the prof,' said Kwame.

The mood soon changed when they got down to business. 'I've met both of the women and one of the men,' said Sandra.

'And I've had a good chat with both of the men,' added Mick. 'How do you want to play it?'

'Let's take the male candidates first,' said Kwame. 'You start, Mick.'

'We have Nelson Evans-Agyei and Kojo Doe, both of the School of Engineering,' said Mick. 'Neither was able to show me anything practical that they are doing but Kojo is playing with AutoSketch engineering drawing software.'

'He'll be able to help with our computer-aided drawing course then,' commented Kwame.

'But not come to Warwick,' said Mick. 'He made no secret of his intention to try and extend his stay.'

'What of Nelson Evans-Agyei?' prompted Kwame.

'Oh he's a real charmer,' said Sandra with obvious enthusiasm.

'He certainly has a smooth way of talking,' said Mick. 'He wasn't as blunt as Kojo, but I would still doubt his motives.'

Sandra wasn't happy, and insisted, 'Nelson's keen to learn more about renewable energy, especially jojoba oil in diesel engines; why don't we give him a chance?'

'Has he done any practical work on jojoba?' asked Kwame.

'No!' said Mick,

'Not yet,' said Sandra, 'but he has researched the literature.'

'What of the two women?' asked Kwame.

'Christy Akyeampong is from the School of Engineering,' said Sandra, 'and Yaa Williams is in the physics department of the Faculty of Science.'

'Let's deal with this first, then,' said Kwame. 'Which one do you fancy, Mick?'

'I've only seen them at a distance,' Mick admitted, 'but I don't need a closer look. Present company excepted, of course, but attractive girls don't generally go into science or engineering.'

'Sandra is the exception that proves the rule?'

'Absolutely!'

'So we can make a purely objective assessment,' said Kwame. 'How do you rate the young women?'

'Not much hope for Christy, I'm afraid,' said Sandra. 'She already has family in London and is very keen to join them.'

'Then she can wait for them to send her a ticket,' said Kwame, 'and we can spend our funds on more deserving candidates.'

'As for Yaa,' continued Sandra, 'I'm not quite sure. She wants to help supply secondary schools in rural areas with locally made basic science equipment. She's made a few samples from recycled tin cans and plastic bottles but she doesn't have much idea about how to produce in quantity or introduce them into the schools.'

'If Yaa is serious, the TCC would certainly help with the extension work in the rural areas,' said Kwame. 'Is she serious?'

'I chatted with her for quite a long time and we had lunch together but I'm still not sure,' Sandra replied. 'She talks about the need to develop the rural areas but she's lived all her life in the town: Accra and Takoradi. I don't think that she knows any more about village life than I do.'

'OK,' said Kwame. 'Let's sum up our discussion. We have two nos: Kojo Doe and Christie Acheampong, and two possibles: Nelson Evans-Agyei and Yaa Williams. Thank you both for your good work. I will pass on your recommendations to the selection committee when we meet tomorrow.'

Kwame invited his two helpers to a last supper at the Senior Staff Club, attended by all their new colleagues from the university. He told Sandra that he couldn't extend an official invitation to Nelson but, if she wished, she was free to invite him as her personal guest. Mick could do the same if his chosen companion was not already on the official guest list.

On Wednesday morning Mick and Sandra set out for Accra on the first stage of their journey home. The selection committee met in the afternoon. Stephen Okunor's visit to Warwick was easily approved. Then there were lengthy discussions about the four younger applicants. Kwame was prepared to give way in the case of Yaa Williams, but she was from the Faculty of Science and the dean of engineering would only agree if one of his candidates was also included. Reluctantly, Kwame agreed to Nelson Evans-Agyei joining the party.

The year's quota of visits under the cooperation agreement was filled. Kwame could score another success, but he knew that he had failed to guarantee that there would not be another absconding. There was nothing more that he could do; his current mission was completed. Now he could let himself look forward to life back in Coventry. Now he could admit to himself how much he had missed Afriyie, Akosua and a big furry dog.

On an August morning in 1995 Kwame strode through the arrival procedures at London Airport feeling guilty that he had not made greater efforts to keep in touch with home during his four weeks in Ghana. He was deeply aware that excuses about pressure of work and difficulties with communications were unlikely to convince others if they didn't convince him. His last letter home had been to congratulate Akosua on success in her GCSE examinations and endorse her choice of science subjects for the first year in the sixth form. He steeled himself to bear criticism with a smile and hoped that the few small presents in his suitcase would help restore his popularity.

He need not have worried. Akosua rushed towards him in her usual boisterous fashion and Afriyie, Tom and Akos Mary all waited patiently for their turn to hug and be hugged. 'All hail the conquering hero!' said Tom.

'Why, what's happened?' asked a startled Kwame.

'We've had a letter from a group of Tema artisans to say that your course in Kumasi was the best thing that has ever been done for them and they want more of the same!'

'So Sam Quaye and his people really meant what they told me,' said Kwame. 'Their enthusiastic support throughout the course really encouraged the others.'

'Where's Takoradi?' asked Kwame, suddenly aware of a certain canine vacuum.

'We left him in the car,' laughed Akosua. 'Uncle Tom wasn't sure he would be allowed inside the terminal.'

'Then we'd better hurry to keep him company,' said Kwame as he struggled with Tom for the handle of his suitcase, and Akosua snatched his hand baggage.

Being Saturday morning, the traffic was light and they were soon in Coventry. At Tom and Akos Mary's they were reunited with little Tom Arthur III and Afriyie's apprentice, Elsie Ntim, who had been caring for the infant in his parents' absence. They all had lunch together before Tom dropped Kwame and his retinue at their home. Kwame was looking forward to a good rest but he promised Akosua that if the weather was fine they would take Takoradi on a long walk on Sunday morning.

Kwame had given Tom a brief written report on Saturday but it wasn't until Monday morning that they had a verbal debriefing. Tom had already heard much from Mick and Sandra and he had the letter from Sam Quaye, so he again congratulated Kwame on the success of their Kumasi mission. Kwame was of the view that the short course had been much appreciated by the participants and had been a stimulating experience for the instructors and helpers. Mick and Sandra had also accomplished some useful supplementary tasks, and he made special mention of Sandra's survey of foundry activity in Suame and Tema.

'So where are the problems?' asked Tom. 'What do we need to improve?'

'There are two things that particularly concern me,' said Kwame. 'One is the matter of fees charged to the course participants and the other is the selection of the people we bring here for training and research.'

'OK, let's take the first one first.'

'Did Sam Quaye put his opinion in the letter?'

'Yes, he thinks that the fee could be increased and the cost of board and lodging reduced.'

'We agreed on some economies, the details are in the report, but there are limits.'

'Like what?'

'I don't want to give up campus accommodation as it confers real benefits, and if we increase fees we must make some provision to help the younger self-employed artisans.'

'Like your little Miss Mfumwa?'

'Oh, you've read about her have you?'

'Did Professor Kwami agree to her repeating?'

'He did.'

Tom agreed that future courses, beginning with the next one scheduled for January 1996, could trial the economies agreed between Kwame and the Tema group of artisans. There would be an increase in the fee but he was happy for Kwame and the TCC director to select up to, say, five younger artisans to be admitted at a reduced rate. These changes would improve the cost recovery but only marginally: from five to ten per cent, perhaps. Real progress towards sustainability could only be achieved if the fees paid to university lecturers could be reduced. 'Can we do anything about this, Kwame?'

'Not as long as the academics know there is foreign funding involved.'

'Can the courses continue after the foreign funding stops?'

'That must be our long-term aim. We might persuade some of the younger lecturers to accept cedi fees, especially those that have benefited from the project in other ways.'

'Right,' said Tom. 'We are agreed about repeating the engineering drawing course in January to cater for those who couldn't be included this time. I want you to go ahead with all necessary arrangements. How do you feel about going back again?'

'No problem, but I would like to make one suggestion.'

'Go ahead.'

'I want to take Greg Anderson. He needs to gain the experience and he could also demonstrate computer-aided drawing and work with Kumasi people to plan a full two-week course.'

'Good idea. Will you take anyone else?'

'Well, Mick is so useful I would always like him around, but I will give it more thought.'

Tom turned to the second of Kwame's concerns about Kumasi people coming to Warwick. 'You've made some changes to the selection procedures and given yourself the key role but you're still not satisfied. Why is that?'

'We're up against university politics, I'm afraid.'

'In what way?'

'Well, although the dean of engineering agreed that we needed to stop absconding, he wouldn't agree to a scientist coming to Warwick unless one of his engineers also came.'

'But Stephen Okunor's an engineer?'

'Yes, but he's technical staff, not an academic – I proposed his candidacy, not the dean!'

'Is your academic engineer reliable?'

'Sandra thinks so. Mick and I have serious doubts.'

'I'm not happy about this, Kwame. We can't have another absconder. Our funders are very concerned about the lady who ran away. They say bringing her here was a waste of money and her action damages all our reputations.'

'I quite agree. I did all I could to prevent it happening again.'

'Well, as you have three people lined up we must try one more time, but if it happens again we must seriously consider winding up that part of the programme.'

Then, much to Kwame's relief, Tom turned to another topic, 'How about your sleuthing, Kwame, is there anything interesting you can tell me?'

'Do you remember Frank Awuah?'

'Vaguely, everything about that first afternoon in Suame is vague.'

'Well, Mick and I visited Frank with another client and we found that Frank was making engine pistons.'

'For your diesel engine?'

'No these were aluminium alloy not cast iron.'

'For motorcycles then?'

'No, these were for cars, Nissans and Toyotas, but they were probably ordered by the Lebanese company involved in the drugs smuggling.'

'Do they sell vehicle spare parts locally?'

'They are linked to a local spare parts store but I don't think these pistons are for local use.'

'Then for what?'

'For concealing drugs bound for the UK.'

'I hope you warned Frank about this possible use of his pistons. The last think we need is for this project to get mixed up with the drugs business. That would be guaranteed to bring everything to an end.'

Kwame understood Tom's concern. It was also a big worry for him. He had always feared that his involvement with Leon's investigations might somehow contaminate his industrial development work. He couldn't see how he could have foreseen his client's engineering products getting mixed up with the trade in narcotics. In the past the drug smugglers had used food items, like kenke balls, coconuts and live snails, and handicraft products such as woodcarvings and traditional woven smocks. Now it appeared they had moved on to the engineering industry and the choice of possible containers was very wide. He could not control the process but he must try to cut it off wherever it impinged on the work of the two universities.

* * *

Akosua had gone off on a summer camp with a party from school so it fell to Kwame to take Takoradi on his evening walks. He had made no effort to contact Leon but he half expected that he might encounter Tam Gordon on one of his turns around the common.

Several days went by and no Twi-speaking Scotsman appeared. Kwame was left free to contemplate the wonders of nature. On a clear evening he watched the sun glide gently along the horizon to a soft landing in the Warwickshire countryside and recalled how a few days before he had seen that same sun crash in a near vertical dive into the forest west of Kumasi. He tried to explain this to Takoradi, but in spite of his name the big dog had never been to Ghana. He was only interested in contemplating his supper and sniffing out scented syringes left abandoned under bushes and benches.

Kwame felt sure that the local police must have grown tired of his frequent calls about drugs detritus on the common. He apologised for harassing them and explained that Akosua's pet was only continuing in retirement what he had been trained to do during his working life. It was the police that were really to blame for having trained him so well. As Takoradi towed him home, Kwame reflected that the scent of heroin must have sharpened his appetite.

Afriyie welcomed him with, 'Your old friend has come.' He hung up his coat and made his way to the lounge, expecting to meet Tam Gordon or Jack Preece. Instead it was David Barney who was sipping tea and reading Kwame's *Independent*. Instinctively applying Mainu's law, he greeted his visitor with, 'You haven't been waiting long then?'

'Not at all; it's good to see you again.'

Kwame welcomed his unexpected guest and Afriyie brought more tea. 'Leon told me you'd been exiled to Scotland,' he said. 'What did you do to get repatriated?'

'You're to blame,' joked David. 'Leon said he needed more people used to keeping you in check!'

'Then we'd better start by seeing if you remember how to eat fufu.' Kwame turned to Afriyie, 'I hope it's ready, I'm as hungry as Takoradi tonight.'

'Leon wants to know when you intend to report on your trip to Ghana,' David said when the meal was over.

'I've been waiting to hear when and how he wants me to report,' Kwame replied. 'Is he coming to Warwick police station or are we meeting in the aviary at the London Zoo?'

'Neither, he'll be at Akos Mary's hairdressing salon at five pm on Wednesday.'

132

'Is Auntie Rose bringing him then?'

'You'll know when you get there.'

In his office next morning Kwame was putting together his formal report on his visit to Kumasi when Tom came in and sat down facing him across his desk. This was unusual enough to alert Kwame that his friend had a personal problem. He pushed aside his papers to remove all barriers to a free discussion. 'Akos Mary and I seem to have encountered our first serious culture clash,' Tom said, 'and you're the only one who can help me.'

'What has happened?'

'She's insisting on baptising Little Tom.'

'Isn't that rather usual here?'

'Not in our family.'

'So your parents aren't religious?'

'Mum told me that when she was a child she was sent to Methodist Sunday School and Dad's family were Anglicans, but they never go to church except to weddings and funerals and I was never baptised.'

Kwame was still puzzled by Tom's problem. How could someone who was normally so level-headed and tolerant be so concerned over such a minor issue? 'I'm sorry, old friend,' he said, 'but I don't see it as a big problem. Sprinkling a little water can't harm the little chap; he'll enjoy it!'

'That's not the point,' said Tom. 'Why perpetuate these ancient customs long after they've ceased to have any meaning or relevance.'

'That's not how Akos Mary will see it.'

'That's the problem!'

Kwame took a deep breath, 'Most of our people are animist by instinct and Christian by default. Animists lay great stress on custom. Long after the meaning of a ceremony has been lost, they feel compelled to repeat it, just in case neglecting it will offend the ancestors or the local spirits. One can call it superstition, like not walking under a ladder or touching wood, but it sets the mind to rest. Make this small gesture to give your good lady peace of mind.'

'Are you saying that I should let her raise my son as a Christian?'

'Little Tom will make up his own mind when he's old enough to ask the questions.'

'What if Akos Mary wants to send him to Sunday school?'

'It didn't harm your mother and it didn't harm me. Surely you will educate Little Tom well enough to be able to differentiate between probability and supposition!'

'Where did *you* learn this, Kwame?'

'From a little man with broken legs and the courage to think for himself.'

Tom rose from his seat in silence and took two paces to the door. There he paused as if about to speak again, but changing his mind he went out deep in thought, quietly closing the office door. Kwame hoped that he had helped his friend come to terms with his problem. He didn't think that Akos Mary would make a big issue over Sunday school but he saw one cloud on the horizon. Since Elsie had come to stay with Afriyie she had persuaded Afriyie and Akos Mary to take her to a Pentecostal church in Coventry. He hoped that the two mature women would soon grow tired of evangelising and leave the apprentice to go alone. Elsie wasn't making much progress with her English and a little more speaking in tongues might do her good.

Kwame kept his appointment with Leon Thornet. As he had supposed, it was Auntie Rose who had arranged the venue, and much to his surprise they were led up stairs behind the hairdressing salon to a comfortable sitting room. Akos Mary brought in a tray of tea and cakes and departed to prepare supper for her two Toms. Kwame was impressed that Leon had decided to do the debriefing himself and not leave it to Jack or David. After all, Auntie Rose must have already reported everything that he had learned in Kumasi.

In his usual manner, now familiar to Kwame, Leon let the small talk go on while the refreshments were taken, seeing everyone relax before introducing the serious business. David Barney came in, greeting the others and signalling to Leon that they were clear to begin. 'You seem to have exceeded our expectations, Kwame Mainu,' Leon began, placing his cup and saucer on his empty plate with studied concentricity. 'Would you like to summarise for us what you learned on your recent trip?'

'First of all,' said Kwame, 'I can confirm that Bra Yaw has been released from prison and is active again in recruiting couriers. He attempted to recruit Kwaku Darko, one of the Kumasi academics who visited Warwick earlier this year. Kwaku told me that he believes that his colleague, Peggy Osei-Wusu, agreed to bring a package to London. This is the lady who avoided going back to Ghana and is now presumably an illegal immigrant.'

'So we know for certain that the Kumasi cartel is busy trying to replace its losses and get back into operation,' said Leon, 'but who is directing operations?'

'We know that Kofi Adjare has gone back to work for Mama Kate, who was also released from prison last year,' said Kwame.

'This is the man you called the *okyeame* and is still the voice of whoever is directing operations in the UK?' said Leon, seeking confirmation.

Kwame nodded, and added, 'But neither Auntie Rose nor I think that it's Mama Kate who is giving him his instructions.'

'I want to come back to this issue,' said Leon, 'but first tell us what else you discovered.'

So Kwame continued, 'One of the drugs couriers who escaped imprisonment, Kofi Boateng, is now a mature student at Kumasi University. We think that he is the cartel's source of information about academic movements under the partnership agreement with Warwick University. I tried to make changes to procedures to make it harder for the cartel to gain this information.'

'What of the Lebanese?' Leon asked. 'What did you find them up to?'

'We found pistons for car engines being made in Suame Magazine that are clearly not for use in real engines. They are probably for supply to Hanabis, the company with at least three directors involved in the drugs cartel. I believe that these pistons are intended for use in smuggling drugs. I advised the manufacturer to stop supplying.'

'Anything else?' prompted Leon.

'I found one young woman, who had recently attended parties held by Lebanese businessmen, who told me that she knew one woman who had become addicted to a hard drug supplied by a Lebanese man.'

'How do you interpret that?' asked Leon.

'As far as I know,' replied Kwame, 'the Lebanese didn't used to supply hard drugs in Ghana. It may be a hint that the partnership in the cartel is breaking down.'

'Do you mean that the Lebanese and Ghanaian groups may be separating?' asked David.

'Yes,' said Kwame, 'the ban on the supply of drugs to Ghanaians may have been part of the original agreement. I sensed growing anger generally that Ghanaians were now becoming addicted.'

Leon turned to Auntie Rose. 'Do you agree with Kwame on the facts, as far as you know them, and on his various deductions?'

'I agree about Mama Kate; she's not capable of directing operations. I think Kwame's probably right about the pistons. As for the Lebanese supplying drugs to Ghanaians, I'm surprised that Kwame consorts with girls who go to those parties.'

Kwame was relieved to see from her expression that she was joking.

wedding he had been a constant source of anxiety. Twice he had emerged from the shadows demanding money and favours. At least now Akos Mary would be free of this threat to her marriage and her peace of mind.

Kwame wondered if he should report Konadu's death to Leon, then immediately realised that Leon must already know. Someone in Leon's team would be detailed to read the Ghanaian newspapers and monitor the TV and radio news bulletins. Konadu operating in the UK would have been an active concern; Konadu repatriated to Ghana would have been a potential threat; Konadu dead was a closed file. Kwame supposed that Leon's only interest would be to know exactly which faction had been responsible for the murder and what further repercussions might be expected.

On a Thursday morning in October the next Kumasi academics were due to fly to London. Kwame had decided to send Mick and Sandra to meet the visitors at the airport and bring them to Coventry. He wanted to be directly involved in Stephen Okunor's project to copy the Mattisson shaping machine attachment. Mick would help Nelson Evans-Agyei with a project in renewable energy, and Sandra was assigned to assist Yaa Williams with her efforts to produce science equipment for rural secondary schools. Kwame was aware that Sandra would have preferred to help Nelson but he judged that a romantic attachment would not be conducive to good work. No doubt the couple would spend much of their off-duty time together.

He had arranged for Nelson and Yaa to stay in on-campus guest accommodation, but Afriyie had agreed that Stephen Okunor could stay with them in their guest room. Stephen was an old friend but Kwame wasn't quite sure if he liked big furry dogs. Apart from this one concern, Kwame knew that he would enjoy long conversations with someone with intimate knowledge of both the university and Suame Magazine. He looked forward to Stephen's arrival.

Kwame was in his office when Mick and Sandra came back with the visitors. After brief introductions to Greg, Kwame suggested that Nelson and Yaa should be taken to their accommodation on campus and he left for home with Stephen. The master craftsman had been trained in Britain in the 1960s but this was his first return visit. Kwame expected to hear much about the changes that had taken place over a period of thirty years.

They were sitting taking tea when Afriyie and Elsie came back from work and began preparing their evening meal. Then Akosua came in from school and fetched Takoradi in from the garden. The big dog lazily scanned the visitor for banned substances, and finding none, fell asleep at his feet. Kwame was relieved that this standard procedure had in no way disturbed his guest. Stephen asked Akosua the name of her dog.

'You guess,' she said. 'It's the name of a town in Ghana.'

'You're from Konongo, is that his name?'

'No.'

'Is it my town, Ho?'

'Wrong again, it's a big port.'

'Then it's either Tema or Takoradi.'

'It's Takoradi!'

Stephen was surprised to be taking fufu on his first evening in England. It wasn't quite the same as back home but quite acceptable. Surrounded by Ghanaians, and with at least half of the conversation in Twi, Stephen had to remind himself from time to time that he had flown three thousand miles to the north in the past twenty-four hours. Kwame knew Stephen was a shy man and he was happy to see him relaxed and obviously at home. In the morning they would begin searching for the gear-generating attachment for the shaping machine.

It was getting late, and Kwame had reminded Akosua that tomorrow was another school day, when Stephen said that he had just remembered that he had something to deliver. 'Not a package, I hope,' said Kwame, hoping that Bra Yaw had not called on Stephen with his usual request.

'No just a letter,' said Stephen. 'A lady called Comfort Opokua asked me to be sure to give it to you in person.' He went up to his room and soon descended again, handing an envelope to Kwame.

'Oh, I hope it's not bad news,' said Afriyie.

'Read it Dad, tell us what Mummy says,' cried Akosua.

'I have asked you to go to bed, Young Lady,' said Kwame, 'I think it's better I read it first; I'll tell you in the morning.'

A subdued daughter reluctantly followed her father's advice. 'I'll leave you to it as well,' said Stephen, and tactfully headed for his room.

Afriyie looked at Kwame. 'Are you going to open it?'

It was quite short.

Kumasi
12 October 1995

Dear Kwame,

This is just a note to let you know that Mama Kate passed away two days ago. As you know, she had been looking frail for some time but her death still came as a shock to all the traders. There is to be a big funeral. *Otumfuo* the *Asantehene* is expected to attend and perhaps even Nana Konadu Agyeman Rawlings.

Best wishes,
Comfort

10

A Shaggy Dog's Story

A few months ago Kwame would not have believed that Mama Kate's death could have affected him so deeply. She had dominated almost twenty years of his life, a formidable figure commanding powerful human and material resources. At first she had been his benefactor, sponsoring his studies at Kumasi Polytechnic and the university. When she tired of his attentions, and he had an opportunity to study overseas, she had tried to recruit him as a drugs courier. Kwame, by not choosing to follow that path and reluctantly helping the British authorities to arrest some of her people, had turned the big lady into a potential enemy who might seek revenge if she learned of his treachery.

Kwame had felt reasonably safe remaining in Ghana as long as Mama Kate and her associates were imprisoned. However, when the market queen secured an early release and sent for him again, Kwame had decided that his family would be more secure back in Britain. It had taken some courage for Kwame to go to visit Mama Kate during his recent visit to Kumasi, but finding the lady in such a depleted condition had aroused his sympathy. His fear had dissolved into something close to affection, and gratitude welled up anew for the start she had given him in his career. And now she was gone! He couldn't begin to imagine what might fill the hole she left in his life.

At breakfast Kwame kept his promise to tell Akosua what her mother had written. 'Do you remember Mama Kate?' he said. 'Mummy used to take you sometimes when she went to buy shoes.'

'Oh yes, she's very big and very rich.'

'I'm afraid she's also very dead.'

'Will Mummy be the next shoe queen?'

'It's possible.'

Kwame was relieved that Akosua did not show any immediate emotional reaction to the news. Maybe she had not had any opportunity to see Mama Kate other than as her mother's business associate.

Stephen Okunor joined them at table and after the usual morning's greetings they sat in silence, each lost in their own thoughts. Then Kwame noticed that Stephen had another buff envelope beside his plate. Nodding towards it, he said, 'Not more bad news, I hope.'

'Oh no,' Stephen replied. 'I brought some photographs of the Mattisson attachment to help identify what we are looking for.'

'They might be very useful, let's go to the office and start the search.'

Kwame had drawn up a list of technical schools which might still be using the Mattisson attachment on a shaping machine, and a list of machine tool manufacturers which might have taken over Mattisson when they went out of business, or might have acquired the rights to make the attachment. Sitting Stephen at a desk with a telephone and a directory he suggested calling people on the lists to find a source of the information he needed. Then he went off to see that the other two visitors were being settled into their new working environments.

He found Mick and Nelson in the alternative fuels laboratory. Nelson had expressed an interest in the use of jojoba oil as an alternative renewable fuel for diesel engines. The laboratory had a variable compression diesel engine on which it had run tests on sunflower oil and was ready to run tests on jojoba oil if a sufficient quantity could be found. While a search for raw material was going on, Nelson was invited to use the library to review the available literature. Kwame knew that a few people had started to grow jojoba in some arid areas of Ghana. If the oil was suitable for diesel fuel it could offer economic and environmental advantages in some of the poorest parts of the country. The project fitted well with his own diesel engine manufacturing project.

Kwame saw the jojoba project as one of a myriad good ideas that seemed to promise great advantages. He also knew that to take such a project from an idea to tangible reality required great effort over a number of years. Nelson would need to take what he learned at Warwick back to Ghana, write a convincing project proposal, find a sponsor and pursue the work with single-minded devotion until the government or private enterprise was willing to take it to the market. He doubted if Nelson would take more than a passing interest in the work. Nevertheless the initiative might inspire someone else to take it on more vigorously.

Kwame had to walk to the physics department to find Sandra and Yaa. He found them in the workshop talking to the chief technician. He was relieved that the two women had decided to take a practical approach. First they intended to discuss with the technicians what instruments were most needed for secondary school physics laboratories and to select what they thought could be made locally in Ghana. Then Yaa would be given help to produce some prototypes, taking care to use only materials and processes known to be available in Kumasi. Seeing that everything was well in hand, Kwame returned to his office where Stephen was busy on the telephone.

Tom came in to greet Stephen and welcome him to the university. Kwame had told Tom much about Stephen, especially when they visited Stephen's private workshop at the Suame ITTU in 1986, but Stephen had not been present and they had not met. Now they greeted each other warmly. It wasn't long before Tom was fully briefed on Stephen's mission. 'So you want to have a go at making the Mattisson gear-generating attachment for a shaping machine,' he repeated to himself aloud. 'What a splendid idea; just the sort of project we want to promote.'

'They're not making them any more so you can't buy new ones but there are some still in use in technical colleges,' Kwame explained.

'Have you tried the Land Rover apprentice training school?' asked Tom. 'They're right here in Coventry. I know the chap in charge; I'll call and arrange an appointment for you to see him.'

'Did I hear you mention Land Rover?' said Greg, drawn away from his computer screen. 'I did my apprenticeship there.'

'Then perhaps you can remember if they had a Mattisson attachment for their shaping machine,' said Kwame.

After Tom had returned to his office, Kwame explained Stephen's mission to Greg. 'Can I be in on this one?' Greg asked. 'If Prof arranges a meeting I'd like to go with you and help show you round.'

'Yes,' said Kwame, 'and when we find a Mattisson attachment you could help Stephen prepare a set of drawings using your AutoCad software. That would tie in nicely with our plans to introduce computer-aided drawing on our next course in Kumasi.'

Both Greg and Stephen looked pleased with this arrangement.

It was Kwame's turn to fetch Akosua and her schoolmates home from Warwick so he asked Stephen if he would like to come along for the ride. Just as they were leaving, Tom came to say that he had arranged for them to visit the Land Rover apprentice school tomorrow afternoon. Mr Dawson, the workshop supervisor, was sure he had what Stephen needed but it wasn't often used and might take some time to find. He promised to detail someone to search the tool store.

Stephen was in good spirits on the drive to Warwick. His project had got off to a good start and he was particularly pleased that Greg had offered to help with the drawings. This was the part of the work that he feared would go slowly and prevent him finishing in time. Now he felt that there were good prospects of completing his mission. Kwame assured him that he would get all the help he needed.

The schoolgirls were waiting and crowded into the Discovery. 'I can't wait to see Takoradi,' said Akosua. 'We have to write an essay about our favourite pet so I need to ask him all about his adventures as a police dog.'

'Does Takoradi speak English or Twi?' laughed Stephen.

'Whichever language comes into my head when I'm hugging him,' Akosua replied.

'It's the same with me and my pony, Dancer,' said one of the other students with a mid-European accent.

There followed a disorganised discussion about animal telepathy. Kwame reflected that Takoradi had certainly been able to communicate information about drugs and that brought his other concern back to mind.

The young women were absorbed in their own chatter, so Kwame asked Stephen if anyone had asked him to bring a package to the UK. 'Only Comfort Opokua who brought your letter,' Stephen replied. Kwame was relieved that at least one person had escaped Kofi Boateng's attention. He wondered how he could find out if the other two had been approached. It was then that he had the idea that Takoradi might be able to tell him.

Later that evening Kwame took an opportunity to ask Akosua if she knew how Takoradi had been trained to signal that he had scented a banned substance. 'We never actually saw him at work,' she replied, 'but I believe he signalled by sitting up very straight on his haunches.'

Next morning Kwame took Takoradi with him to the office on the pretext of having nobody to leave him with at home. After a good sniff all around to check out the office, the old dog lay down to rest. Kwame knew that he couldn't wander round the campus with Takoradi but he could call the visitors to his office. First he called Sandra, who came to sit across his desk in the visitor's chair. He told her that he wanted to be sure that Yaa had everything she needed but before he could ask her to bring Yaa to the office Takoradi decided to repeat his patrol, including a somewhat startled Sandra in his survey. The old dog snapped to attention sitting upright beside her chair.

Kwame had not expected Takoradi to react so soon and certainly not with one of his colleagues. Had Sandra picked up a scent from someone else? Then he remembered her pleading in Kumasi for Nelson to come to Warwick. Maybe she had spent time with Nelson the previous evening. He decided to go ahead with his plan and see what else Takoradi could tell him. After Sandra had departed on her errand he slipped a biscuit to his canine friend.

Yaa came back with Sandra but as far as Kwame could tell it was only Sandra who drew the dog's attention. Then he repeated the procedure with Mick and Nelson. This time it was quite clear that it was Nelson who attracted Takoradi's interest.

Kwame knew that he was far from being a trained dog handler. Takoradi's signals could only be grounds for suspicion but it seemed possible that Nelson had carried a parcel for the cartel and the scent had been retained on his clothing. He was sure that Leon would not approve of his initiative and would probably discount the results, but it gave him grounds to suspect that the cartel still had access to inside information on Kumasi University's envoys to Warwick. Stephen might have been missed because he was not on the original list of candidates but had been added separately by Kwame.

Kwame took Takoradi home at lunchtime and returned to take Stephen and Greg to the Land Rover apprentice school. They were welcomed by Mr Dawson who asked after Professor Arthur. 'I'm afraid that we're still looking for the Mattisson attachment,' he said. 'Would you like to look around the plant while you're waiting?' Kwame, who had always loved Land Rovers, eagerly accepted this offer. He had long wanted to see how his favourite vehicle was made.

It was as impressive as he always imagined it would be. Long lines of vehicles slowly advancing as teams of workers added parts to turn a bare steel chassis slowly into a completed product. He recalled how his own Land Rover back in Tema had once made this journey, as had all the TCC and GRID Land Rovers in their day. As he watched the original model, now called the Defender, coming off the production line he tried to imagine a continuous stream of vehicles stretching back nearly fifty years to when the production first began. Of all those hundreds of thousands of vehicles, he was told, more than half were still in use, on-road and off-road in every country in the world.

When they returned from the tour of the plant, good news awaited them. The much sought-after attachment was standing on a work bench. 'We don't use it much these days,' explained Mr Dawson, 'because most of the production gears are made on hobbing machines and prototype gears are usually milled.'

'Did Professor Arthur tell you what we need it for?' Kwame asked.

'He said that you want to make them in Ghana.'

'That's right; can we borrow it for a few days to make some drawings?'

'If you bring it back in the same condition.'

'There you are,' said Kwame to Stephen and Greg. 'That should keep you busy for a while!'

Mr Dawson found a suitable box to protect his precious antique and soon the team was heading back to base feeling that they had accomplished the first phase of Stephen's project. Now the machine could be dismantled and every part carefully measured so that accurate production drawings could be produced. Expert help would be sought to determine the specifications of all materials and to identify the appropriate machining and assembly operations. Then Stephen would decide what could be done at his workshop at Suame Magazine, and remedies would be found for any perceived shortcomings. Even with Greg's help this work was expected to occupy the whole of Stephen's stay in Coventry.

Kwame was not surprised that Leon would want to discuss the implications of the deaths of Mama Kate and Mr Konadu. He was summoned to a meeting at Warwick police station on his next school run. Leon was accompanied by David Barney and Tam Gordon. Once again the team was settled in comfortable chairs and provided with refreshments before getting down to business.

'Gentlemen,' Leon began in his somewhat ponderous way, 'it seems that we are faced with a rapidly changing situation tied to the deaths of two members of the Kumasi cartel. While this might seem to imply a short-term weakening of the immediate drugs threat, it may bring nearer a longer-term threat that could be much greater. For this reason it is essential that we try to understand just what is happening in Kumasi and Ghana generally. Tam has just returned from Ghana where he has been investigating the fate of Mr Konadu. Please tell us what you found.'

'I followed Mr Konadu back to Ghana when he was deported,' said Tam. 'This was after he had been exposed as an illegal immigrant. It isn't clear what Konadu had been up to in England but he may have started with the Kumasi cartel and then been recruited by a rival group. I think that he might have tried to go freelance in the case of Kwame's snails.'

'I must protest at them being referred to as my snails,' Kwame said, half in jest. Leon frowned and asked Tam to continue.

'If my supposition is correct, Konadu could have been exposed by either group but I don't believe that his murder was the work of Ghanaians. Konadu was reported to have been shot and we have no record of Ghanaians using guns in the past. They have even refrained from using violence in a few cases where some degree of violence might have been expected.' Kwame joined in unanimous nodding.

'So are you saying that it was the South American drugs group that both exposed and murdered Mr Konadu?' asked Leon.

'Yes,' said Tam. 'That's what I think based on our present knowledge.'

'Now what can we deduce from the death of Mama Kate?' Leon continued, looking at Kwame.

'Not much,' he replied. 'We had already formed the impression that Mama Kate wasn't leading the Kumasi cartel. In that sense her death changes nothing. We know that Bra Yaw is still recruiting couriers, and some drugs are still getting through, but the Kumasi cartel seems to be leaderless as far as Ghanaians are concerned.'

'How about the Lebanese?' prompted Leon. 'What are they up to?'

It was Tam who cut in. 'From what I learned in Ghana I would say that the Lebanese are trying to work with the South Americans. They may not have cut all their contacts with the Kumasi cartel but they must regard their Ghanaian partners as a wasting asset.'

'I agree,' Kwame said. 'It's a mystery to me how the operation keeps going.'

'But it does keep going, doesn't it?' It was Leon who asked this question, looking pointedly at Kwame.

'Bra Yaw keeps recruiting couriers.'

'From among your university visitors.'

'That worries us too.'

'First Miss Osei-Wusu and now Mr Evans-Agyei are suspected of having arrived with contraband. If this goes on we may have to ask the university to close the programme.'

'I did what I could to prevent it,' said Kwame, 'but the cartel seems to have a mole in the School of Engineering.'

Kwame would have liked to ask why Leon suspected Nelson Evans-Agyei of being a drugs courier but he was reluctant to say how he had used Takoradi to lead him to the same suspicion. He realised that he still had more to do to plug the information leak from the School of Engineering, but he would have a chance to do more during his visit to Kumasi in January and no more visitors would come to Warwick until after that time.

Leon asked Kwame to listen to a few recently recorded telephone calls from Ghana and he was able to interpret that there had been a delivery of cocaine by a migratory bird, probably referring to the involvement of Evans-Agyei. It was clear that the same cultured *okyeame* voice was passing on instructions, but they were still no nearer to knowing who was directing operations.

Kwame had to bring Akosua and her friends home from school early in the afternoon so he decided to stay in Warwick. Hearing this, Tam suggested they take lunch together. 'It will give me a chance to return some of your hospitality,' he said. 'I know a nice quiet place where we can chat in peace.' Leaving their cars at the police station they walked a few hundred metres to one of Tam's favourite watering holes.

'How's Takoradi doing these days?' Tam asked, while they waited for the food to arrive.

Kwame was tempted to mention Takoradi's role in casting suspicion on Nelson Evans-Agyei. 'Keeping up his old tricks,' he replied.

'Still sniffing syringes on the common, eh?'

'And the rest!'

'Tell me more.'

Kwame told Tam how he had taken Takoradi to his office one morning and the dog had shown special interest in one of their visitors recently arrived from Ghana.

'Was that this Evans-Agyei mentioned by Leon?'

'The very same!'

'You should have told Leon.'

'I thought I might get blamed for exceeding my brief.'

'Yes, you might, but don't worry, I'll pass it on diplomatically.'

Kwame asked Tam about his recent trip to Ghana.

'You know I can't tell you much about that,' Tam said. 'It was as hot and humid as ever and much more dangerous.'

'Especially for poor Konadu!'

'That was a bad business. Before he could lead us to any of his contacts he was gone.'

'He wasn't a clever man.'

'Not clever enough to play games with the Venezuelans.'

Kwame looked at his wristwatch; lunch had taken longer than he expected. 'I must dash to collect Akosua from school – thanks for the lunch.'

'My pleasure, old boy. Remember me to Akosua and Takoradi – and your good lady.'

'They will all hear,' said Kwame in Twi.

Akosua was waiting with her friends. 'You're late, Dad, we were getting worried.'

148

'Sorry, I ran into Uncle Tam and we had lunch together.'

'Did he ask about Takoradi – if I was taking good care of him?'

'He asked about you both.'

Akosua usually clambered into the back of the vehicle with her friends but today she sat in front with Kwame. He suspected she had something on her mind. 'It's the essay about Takoradi,' she said. 'I'm not sure how to end it.'

'Have you said that he's retired but still finds syringes on the common?'

'Yes Dad, but I want something more exciting.'

'Then why not speculate on how he still might detect a drug smuggler or dealer?'

'Thanks Dad, that's a good idea – do you think he could still do it?'

'I think he could.'

Akosua was silent for a while but Kwame knew her questions had not ended. After a long pause she said, 'Some girls have been expelled for taking drugs.'

'From your school?'

'They say some dealers hang around outside.'

'Have the police been informed?'

'Yes, but they haven't found the dealers.'

'That's very bad.'

'Maybe Takoradi could help.'

'No, that would be very dangerous.'

Now Kwame felt embarrassed. He had used the old dog in the role that he had refused to his daughter, but he believed that there was little danger in testing a first-time courier newly arrived from Ghana, whereas confronting professional criminals in a public place could be suicidal. He realised that the success of his initiative might have tempted him to move on to more serious investigations, but Tam's warning and Akosua's extreme request convinced him to leave the old dog undisturbed in his retirement. He resolved to tell Leon about the drugs dealers hanging around the school and ask for his support in provoking action from the police. The work must be left to the professionals.

One evening after dinner Stephen asked Kwame if he could get some patterns made while he was in Coventry.

'You need them for the major parts of your gear-generating attachment, do you?' Kwame asked.

'Yes,' said Stephen. 'If I can take a few wooden patterns back with me I can easily get some castings made at Suame.'

'Do you have drawings of the parts?'

'They should be finished by tomorrow.'

'Then I'll ring Martin Hutchinson at the foundry training school. He's already offered to help us and they have an excellent pattern-making shop.'

Next morning Kwame contacted Martin and arranged for Stephen and Greg to visit the foundry school that afternoon. Even though pattern-making was a slow process there should be enough time to get Stephen's patterns made ahead of his departure. Failing that, they could be sent later by parcel post, or Kwame could carry them to Ghana on his next visit in January. He reflected that it was good thinking on Stephen's part to anticipate this problem. He knew only one skilled pattern-maker in Ghana and he was employed at the Tema ITTU. With GRID's reluctance to work with the university in Kumasi, Stephen might have experienced a long wait if he had ordered his patterns from Tema.

Kwame called Mick and Sandra to his office to check on the progress of Nelson and Yaa. Mick reported that he had helped Nelson obtain a sufficient quantity of jojoba oil for him to begin some tests on the variable compression diesel engine. However a literature search had suggested that there could be problems with waxy compounds in the oil causing filter blockages and it might be necessary to pre-treat the oil to remove these compounds. Nelson was consulting chemists for ideas on how this might be done.

Kwame was reassured that, whatever the technical problems, Nelson was being helped to work steadily towards appropriate solutions. He turned to Sandra to ask how Yaa was progressing. 'She seems to be struck with the potential for making laboratory glassware locally in Ghana,' Sandra told him, 'Glass being very fragile, savings could be made on the cost of packaging, transport and breakages. She is proposing that a technician should come from Kumasi to learn how to make standard items like flasks and retorts.'

'Is she planning to take any lessons herself?'

'I don't think so.'

'Then why don't you suggest it?'

Kwame wondered why his compatriots were shy of gaining hands-on experience of craft work. When they tried, they often found a hidden aptitude and derived unexpected satisfaction from their accomplishments. His training at the Suame ITTU had convinced him that practical involvement always led to a better understanding of materials and processes. He was sure that Yaa would enjoy a little practice in glassblowing.

Takoradi burst into the office, completed his sniffing circuit and sat at attention beside Sandra. Afriyie put her head round the door to say

150

that she hoped she wasn't interrupting anything important but she had just passed her driving test. Kwame had forgotten that today was the big day but he was very pleased with the news. He and Sandra both voiced their congratulations. 'Are you going to drive us home?' he asked.

'Just try to stop me,' was Afriyie's cheery reply.

Mick and Stephen soon came in fresh from their visit to the foundry school. 'They'll have my patterns ready in two weeks,' Stephen reported happily.

'That's fine,' said Kwame, 'but are you up to being driven home by Afriyie?'

'I'll face any challenge to enjoy another of her fufu dinners,' said the master craftsman gallantly.

'Fufu dinners?' said Tom. 'That's just what I wanted to discuss with you.' He had seen Afriyie come in and had followed her to Kwame's office. 'Have you made any plans for Christmas?' Mick and Sandra left quietly on hearing their seniors switch to domestic matters.

It was Afriyie who responded, 'Akos Mary and I want to invite your parents, Tom, to return last year's hospitality. They will stay with you, of course, and Akos Mary will plan an English Christmas Day, then you will all come to us for a taste of Ghana on Boxing Day.'

'What a splendid idea!' said Kwame.

'And a great relief!' added Tom. 'The girls have it all worked out! I will invite Mum and Dad before they make any other arrangements.'

Tom returned to his office to make the telephone call and Kwame gathered his party for the journey home. 'Where's Takoradi?' he asked.

'He came in with me,' said Afriyie, 'I thought he was still here.'

'He followed Sandra when she went out with Mick,' said Stephen.

Kwame, fearing the worst, said, 'Please wait here, and I'll go to fetch him.' He hurried to the office that Sandra shared with Mick and Greg. Much to his relief the research assistants had all left for home. The sole occupant was the big furry dog sitting smartly to attention before a filing cabinet. Patting him affectionately on his head by way of reward, Kwame used his master key to release the drawers and drew open the bottom one. He slid the numerous files forward on their rails, compressing the contents and expanding the space behind. There, under a pile of unsorted papers, he found a carved wooden elephant. He had no doubt that this was the source of the scent that had attracted Takoradi's interest.

Kwame knew that he needed to do something – but what? He decided that the first thing was to gain some time to think. So he went back to the others and asked Afriyie to drive home with Stephen. He asked her

celebrating the award of her driving licence, Stephen was pleased with the progress of his project and all three women were excitedly discussing the newly hatched plan for Christmas. Akosua had been praised for her essay on elephants and their role in Akan culture but Kwame was beginning to wish that at least the wood carvers had ignored them.

11

Two Elephants

Next morning Kwame told Tom that he needed some time with him to discuss a serious issue, so Tom rearranged his programme and they met in Tom's office after lunch. 'I hear that Afriyie passed her driving test yesterday,' Tom said. 'I'm sorry I didn't know yesterday when we met but please give her my congratulations.'

'Yes I will, she's very excited.'

'Akos Mary also said that Afriyie drove your car home last night but you worked late.'

'That's what I need to tell you about.'

Kwame told Tom how Leon's people suspected that Nelson Evans-Agyei had been recruited by the Kumasi cartel to bring a consignment of drugs to the UK, and how he had been alerted to this possibility by Takoradi first reacting to Sandra Garg and later to Nelson. 'Sandra and Nelson,' Tom said, 'are they in a relationship?'

'It looks like it. It seems to have started in Kumasi.'

'Is Sandra involved with drugs?'

'She's involved, but probably doesn't realise it.'

'How do you mean?'

Kwame then explained how Takoradi had led him to the wooden elephant in Sandra's filing cabinet.

'You think that there are drugs inside the wood carving?' Tom was almost shouting. 'Don't you think that Nelson might have brought a gift for his girlfriend?'

'Oh, please calm down,' said Kwame, 'until I've told you all I know.'

Tom's secretary brought in two cups of tea and this provided a convenient pause in which to re-establish equilibrium. 'I'm sorry,' Tom said, 'please go on.'

'We think that there are drugs in the carved elephant because Takoradi followed his nose to it and because a dog at the airport had already picked out Nelson as a suspect drugs courier.'

155

'But why should Nelson give the elephant to Sandra.'

'I can only surmise that for some reason he couldn't hand it over as instructed and wanted help in hiding it.'

'It wasn't very well hidden.'

'No, and that suggests that Sandra doesn't know what's inside.'

'So what happens now?'

'Leon's people have taken the elephant away for investigation and it's been replaced in Sandra's filing cabinet by a similar wood carving.'

'Won't they notice the difference?'

'In time, maybe, but it could buy Leon a few days to complete his work.'

'Then what?'

'They will want to talk to Nelson and Sandra but officially we know nothing about it.'

Tom sat looking glumly at Kwame. 'So we carry on as if we know nothing about what's going on until the whole thing explodes in our face?'

'I'm sure Leon will handle the matter very tactfully.'

'I'm not so sure about the project management committee, the faculty board and the university council.'

'They'll think Professor Thomas was right about being twinned with a den of thieves,' said Kwame, sorrowfully recalling the remark made at his job interview.

'It could jeopardise the whole partnership programme.'

'I'll do everything I can to prevent that,' said Kwame grimly.

A few days later, Mick came into Kwame's office to tell him that police had come to the diesel engine laboratory and Nelson had been arrested. He was closely followed by a distraught Sandra who placed a carved wooden elephant on Kwame's desk. Kwame couldn't help smiling; he hadn't expected to get his carving back quite so soon. Misinterpreting his smile, Sandra said that she wasn't giving him a present but she suspected that the wood carving had something to do with Nelson's arrest and she wanted nothing more to do with it. In answer to Kwame's questions she said that Nelson had asked her to hide it for him but he had not told her why. That evening the elephant was back on its shelf in Kwame's guestroom. Stephen, absorbed with his gear-generating attachment, had not noticed that it had been missing.

Next day, more hand-crafted artefacts were brought to Kwame's desk.

Yaa was keen to show off her newfound skills in glassblowing. Kwame was delighted to see the enthusiasm that his suggestion had generated and was thankful that at least two out of three assignments were going to plan. He could see that a small-scale glassblowing unit could serve a useful purpose in producing laboratory equipment to order for school and college laboratories. In the hands of students breakages were inevitable, but long delays could be avoided if replacements could be made locally. He congratulated Yaa on her progress and encouraged her to take full advantage of her remaining time in Coventry.

Kwame checked that his office door was closed and he could not be overheard. 'Yaa,' he said, 'can I ask you something that's not directly connected to work but could affect our work?'

'OK.'

'In Kumasi, before you started your journey, did anyone ask you to carry anything to the UK?'

'Yes they did, but I had been warned to be careful and I refused.'

'You did the right thing. Can you tell me who asked you?'

'He was a man about your age but he didn't give a name.'

Kwame concluded that it was probably still Bra Yaw who was contacting the Kumasi people scheduled to travel to Britain. The fact that they had all been approached except for Stephen confirmed his theory that somehow Kofi Boateng or Bra Yaw were getting access to the list of people nominated by the School of Engineering, perhaps even before the final selection. It was at the school that he would need to concentrate his attention during his next visit to Kumasi.

It was a few days later that the expected call came from Leon. Once again, after dropping Akosua at school, Kwame drove to Warwick police station. This time only Leon and Auntie Rose were present and Leon got straight down to business.

'You must be wondering what Mr Evans-Agyei told us,' he said to Kwame. 'He said that he'd been expecting someone to collect the wood carving but when nobody came he asked Sandra to help him hide the artefact. We appreciate your help in discovering what happened after that.'

'Do you think that it was Konadu who was expected to collect the elephant?' asked Kwame.

'Yes, we do,' replied Leon.

'Then it looks as though Konadu was working for the Kumasi cartel at the time this was all arranged.'

'Yes, and once Konadu was gone they had no way of contacting Evans-Agyei to change the plan; the couriers are not in touch with your *okyeame*.'

Kwame ignored the jest. 'Then they are in serious disarray,' he said.

'Was the lady, Miss Williams, also asked to carry a parcel to the UK?'

'Yes, she was, but she refused.'

'So they're still trying hard in Kumasi but not connecting at this end,' Leon summarised quietly to himself.

'I don't think Sandra knew there was anything hidden in the elephant,' Kwame said.

'In Evans-Agyei's case,' Leon replied, 'we think he suspected something but didn't know for certain.'

'Yes,' added Auntie Rose, 'he suspected that it might be wee.'

'And was it cocaine?' asked Kwame.

'Need to know, I'm afraid, old boy,' laughed Leon, tapping the side of his nose.

This time Kwame too laughed at the joke, recalling how Peter Sarpong had put them on the trail of Oboroni, alias Crispin Russell, in 1987.

'But will you be taking any action against Sandra?'

'Auntie Rose will have a quiet chat with her.'

'And Nelson?'

'I'm afraid Mr Evans-Agyei will have his day in court. If he can persuade the jury that he didn't know what was in the wood carving, he could be let off with a light sentence.'

'Will he be held in custody?'

'The magistrate will decide but it's most likely that he will.'

On his arrival back in Coventry Kwame decided to tell Tom straight away what damage this news was likely to do to their programme. He found the professor in his office.

'I'm afraid Nelson has been arrested,' he said, 'and will be charged with bringing narcotics into the country.'

'Oh no,' groaned Tom, 'out of five people we have brought from Kumasi, one has become an illegal immigrant and one has been arrested for drugs trafficking. We must certainly stop bringing people here until we can do something to guarantee their good conduct. I must write to Kumasi and tell them the bad news.'

'I'm sure the cartel has an informant in the School of Engineering,' said Kwame. 'If that person can be exposed we can stop this trouble. These people aren't all bad. Two were approached but refused to help the traffickers, and the two who carried drugs didn't know what they

158

were doing. The couriers are told almost nothing by the cartel. If they had known that hard drugs were involved I don't think they would have agreed. They were led astray by the lure of easy money.'

'I believe you, Kwame,' said Tom, 'but I will have difficulty convincing the management committee, especially Professor Thomas.'

'There is some hope of a better future as far as the university is concerned,' Kwame said. 'We think that the Kumasi cartel is now quite weak. Their failure to collect the goods from Nelson suggests that they are losing control of the people at this end. When this is fully realised in Kumasi they may stop sending the couriers – at least for some time. That might give us a chance to block recruitment within the School of Engineering.'

'I certainly hope you're right,' said Tom glumly.

On his way back to his own office Kwame called Mick to follow him. 'I'm afraid Nelson will be held in custody and will probably be prevented from doing any more work on his project,' he said. 'I want you to ensure that we collect all his notes and documents and file them for future reference.'

'I'll do that right away, but what has Nelson been doing to get himself arrested?'

'Let's just say that he brought something from Kumasi that he shouldn't have.'

'Poor Sandra, she's very upset.'

'Then we must all do what we can to restore her spirits.'

Kwame wanted to talk to Sandra but he decided to delay a few days to give Auntie Rose a chance to speak to her first. So he called Greg and asked how Stephen's drawings were progressing.

'We've finished all the drawings of the castings and sent them to the foundry school for the patterns to be made,' Greg said, 'and I've nearly finished drawing the other parts. Basically, I've only got the general arrangement drawings to do. Stephen will have everything he needs by next week when he goes home.'

'The time has passed quickly,' said Kwame, 'but you have done well to help him achieve his objective.'

'I can't wait to get there in January to see how far he's got with the work.'

'Don't expect too much; things go slowly in Ghana.'

'Yes, but Stephen's an exceptional craftsman. He'll keep things moving along.'

'That's why I brought him here,' said Kwame with a smile.

Kwame knew that Stephen's visit would be regarded as a big success by Tom and the other engineering professors. If only he could bring more people like Stephen the programme would achieve much more and avoid the disasters of absconding and drugs. Knowing the engineering industry as he did, Kwame was sure that he could fill the whole programme with people like Stephen: highly skilled, mid-career, self-employed family men, dedicated to promoting their industry and meeting their broad social responsibilities. Through their efforts, hundreds and thousands of young men and women were receiving training and employment and many of their protégés went on to found their own small enterprises. These champions of the grassroots industrial revolution had benefited greatly from the help of the TCC and would achieve even more with the sort of help that Stephen was receiving.

What was preventing such an inspiring path to progress? Basically, Kwame felt, it was the desire on the part of Kumasi University to preserve the benefits of overseas visits for its own academic staff: junior lecturers with university degrees but little practical experience and few social responsibilities. Many of these young people had taken their academic posts to bide time until an opportunity arose to escape overseas. Kwame realised that he had been aware of this danger from the outset. What he should also have anticipated was the temptation offered by the drugs smugglers. He had underestimated the determination of people like Bra Yaw to exploit a programme of free travel to the UK.

Kwame realised that it would have been better if it had been possible for the TCC alone to select the candidates for the visits to Warwick. Then it would have been largely self-employed craftsmen who would have been nominated. The university would not have agreed to this because it wanted the benefits for its own people, not for outsiders. It now seemed possible that recent disasters might persuade the authorities in Kumasi to include more people like Stephen Okunor in the programme. If so, present problems might yield future benefits. In this more optimistic frame of mind Kwame returned to his routine duties.

Stephen and Yaa completed their assignments in Coventry and returned to Kumasi on schedule and in time to spend the Christmas festivities at home. This time there was no attempt to resist repatriation.

Kwame and Tom's families combined their resources to provide a suitable Christmas celebration for themselves and for the older generation of Arthurs. Elsie proved to be a big help to Afriyie and Akos Mary, especially in the preparations for Ghanaian festivities on Boxing Day. Kwame was delighted that he managed to achieve total surprise when he presented Afriyie with a new car on Christmas morning. 'It's my best Christmas present ever,' she cried, as Akosua and Takoradi scrambled in for a test drive.

'Will you be taking me to school now?' asked an excited Akosua, to which Afryie replied, 'Whenever your father will let me.'

Kwame was hoping that Afriyie would now do most of the school runs to Warwick. He would still have to serve as chauffeur whenever he was summoned by Leon but that was not too often, and he really shouldn't mind. It was the extra income provided by his sleuthing that made generous Christmas presents possible. These days Kwame had few financial concerns and his savings were mounting steadily. He knew that when at last he felt free to take his family back to Ghana, building a house even to Comfort's exacting specifications would be no problem.

Akos Mary and Afriyie had asked Auntie Rose to join them on Boxing Day for the Ghanaian festivities. Kwame was pleased when she accepted the invitation because he felt that he would like to know the lady better, but hitherto she had seemed determined to keep her relationships largely on a professional basis. Maybe she believed that she could face the dangers of her work more easily if she remained detached from family and friends. Akosua Akomwa, the little welder in Tema, seemed to be her only living relative.

Kwame had a growing feeling that the Ghanaian faction of the Kumasi cartel was close to disintegration. He wondered if an opportunity might arise to persuade the few remaining members to change their ways and stop their illegal activities. If he attempted such a task he believed that Auntie Rose would be an invaluable ally. This was work that only Ghanaians could undertake. Not even Tam Gordon with his passable Twi could be much help. Comfort, he reflected happily, would wholeheartedly agree that here was something to be done for our people by our people.

In a short break from the festivities Kwame managed to ask Auntie Rose if she would be in Kumasi during his forthcoming visit. 'Oh yes,' she replied with a smile. 'Leon wouldn't let you go on your own.'

'Will you be staying with Comfort again?'

'If she'll have me.'

'Is the cartel still active?'

'As far as we can tell.'

'Do we know yet who's in charge?'

'That's still a mystery.'

'I've an idea; could we meet for a serious chat sometime?'

'With Leon?'

'No, I want this to be between ourselves.'

'Leon will have to be told.'

'Yes, but I want us to chat first.'

'Then come to the hairdresser's on the first Wednesday evening of the New Year.'

They hadn't rested for long after a heavy lunch when Akosua raised the topic of Takoradi's daily exercise. She was both eager for the walk and reluctant to leave the party. Uncle Tom gallantly volunteered to go with her wheeling Little Tom in his pushchair. 'Why don't we all go?' suggested Akos Mary, 'It will do us good to get some fresh air.' So wrapped up in overcoats, scarves and gloves they erupted onto the street in a cloud of condensed Twi complaints about the cold.

Taking pity on Tom, Kwame took up station beside him and began translating the banter of the five women all speaking at once. He was happy that they were in such high spirits but his task as interpreter soon overwhelmed him.

'Don't worry about me,' said Tom. 'If you want to join in the ladies' chat I'll talk to Little Tom.'

'Does he speak both languages?'

'That's what we both want but we're worried that he won't hear much Twi once he starts school.'

'Then we will all help to ensure that he hears plenty at home.'

'Thank you, Kwame, we'll both appreciate that.'

They reached the common and the ladies were throwing a ball for Takoradi to chase. 'I wonder if he'll find any syringes,' said Tom.

'As far as I know the habit isn't seasonal,' replied Kwame, 'so he can be expected to find them all year round.'

'What about the supply situation? You say your people aren't so active these days.'

'It's not only my people, as you call them; there are plenty of other suppliers. The Kumasi people seem to have concentrated on cocaine recently, and two shipments have been intercepted, so that could be in short supply, but the syringes are for heroin and I've no idea how that market is faring.'

'I'm sorry for the slip of tongue, Kwame. I know there are other drugs traders. It's just that the Kumasi business is a big worry just now with half our academic visitors being turned into drugs couriers.'

'I'll stop it while I'm in Kumasi this time,' said Kwame determinedly.

'You're taking Greg with you aren't you?' said Tom.

162

'Yes, he's waited a long time for his chance.'

'You're repeating the engineering drawing course and Greg will introduce them to computer-aided drawing?'

'That's right.'

'Let's brief Greg to make a survey of their computer and IT needs. We could supply some electronic equipment and software with the money we might not spend on visits.'

'Help them prepare for a future course in computer-aided drawing?'

'That's the idea. Would they regard that as fitting compensation?'

'Yes, on the whole, I think they would.'

'Except for the people who miss the visits?'

'You said it!'

The holiday passed more quickly than anybody wanted and they were soon all back at work and school. On the Wednesday, at the close of work, Kwame made his way to the hairdresser's for his meeting with Auntie Rose. She was waiting in the small back office; only Leon, it seemed, had access to the more spacious and comfortable room upstairs.

After the usual elaborate greeting and water ritual Auntie Rose recalled what Kwame had said about an idea for resolving the situation in Kumasi. 'Leon was very interested; it was difficult for me to come alone on this one.'

'He'll want a full report then?'

'I'm afraid so.'

'I must say immediately that my idea will only work if we do it on our own.'

'If I like your idea I'll do my best to get him to agree.'

Kwame asked, 'How many Ghanaians do we think are still active in the cartel in Kumasi – excluding couriers, of course?'

'We only know two for certain: Bra Yaw and Kofi Boateng.'

'And Kofi Adjare, the *okyeame*.'

'Yes, but he's only the *okyeame*.'

'That's an essential role. If he could be persuaded to stop, it would bring all activities to a standstill.'

'Only until they find another *okyeame*.'

'Finding a replacement for Kofi won't be easy; in their weakened state it might collapse the whole operation.'

'What about the Lebanese?'

'They will probably go on but that's up to them. We should concentrate on getting our own people out of it.'

'How do you think Kofi Adjare can be persuaded to stop working for the cartel?' asked Auntie Rose.

'Our main argument should be that hard drugs are now being sold in Ghana. This is corrupting our youth and will eventually destroy the traditional culture that he loves so much. It would be better to work with the *abrofo* to try to stop the international trade in drugs.'

'Don't you think he knows this already?'

'When he was arrested in England with the others in 1988 he was given a lighter sentence because the *abrofo* believed that he didn't fully realise what was going on. If he didn't know then, maybe he still doesn't know.'

'I think we'd be taking a big risk.'

'What danger do you see?'

'Whoever is giving Kofi his instructions is sure to be enraged.'

'We're not doing anyone any harm; nobody will be arrested or sent to prison. We're just seeking a peaceful end to the situation.'

'Well, if things go wrong there's one thing we can do.'

'What is that?'

'We can seek the protection of our king, *Otumfuo*, the *Asantehene*,' said Auntie Rose.

Kwame flew to Accra with Greg and Mick in the afternoon of Friday 12 January 1996. This time they avoided the long road journey by taking a connecting flight to Kumasi. Kwame had told Tom that he wasn't sure that Mick would be needed but as the time of the mission approached he realised that the young engineer had made himself almost indispensable. During his previous two trips to Ghana, Mick had acquired a fund of useful local knowledge and he had won the confidence of the local people, not least through his interest in learning Twi. Now that Kwame knew that he must give priority to stopping the recruitment of drugs couriers, he needed Mick to provide full technical support to the training programme.

Kwame had every confidence that, if necessary, Mick and Greg could coordinate the forthcoming two-week course without his direct involvement. To prepare for this eventuality he handed Mick the cash he carried to meet expenses and the notebook in which all expenditure was recorded. He asked Mick to help Greg settle in and to ensure that he was given all the support he needed to play his part in the present course and to prepare for a future course in computer-aided drawing.

Kwame told Greg about Tom's suggestion to review the IT status of the TCC and the School of Engineering and identify any computer equipment and software needs that might be met from the partnership agreement with Warwick. He made no mention of the funding coming from a permanent cut-back in the visitors' programme as he didn't want this possibility to disturb their relationship with colleagues in Kumasi. It was Kwame's own priority task to try to ensure that this possibility did not arise.

Leaving Mick and Greg to handle the preparations for the course, Kwame set up a meeting with the TCC director and dean of the School of Engineering. He had decided to convey the grave concern of Professor Arthur and his board in Warwick and to request immediate action to stop the drugs traffickers learning the identity of academics travelling to Warwick.

'You will recall,' he began, 'that both the initial visitors were asked to carry drugs to the UK. One of them is believed to have helped the traffickers and the lady has so far failed to return to Ghana. Of the three who recently visited Warwick, two were approached and one carried drugs. This man has been detained by the authorities and might be convicted and sentenced to prison.

'This situation is a disgrace to Kumasi, and is regarded as a disgrace to Warwick. We must take urgent action to prevent any recurrence or the visitors' programme will be cancelled and the whole partnership agreement could be threatened. Warwick doesn't want this to happen and will help in any way it can, but it is essentially a problem for Kumasi to solve. As one of your sons I am here to help for as long as it takes.' Kwame could see from the frowns on the faces of his companions that his words had conveyed the full measure of his concern.

'We appreciate that the situation is serious,' said the dean, 'but what can we do to improve it?'

'It's clear that you have someone in your office giving names to the drugs cartel.'

'Why should someone do that?'

'I'm sure the cartel pays them very well.'

'How can we find who it is?'

'I admit that is difficult, and it might be easier to cut them out.'

'How do you mean?'

'Couldn't you handle the matter personally with the staff members involved and not use any secretarial staff until after the visitors have left the country? Furthermore, you could warn travellers of the dangers of drugs trafficking and point out that most couriers get caught, especially now that the British authorities are on the watch for Kumasi to Warwick travellers.'

'Yes, that's all possible.'

'Is there anything we could do to improve the selection of visitors?' asked the TCC director.

'Yes,' replied Kwame, 'Stephen Okunor was not approached by the drugs traffickers, presumably because I proposed him during my last visit and his name didn't appear on the original list of candidates. However, I want to make a more important point. Stephen took his opportunity in Warwick very seriously. He achieved what he needed and was keen to come back here to put his new knowledge to immediate use in his business. His focus was entirely on his mission. Such people are immune from the temptation to abscond and much less likely to be tempted by the drugs traders.'

'You mean we should send more workshop owners?'

'Yes, I think we should.'

'But the programme is intended to develop academics,' protested the dean. 'We made an exception for Okunor because he runs our mechanical workshop but we couldn't include outsiders.'

'You don't gain much from developed academics who run away!'

'They don't all run away.'

'Out of four so far, one succeeded in absconding and one carried drugs and might well have run away if not arrested. A third was seriously tempted to abscond but I conducted him through London airport and practically pushed him onto the plane.'

'You're a Ghanaian; don't you want to help our people?'

'Of course I do, but this is not the way.'

'What is the way?'

'To help people like Stephen Okunor develop basic technical skills to produce the goods and services the people need.'

'That's a very slow process and doesn't help the university.'

'I think you mean it doesn't help the people who work in the university.'

'Isn't that the same thing?'

'You might think it is, but I don't.'

'Reach your chests down,' broke in the TCC director in Twi. 'It won't help to solve the problem if we end up fighting.'

The dean looked chastened and Kwame felt the same. It achieved nothing to get into an argument in which both parties became deaf to the other.

They had dug deep to the bedrock of the development dilemma, the one that had haunted Kwame all his adult life: How do you persuade an educated person to forego the fast route to a personal fortune to help in the slow process of community development? He felt that he had resolved this problem in his own heart and mind but to what extent was this due to the accident, as it seemed, of material security. He must be slow to judge others while at the same time seeking to work with those who felt some obligation to help the community which had supported them thus far.

'I apologise for any offence caused by the heat of my argument,' Kwame said. 'It's just the seriousness of the problem and the threat it poses to our partnership agreement that angers me.'

'I feel the same,' said the dean, offering his hand. The director's smile blessed the handshake that he had engineered.

Kwame's next task was to meet Auntie Rose and Comfort to discuss the options for pursuing Kwame's idea of an approach to Kofi Adjare. He was relieved to find that Auntie Rose had already taken up residence in the Nhyiasu house, so he drove there after dark the next evening. His ring on the doorbell was answered by Auntie Rose who told him that Comfort was out but would soon be back. They decided to wait for Comfort before reviewing the local situation. Kwame settled back in a well-upholstered armchair with the *Ghanaian Times*.

With the newspaper exhausted, and still compelled by Mainu's law to wait, Kwame let his mind drift back eighteen months to when he first saw his former wife's mansion. He had never imagined himself living in such a house and at that time the possibility had seemed remote. Yet his good fortune since his return to England meant that he would soon be in a position to make his ex-wife an offer or to construct a rival edifice across the road. He wondered idly what effect this realisation would have on Comfort.

'I think she might take you back if you asked her,' said Auntie Rose. Kwame didn't know what to say in reply. Had she read his thoughts? Had he been thinking these thoughts? He didn't think so, but who knows what is swirling in the subconscious mind? Only a woman, it would seem, could unwind that vortex. Auntie Rose had forced open a door on painfully stiff hinges to release a tribe of *mmoatia* intent on his destruction. He stared back at the *mmoatia* queen with what he hoped was a startled expression.

It was Comfort's arrival that persuaded Kwame once again of the correct orientation of Auntie Rose's toes. 'Why didn't you give the man a drink?' Comfort said to Auntie Rose, who replied in self-defence, 'He said he wasn't thirsty.'

'Well he looks thirsty now. Why don't you both have a drink while I take a quick shower?' Their hostess ran out as quickly as she had run in.

'Where has she been?' asked Kwame.

'They've opened a new fitness club in Harper Road. Comfort is trying to lose weight.'

'You don't have that problem!'

'No, and that has been an advantage in the past.'

'How do you mean?'

'There was a time when we were told to carry the drugs in padded bras.'

'You did that?'

'Not for long; they decided I was too short to be fully padded out. They preferred tall women with flat chests; they could carry the most.'

'How much could they carry?'

'One woman I knew carried about 1000 grams of cocaine.'

'What happened to her?'

'She got through several times until one day she was strip-searched.'

Kwame was surprised that Auntie Rose was speaking so freely about her past activities. She had always seemed reluctant to discuss her past in any detail. Maybe the Christmas hospitality had served to break the ice, or perhaps it was their shared mission that had changed her attitude.

'What's this about being strip searched?' Comfort asked, returning from her shower.

'Oh, Auntie Rose was just telling me about some of the tricks of the drugs couriers,' Kwame replied. 'How some used to stuff their bras with cocaine.'

'Used to? Some are still doing it aren't they?'

'Yes, those that look respectable enough can get away with it,' said Auntie Rose.

'Have you discussed my idea with Comfort?' Kwame asked Auntie Rose.

'Yes,' said Comfort. 'I think we know Kofi well enough to risk talking to him.'

'How can we meet him?'

'Well, I'm trying to persuade him to be my driver again.'

'What's he doing now?'

'Since Mama Kate died he hasn't taken any other job as far as I know.'

'But he's still acting as *okyeame* for the cartel.'

'Auntie Rose told me; I wonder who's giving him directions?'

'That's a continuing mystery.'

'Where is Kofi staying?' asked Kwame.

'He's still living in boy's quarters at Mama Kate's,' replied Comfort, 'but I know her heirs want to get him out. They want everybody out so that they can sell the house and share the money.'

'Then he's likely to accept your offer to get new accommodation,' said Kwame.

'That's what I was hoping but he hasn't agreed yet.'

'Could you call him here for another chat and we'll all speak to him?'

'That's what Auntie Rose and I were thinking.'

'Then please call me when the meeting is arranged.'

Kwame spent a day reviewing the preparations for the re-run of the engineering drawing course. He visited the TCC and the School of Engineering, and discussed progress with Mick and Greg. Mick was determined that all the improvements that had been proposed at the end of the first course should be incorporated into the second. He had made a list and was checking off items as opportunities arose to see the people concerned. Kwame was pleased; it was too easy for instructors to repeat a course without putting in much effort and this often led to a fall in quality. Ensuring that improvements were made kept everyone focused on the task ahead and refreshed the content of each presentation.

As Kwame had feared, the course director made an appeal for the lecturers' fees to be raised. The fees were paid in pounds sterling, not local currency, and Kwame considered them to be rather generous. He pointed out that the re-run required much less preparation than the first course. This was countered by the argument that some of Mick's required improvements amounted to virtual redrafting of presentations. He knew that this was unjustified exaggeration but he was anxious to preserve the goodwill of the instructors and agreed to a modest increase.

Kwame's old fears returned; this circle will never be squared, he thought. Fees paid by participants could never amount to the sum required for full cost recovery as long as the professionals demanded international levels of remuneration. He would satisfy himself that the economies negotiated for the participants' board and lodging would be fully implemented, but the saving would be negligible. Local sustainability for the courses seemed as far away as ever.

Kwame asked to see the list of participants. It was a little shorter than for the first course. He recognised all of the enterprises and most of the individuals, smiling as he came to Akosua Akomwa at the bottom of the page. She was the only repeater, but this time not the only woman. Two Tema companies, Kofi Asiamah's Redeemer and Samuel Quaye's ENTESEL, were each sponsoring a female apprentice. These two engineering entrepreneurs, who had both come on the first course, had been stalwart supporters of Kwame's 'Women in Engineering' project and were now extending their support to the engineering drawing courses.

The first course had attracted self-sponsored workshop owners and master craftsmen. The second course would mostly include technicians and apprentices, male and female, sponsored by their employers. This was an encouraging trend, confirming that the employers valued the training and the enhanced skills it would bring to their workshops. The programme was strengthening enterprises from widely dispersed centres and a variety of engineering specialisations. Kwame felt that he was still privileged to play a key role in Ghana's grassroots industrial revolution.

12

Kofi's Conversion

Greg had been counting computers. 'I've searched the School of Engineering and the TCC but I've not found enough suitable machines to mount the computer-aided drawing course,' he complained. 'Some of the machines are old and don't have a hard disc.'

'Maybe that's why Professor Arthur wanted you to survey their IT needs,' Kwame replied. 'There's time to send down a few more machines before your course comes on in July.'

'I was hoping they could each have their own computer on the present course.'

'You can ask them to take turns in groups of two or three.'

'Yes, I guess that's OK for a demonstration.'

'Do you have any other problems to discuss while I'm here?' asked Kwame.

'Yes,' Mick said. 'I've been wondering about visits to workshops. Last time we visited the Neoplan bus assembly plant. They learned a lot but some said that it was too remote from their own work. I was wondering if there is a smaller engineering enterprise that we could visit – something that is more on their scale of operation.'

'That's a good idea,' Kwame said, 'but the reason we are mounting these courses is because the small engineering shops do not use engineering drawings. I only know one company here in Kumasi where I have seen drawings being prepared and that's Solomon Djokoto's SRS Engineering. Let's pay them a visit tomorrow morning.'

The next day Kwame drove with Mick and Greg to Carpenters' Row, Anloga, where the SRS workshop was located. Kwame knew that Solomon produced drawings of the new machines he designed, but he wasn't sure there would be enough to show the course participants and make their visit worthwhile.

They found junior partner and brother, Ben, at work on his books of accounts. He said that Solomon was out on a job for one of the neighbouring carpentry shops but he would soon be back. Kwame explained their mission and Ben pointed to a pile of large sheets of drawing paper, dusty and browned by exposure to the harsh environment. 'Those are Solomon's drawings,' he said. 'He only does them when we have an order for a new machine.'

'Is that his drawing board?' Mick asked, pointing to a long-neglected board on a metal stand in a corner of the office. Greg was idly lifting a few of the top sheets of drawing paper, shaking and blowing off a patina of pink dust. 'These drawings have been well used,' he said. 'Look! Oily finger prints and even a few scorched holes from welding splutter.'

'Yes,' said Ben. 'Solomon issues the drawings straight to the workers.'

'Did I hear my name?' Solomon said, coming into the office. Seeing Kwame he greeted him warmly and turned to welcome his other visitors. He put a wooden coat hanger down on his desk and, dispatching a minion to fetch bottles of cold soft drinks, he asked about their mission. After listening to Kwame and Ben he said that although he did drawings of new designs he didn't follow proper drawing office procedures. He didn't print copies of his drawings and he didn't always take proper care of the originals. However, there were more drawings stored in the drawers of the large cabinet next to the drawing board.

They sat for some time trying to work out what could be done with this limited material. 'We could tidy up the drawing board and have a new drawing in progress,' Solomon said, 'and we could display some drawings around the office.'

'Then you could show the participants how you use the drawings in the workshop,' added Kwame, 'and relate a few drawings to actual stages of manufacture: on a lathe, welding and so on.'

'Finally, could we ask the participants to discuss how the procedure could be improved?' suggested Mick. 'They might like to do the same, only better.'

'Yes,' said Kwame. 'I think we have enough to make a short visit worthwhile.'

Solomon was sitting at his desk smiling contentedly at his circle of guests. He liked to get involved in university activities and repay in small measure the help he had received over many years from the TCC. Smiling back, Kwame saw the coat hanger on the desk before him and asked if Solomon was working on a new project. 'Yes,' he replied. 'A carpenter wants a routing machine to produce this new type of wooden coat hanger.'

Kwame noticed that the pattern was made in two halves, abutted together and held by elastic bands. Removing the bands, Kwame looked at the two halves of the coat hanger. Each was deeply grooved on the mating surface so that when the two halves were glued together a hollow space would remain inside. 'Hollow coat hangers,' he observed.

'For lightness, I guess,' said Solomon.

'It doesn't lose much weight,' said Greg, 'and in any case who needs a lighter hanger?'

'Air travellers might,' suggested Mick.

'Oh no!' groaned Kwame. 'They wouldn't be for *Sika Ye Na*, would they?'

'The carpenter didn't tell me who they're for,' said Solomon, 'and I doubt if he will tell us if we ask.'

'Not if we all go,' Kwame agreed, 'but you're going to make the production machine, not the product; you're going to help him, not become a competitor. He should be willing to tell you; tell him you want to be sure to meet the customer's quality standards.'

'I'll do my best,' said Solomon, leaving to consult his client.

'Shall we have some more drinks while we wait?' asked Ben. In the hot dusty air of Anloga, flavoured by the fumes from the charcoal burners in the valley behind, they all agreed that more ice-cold drinks would be very welcome. The drinks didn't last long but Solomon was soon back. 'The coat hangers *are* for *Sika Ye Na* enterprise,' he announced triumphantly. Kwame could only groan again.

Kwame was late for the meeting with Kofi Adjare. It wasn't his fault; the summons had come late. It appeared that Comfort had not been sure Kofi was coming until she saw him walking slowly up the drive to her front door. Kwame found the albino *okyeame* sitting with the two women. He took care to exhaust the full ritual greeting before sitting down. There was something venerable about Kofi that demanded observance of tradition. 'Has Comfort offered you your old job back?' he asked.

'The rat doesn't refuse palm nuts,' the old man solemnly intoned.

'That's true. So you've accepted! Congratulations to both of you!'

'Thank you Kwame,' said Comfort.

The three conspirators looked at one another, each wondering who would lead the discussion. Now they were sitting with their quarry, nobody seemed to know how to start. Kwame realised that the ladies were looking to him to speak first so he took a deep breath and plunged in with, 'Is it lawful to make war before the *Asantehene* sets foot across the Pra?'

'It is lawful to defend the way of the ancestors.'

'Are you defending the way of the ancestors?'

'I am spoiling the way of the *abrofo* as they have spoiled our way.'

'How have they spoiled our way?'

'They have made our children strangers, unworthy of carrying the head of their father's corpse.'

'Is it good to send the *abrofo* bad medicine?'

'The bad medicine strengthens the curses of the fetish priests.'

'Can your bad medicine and juju defeat the powerful magic of the *abrofo?*'

'One iron cuts into another iron.'

Kwame smiled at the proverb suggesting that the clash will tell whose magic is the stronger. Now Kwame realised that Kofi was helping the drug traffickers out of hatred for European culture and the damage it had done to his traditional way of life. He wanted to corrupt the youth of the foreigners to exact retribution for the distortion of the language and false aspirations of modern Akan youth; a corruption of mind that alienated them from their forebears. This explained why Kofi served the cartel without showing any interest in material reward; being a man content to live in boy's quarters and walk in sandals when not driving someone else's car. He was inspired by a thirst not for wealth but for revenge.

Kwame had never believed that Kofi was helping the cartel to share in the spoils of the drugs trade, but he had often wondered about Kofi's true motivation. Now, with this new understanding, what arguments could he use to convince Kofi to change his ways? Maybe he should try to convince the *okyeame* that the legacy of colonial rule included many useful things that could exist harmoniously alongside the indigenous culture. This threat to the traditional way of life could be resisted. The sale of drugs to the youth of Ghana, on the other hand, would constitute a much greater threat to all that Kofi cherished, as well as to all hope of improving the wellbeing of the people.

Kofi Adjare earned his living as a driver. His choice of profession contrasted strangely with his love of traditional wisdom but it now presented Kwame with an opening gambit. He remembered that it was said that the *mmoatia* cannot stop a motorcar.

'The powerful magic of the *abrofo* has become your magic,' he said. 'The *mmoatia* cannot stop a car, but you can stop a car! You are the master of all cars and all cars are your slaves. Has this new power done any harm to the rich culture of the ancestors that you carry in your head and in your heart? Has your power to fly to Accra in four hours prevented you from preserving the heritage that we all honour?'

The old albino said nothing. For once his rich store of proverbs seemed to have deserted him. He was listening intently so Kwame pressed on. 'I agree with you that our culture is under attack. We have allowed the language of the *abrofo* to pollute our Twi and their religion to supplant our ancient beliefs, but we can defend ourselves against further encroachment. A far greater danger is that your bad medicine is now being turned against our own youth and only for the purpose of making a few men rich. Once our youth are sick from this bad medicine the culture of our ancestors will die much more surely than from the assault of a few English words and an ancient black book of *anansesem*. I implore you in the name of Okomfo Anokye and the great King Osei Tutu to stop sending bad medicine to *aborokyiri* and help us build a fence around our own children to protect them from this dreadful scourge.'

Tears were running down the old man's pale cheeks. 'We called your father a fool,' he said, 'but we were the fools. Your father called upon us to preserve our culture but also to keep the best of all the *abrofo* brought us. Truly he used to say that "wisdom isn't gold that you wrap and hide in the ground". Were you the only one who understood? I grieve for you in your loneliness.'

Now tears were also dribbling down black cheeks and both women were looking at Kwame. Comfort was staring with the eyes of a child and he had no strength left to bear the emotion it aroused. He drew a deep breath and fought to regain his composure.

During the break that ensued, Comfort asked her maid to bring some drinks and they were all glad of the excuse to concentrate on their glasses. As the liquid levels fell Kwame became aware once more that all were expecting him to continue the discussion. 'If we stop sending drugs to *aborokyiri* the *abrofo* are prepared to teach us their powerful magic to help us stop other foreigners sending drugs to Ghana for sale to our young people. Will you join us in this quest?'

'One head cannot stand,' said Kofi, implying that people must pool their ideas if the best way ahead is to be found.

'Tell me,' said Auntie Rose to Kofi, unable to contain her curiosity any longer, 'who has been telling you what messages to send to *aborokyiri* these last few months?'

A puzzled look crossed the albino's face. 'You mean since Mama Kate became ill?' he asked. The little lady nodded. 'I was left alone to do the work and very little could be done.'

'But you sent me some snails and later a carved elephant,' prompted Kwame.

'Yes, I'm sorry about the snails. As for the elephant, the one who fears the worm keeps on sending people with wood carvings, but not much is getting through. Too many people are getting caught. I'm glad to stop it.'

'What about the Lebanese?' asked Comfort.

'The camel herders will follow their own path. It was Mr Russell who brought them in. I didn't speak to them.'

'But your people were selling drugs in the UK for the Lebanese, weren't they?'

'Not since Mr Russell was locked away.'

Auntie Rose still had some questions to ask. 'Is it true that only Bra Yaw and Kofi Boateng are active these days?'

'That's all.'

'What will they do now?'

'They won't work with the camel herders.'

'Are they dangerous?'

'The camel herders are.'

After Kofi Adjare had left, Comfort and Auntie Rose were quick to tell Kwame how well he had done. With Kofi leaving the cartel, the Ghanaian element was likely to cease to function. There was a fear that the few drugs traders remaining in Kumasi seemed likely to join the Lebanese, and if the Lebanese were linking up with South Americans a new cartel could come into existence. For the moment, however, the network of Kumasi-based agents still at liberty in the UK was bereft of any coordination and control and deprived of fresh supplies of contraband.

Kwame had discovered evidence of the Lebanese working hard to introduce new methods of transport to the UK, including engine pistons and now hollow coat hangers. No doubt such efforts would eventually enable increasing quantities of hard drugs to get through. However, in the interim, the Lebanese faction would be deprived of the distribution and sales network previously provided by the Akan diaspora. Until a new network could be established Leon and his people could expect a welcome hiatus in the supply of narcotics flowing from Kumasi to the streets of Britain.

On the day after the meeting Comfort rang to tell Kwame that Kofi had left his room in the boy's quarters at Mama Kate's house in Manhyia and moved into similar quarters at Comfort's house in Nhyiasu. She hastened to add that she would soon ensure that Kofi was provided with accommodation more suited to his status as chauffeur and spiritual counsellor. She said that Auntie Rose had been in touch with Leon on a secure telephone and he was very pleased with the outcome of yesterday's meeting. He suggested that sometime before Kwame's return they should meet again with Kofi for a more thorough debriefing. He felt there was still more to learn about past and present activities of the cartel.

Kwame was eager to see how Stephen Okunor was progressing with the gear-generating attachment. Knowing that the two *oboroni* engineers were equally interested he waited until Mick and Greg could spare an afternoon for a trip to Suame Magazine. When they reached the ITTU they took the narrow dark stairs down to the basement workshop that was rented by GAMATCO, Stephen's company.

The trio from Warwick received a warm greeting from Stephen who announced to his workers that here were the engineers who had helped him during his recent visit to *aborokyiri*. 'I gave the patterns to Edward Opare,' he said. 'Let's go and see if he has cast them yet.' They walked out of the back of the workshop into the bright sunlight and round the outside of the building to the Enterprise of Technology foundry.

Edward Opare was the father of all the iron foundries that had sprung up in Suame Magazine since 1982. He had been chief technician of the Suame ITTU throughout the technology transfer programme. Now in retirement, he operated his own foundry. Edward did not produce hundreds of corn mill grinding plates like most of the other foundries. Instead he concentrated on more intricate high-quality castings, many of them replacement parts needed for the large machines of the mining and construction industries. Kwame agreed that Stephen had chosen the best place to cast his parts.

'Your castings are on the bench over there,' Edward said to Stephen, 'I was just waiting for them to cool before bringing them down to you.' Mick couldn't resist briefly touching the smallest part, hoping it had cooled enough to pick up. It hadn't, and he withdrew his hand with a yelp. Edward said there was a first aid kit at the ITTU and led Mick away while the other three gazed at the castings.

'We will only know if they are good after they're machined,' said Stephen.

'Oh, don't worry,' said Kwame, 'Edward was also trained in Coventry, they will be just fine.'

'Were you both trained at the same foundry school?'

'Yes, but Edward went two years before me.'

'So the patterns and the craftsman came from the same place.'

'The results are bound to be good!'

They walked back to GAMATCO and Kwame went next door to see Frank Awuah. 'What's happening with the pistons for *Sika Ye Na*?' he asked.

'Oh, I've stopped making them as you advised,' Frank said, 'but I fear that other people will make them.'

'The TCC has sent out a warning notice to the workshops that are clients of the ITTU,' said Kwame. 'Could you do the same through the Suame Mechanical Association?'

'I'll try, but the association is not always good at communications and is always reluctant to tell members to turn away business.'

They were joined by a rather crestfallen Mick with a bandaged finger. 'I thought it might have cooled down,' he said feebly.

'Oh, every apprentice does the same,' said Edward, which didn't help Mick's singed pride. To divert attention away from his self-inflicted wound, he said, 'Why don't we bring the participants on the drawing course to see what Stephen is doing? He has a full set of drawings as well as the wooden patterns and now the first castings.'

'That's a good idea,' said Kwame, 'but we have suggested taking them to SRS Engineering; how can we combine the two visits? If we take them to Anloga and also to Suame we'll waste too much time travelling.'

'Why not take Stephen's exhibits to SRS and make a display of his work there?'

'Right, can I leave it with you and Greg to arrange with Stephen?'

'Yes, and we'll liaise with SRS as well.'

Mick never stops thinking about the work, thought Kwame, very happy with this latest idea. He had felt that the planned visit to SRS would be short of content but Mick's idea solved this problem with a valuable addition. The participants would get a good impression of how engineering drawings were beginning to be used to upgrade practice in two grassroots workshops. They should be motivated to follow the same procedures in their own businesses.

On Sunday afternoon the participants began to arrive. Kwame, Mick and Greg joined the reception committee in the TCC car park. One by one and two by two, the participants were taken to their temporary accommodation by designated attendants. Once again the Tema party arrived in one overloaded vehicle, this time with half the occupants female. Akosua Akomwa came over to Kwame waving a large drawing. 'They want me to make this cassava grater,' she announced.

'Who does?'

'UNIFEM, they have a women's project at Kpandu.'

178

'They gave you the drawing?'

'Yes, it came from Nigeria. When I can understand it properly I will make it for them.'

'Then you must study well.'

Kwame was intrigued by this early success for his pioneering female engineer. He understood from what Akomwa told him that UNIFEM was sponsoring a women's gari making project at Kpandu in the Volta Region and wanted to introduce a new cassava grating machine that had been recently developed on a similar project in Nigeria. No doubt they found it fitting to ask a female engineer to make the prototype. He called Mick and Greg and asked them to ensure that the little welder was given extra help to interpret her drawing.

When all the participants were in, Kwame walked back to his Land Rover. His mobile telephone was ringing. It was Comfort.

'Kwame, can you come quickly? It's Kofi; we think he's been kidnapped!'

'Is Auntie Rose with you?'

'Yes, and an old white man called Tam Gordon.'

On the drive to Nhyiasu the questions were churning around in Kwame's head. Had Kofi really been kidnapped, and if so, by whom? What was Tam Gordon doing at Comfort's house? Did Auntie Rose know that Tam was in Kumasi? He realised that he might soon have some of the answers but this did not quell the mental turmoil. He had been very happy that it had been possible to persuade Kofi to stop helping the cartel and he certainly didn't want any harm to befall him. Now he must do all he could to help restore the situation.

The maid answered the door and Kwame entered the lounge to find his three associates deep in conversation. After the briefest of greetings they hurried to tell Kwame what had happened. Two men had called at the house while Comfort and Auntie Rose were at market. They had forced Kofi Adjare into a car and driven off. The maid thought that the car was like one she had seen Mama Kate riding in. 'Tam also saw them leave,' added Auntie Rose.

'Yes,' said Tam, 'the car was a new Alfa Romeo.'

'Mama Kate definitely had an Alfa Romeo,' said Kwame, 'and Kofi Boateng used to drive it. Maybe the two men who took Kofi Adjare were Kofi Boateng and Bra Yaw.'

'Are we sure we know why they took Kofi?' asked Kwame, although he thought he knew several possible reasons.

'Yes, provided Prof gives it his backing.'

'I'll look for a cheap second-hand machine to bring down for a demonstration.'

'We'll ask Prof to designate some funds.'

'What about Kwaku coming to Warwick on the short-term training programme?'

'He can apply through his dean. I would have no objection.'

'Thank you, Mr Mainu – er, Kwame,' said Kwaku happily.

Kwame thought that Kwaku reminded him of the enthusiastic young man he used to be. If only I could select all the people to come to Warwick one by one like this there would be no problem of absconding, he thought as he left the laboratory. At the same time he knew that the dean would not easily agree to Kwaku's nomination. In the university hierarchy Kwaku was classified as senior staff but not as academic staff. Nevertheless, the dean had agreed to Stephen Okunor's nomination, and he was not on the academic staff either. Kwame resolved to push hard for Kwaku when the time came for the final selection meeting.

As he was still in the School of Engineering he called in at Sam Sander's office. He wanted to know how AT Ghana was faring since his departure and, in particular, how the survey of engineering industries was progressing.

'We're about half way through,' said Sam, 'and it's going smoothly now. We should be finished in another year.'

'Will you write the final report?'

'No, I've an opportunity to travel to the USA to do a PhD. Dan Nyarko and Dr Jones will draft the final report in Tema.'

'Congratulations! When will you leave?'

'In September.'

'From the work you have done so far on the survey, can you identify any pressing needs?' asked Kwame. 'I'm looking for ideas for future short courses.'

'My main concern is for better management,' said Sam. 'Some of the enterprises seem to have reached a glass ceiling at about 25 to 30 employees. In my view further growth will be impeded until more modern management methods can be adopted.'

'Can you give me some examples?'

'Workshop proprietors must learn to delegate some of their functions like production supervision, inspection and quality control, accounting and marketing. We could offer short courses to help prepare senior staff to manage these sections of the businesses.'

'It's not as simple as that, is it? Proprietors like to keep everything in their own hands. They don't trust others to take over management responsibilities.'

'That's true, so maybe we should begin by offering a course for proprietors in modern management and its benefits for growing the enterprise.'

'Anything else?'

'Yes, the proprietors all complain that they can't get bank loans to expand their businesses, invest in new equipment and introduce new products. The banks all demand a business plan. The proprietors don't know how to draft a business plan nor can they afford to employ an expert to do it for them. It would help the small enterprises if we ran short courses in business planning.'

Later, back in his guest chalet, Kwame reflected on what he had learned. He was pleased with the progress of the survey and Sam had given him enough new ideas for short courses to keep the programme running for several years. Some of the more far-sighted entrepreneurs had already asked Kwame for help in upgrading their business management. They realised that they were trained as artisans and their skills were mostly technical and practical. They had no formal training in basic business skills like accounting, marketing and human resource management.

Kwame had noticed that delegation of functions had already begun in a few companies. This was usually in accounting, and invariably involved a close relative, such as a junior brother at SRS Engineering in Kumasi or a daughter at ENTESEL in Tema. As he had told Sam, the crucial issue was the matter of trust. Many enterprises employed only members of the owner's extended family. The challenge was to extend the trust placed in a close relative to the delegation of responsibility in other areas of the business where more distant relatives might need to be employed.

Unfortunately there were too many examples of sons and nephews stealing from their fathers and uncles to allow trust to grow easily in the community of small enterprises. In most cases the purpose of the theft was to fund an escape overseas, so the entrepreneur lost a relative and senior staff as well as money. Perhaps the intention of the escapee was to repay the loan from the riches of *aburokyiri*, but as Kwame had found, riches come slowly to those with no formal qualifications unless they continued to run the risks associated with a life of crime. Most of the absconders gained little advantage to compensate for the wrecked businesses they left behind at home. This was the danger small enterprise owners feared and the reason why they kept a firm grip on every part of their businesses.

Kwame understood only too well the desire of his compatriots to escape to greener pastures. He had been afflicted by the same passion for many years in his youth. He had been lucky to find interesting work and legitimate opportunities to travel overseas and he felt compelled to admit that his good fortune had resulted largely from the help he had received outside of Ghana. So why did he concern himself so much with efforts to prevent others following in his footsteps? It could only be from consideration of the damage the haemorrhage of so much talent and youthful energy was doing to the much larger community left behind.

Could he be sure that the damage caused by mass emigration outweighed the benefits? The successful absconders sent much money back home to build large houses, buy taxis and tipper trucks and finance small enterprises. Most of the financially successful emigrants, who weren't actual criminals, were professionals who had received many years of education at the expense of the Ghanaian taxpayer. The benefits they returned to Ghana from overseas were narrowly focused on their own families, whereas the benefits that might have accrued from their professional careers in Ghana, working as engineers, doctors, lawyers, etc, would have been spread much more widely in the community.

Kwame concluded that the loss to the community did outweigh the benefits and he was justified in doing what he could to discourage emigration. He continued to rationalise his personal situation, first on the grounds that his emigration was enforced and second that his work was still focused on the development of his homeland. He might soon need to reassess his position in the light of current developments, but first he must play his part in the rescue of Kofi Adjare.

On Tuesday morning, Kwame went with Comfort and Auntie Rose to their audience with the Queen Mother of Ashanti. Although the Queen Mother's court was less formal than that of the King, there were still protocols to be observed. Kwame was glad Comfort had kept one of his old Kente cloths so that he could appear before Nana suitably attired. He relied on Comfort to guide him gently through the long-established procedures and at length he had an opportunity to state his business.

He found himself presenting his case before a council of benign grandmothers, sitting attentively in line on either sides of their *ohemaa*. He felt immediately at ease in this gentle feminine ambience. Not being sure how the royals viewed the drugs trade, he decided to take a detached position. He explained how Kofi Adjare, an outstanding linguist, had been engaged in a Kumasi-based business exporting to the UK. While Kofi was working in Britain some problems had arisen with the authorities that resulted in Kofi and others being imprisoned. After his release and return to Ghana, and the deaths of two elders, Kofi realised that the business was failing and decided to leave and take up an appointment as Comfort's driver. However he had been kidnapped by his former associates. As Kofi's friends they were pleading for an audience with *Otumfuo,* to seek his help in gaining Kofi's release.

The Queen Mother consulted her council of elders and asked Comfort if this export business was in any way connected to the import of shoes. Comfort replied that although there had been a link in the days of Mama Kate the link was now broken. She assured the Queen Mother that if she were permitted to be enstooled as shoe queen she would guarantee that there would be no reconnection of the two activities. This brought a faint smile to the royal lips and approving nods along the line of councillors.

After more whispering among the council members the Queen Mother said that she could see that the matter was urgent, as Kofi could be in danger. They would do all they could to preserve his linguistic skills and store of oral literature. She would grant them an emergency audience with the King on the next day. Kwame expressed his gratitude and asked if it would be a formal interview requiring him to bring a linguist. The Queen Mother smiled again and said it seemed to her that Kwame was well able to speak for himself. He thanked her for this gracious compliment.

13

Ashanti Affairs

Wednesday afternoon brought them back to Manhyia for their audience with the King – *Otumfuo* Opoku-Ware II, *Asantehene*. Kwame was again relieved that he was not faced with the full traditional formality of the King's court. *Otumfuo*, the powerful one, sat with just three or four of his elders. Opoku-Ware II was a man of mature years and of a stature that befitted his title. A little lighter in complexion than the majority of his subjects, he had a large, round, kindly countenance with twinkling eyes and a welcoming smile. One could not doubt the presence of majesty: an aura of power that was all embracing and protective.

At the appropriate point in the proceedings Kwame again presented his case and made his plea. An elder leaned over to whisper something in the royal ear and the King asked, 'This man, Kofi Adjare, is he an albino and a great linguist?'

'Yes Nana, he is a guardian of our language, *mmebusem* and *anansesem*.'

'Such a man must not be harmed. Truly it would be said of him "The death of an elderly man is like a burning library".'

'Yes Nana.'

'We will issue instructions that whoever is holding him must release him at once.'

'Thank you Nana.'

At Comfort's house, after their return from the palace, Tam wanted to know what had transpired. Kwame was in a buoyant mood. It seemed to him that their problem was solved. The two women were also happy. 'Why are you so certain that Kofi will be released?' Tam asked.

'Do you remember the visit of the Prince of Wales in the late 1970s?'

'When *Otumfuo* held that big durbar?'

'Yes. A Canadian journalist had his expensive camera stolen.'

'I don't remember that.'

'The theft was reported to *Otumfuo.*'

'What happened?'

'*Otumfuo* ordered the return of the camera.'

'Was it returned?'

'Yes it was.'

'If the *Asantehene* can cancel crimes just like that, why are more crimes not brought to his attention?' asked Tam.

'Crimes are the concern of the police and very few are brought to *Otumfuo,*' Kwame replied. 'He is only concerned with crimes that might damage his reputation or the culture and traditions of Ashanti. In the case of the stolen camera the theft would have disgraced the durbar and the golden stool. In the case of Kofi we based our plea on the hope that his role as an accomplished linguist and a guardian of our culture would interest *Otumfuo.*'

'The *Asantehene* has no legal power to enforce the law, does he?' Tam still needed help to understand what was happening.

'No,' replied Kwame, 'but he has great moral authority, especially over Ashantis. We expect our plea to be successful because we think that the people holding Kofi are Ashantis. They will release him either out of loyalty or out of fear of retribution by the King's men.'

'The King's men?'

'I guess you might call them the vestigial remains of the Ashanti army.'

'Are they still feared?'

'They are, especially immediately after the death of an *asantehene,* when it is rumoured they roam at night seeking victims to serve *Otumfuo* in the next life.'

'That's rather creepy!'

'Don't worry, they are not supposed to kill white men.'

'Not even those who speak Twi?'

'Not even those.'

Kwame was beginning to feel rather irritated by Tam. What was Tam supposed to be doing in Kumasi? He said that Leon had sent him to watch Kwame's back. Did his back need watching? When Tam had switched to guarding Kofi he had not been very effective.

Tam had obviously spent long periods in Ghana and had acquired some degree of fluency in Twi but not enough to pass off as a Ghanaian. Even if it had been possible to further darken his tanned complexion, his English accent would have given him away. It must be difficult for him to move about unobserved, Kwame thought, although he had to admit that for some time Tam had kept out of sight rather effectively.

the King's men for the living to take their share. They marched off in less order but in higher spirits than they had arrived, taking their recently freed prisoners with them.

Kwame and the two women escorted Kofi to Comfort's house for softer refreshment and a review of the situation. Everyone congratulated Kofi on his release and homecoming and then he returned to his quarters to rest.

'I feel really sorry for Bra Yaw and Kofi Boateng,' said Auntie Rose. 'After losing Uncle George and Mama Kate, Kofi's defection must have left them feeling completely abandoned by their elders. It was foolish of them to kidnap Kofi but they must have been confused and very desperate. To suffer the humiliation of arrest by the King's men, and being made to grovel at their victim's feet, was the ultimate loss of face. Short of execution it's hard to imagine a worse punishment.' The others all nodded in agreement.

Tam joined the party. He was told what had transpired but wasn't convinced that the danger had been removed. 'Don't you think that Bra Yaw and Kofi Boateng will seek further revenge in the future?' he asked.

'No, I don't think so,' replied Kwame. 'They are now known individually to the King's men so they would be very foolish to repeat their action. Their organisation has been virtually disbanded and if they want to return to their old ways they will need to join another cartel. Hopefully, any new organisation would have no reason to threaten us and would prevent its recruits from starting a new war.'

'I hope you're right,' said Tam.

'How do you think Leon will view what we have done?' asked Kwame.

'I think he will be very pleased,' replied Tam. 'The Kumasi-based distribution system in the UK has been seriously disrupted and will be out of service for some time. This will give Leon's people a breathing space to hunt out the stores of hard drugs that will be accumulating from the continuing export efforts of the Lebanese.'

'Do you think Leon will want us to work on that now?'

'The Lebanese exports? Why, have you found something more?'

'They are ordering hollow coat hangers from local carpenters.'

'Are they? We must add that to our list of suspect goods.'

'Coat hangers could be sent by several routes, couldn't they?'

'You mean in bulk for general sale or in travellers' suitcases?'

'Yes, or with Ghanaian clothes exports or as hand crafted wood carvings.'

'They'll probably be used in all these ways and some are likely to get through.'

'From what you reported,' Tam said, 'Hanabis uses this agency *Sika*

Ye Na enterprise to collect the various hollow goods. Is there any way to find out what else they are ordering?'

'Someone could call at *Sika Ye Na* on the pretext of looking for auto parts but I don't suppose the special goods will be on display.'

'What about a break-in at night?'

'I would expect the place to be well guarded; night watchmen are cheap here.'

'Cheap, but not necessarily loyal.'

'No, but fearful of retribution.'

The discussion continued for some time but in the end no viable way had been found to reveal what other devices the drugs smugglers might be introducing in their continuing war with the UK customs. Kwame resolved to keep on looking out for clues in his interactions with grassroots industries. He also agreed to alert the participants on the engineering drawing course of the dangers of being approached to produce goods that could be used in drugs trafficking.

Kwame wanted to follow up the progress of the academics who had visited Warwick under the partnership agreement. He had already called on Stephen Okunor at his Suame workshop. Of the other four, Peggy Osei-Wusu and Nelson Evans-Agyei had remained in the UK. This left Kwaku Darko, who had studied electric motor rewinding, and Yaa Williams, who was investigating the local manufacture of science equipment for secondary schools.

After an early morning call on the engineering drawing course, Kwame made his way to the electrical engineering laboratory where he expected to find Kwaku Darko. The laboratory was deserted but a solitary technician told Kwame that Mr Darko did not have a lecture that morning. The young man couldn't be sure when Mr Darko would next come to the laboratory. Kwame asked about the electric motor rewinding unit and was shown a small workshop across the yard from the main laboratory. The door was locked. Only Mr Darko and one technician had keys and neither was available. Kwame was advised to come back another time.

He walked across to the physics department hoping for better luck. It was time for the mid-morning break so he headed for the staff common room and looked inside. Yaa was sitting with a group of colleagues. Recognising Kwame she came to greet him and invited him to join them relaxing with coffee and biscuits. It was Kwame's first social visit to the faculty of science and he was impressed with the recreational facilities.

'You scientists know how to look after yourselves,' he said. 'We never had coffee breaks at the TCC.'

'Welcome to civilisation.'

'You've destroyed my illusions of scientists sipping tea from a glass flask in the laboratory as they read their instruments and record data in tea-stained notebooks.'

'You can have tea if you prefer it.'

'No, coffee will be fine.'

'Come and see what I've been doing since I came back from Warwick,' Yaa said as the coffee break drew to a close. 'It's not been long but we have a few things under way.' She showed him some prototypes made in the mechanical engineering workshop that she thought could be made by local industries. These were made of steel and included tripod stands, retort stands and a variety of clamps. 'You said the TCC could help get them made commercially; could they take over from here?' she asked.

'They could, but wouldn't you like to take it a little further yourself?'

'How do you mean?'

'Wouldn't you like to learn more about the local market?'

'There are plenty of secondary schools.'

'They're not all the same. I think you should do some market research.'

'Where do I start?'

'Go to see Solomon Djokoto at SRS Engineering in Anloga. He started in business making schools science equipment but encountered difficulties with the marketing. Find out the problems he faced and try to devise a strategy for overcoming them. Then you will be in a better position to go to the TCC and if they introduce you to an interested company you won't mislead them about the market potential.'

'Thanks, I'll take your advice.'

The man approaching with a broad smile and a white coat reminded Kwame of Uncle George but with considerably more hair. 'This is Kwabena Addai, he's our glassblower,' Yaa said. 'Kwabena, this is Mr Mainu who arranged my visit to Warwick.'

'Pleased to meet you, Mr Mainu,' said Kwabena, holding out his hand.

'Call me Kwame. I'm very pleased to meet you and see what you and Yaa have been doing.'

Yaa told Kwame that Kwabena was employed to make special glassware that was needed for teaching or research in the faculty of science. Standard items were usually purchased in bulk from overseas but they both felt that these could be produced locally for supply to schools, universities and research laboratories. Kwame asked if they had drawn up a list of

192

ASHANTI AFFAIRS

what they considered to be standard items and Yaa replied that they had a list and samples of each item.

Kwabena showed Kwame the flasks, burettes, pipettes, stills and condensers that he had made to Yaa's specifications. Kwame agreed that it would be a good idea to establish local manufacture and asked what was required to help local private companies to get started. 'Isn't the first problem that there are no trained glassblowers working in these enterprises?' he suggested.

'Exactly,' said Yaa. 'We want to set up a training programme to meet the need and we are wondering if it can be done under the cooperation agreement with Warwick.'

'What sort of help would you need?' asked Kwame.

'First, we feel that Kwabena needs to be introduced to some mass production techniques. He works by hand and on a one-off basis but commercial production will need greater use of tools, dies and moulds to ensure standardisation. Perhaps he could learn the basics at Warwick. Then we would invite a group of about six students or apprentices from interested companies for training here under Kwabena's instruction. Perhaps Warwick could send down an experienced production glassblower to assist with the start-up.'

'That sounds like the outline of a suitable project,' said Kwame. 'Please write it up with cost estimates and let me have it to discuss with Professor Arthur.'

Yaa and Kwabena both looked pleased at this response to their proposal. 'You have made good use of your opportunity to visit Warwick,' Kwame told Yaa. 'This is just the sort of follow-up activity we hoped for when we planned the cooperation agreement. I am sure that Professor Arthur will be interested in your proposal and I look forward to following its progress.' At last, he said to himself, with Stephen and Yaa we have some success to report for our visitors' programme.

Then a sudden thought struck Kwame. 'Do you do any decorative work?' he asked Kwabena. 'You know, like paperweights and ornaments?'

'Yes, I do some private work to earn a little extra,' Kwabena replied. 'Would you like to see some?'

He led Kwame into a small room off the main laboratory. Here, as Kwame suspected, were glass globes with internal swirls of colour and small antelope with spindly legs. He examined them carefully, looking especially for concealed cavities. Finding none, he asked, 'Have you ever made anything for *Sika Ye Na* enterprise?'

Kwabena looked puzzled, 'There are a number of businesses with that name but I don't remember any one of them buying anything from me.'

'If you should get such an enquiry would you let me know?'

'Yes, I will.'

It had been a very long shot. He felt that it was unlikely that the drugs traffickers would use one of Kwabena's glass ornaments to conceal their wares. The basic raw material was transparent, and fully opaque colouring might look unusual enough to arouse suspicion. Then Kwabena's products were small and produced one at a time, whereas the Lebanese seemed to be ordering mass produced items of somewhat larger size and carrying capacity.

Kwame remembered how the TCC had worked with the glass bead makers of Dabaa and Asaman. These traditional Ashanti beads were made of opaque glass. The beads were larger than European beads and produced in great numbers. According to custom they were worn round the waist by Akan women, loosely strung 'to talk as they walked'. They were now exported as African artefacts and sold in Ghana to tourists. Although usually solid, apart from the stringing hole, a whole necklace of hollow beads could conceal a significant quantity of contraband. He made a mental note to mention this possibility to Tam or Leon.

Kwame made his way back to his guest chalet to write up his notes and take some lunch. Two men were waiting at his door and as he drew nearer he recognised them as Bra Yaw and Kofi Boateng. Did this portend trouble? Had they come to exact revenge? Then a cooler voice told him that this was unlikely so soon after their arrest by the King's men and in the bright light of noon on a busy campus. So he strolled boldly forward and gave his visitors what he hoped was a jovial greeting. They responded in the same spirit. 'Who showed you my hideaway?' Kwame asked, still trying to sound more jocular than he felt.

'Auntie Rose brought us here,' said Bra Yaw. 'She'll be back in a moment. She went off looking for a groundnut seller.'

Kwame unlocked his front door and invited his visitors inside and before the door was closed again Auntie Rose was back. She had brought enough roast plantain and groundnuts for them all and Kwame produced Club beer for Kofi, Star beer for Bra Yaw and Auntie Rose and a soft drink for himself. They chatted amicably about nothing in particular until the refreshments were exhausted and Kwame was left wondering what had prompted this unexpected meeting.

Realising that the last groundnut was gone and she was left only with deceptive pink husks that fluttered away in the draught of the ceiling fan, Auntie Rose said to Kwame, 'These gentlemen have something to say to you.'

The two gentlemen looked at each other as if undecided who should speak. Then, accepting the role of the senior partner, Bra Yaw said, 'We have come to apologise for all the trouble we have caused you over the years and especially for the foolish act of kidnapping Kofi Adjare. Kofi helped us to realise that we were wrong and we should now join the fight to prevent hard drugs being sold on the streets in Ghana.'

Kwame couldn't believe his good fortune. It seemed that all his fears for himself and his family had been swept away in a few dramatic days, but he still wanted to learn more about how this rebirth had come about. 'I am happy to accept your apology,' he said, 'but why did you involve yourselves for so long in sending drugs to *aborokyiri*?'

'For the money,' replied Bra Yaw. 'We thought that if the *abrofo* want cocaine and heroin why not send it to them. They have plenty of money and it was an easy way to get some of it for ourselves.'

'It was also a risky way!'

'Yes, but even taking account of my years in prison, I still earned much more money than I could have earned in a lifetime in Ghana.'

'So why have you changed your minds?'

'Kofi told us what you had said to him about foreigners now coming to Ghana to sell the drugs here. Our people don't have money, but to buy the drugs they will get into so many crimes. In *aborokyiri* they can afford to fight the drugs trade, seize the drugs coming in, lock up the dealers and even rehabilitate some of the users. But here the government won't do anything, the police can be bribed, and soon the whole country will be ruined. We don't want to be part of that.'

'I'm very glad to hear it.'

Kwame was wondering how much he could learn about the activities of the cartel. Were there any Ghanaians still working with the Lebanese? What could Bra Yaw and Kofi Boateng tell him about the ongoing activities of their former associates? However, it was Auntie Rose who asked the first question. 'Have you split up with your Lebanese friends?'

'It was Mr Russell who brought us together. After the arrests, all the seniors were out of the work: Mr Russell, Uncle George, Mama Kate and the Hanabis directors. The two sides drifted apart. Mama Kate tried to revive the partnership but she was too tired. When she died Kofi Adjare broke away completely. He never liked the camel herders, as he calls them. We tried to keep our few people in *aborokyiri* supplied with drugs but most of what we sent was caught by the *abrofo* customs. It wasn't worth continuing. It was time to stop.'

'Are the Lebanese still sending drugs?' asked Kwame.

'We believe so,' replied Bra Yaw, 'but we were never told much about what they were doing. Kofi and I were trying to send supplies to our people and we knew the camel herders were sending more but we were never told how they were doing it.'

'Can they sell the drugs in *aborokyiri* without the help of your people there?'

'I think we were selling some of the drugs for them but now I don't know what they are doing.'

'What can you tell us about Mr Konadu?'

'Kofi mentioned a Mr Konadu to us once. It seems he was helping us in *aborokyiri* but he wasn't trustworthy and that was causing trouble.'

'Did he help the Lebanese?'

'Either that, or he tried to work on his own.'

'Did you know he was sent back to Ghana and someone murdered him?'

'No, we didn't know that.'

Kwame was forced to accept once again that the junior partners in the cartel were told very little about overall operations. What Bra Yaw had told him confirmed his suspicions but added little more. From his personal point of view it was good to know that the Ghanaian faction formerly led by Uncle George and Mama Kate had ceased to exist and no longer posed a threat to himself or his family. Peter Sarpong remained a potential danger but he would stay in prison in the UK for several more years. Kwame realised that the way could now be open for him to return to work in Ghana. He might soon need to reappraise his plans for the future.

Dragging his mind back from these sunlit uplands, Kwame realised that Kofi Boateng would no longer be trying to turn the academics visiting Warwick into drugs couriers. 'Can I assume that you will stop asking my people coming to Warwick to carry your parcels of kenke?' he said to Kofi.

'Yes, we are stopping everything to do with drugs.'

'Will you tell us who in the past agreed to help you?'

'Of the first group, only Miss Peggy carried drugs for us.'

'Did you know she is still in *aborokyiri*?'

'No, I didn't know that.'

'What about the second group?'

'In that group it was only Mr Nelson who helped us.'

'He is also in *aborokyiri*, under arrest and awaiting trial.'

'I'm sorry.'

Kwame was happy that he need no longer fear his academic visitors might be drugs couriers. This would not guarantee that there would be no more absconding but it did avoid any further disgrace to the programme from association with drugs trafficking. Tom would be relieved to hear this news and it should enable him to continue the programme with only the present temporary interruption. Kwame had told Tom that he would stop the drugs couriers but at the time he had only a vague idea about how this could be accomplished. Now it was done he was grateful that fate had made it possible to keep his promise.

Kwame had left Mick and Greg to look after the engineering drawing course but he felt compelled to call in and check on progress. He was happy to find that his two assistants had everything under control. He spoke to some of the participants and found that they were content with the arrangements, even though the catering and accommodation were less lavish than on the first course. Akosua Akomwa, who had attended both courses, told him that the downgrading made little difference in practice. She showed him the drawings that UNIFEM had given her and said that she was now confident that she could make the cassava-grating machine.

Kwame asked Greg how his list of IT equipment needs was progressing. Greg said that he had everything well in hand but not much would be needed from Warwick. The university had placed a large order for computers that was expected to arrive ahead of the computer-aided drawing course. He told Greg that this was fortuitous because it now seemed likely that the visitors' programme would resume earlier than had been expected and the funds available for IT equipment would be correspondingly reduced. He hoped that nobody would be disappointed by this change of plans. 'Does this mean that Kwaku Duah will be able to come to Warwick?' asked Greg.

'That's what I'm hoping,' said Kwame.

Even though Tom had decided to halt the visitors' programme until the outcome of Kwame's trip became apparent, Kwame felt it would be useful to hold a meeting of the selection committee to review the situation before he returned to Warwick. He was able to tell the committee that, although there was still some concern about visitors absconding, the danger of visitors acting as drugs couriers was considerably reduced. As a consequence he was now expecting that Professor Arthur would allow the programme to resume. He would like to have a provisional list of recommended people to submit to Professor Arthur so that the delay to the programme would be minimised.

The dean said that as the programme had been suspended he had not asked for applications so he had no names to put forward.

'Would you be prepared to support the application of Kwaku Duah?' Kwame asked. 'According to our IT expert, Greg Anderson, Duah is a skilful and enthusiastic young man who with a little training would be capable of helping to introduce computer-controlled machine tools. He's a great asset in helping to prepare for the computer-aided drawing course and in the future he could keep the course running after the end of our partnership agreement.'

The dean smiled. 'You like to push the cause of technicians, don't you?' But before Kwame could respond he added, 'I see the value of transferring these practical skills to our local industries and I agree that Duah is a promising young man.' The TCC director said that they were keen to start demonstrating numerically controlled machining centres at Suame ITTU and the training of Duah would be a useful first step. 'But we need a machine as well,' he added. Kwame said that he and Greg had already discussed with Duah the possibility of bringing in a demonstration machine. He would put this proposal to Professor Arthur and ask for funds to be made available. Both dean and director looked satisfied.

Kwame was emboldened to make a further proposal. 'Now can I suggest another highly skilled technician?' he asked. 'You will remember that one of our latest visitors was Yaa Williams of the physics department. Since her return she has produced a number of prototypes of schools science equipment that could be locally manufactured. At Warwick she showed a special interest in glassblowing and since her return she has had some items produced by Kwabena Addai, the department's glassblower. Now it would be useful to familiarise Addai with techniques for mass producing these items.'

'How do you mean?'

'Traditional glassblowers produce individual hand crafted-items; there is visible variation in size and form. Mass produced items for general sale should be identical within close limits. Addai could be shown how this can be achieved with a few basic gauges and moulds.'

'I agree that having sent Miss Williams with good results we are justified in building on her achievement by sending Mr Addai,' said the dean.

The director nodded his agreement but raised a caveat. 'SRS Engineering started by producing schools' science equipment but gave up due to marketing problems. Has Miss Williams been advised to talk to Solomon Djokoto about his experiences?'

'Yes,' said Kwame. 'That was also my concern. We mustn't let them go blindly forward without a strategy to avoid repeating past mistakes, but I don't think that should prevent us going ahead with Addai's visit.'

Kwame couldn't be certain that Tom and his senior colleagues in Warwick would agree to the resumption of the visitors' programme, but if they did, he had the next two visitors agreed by the selection committee in Kumasi. It would be up to him to convince Tom that future visitors would not be carrying drugs. He felt that he had a good story to tell and that the outcome would be positive.

These few weeks in Kumasi had transformed Kwame's life. Fears that had haunted him for years had been swept away and largely through his own effort. He felt proud that he had shown the resolve and courage to face the situation squarely and engineer a satisfactory outcome. He knew that he had taken a significant step forward in confidence and maturity, both in his professional work and his efforts to combat the drugs traffickers. He was nearly thirty-nine, his following birthday would be his fortieth and he felt ready to start a new life.

A new life could bring new joys but it would also bring new challenges. He would need to decide when to return to Ghana, and that meant taking account of the needs of Akosua and Afriyie as well as his own. Then there was the question of loyalty to Tom; he wouldn't want to damage the partnership agreement now that it had good prospects of achieving its objectives. Last, as well as first, there was the siren call of reunion with Comfort.

He couldn't free his thoughts from the words of Auntie Rose repeating endlessly in his head, 'I think she might take you back if you asked her.' Part of him rebelled at facing this complex issue but another part remembered the joy of sunlit afternoons, lively conversation and timely advice from a sharp intuitive mind.

14

Seismic Activity

Kwame returned to London with Mick and Greg. They were content with what had been achieved during their visit to Kumasi. The engineering drawing course had gone well, preparations were in hand for Greg's computer-aided drawing course and they had seen some positive outcomes from the visitors' programme. They all hoped that Professor Arthur and the authorities at Warwick would be reassured about the value of the partnership agreement and fully restore the scheduled activities.

Much to Kwame's surprise, Tom was waiting for them at the airport. 'I couldn't wait to hear what you have done about this wretched drugs business,' he whispered in Kwame's ear.

'Stop worrying, it's all fixed,' was the barely audible reply.

There was lively conversation in the Range Rover all the way to Coventry. 'Straight to my office,' Tom said to Kwame as soon as the other two had collected their bags and taken their leave.

'I hope what you told me at the airport is the whole truth,' Tom said as soon as they were seated. 'I've had no end of trouble from Professor Thomas and the other doubters since you left. The den of thieves has become the nest of vipers or worse in some of the rhetoric that's been thrown at me. They've set up a review meeting of the management committee in two days' time and you are ordered to attend.'

Kwame had not expected the situation to become so serious but he realised that he should not be surprised. As he had pointed out in Kumasi, of five visitors to date, two were suspected of having carried drugs, one had been arrested and one had overstayed her visa. These were the blunt statistics the professors had seen. Who could blame them for thinking that the university's reputation was in danger of being seriously damaged?

Kwame hurried to tell Tom what had transpired in Kumasi, explaining that the Ghanaian command and control centre had been disbanded and no more university visitors would be approached and asked to carry drugs to the UK. He realised that not all the details about the drugs cartel and its demise could be given to the management committee and he asked Tom's view on how best to present their case.

'You could say that the person within the university who was contacting the visitors has been identified and prevented from repeating his actions.'

'Don't you think that sounds rather weak? They will ask for more details.'

'Then say that you took the matter to the *Asatehene* and he used his traditional authority to have the man arrested.'

'That is near enough to the truth to be convincing.'

'That's a big relief, Kwame,' Tom said. 'You did really well to bring about this outcome. The master sleuth must be very pleased with you.'

'I've not reported to Leon directly but I guess he's heard most of it from Auntie Rose and Tam Gordon.'

'Were they both in Kumasi? You're like a magnet dragging iron filings!'

'That's what it felt like most of the time.'

'Did they help much?'

'Not much, it was Comfort who helped me more.'

'Rekindling old flames, eh?'

'I'm trying not to get burned.'

'As for your official duties,' Tom said, 'I'll get most of it from your written reports.'

'Everything went well and our two young men performed splendidly. They've both made themselves popular at the university and after three trips and more Twi lessons Mick is practically a native.'

'Your next course will be Greg's computer course in July, won't it?'

'That's right.'

'Would you mind if I came down for that one?'

'Of course not – it will be like old times.'

Afriyie came with the Discovery to take Kwame home where he received an enthusiastic welcome from Akosua and Takoradi. Elsie brought in the supper but her greeting was somewhat muted. Kwame sensed a tension between the apprentice and her mistress. It was not until Elsie had retired to her own room and Akosua and Takoradi were doing their homework that Kwame had a chance to ask Afriyie if there was a problem.

'She's demanding what she calls English wages.'

'Is she taking into account the full cost of bed and board?'

'She wants more money in her hand.'

'Apprentices aren't paid much and if you deduct the cost of bed and board there won't be much left even from English wages.'

'That's what I told her.'

'Where is she getting this attitude from?'

'Her friends at the Pentecostal church'

'Aren't they your friends as well?'

'Not any more.'

Kwame thought there was a simple answer to this problem. 'We'll find out what a second year apprentice in the sewing industry is paid,' he said. 'Then we'll take the standard rent for one room around here and estimate the cost of her meals. The next time you pay her, show her the full amount in cash and deduct the cost of bed and board. If there is any balance, give it to her. That way she should understand the real economics of life in *aborokyiri*. I think she'll opt to go back to being a member of the family rather than an employee-lodger.'

Akosua rushed in with, 'We've finished my homework!'

'How much did Takoradi help?' Kwame asked.

'Heaps, Dad. It was an essay on working animals and he told me about his adventures with the police.'

'Didn't you write about Takoradi before?'

'We've moved on a year, Dad; what we do now is much more sophisticated.'

'I hope my sophisticated daughter worked hard at school while I was away.'

'Of course, I've got end-of-year exams in June.'

'Any problems?'

'I need a bit of paternal coaching in maths and physics.'

'Well, *pater* is home now; call when you need me.'

Kwame had been expecting an early call from Leon to review his trip to Kumasi but he had not expected to be summoned once again to the hairdressing salon. They met in the comfortable upstairs room and Auntie Rose, David Barney and Tam Gordon were all in attendance. Leon produced a bottle of wine and said that Kwame deserved a celebratory drink for what he had been able to achieve. 'Since my trouble with a stomach ulcer, I'm not supposed to drink alcohol,' Kwame said, 'but if you're all joining me I will allow myself to take a small glass.' They all laughed.

Leon poured the drinks and then said, 'Let's drink a toast to Mr Kwame Mainu: congratulations, good health and no more stomach ulcers.' This was greeted by 'hear-hear' and '*hwe*' from Auntie Rose.

Kwame beamed at his companions and thanked them for the toast but he hastened to tell them, 'I shouldn't be given all the credit. I was much helped by my ex-wife, Comfort Opokua, by the Queen Mother of Ashanti and by the King: *Nana Otumfuo, Asantehene.* The support of Auntie Rose and Tam was also a great help.'

'I'm afraid I wasn't much use,' said Tam. 'I guess I'm getting too old for tropical duty and should follow Takoradi into retirement.'

Leon waited for the glasses to be drained before beginning the formal discussion. 'We now have a greatly changed situation in Kumasi,' he said. 'It must be carefully assessed in order to determine our future strategy. It seems that the former cartel has split up with the Ghanaian group completely disbanded. This means that the dispersed network of drugs dealers in the UK is no longer receiving directions from the cartel in Kumasi. For the moment we can expect sales on the streets to be much reduced.'

Leon paused to see if anyone wanted to make a comment and then continued. 'It seems that the last three members of the Ghanaian group: Kofi Adjare, Bra Yaw Aidoo and Kofi Boateng, have come over to our side, as it were, and we will return to consider if and how we might employ them. On the Lebanese side, however, we have evidence of renewed activity in devising new ways of bringing drugs to the UK, including hollow coat hangers and, Kwame suggests, strings of Ashanti waist beads. As the Lebanese group is now cut off from its former sales network it is likely that stockpiles of unsold drugs are building up.'

Again he paused and surveyed the meeting, but finding only an attentive audience he continued, 'We must ask ourselves the question: where do we go from here? What must be our number one priority?'

'The future threat will come from the Lebanese,' Tam said. 'We must find out more about their plans, especially with regard to re-connecting to a sales network in the UK.'

'Will they try to re-connect to the Ghanaian network, or to another existing network, or will they try to establish an entirely new system?' Leon asked.

'I believe their first choice will be one of the first two,' said Kwame. 'If they go on alone my guess is they will try to re-connect to the Ghanaians and Nigerians who were helping them before. If they join the Venezuelans they will probably share one of the networks the South Americans already operate here.'

'I think Kwame is right,' said David Barney. 'Setting up a new system will take longer and cost more.'

'So it all hinges on what the Kumasi Lebanese will do,' Leon mused aloud. 'Is there any way we could find out?'

'First of all, we have three names,' said David. 'Suleiman Hannah, Bashir Abizaid and Omar Issah.'

'What do we know about them?' Leon asked Kwame.

'Bachir Abizaid left Ghana after the first Rawlings coup in June 1979. The other two were arrested in Ghana in 1988 and served a prison sentence until they were released in 1993.'

'Where are they now; do you know, Kwame?'

'As far as I know, Hannah and Issah are still in Kumasi and Abizaid is still outside Ghana.'

'I've done a little research,' David said. 'The Lebanese community in Ghana is about six thousand strong, there are nearly ten thousand in Nigeria but the Lebanese in Venezuela number more than three hundred thousand. If the Lebanese in Kumasi are linking up with Venezuelans, aren't they likely to be fellow Lebanese? Could Abizaid be in Venezuela?'

Leon looked sternly at David. 'We must avoid drifting into idle speculation,' he said. 'Is there anything we can do to gather more facts?' He gazed hopefully at Auntie Rose.

'You mean go back to Kumasi and offer to work with them?' she said in a tone that expressed incredulity.

'I don't mean you personally, but could Mr Aidoo or Mr Boateng be persuaded to help us?'

'They might be willing to help but they've had no training. We're proposing dealing with Lebanese, not Ghanaians, the mission would be too dangerous.'

Kwame didn't like the idea either. 'Could we try another approach?' he suggested, 'Could one of the Lebanese partners be persuaded to come to the UK? I'm sure you would like a little chat with the gentleman, Leon.'

'Even if one of them came here we would need enough evidence to charge him with an offence.'

'They were imprisoned in Ghana on evidence provided by Bra Yaw.'

'And now we have Bra Yaw on our side!'

'And you also have Crispin Russell, alias Charles Richards, alias Oboroni. He was almost certainly the link between the Lebanese and Ghanaian groups in the past and the Lebanese might feel that he could re-connect them to the UK distribution network. They might be very keen to talk to him again.'

'Let's get this straight,' said Leon. 'You are proposing a deal with Crispin Russell to entice Hannah or Issah to Britain and using evidence provided by Aidoo to arrest and question the gentleman.'

'That's a neat summary,' said Kwame. 'Don't you think that it sounds less hazardous than sending Aidoo or Boateng into the thieves' den in Kumasi?'

'It might work if it was well prepared,' David said. 'We could begin by inviting Mr Aidoo to come here.'

'I'll have to check to see if we could offer him immunity from prosecution,' said Leon.

Kwame had not been looking forward to the meeting with the management committee, and following closely on the meeting with Leon he had not had much time to prepare. The chairman greeted him as warmly as ever and thanked him for coming. Kwame reflected ruefully that Tom's invitation hadn't given him much choice but he was soon to realise that hard lobbying by Tom ahead of the meeting had done much to soften the mood.

'This emergency meeting has been called to review the situation with our visitors' programme which has been suspended due to certain police investigations,' the chairman began. 'It seems that Mr Nelson Evans-Agyei, who came from Kumasi to study alternative renewable fuels for diesel engines, has been arrested by the police on a charge of bringing narcotics into the country. Furthermore we are told that an earlier visitor from Kumasi, Miss Peggy Osei-Wusu, failed to return to Ghana and is now an illegal immigrant. Miss Osei-Wusu is also suspected of having brought in contraband. Three other visitors, I might add, completed their assignments and returned to Ghana on schedule.'

'Are you saying that we should accept a sixty per cent success rate?' Professor Thomas demanded roughly.

'Not at all, Professor,' said the chairman. 'I was merely presenting the full picture.'

'Then can we concentrate on the forty per cent of serious failure?'

'Would you like to lead the discussion, Professor?'

'Can Mr Mainu tell us how the visitors were selected?'

'Most of the names were put forward by the dean of the School of Engineering and then finally approved by a selection committee.'

'Were you a member of the selection committee that approved the drugs traffickers?'

'The committee approved the second group of three visitors including Mr Evans-Agyei.'

'So how did you come to select a drugs trafficker?'

Kwame explained that the selection committee had no way of knowing who might carry drugs. The traffickers had access to the approved list of visitors and approached them individually. Of the four that were approached, two are suspected of having agreed to carry drugs and two refused. The fifth man, Stephen Okunor, had been proposed independently by Kwame and had not been asked to carry drugs.

'I understand, Mr Mainu,' the chairman cut in, 'that during your recent visit to Kumasi, certain steps were taken to eradicate the problem. Can you now guarantee that there will be no recurrence of this unfortunate situation?'

'Yes,' Kwame said, 'the two people involved were identified and prevented from repeating their actions.'

'How can you be sure?' It was Professor Thomas again.

'We called upon the King of Ashanti for his support and he had the men arrested. I now have their personal guarantees that they will do nothing further to assist the drugs traffickers.'

'Correct me if I am wrong, but Ghana is a republic with a strong central government; how much authority does your king really have?'

'You are right, the *Asantehene's* power is purely traditional but it is very strong within the Ashanti community. The men concerned are members of that community.'

The chairman seemed satisfied and moved to draw the meeting to a conclusion. 'I want us to record our thanks to Mr Mainu for travelling to Kumasi and taking swift and resolute action. I understand from Professor Arthur, who has some knowledge of the Kumasi scene, that Mr Mainu's mission involved some risk and was accomplished with both courage and resourcefulness. Now we have heard Mr Mainu's report for ourselves, can I move to lift the suspension order on the visitors' programme?' The resolution was passed with one abstention.

'Well done, Kwame!' Tom said immediately after the meeting. 'Now we can go ahead with your next two hand-picked candidates. With your prompt action in Kumasi the programme has only been delayed by a few weeks and we can easily make up the lost time.'

'Yes,' Kwame said, happy to see Tom in a much better mood. 'I have every confidence in Kwaku Duah and Kwabena Addai. Can we go ahead with the arrangements?'

'Yes, as soon as possible.'

Back in his office Kwame called his three assistants, but only the two men came. 'We have a go-ahead on the visitors' programme,' he said. 'I'm sure, Greg, that you will want to arrange the work experience of Kwaku Duah. Let him divide his time between helping with preparations for the computer-aided drawing course and gaining some experience with numerically controlled machine tools. Take him to the Land Rover training school for the hands-on part.

'Our other visitor is Kwabena Addai,' he continued. 'He's a glassblower working with Yaa Williams. As Sandra looked after Yaa, I was hoping she would also follow up with Kwabena, but as she is not here I would like you, Mick, to start the ball rolling. Please check with the physics department to see if they can host a glassblower for four weeks. Sandra can join in when she is ready. Where is she, by the way?'

'Haven't you heard?' said Mick. 'Nelson has been sentenced to two years imprisonment. Sandra is very upset – she hasn't been in for the last two days.' Mick showed Kwame a copy of a local newspaper with a brief account of Nelson's trial on a charge of drugs trafficking under the headline 'Jumbo Cocaine Haul'.

Kwame read the account closely hoping that it would not present the university in a bad light. He was relieved to find that Nelson had admitted bringing in the carved elephant and no mention was made of how its contraband content had been detected. Hopefully the incident would attract no more publicity and neither the university nor the partnership project would be damaged.

Akosua's sixteenth birthday passed, quickly followed by Kwame's thirty-ninth, and life for the Mainus returned to what they accepted as normality, even though they hadn't experienced too much of it. Kwame's work reverted to the traditional nine to five routine and Akosua was working hard at school in the sixth form. Afriyie's dressmaking was earning her a useful extra income and apart from the difficulties raised by Elsie over her salary the business was progressing smoothly. On the surface life seemed tranquil but deep down Kwame was aware of seismic activity.

With the changed situation in Kumasi, Kwame felt that he was now free to return to work full-time in Ghana. He had come to Britain because he feared that there was danger to his family if he remained in Ghana. That threat was now removed. He could hear his father calling him back to serve his homeland. At the same time his successful and comfortable life in Coventry pulled him strongly in another direction.

He wanted Akosua to complete her education in the UK and he was reluctant to leave her on her own until she was at least two years older. He also felt that out of loyalty to Tom he should serve out his three-year contract with the project. His work was still focused on assisting the economic development of his country and in his present position he could do as much for Ghana as in his former full-time employment in Tema. By these arguments he rationalised the undoubted attractions of his affluent and relaxed life in exile.

He knew that Afriyie wanted to stay longer in Coventry with her comfortable home, her business and her friend, Akos Mary. She was also looking forward to having her first baby in the UK. This was becoming an increasing concern. In spite of much effort no pregnancy had resulted. Afriyie would soon be thirty-four and she was beginning to hint that her best years for starting a family were passing by.

It was more than a year since Kwame had agreed to Afriyie's request and now since his latest visit to Kumasi his emotional commitment had changed. Did he want to further strengthen his ties to Afriyie? Wouldn't a child with Afriyie close the door to any prospect of reconciliation with Comfort? During his last two visits to Kumasi he had felt his feelings for Comfort steadily reviving. He realised that in spite of all the pain she had inflicted, his love for his wife had never died and it was now restored almost to its pristine level.

Comfort had been his first love and the only love he felt that he had freely chosen. She was the love he had shared with his father and the love his father had tacitly approved. Without her protection he might well have drifted into becoming a drugs courier and suffered the fate of Bra Yaw or Peter Sarpong. Comfort had often accused him of infidelity but Kwame knew that he had never yielded to the temptation to take another girlfriend during his long years alone in England. He had worked hard in all his spare time to earn money to provide the house she always wanted. In helping to break-up the drugs cartel in the UK he had done some things that Comfort didn't like, but he had never intended to hurt her by any of his actions and had gone to great lengths to avoid causing her pain. He had always striven to meet her demands and keep their marriage intact. The break-up of their relationship, leading to six years' loss of contact, had been entirely her decision.

Kwame had struggled to understand Comfort but he also felt she had failed to understand him. During his recent visit to Kumasi, however, he sensed that a deeper understanding had evolved through their mutual effort to pull Kofi Adjare from the debris of the cartel. He sensed that his resolute action in rescuing her old friend and adviser had inspired in Comfort a new respect and admiration. She did not appear to have formed any other long-term relationship and their traditional marriage had never been formally dissolved. According to ancestral custom they were still man and wife. Akosua was the child of their union; with a claim on both their lives. She would surely welcome the restoration of the traditional nuclear family.

At the same time that these emotions surged, Kwame knew that he must also give due weight to the needs and aspirations of Afriyie. They had drifted together partly by chance and partly by feminine guile. Their relationship was more one of convenience than of passion, although passion had played its part. When presented with the challenge of marrying at the same time as Tom and Akos Mary, Kwame had pulled out after months of indecision. Yet he knew that he owed Afriyie a great debt of gratitude.

Afriyie might lack Comfort's quick wits but her steadier temperament made her a more dependable sexual partner. She had kept house for Akosua and himself for almost eight years, remaining totally loyal and asking for little in return. She had worked hard at her sewing business, contributing to the family income, and she had willingly accompanied him back to Britain. In short, she had done nothing to deserve his rejection.

Kwame reflected ruefully that some people might say that his emotional turmoil was a form of mid-life crisis. If so, it did not quite fit the usual pattern. Apart from coming a few years too early, his fantasy involved returning to the wife of his youth rather than seeking his lost youth with a new wife. Nevertheless, it was still an attempt to turn back the clock. Was his desire to go back to Comfort a mirage that would fade as it was approached, leaving the rest of his life a barren desert? Was it just a selfish indulgence that in time he might come to regret? Of one thing he was sure: such a major life changing decision needed time to mature. He could afford to wait upon events to provide the answer or change the question.

Although Comfort had been much in his thoughts Kwame had not expected that she would write him a letter. It came to hand one morning in his office at the university.

At Home
4 May 1996

Dear Kwame,

Don't be disturbed to receive my letter; nothing terrible has happened. I just want to pass on some information that could be relevant to your mission.

I was in the foreign exchange shop the other day and I met Bachir Abizaid. He has grown much fatter and lost his hair and at first I wasn't sure that it was him. He recognised me and said he was happy to be back in Ghana after nearly seventeen years away. I asked him where he had been but he just said that he had been moving around in Lebanon, Europe and South America. When I asked if he was going back to Hanabis he said that he had never left the company but had remained a director throughout. He asked if I ever heard from Mr Russell (Oboroni) and I told him not since they both left Ghana in June 1979.

I enjoyed our adventures on your recent visit. Are you coming back in July?

Please give my regards to Auntie Rose and my love to Akosua.

Best wishes,

Comfort

Kwame made a photocopy of the letter and rang David Barney to tell him he had some information to pass on. He waited in his office and David came in just after the others had left for home.

'Leon will be interested in this development,' David said. 'He will want to know where Abizaid has been all this time.' He read the note a second time and then asked, 'Abizaid enquired after Mr Russell; could he be the one we try to invite to the UK?'

'Oh no, I don't think so. It was the other two Lebanese directors of Hanabis that were convicted on Bra Yaw's evidence in Ghana in 1988. It's very unlikely that Bra Yaw could provide evidence to incriminate Abizaid. He left Ghana in 1979 and Bra Yaw's knowledge of the cartel dates from the mid 1980s.'

'Could Russell incriminate Abizaid, assuming that Russell is prepared to provide evidence?'

'It's difficult to say. They both left Ghana in 1979 and I have no idea if they remained in contact after that. We don't know what Abizaid was doing between 1979 and 1988 when Russell was imprisoned. He might have been deeply involved with Russell in Britain or he might have been far out of it attending to other areas of Hanabis's business.'

'What do you suggest Leon should do?'

'First, let him talk to Oboroni; he might tell us what Abizaid was doing. Then decide which Hanabis director to go after. I would still prefer Hannah or Issah, using Bra Yaw's input, to relying only on Oboroni.'

'That makes sense to me,' said David.

Not for the first time, Kwame wondered why the British officials sometimes asked him to suggest the next move in their enquiries. He decided that after all the years of working together he could ask David Barney and expect a frank reply.

'Why do you people sometimes ask me to suggest your next move? I thought my role was limited to Twi translations and providing information on the Ghanaian involvement in the drugs cartel.'

'What you say is true. Back in the 1980s we might have wanted to test your reliability but more recently we have come to value your suggestions. Leon is impressed with what you have achieved during your last two visits to Kumasi. Please don't look for ulterior motives. If we ask for your advice these days it's only because we value it.'

'Thank you for your compliment and for giving me a straight answer,' Kwame replied, 'but I would also like to be frank and remove any misunderstanding. My aim is to help my people get out of the drugs business and resist a domestic drugs trade taking root in Ghana. I am only interested in the fate of the Lebanese directors of Hanabis to the extent that they are involved with Ghanaians. I understand that communications in Twi have stopped and are no longer a factor in the distribution system in the UK. My role here has evaporated. I would like to restrict my involvement to what I can do for my people in Kumasi.'

'I understand, and I'm sure Leon also understands, that our war with the Lebanese drug traffickers is not your personal concern, but for the moment we cannot rule out the re-establishment of contact with a Ghanaian distribution system in the UK. That is the reason why Leon would like to keep you on the team.'

'Is there something you're not telling me?'

'Well, there is the matter of Mr Sarpong.'

'Peter Sarpong?'

'Yes, he's applied for early release on the grounds of good behaviour.'

Peter Sarpong's release from prison was the one event that Kwame feared. With the deaths of Mama Kate and Uncle George, and the conversion of Bra Yaw and Kofi Boateng, for the first time in almost a decade, Kwame had felt safe from the revenge of his compatriots. Now the possible release of Peter Sarpong brought the fears flooding back. Did Peter suspect that Kwame was involved in his arrest and imprisonment? Had Akos Mary had any opportunity to tell him of Kwame's role in her arrest? Did Peter suspect that Kwame had played a part in the arrest of his uncle which led to Uncle George's death in Nsawam prison? Peter might come out of prison to find his former organisation disbanded, but he could have several personal reasons for seeking revenge on Kwame and his family.

Kwame hoped that one question could be answered by Akos Mary. This could be the key to whether Peter Sarpong knew or suspected his involvement with the British customs investigation. Ever since Akos Mary had forgiven him for his part in her own arrest he had been seeking an opportunity to ask her. Now the issue had taken on a new urgency, so one day at the close of work he made his way to the hairdressing salon.

Kwame found Akos Mary clearing up and they chatted in the back office about Little Tom's progress, Akosua's forthcoming examinations and Afriyie's problems with Elsie. Then Kwame broached his major concern, 'I hope you can help me,' he began.

'Oh Kwame, don't look so worried. You know I will do anything I can to help. You have always helped me in times of trouble.'

'Ever since you forgave me for the part I played in your arrest I've been wanting to ask you another question.'

'Go ahead.'

'At the time of your arrest you were very angry and you called me "*oboroni*".'

'I remember.'

'Did you see Peter Sarpong after that?'

'Do you mean at the police station?'

'At any time?'

'I didn't see him at the police station but I saw him at his trial.'

'Did you ever speak to him?'

'I gave evidence, that's what shortened my sentence.'

'But did you ever speak directly to Peter?'

'No.'

'You never told him about me?'

'Oh no, nothing like that.'

Kwame was relieved to hear these answers but he wanted to be very sure. 'Akos Mary,' he said, 'I hear that Peter may soon be released from prison and I'm afraid...' He stopped abruptly as he saw the terror in her eyes and realised simultaneously what had provoked it.

'*You're* afraid, Kwame? I was the one who gave evidence against him at his trial!'

'Oh I'm so sorry, I hadn't intended to alarm you; I was thinking of myself and Akosua.'

'Peter may *suspect* you, but he *knows* I helped to convict him!'

He struggled to calm his friend, telling her that the appeal for early release would take several months to process. They were not in immediate danger and there was time to plan for the eventuality. Peter's appeal might well be unsuccessful.

Kwame warmed to his theme, encouraging himself but leaving his companion in distress, his words drowned in her ears by the nightmare cries of Little Tom.

'What can we do?' sobbed Akos Mary.

'We may be able to get an appeal lodged against his early release.'

'How can we do that?'

'I know a way.'

Kwame realised that his appeal to Akos Mary had changed nothing. The release of Peter Sarpong presented a threat to her if not to him. He must do all he could to prevent the early release. He decided to ask Leon to oppose Peter's release and he began to rehearse in his mind the arguments he would propose.

Next morning in his office Kwame was again on the telephone to David Barney. This time he was requesting an early meeting with Leon. 'Shall I come to the usual place on Thursday morning?' he asked David.

'No, I'll meet you in the parents' car park at the school.'

Sandra came in as Kwame put down the telephone. It was the first time he had seen her since the conviction and imprisonment of Nelson Evans-Agyei. 'Did you enjoy your leave?' he asked.

'Yes thank you,' she replied. 'I was able to spend a few days at home in Leicester with my parents.'

'What do your parents do?'

'Mum is a doctor and Dad is a nurse,' Sandra said, and anticipating his smile she added, 'Yes, I did get that the right way round!'

'They let you become an engineer?'

'They pride themselves on being modern parents.'

Kwame wondered if they knew of their daughter's infatuation with an African man.

'According to Mick you want me to take over the support of Kwabena Addai,' she said.

'Yes,' said Kwame. 'Kwabena works with Yaa Williams. He's a glassblower, over here to learn some techniques to help them produce laboratory glassware in larger quantities.'

'So we're following up on what Yaa started.'

'That's right. Yaa and Kwabena have produced some good prototypes but now they want to move on to small-scale commercial production.'

'Kwabena is based in the physics department; is that OK?'

'He should also spend some time with a commercial glassware producer. I want you to telephone around and see what you can arrange.'

'How long should his attachment last?'

'At least two weeks; more if possible.'

Sandra stood up and walked to the door but then turned back, 'Have you heard about Nelson?' she asked.

'Yes, Mick showed me the press cutting.'

'What will happen to him?'

'He will serve his sentence and then be deported back to Ghana.'

'Will he be in prison for two years?'

'That was the sentence, but most people seem to be released early if they behave well.'

'I'm sure Nelson won't cause any trouble.'

'Then he will be let out early.'

'Can they have visitors?'

'Oh yes, why don't you write to ask to visit him?'

'Do you think he'd like that?'

'I'm sure he would.'

She sat silent for a while, eyes focused on infinity. Kwame waited patiently, savouring the irony of the situation. Sandra was willing Nelson's release to come early while he was scheming for Peter's release to be delayed. If the human will could affect the flow of time, he thought, we'd all get seriously out of synchronism.

At length the young woman returned to the present with, 'You say he will be deported back to Ghana.'

'That's what usually happens.'

'But I will be able to visit him there.'

'Of course, if that's what you both want.'

'Could he ever return to England?'

'Yes, I think so, if he commits no further offences.'

There was another long pause and Kwame tried hard to hide any signs of impatience. 'He was tricked, you know; he didn't mean to do anything illegal.'

'I'm sure you're right. He won't do it again.'

'Thank you, Kwame.'

'What for?'

'For listening – for understanding.'

This time she not only reached the door but succeeded in opening it and passing through. Kwame hoped that he had helped to put her mind at rest but he wasn't quite sure that Sandra would be able to function efficiently. He realised that as a man from a different culture there was only so much that he could do to help her. Did she have a female friend from her own culture to turn to in times of emotional stress? He thought that Mick might know so he called him to his office.

'I've briefed Sandra on what we can do for Kwabena Addai,' Mick said. 'Should I hand over to her or do you want us to work together?'

'She's still upset about Nelson. I think it would be good if you could support her for the moment.'

'We're all worried about her.'

'I've done what I can, but she needs a shoulder to cry on. Does she have a female friend, perhaps an older one?'

'She's friendly with Mrs Gupta, Professor Thomas's secretary.'

'Then we must hope that she's getting the support she needs.'

15

Fertility Dolls

The girls got down from the Discovery and the happy chatter diminished in volume as they moved away. Kwame let his ears adjust to the drop in the sound level. His trips to Warwick were always noisy affairs with heated discussions of homework, the handsome young physics master or the latest pop music. More ominous for Kwame was excited talk of boyfriends, though Akosua still seemed more interested in Takoradi than males of the two-legged variety. He wondered how long this would last and how he would cope with his daughter's first romance.

You couldn't hear the radio when Akosua and her friends were in the car but now was a chance to catch up on the news. He pressed the button and leaned back to listen to the *Today* programme on BBC Radio 4, wondering idly if quality radio was as effective as a broadsheet in shortening a waiting period. Sure enough, even before the news summary had finished David Barney's Ford Mondeo slipped silently into the adjacent parking space. Mainu's law works for radio too, he reflected as he waved a greeting and drew out the ignition key.

'Leave your car here and come with me,' David called through a half-open widow. 'I'm afraid we've got a longer ride than usual,' he explained as Kwame fastened his seat belt, 'because Leon wants you to meet one of the lawyers preparing the case against Peter Sarpong's early release.'

'That's good,' Kwame replied. 'I'm happy to go an extra mile for that!'

'Tam's a lucky blighter,' David said as he filtered into the stream of fast-moving vehicles on the motorway.

'Why do you say that?' asked Kwame, surprised at this unprofessional outburst revealing David's personal feelings.

'He gets all the trips to Ghana.'

'You'd like to have a chance, would you?'

'We all would, but its only Tam who ever goes.'

'He's the only one who speaks Twi.'

'Yes, but is that really necessary?'

216

'It's not essential but it helps, especially if you need to talk to illiterates and rural people.'

'How widely is English spoken in Ghana?' David asked.

'It's the official language, the language of government and most newspapers and books, and it's the language of education in schools except for the first year of primary school in Ashanti Region,' Kwame explained.

'But what about people in the street; do you hear much English?'

'You mostly hear Twi with many English words mixed in.'

'Can you give me an example?'

'We were once waiting for a meeting to begin and one person looked at his watch and said "Time *ben yebe starti*?" I guess you don't need to speak Twi to understand that question.'

'No, but is the general standard of English improving?'

'I'm afraid not. There has been a general decline in the standard of English speaking, especially since the introduction of junior secondary schools, called JSS or Jerry's Special Schools after Jerry Rawlings, former military dictator and now president.'

'What's the problem?'

'I suppose it's basically a shortage of teachers and large class sizes, as well as teachers needing to have a second job or a private business to earn enough to support themselves and their families.'

'So are there proportionally fewer English speakers than formerly?'

'I'm afraid so.'

'Then Tam might be needed even more than in the past.' David mused aloud, seeing his chances of being sent to Ghana growing ever dimmer.

'If Tam's role is to gather information from common talk in the streets and public places, his Twi will be very useful,' Kwame said, 'but I must admit I couldn't really understand why he was in Ghana recently.'

'I've got Leon's permission to tell you,' David said. 'He was there to try to determine to what extent hard drugs are being sold on the streets and, if sales are increasing, to try to find out who's selling them.'

'Yes, why didn't I think of that? He might meet many situations in which people will think that they can speak freely in Twi and *oboroni* won't hear them.'

'You like the idea then?'

'I do, and it explains why Tam can pretend he knows less or more Twi depending on the situation.'

'The old man is brighter than he seems, eh?'

'You're telling me!'

'So that story about Tam watching my back was only partly true,' Kwame said, 'and I now see why I saw so little of him. He was walking the streets, mingling, listening and watching. What did he find?'

'He confirmed our suspicions, I'm afraid. The sale of hard drugs on the streets and in bars and cafes is on the increase. He even found a few cases of selling to school children.'

'I suppose that if Tam has been going to Ghana over many years his impression of trends is reliable.'

'And that's why it's always Tam who is sent.'

Kwame realised that David had answered his own complaint. It was a timely moment to close the circle because the Mondeo was drawing to a stop in the car park of a large hotel on the outskirts of Oxford. 'Leon has hired a room,' David said, and led the way to the lifts.

Leon was alone with a scholarly looking gentleman who was introduced as Mr Claude Demaine, the lawyer representing the Crown Prosecution Service in the case of Peter Sarpong. Kwame was offered a seat with his usual glass of water already in place on a side table. The others were busy with coffee and biscuits and Kwame was invited to join them.

'Mr Demaine and I have already reviewed the case,' Leon said, 'and it seems that the appeal for early release is well founded. Mr Sarpong has been a model prisoner, well behaved, studious and hard working. We are warned that with the present situation of over-crowding in our prisons we will need a powerful argument to succeed in opposing his appeal.'

Kwame knew that he looked glum and wanted more time to think. He was relieved that Leon continued, 'It seems to me that our main case is based on the recent demise of the Kumasi communication centre and consequent loss of effectiveness of the Ghanaian distribution network in the Coventry-Warwick area. In our estimation, if Mr Sarpong is repatriated to Ghana there is real danger of a revival of activity in Kumasi. In the unlikely event of his being allowed to remain in Britain, there is a danger of a revival of drug sales in the Coventry area.'

'This argument is unlikely to prevail,' said Mr Demaine, 'because it could apply in the case of every criminal: they could all be suspected of going back to their old ways. Mr Sarpong has paid the penalty for his past crimes and cannot be further punished for crimes not yet committed. We need something more: a special reason for suspecting him of returning to his old ways.'

Leon looked at Kwame. 'What else do we have?'

'Professor Arthur's wife, Akos Mary, who gave evidence against Sarpong at his trial, fears that he may take revenge on her or on her family.'

'Mrs Arthur is in England, am I right?' It was Mr Demaine who asked the question. 'Yes,' said Kwame.

'Would she be in danger if Mr Sarpong is deported back to Ghana and denied re-entry?'

'Mrs Arthur will want to return to Ghana from time-to-time, and if she did, she could be in danger. I would also question whether the restriction on travel to the UK could be permanently applied to Peter?'

'I can't be sure about that.'

'Then the danger persists.'

'Do you have anything else, Kwame?' Leon asked.

'I'm also afraid for myself and my family,' Kwame said. 'Peter Sarpong might suspect that I had something to do with his arrest and the arrest of his uncle, George Debrah.'

'He died in prison in Ghana, didn't he?' asked the lawyer.

'He did.'

Mr Demaine turned to Leon. 'We might have something here. It could be argued that we can provide protection in the UK but we cannot guarantee protection in Ghana. Both Mrs Arthur and Mr Mainu are Ghanaians who might return to Ghana with their families at any time. So Mr Sarpong free in Ghana could pose a danger. We can argue this point but I fear that in the absence of a specific threat it is still a weak case.' The lawyer paused to contemplate this bleak outlook and then asked Kwame, 'Before his arrest, did Mr Sarpong ever threaten you directly?'

'Yes he did, they were what you call "veiled threats" but I understood them clearly enough and they were directed against my family, especially at the time when I was here as a student but my family was still in Ghana.'

'Why did he need to threaten you at that time?'

'He tried to recruit me to help market the drugs and I took it that he was warning me not to pass on any of the things he had told me.'

'What had he told you?'

'He said that he could supply cannabis, heroin and cocaine; that he was aiming to expand his sales force and target sales more on young people in schools, clubs and discos.'

'That sounds like a serious reason to threaten you.'

'We took these threats to Mr Mainu and his family very seriously at the time,' Leon added, 'and we provided safe accommodation for his family until after the arrests.'

'Then I believe we have a stronger case,' said Mr Demaine. 'Can you let me have signed statements of what you have told me?'

'We will produce them today and send them to you directly,' Leon assured him.

Mr Demaine took his leave and Leon turned to his companions to announce that he had ordered lunch and they would be joined by Auntie Rose and Tam Gordon. There was a knock on the door and two waiters came in to set the table. They were closely followed by Auntie Rose and Tam. Leon waited until everyone was settled with a full plate and then he said to Tam with a grin, 'I think young Kwame has learned to respect his elders.'

'Who's been telling tales then?' replied Tam in the same vein.

'I asked David to complete his education,' Leon replied with his grin turned on Kwame.

'Trouble fears a beard!' Kwame said to Tam in Twi.

'What's that?' said Leon, looking confused.

'Kwame is telling me in a proverb that his culture teaches him to respect the wisdom of elders,' said Tam. 'I guess he didn't need any further education on that point.'

'No,' said Kwame, 'but I now understand much better what you've been doing in Ghana recently.'

Tam's grin faded to be replaced with a look of concern, 'The situation is declining quite rapidly. Hard drug usage is on the increase. Maybe it's relatively easy to persuade wee smokers to try something stronger.'

'The important question is: who's behind it?' Leon said. 'Is it South American traders moving in, Lebanese from Ghana and South America or our old Lebanese friends in Kumasi changing markets because of loss of cooperation from their Ghanaian associates?' He turned to Kwame, 'You tried to find out something about the Lebanese in Kumasi, didn't you?'

'Yes,' Kwame said, 'I talked to one young lady who had recently attended Lebanese parties. She told me of one Ghanaian woman who had become addicted to a hard drug supplied by a Lebanese man, but I saw no sign of systematic marketing by the Hanabis people in Kumasi. On the other hand, they seemed to be hard at work trying to find new ways to smuggle drugs to the UK.'

'Your motor pistons and coat hangers, eh?'

Leon tried one of his sweeping summaries. 'So our present understanding is that the Hanabis people are intent on re-establishing sales in the UK and the people developing the domestic market in Ghana are a new group yet to be identified. Whoever they are, they constitute a threat to peace and security and should be of increasing concern to the Ghana government. How can we come to an agreement in which our two countries collaborate in the war against drugs?'

'It won't be easy,' said Kwame. 'Members of Rawlings's government have been implicated in drug cases brought to court in Europe and the USA. These may be a few rogue individuals. Collectively, the government should be concerned about a growing scourge in their own country.'

'In the past you've hinted that we might need to wait for a change in government. Isn't there anything we could do now?'

'I see just one possibility but I'm not sure you would approve of it.'

'Let's hear it.'

'Well, it's widely known that Rawlings never makes a move without first consulting the fetish priests.'

'Go on.'

'We now have Kofi Adjare working with us and he is a wise man steeped in our traditional culture. It's just possible that he might be able to alert Rawlings's advisers to the dangers to our youth and through them persuade the president to negotiate your agreement.'

'Use black magic to fight the drugs trade?'

'It's a matter of using what influences people.'

'When are you next scheduled to go to Ghana?' asked Leon.

'We have a training course scheduled in Kumasi in July,' Kwame said. 'Strictly, I need not go, but I will go if I can do something useful.'

'I think you should go and have a chat with your friend Kofi Adjare. Please tell Professor Arthur to send us the bill in the usual way.'

Back in the King's School car park in Warwick, Kwame had a short wait before his Discovery was rocking to the excited clambering of five young women coming aboard with their scholarly impedimenta. Reluctantly he switched off the radio and speculated on the chances of some mature discussion emerging from the discordant babble. Tonight he was in luck, at least for the first part of the journey.

'Dad we need your help,' Akosua said, as she slammed the car door and searched for the seat belt socket.

'More jumbo tales?' Kwame asked with a laugh.

'No Dad, be serious; we have an assignment about trees.'

It was always a slow drive home and the traffic was as heavy as usual. Kwame was glad to have something to occupy his mind other than reading and re-reading the registration plate of the stationary vehicle ahead and trying to convert the three letters into a suitable acronym. 'How can I help you about trees?' he asked.

'We have to write an essay about trees in popular culture. We have loads of references to trees in English literature but we thought that we would like to do something different like we did with the elephants.'

'You mean give it a Ghanaian flavour?'

'Yes Dad, what can you tell us?'

'Well, have you thought why so many towns and villages in Ghana have names ending in "*ase*" meaning "under"?'

'Because they were founded under trees?'

'That's right. Can you think of a few place names like that?'

'There's Odumase or under the *odum* or iroko tree; Abease, under the oil palm; Besease, under the cola nut tree, and lots more.'

'Well done!'

Akosua wasn't satisfied, 'We need more than that Dad; can you think of any stories about trees?'

'You know the story about how Kumasi got its name.'

'Tell my friends, Dad.'

'Kumasi was established as the capital of Asante during the reign of Otumfuo Nana Obiri Yeboa who was *Kumasihene*, King of Kumasi, from about 1660 to 1680. There is a legend that one day the king asked his chief fetish priest where he should build his capital city. There were two suitable sites, so the king was advised to plant two *kum* trees, one at each location. One *kum* tree died so they called that place Kumawu, the kum tree has died. The other *kum* tree thrived so that was where they built the great city of Kumasi, the *kum* tree has stood. The very next *Kumasihene* was the first to take the title *Asantehene*, King of Ashanti.'

'Oh that's a good story,' said one of Akosua's companions. 'Can you tell us any more?'

'We have many stories called *anansesem* or spider stories. Many of them feature a central character, Ananse the spider, but many others are about other animals, people and gods. One is about how men came to learn the usefulness of the *odum* tree.'

'Tell us the story,' said a chorus of voices.

'It's quite a long story and Akosua has it in a book at home. We can ask her to write a summary for your assignment. I will give you just an outline.'

Kwame paused as he concentrated on negotiating a roundabout, weaving between lines of static traffic heading in other directions. Then he continued, 'Long ago, Nana Nyankopon, the creator god, lived on earth with his three wives. His favourite wife, Kraa, the youngest and most beautiful, gave birth to three sons called Gold, Silver and Copper but the senior wife, Akoko Antwiwaa was jealous and hid the newborn babies in the hollow of an *odum* tree. At the end of a long story Nana Nyankopon is told what has happened and Akoko is punished by being turned into a chicken.'

The young women sat silent for some time, a unique experience for Kwame who thought to himself: they're wondering which question to ask first. Then they were all talking at once.

'Can men marry three wives in Ghana?'

'In the Bible, Abraham had three wives.'

'I don't want my husband to have two more wives.'

'What is the moral of the story?'

'You shouldn't be jealous.'

'How does it tell us the usefulness of the *odum* tree?'

'It doesn't, it only draws attention to the tree.'

'How dreadful to be turned into a chicken!'

'How wicked to hide babies in a tree!'

Kwame listened as his daughter struggled to answer her friends' questions and comments but gradually his own concerns flooded his thoughts. Polygamy could be the answer to his problem. He had lived with Gladys and Afriyie for some time in Tema before he came to England; how pleasant it would be if he could live with Comfort and Afriyie. Jealousy would be the problem. If God's wives couldn't live in harmony how could he expect his wives to live in peace?

On the other hand, many men in Ghana succeeded in maintaining some sort of domestic harmony with multiple wives. Moslems had developed a system that encompassed up to four official wives under one roof and Christian men solved the problem by maintaining more than one household, one for the official wife and one for each junior wife or girlfriend. Polygamy was allowed under customary law in Ghana; it was left to each man to adjust his lifestyle to his particular circumstances.

Kwame knew that his father was against polygamy. Kwesi Mainu had only one wife and never married again after he had been abandoned. In such circumstances polygamy could have provided benefits. If Kwesi had had two wives maybe one would have stayed to care for husband and son. The arguments seemed finely balanced, and as always Kwame decided to give himself plenty of time to come to a decision.

The lively discussion he had provoked with the *odum* story continued unabated until one by one Akosua was deprived of her disputants and father and daughter drifted the last few hundred yards to their house in silence. As the exhausted pair tumbled down from the vehicle they were greeted by a distraught Afriyie with the news that Elsie had run away.

budgetary implications. They met regularly to review work progress and discuss future plans.

'How are the preparations for the July course coming along?' Tom asked as the deadline for travel arrangements approached in June 1996.

'They're going well,' Kwame said. 'Greg has an able helper in Kwaku Duah and with Mick's support I'm sure we will achieve another success.'

'They don't really need you then.'

'No, they can handle everything.'

'You know I plan to go with them this time.'

'We'll all go together.'

'Does Leon Thornet have work for you?'

'He does. I won't need the project to fund my travelling expenses.'

Tom sat silent for a while looking at the project budget so Kwame took the opportunity to make a suggestion. 'Our expenditure is a little short of budget, isn't it?' he said. 'We've received fewer visitors from Kumasi than planned and we've been saving on my trips.'

'Come out with it Kwame, what do you want to spend money on?'

'I would like to keep Duah here until we all go to Kumasi.'

'He's at the Land Rover apprentice school, isn't he?'

'That's right, and Greg and I would like him to stay there two or three weeks longer. There's a lot to learn. He's a bright young man and very enthusiastic; he won't waste his time.'

'Then it's OK with me.'

Again Tom lapsed into silence and Kwame waited patiently for his old friend to raise the next topic.

'Would you mind if I brought Akos Mary along?'

'Not at all, why do you ask?'

'Well, we want to leave Little Tom behind this time and we were wondering if your three girls could look after him.'

'I'm sure Afriyie and Akosua will be delighted to have Little Tom all to themselves.'

'And Elsie?'

'Oh sorry, I haven't told you. Elsie has run away.'

'Have you contacted the police?'

'No, Afriyie didn't want to do that. Elsie is an adult and free to do whatever she wishes.'

'But she doesn't speak much English.'

'That's true, but we suspect that she has gone to stay with other Ghanaians.'

'Will you try to trace her?'

'We will make some enquiries through the Pentecostal church.'

'Then I wish you the best of luck!'

'How is the project management committee these days?' Kwame asked.

'They've calmed down,' Tom said. 'They've seen that we've had no more trouble with visitors and the courses in Kumasi have been going well. I hope we can keep it like that.'

'How's my friend Professor Thomas?'

'He was asking about your diesel engine.'

'Ah yes, I wanted to talk to you about that.'

'I'm listening.'

'Mick and I have gathered all the information we can at this end and we've identified the foundries and machine shops that we will work with in Tema and Kumasi.'

'What's the next step?'

'We feel that we need to spend about six months in Ghana constructing and testing the prototypes.'

'They can't do it on their own, then?'

'We need to be there to keep the work going.'

'You *and* Mick?'

'I'm afraid so.'

'That's an expensive undertaking; I must give it some thought.'

When Kwame returned to his office he found a young man waiting for him whom he recognised as one of the technicians from the diesel engine laboratory where Nelson Evans-Agyei had been on attachment. 'Oh no, not another wood carving,' groaned Kwame, as he was handed a fertility doll of the type mass produced for the tourist trade in Ehwia and other Ashanti villages. It was carved with a small body and a big round head in the form of a flat disc. This one looked rather worse for wear, oil stained and indented.

'Didn't the police search your laboratory?' Kwame asked.

'They did, and very thoroughly too,' the young man replied, 'but this was found in a storeroom we use in another building. I guess the police missed the storeroom because nobody mentioned it to them.'

'How did it get in this state?'

'It was found underneath an engine when we were clearing out old stuff we didn't need. Nelson must have used a lever to raise the engine and slide the carving underneath. The engine was leaking oil and its weight must have indented the wood.'

'Thanks for bringing it to me; I will report it to the authorities straight away.'

Once again David Barney was summoned to Kwame's office. He arrived late in the afternoon. 'What have you got for me this time?' he asked. 'Another elephant?'

'No, this is called an *akuaba* or fertility doll.'

'Could it be stuffed with contraband?'

'That's for your people to find out.'

'Nelson didn't give this one to his girlfriend to hide?'

'No, he didn't want her to get pregnant!'

It had been a day of surprises but next morning an even greater surprise awaited Kwame when he reached his office. Sitting on his guest chair with her voluminous violet sari overflowing on both sides was Professor Thomas's secretary, Mrs Gupta. Kwame greeted his visitor, called for some tea to be brought, and settled himself behind his desk. It was when Mick brought in the tea that Kwame realised that he had not seen Sandra Garg for some time and this might be connected to Mrs Gupta's visit. 'Have you come about Sandra?' he asked.

'Yes, she has asked me to tell you that she is taking six months' leave.'

'She should have applied for leave in advance in the usual way.'

'Yes, she asked me to apologise on her behalf but she has been called home by her father.'

'Six months! She's already taken some leave. I doubt if she has that much leave due to her? I must check.'

'This will be maternity leave.'

So the *akuaba* had cast her spell in spite of Nelson's precautions! Kwame told himself that he didn't believe in that superstitious stuff but this was a startling coincidence. He struggled to formulate an appropriate response. 'Are we sure of the facts?' he asked.

'Oh yes, it's more than seven months and quite definite.'

'Her family is supporting her?'

'Yes, I persuaded her to tell her parents and they responded sympathetically. They pride themselves on being modern people, both in the medical profession, but this will be a challenge for all of them.'

'Well, thank you for helping Sandra. We were concerned about her welfare and hoped that you would help her but we didn't anticipate this outcome.'

Mrs Gupta's departure returned Kwame's office to its familiar monochrome. First he called Mick to let him know that Sandra had left the scene. 'I will need you to tie up Kwabena Addai's attachment and arrange his trip back to Kumasi,' he told him. Then he hurried to tell Tom of the sudden reduction in the strength of their team. They had expected Sandra to guard the home base while everyone else was in Ghana for the computer-aided drawing course. Now, at least one person would have to stay behind.

'Can we manage in Kumasi without Mick?' asked Tom. 'I wouldn't want to disappoint Akos Mary.'

'Now Duah is doing so well I'm sure he and Greg can look after things. I will fill in any gaps, but Mick will be disappointed.'

'He's been to Ghana three times, that's not bad.'

'No, he's been luckier than the others so far; he can't complain.'

Early in July, when Kwame was preparing to leave for Ghana again, he was asked to see Auntie Rose at the hairdressers' salon. This time they met in the comfortable upstairs room. 'Has Leon taken over this place as his Coventry base?' asked Kwame with a laugh.

'Leon does what he needs to do,' replied the little lady, half filling the big easy chair with her forward-pointing toes stretched out before her.

Kwame had got used to Auntie Rose's changeable behaviour, sometimes distant, sometimes close, so he tried to adjust himself to her serious demeanour. 'Do you go to church?' she asked.

'No, you know I don't.'

'Then why do you send your daughter?'

'Oh, you mean the Pentecostal church.'

'Why does she go there?'

'Why does anybody go to church?'

'Don't be flippant with me, Kwame Mainu.'

'Afriyie's apprentice, Elsie Ntim, ran away last month,' Kwame said, 'and Akosua thought that she might learn something of her whereabouts through the church.'

'Elsie doesn't attend the Coventry church anymore.'

'No, but some of her friends might still go there.'

'They'll be suspicious of Akosua, an educated *dadaba*.'

'She'll hide her English and play the part of a bush girl, a *kuraseni*.'

'So far she's succeeded, but I'm worried that one day she'll give herself away.'

Kwame realised that Auntie Rose must have seen Akosua at the Pentecostal church so he asked, 'What takes you to the den of charismatics?'

'What takes me everywhere I go?'

'The war on drugs?'

'Precisely.'

'So you think the place could be dangerous for Akosua?'

'It will be if the traffickers get re-established there.'

'Will you warn us if that happens?'

'Yes I will, but have you warned Akosua?'

'I've told her that if she sees or hears anything illegal she should stop immediately.'

'Good, then we'll leave the young lady to her academic assignment. Who knows? One day she might be a recruit for Leon's team.'

'I'm off to Ghana again next week,' Kwame said. 'Can I expect to see you in Kumasi this time?'

'Ah yes, your venture into juju! I shall miss seeing how that goes.'

'So you won't be going this time?'

'Comfort will manage very well without me.'

'How do you think Kofi Adjare will respond to my suggestion?'

'He'll not want to get mixed up with Ewe *okomfo*.'

'You may be right but it's worth a try.'

'Good luck!'

'By the way,' Kwame said, 'is there any news of the fertility doll?'

'As you suspected, it was filled with cocaine,' replied Auntie Rose. 'I hear that the girlfriend is pregnant. So they do work after all!'

'Don't tell me that,' said Kwame, 'I'm having difficulty staying rational as it is. These were two healthy young people who took no proper care. It was bound to happen!'

'With the help of *akuaba*!' insisted Ms *Mmoatia*.

'Will it mean a second offence for Nelson?'

'He was foolish not to mention the *akuaba* at his trial but I doubt if they will bother to prosecute a second time. After all, the drugs didn't reach the streets.'

'I doubt if there's a market for cocaine soaked in old engine sump oil!'

'Regrettably, some people would buy even that.'

16

African Anatomy

Kwame felt that he should pass on Auntie Rose's warning to Akosua and so that evening after dinner he asked to see her logbook. She showed him the three entries that she had made after attending three regular Sunday services. So far, she admitted, she had not made much progress in making friends of other girls her own age. There was the usual attention from middle-aged men that an educated *dadaba* found easy to brush off, but disguised as an illiterate bush girl she found more difficult to handle. It was easy to pretend not to hear English but less easy to decline sympathetic offers of generous help in Twi. 'Don't worry, Dad,' she said, 'they won't get anywhere.' Kwame hoped that she was right.

Akosua thought that Takoradi might help her get to know the other teenagers but she couldn't take him to a service. She wanted Afriyie or Kwame to bring Takoradi to meet her one day after a service as they were all coming out. 'I'm sure there will be some who can't resist him,' she said confidently.

'Let's hope he smells no drugs,' Kwame said, and then he warned her again about stopping at once if she detected anything illegal.

Kwame pondered for some time on this conversation. It was the mention of older men that played on his mind; not directly as a threat to Akosua but as a possible factor in Elsie's departure. He had never considered Elsie to be attractive to men but tastes varied, and if the lure was not sex but drugs, appearance and personality might be immaterial. So far they had assumed from what Elsie had told Akosua that Elsie had been influenced by peer pressure: what the other young women were saying and doing. He decided that if there was any hint that Elsie had been lured away by an older man he would tell Akosua to stop her investigation. He was glad that Auntie Rose was also monitoring the situation.

Kwame had not expected to see David Barney back so soon. This time he came early in the morning, just after they had all arrived at the office. Kwame finished a brief review of the day's tasks with Mick and Greg and went back to his office, closing the door. He sat down opposite to his waiting guest. 'I guess you're not the bringer of good tidings,' he said.

'No, I'm afraid not. We've found another fertility doll.'

'Where? How?'

'After the first one was found in the diesel engine storeroom, Leon ordered a thorough search of the place.'

'Was it in the storeroom?'

'Yes, in a bath of used engine oil underneath some old engine parts.'

'He must have been desperate to hide them quickly. Do you think there's more to find?'

'No, the search was very thorough.'

'Did this one contain cocaine like the first?'

'I'm afraid so.'

'Sandra is convinced he didn't know what was inside the elephant.'

'No, we have the impression that most couriers from Ghana think that they are carrying wee, cannabis, not hard drugs, but that's still illegal.'

'Has there been any progress with the plan to bring Bra Yaw here as a guest of Her Majesty's Government?' Kwame asked.

'Oh yes, Leon has got him immunity from prosecution.'

'When can we expect him?'

'We thought you might like to bring him home with you after your next trip.'

'He's no special friend of mine.'

'No, but we need you here when we talk to him.'

When David had gone Kwame walked to Tom's office to tell him about the fertility dolls. 'He has Professor Thomas with him,' Tom's secretary, Alice Brown, said. 'He's usually not long, it might be worth waiting.' Kwame picked up the *Telegraph* and settled to read but it was impossible to ignore the raised voices from the inner office.

'Does Prof Thomas have a new problem?' Kwame asked.

'He's heard about Miss Garg from Mrs Gupta and now he wants to travel to Ghana with Prof,' the secretary replied.

The inner office door opened and a red-faced professor emerged. Ignoring the occupants of the outer office, he marched straight ahead through the outer door.

'Ah Kwame,' said Tom, 'just the man I need.'

'It's good to be needed.'

'Did Alice tell you?'

232

'About Prof Thomas wanting to come to Kumasi?'

'Yes.'

'Why don't you let him come? Everyone falls in love with Ghana. He won't trouble us any more after that.'

'It's a heavy expense the project can't afford.'

'But Mick isn't coming.'

'Prof will cost us more; he likes to travel first class!'

'It will be worth it in the long-run.'

'I'm sure you're right, Kwame.'

'You didn't come here to talk about Prof Thomas,' Tom said.

'No, I came to tell you about the fertility dolls.'

'Is that what you call *akuaba*?'

'Exactly.'

'Still not managing it then, Kwame?'

'They're not for me; they were brought by Nelson.'

'With cocaine filling like the elephant?'

'That's what they tell me.'

Kwame explained to Tom how the first doll had been found by the laboratory technician when he was clearing out the storeroom. 'I should have told you earlier but it slipped my mind when we discussed Sandra's leave. At that time it hadn't been confirmed that it contained drugs.'

'Who found the second one?'

'Leon's people, they carried out a thorough search.'

'And they both contained cocaine!'

'At least none of it was sold on the street.'

'No, but all of it was found on our campus.'

Tom sat in silence, looking glum, but Kwame tried to see the glass half full. 'It's still the same case, not a new one,' he said, 'and Leon's people believe that the Kumasi couriers thought they were carrying wee, not hard drugs. We don't expect any other cases to arise. Let Prof Thomas come and see for himself. We'll explain everything that has been done in Kumasi to stop the drugs couriers as well as to select reliable visitors who won't become illegal immigrants.'

'Or impregnate our female staff?'

'There's not much we can do about that.'

'Speaking of absconders, is there any news of Elsie?' asked Tom.

'Nothing definite, Akosua is trying to trace her through the Pentecostal church.'

'Couldn't that be dangerous?'

'We hope not, but Auntie Rose is monitoring the situation.'

'It's good our girls have stopped going there.'

'Yes, but I'm not sure why they stopped.'

'According to Akos Mary, a woman was accused by several others of being a witch and they conducted a purification ceremony,' said Tom.

'More than they could stomach, eh?'

'I think they feared that one day one of them might be accused of witchcraft.'

'Yes, it's a danger facing anyone who seems to be better off.'

'Then it's my fault; I let Akos Mary drive there in the Range Rover.'

'Look on the bright side – your car might have saved your marriage!'

After a few moments reflection Kwame said, 'I'm sorry that my people have brought all this mumbo-jumbo to England. We Africans seem to have taken over many of the churches and used them to transfer our juju beliefs.'

'Don't take it too much to heart, Kwame. European missionaries took Christianity to Africa first. Our people started it!'

'It's a shame though that people with a religion seem to like the bad bits more than the good bits.'

'How do you mean?'

'Well, take blood for instance.'

'I'd rather not.'

'African fetish religions stress the power of blood in purifying and pacifying evil spirits, formerly with human sacrifice and these days with animal sacrifice. So they like the idea in Christianity of human sacrifice and the blood of Jesus providing cleansing of sins and protection from hell. They say "*Yesu mogya nka w'anim*", let the blood of Jesus splash your face!'

'Oh stop it Kwame, you're turning my stomach over!'

'Is there any reason for this revived morbid interest in religion?' asked Tom.

'It's connected with an idea I have for persuading the Ghana government to cooperate with the UK authorities over the control of drug trafficking,' said Kwame. 'The Rawlings government is fond of consulting fetish priests before deciding on a course of action. We are wondering if we can find a way of influencing policy by that route. So, I've been reading my old notes and realising anew how ridiculous it all is, but it's all for a good purpose.'

'Now you sound like Winston Churchill.'

'What did he say?'

'It was after Hitler invaded communist Russia. Churchill said that if Hitler invaded hell, he would at least make some favourable mention of the devil in the House of Commons.'

'The end justifies the means, eh?'

From black magic to the 'witchcraft of the whites', thought Kwame, wondering how Kwaku Duah was progressing in programming numerically controlled machine tools.

He made his way to the Land Rover apprentice training school where he found Mr Dawson, the workshop supervisor, in a jubilant mood. 'Your man is doing really well,' he said. 'I wish we had more students who took full advantage of their opportunities like your people do. Keep sending them to us; they encourage the others.'

'We're very grateful that you take them and make them feel at home,' said Kwame.

They walked through the workshop and found Kwaku hard at work on an NC milling machine. 'Are there many of these machines in British factories?' Kwame asked. 'The numbers are slowly increasing,' Mr Dawson replied, 'but we are still a long way behind Japan, the USA and Germany. Our labour costs are high and we must use many more NC machines and robots if we are to raise our productivity to the level of our international competitors. Seeing the enthusiasm of young Mr Duah I wouldn't be surprised if computer-controlled machines brought rapid industrialisation to countries like Ghana. You could soon be taking over production from the old country.'

'How do you think our people at home will receive NC machines?' Kwame asked Kwaku.

'They'll love them,' Kwaku said. 'We all like easy ways of doing things and workshop owners always want to manage with as few employees as possible. Fewer workers means fewer people to watch. These machines will work for you all day, never make a mistake, never ask for a pay rise and never steal any tools or materials. What more could you want?'

Kwame was reminded of a story Dr Jones had told him about a visit to Nairobi in the early 1970s. There the TCC director had met a lady who owned a single automatic machine of the pre-electronic era. The machine produced dressmaker's pins at a rate to meet the whole market demand of Kenya, Uganda and Tanzania. The lady was sitting in a shed beside her prized possession watching her one employee: a technician who maintained the machine and kept it supplied with raw material. The lady was growing rich but the industry provided employment for only one person. Could this be the future of industry in Ghana? If so, the benefits would be narrowly focused, and wide-scale poverty would be likely to persist. With a shudder, he turned again to Kwaku.

'Are you ready to fly home with us next week?'

'Yes, I've learned a lot, but now I'm keen to return to Kumasi and help Greg with the computer-aided drawing course.'

The day before he was leaving for Ghana, Kwame received a note from Sandra.

Leicester
12 July 1996

Dear Kwame,

I was sorry to leave so suddenly but I know that Mrs Gupta has explained the circumstances. I have much appreciated your kindness and understanding and look forward to rejoining the team in the New Year.

The twins are due on 25 July!

Regards,
Sandra

It was by far the largest exodus in which Kwame had taken part. In addition to Kwame, Tom and Akos Mary, there were Professor Thomas, Greg Anderson and Kwaku Duah. Professor Thomas had been persuaded to forgo his first-class seat for business class, but as Tom and Akos Mary felt obliged to accompany him, the cost was still far above budget. Kwame settled into his tourist-class seat with Greg and Kwaku as his companions. He sympathised with Greg as they both manoeuvred their long legs to adjust to the less-than-generous seat pitching. He envied Kwaku his modest stature.

Tom had confided in Kwame that he hoped Prof Thomas would restrict his consumption of alcohol on the flight because he knew that his academic colleague was quite unprepared for the hot damp blanket that would envelop them as they emerged from the aircraft in Accra. 'It'll be up to you to catch him,' Kwame said, 'I'll be too far back in the exit queue to be of any assistance.' When the time came, he watched with his nose to the window as Tom and Akos Mary supported the red-faced portly professor on their way down the steps from the aircraft and across thirty metres of tarmac to the air-conditioned terminal building.

Kwame and his tourist-class companions caught up with the business-class trio as they waited for the solitary carousel to deliver their luggage. The rugby scrum around the carousel was as intense as ever and Professor Thomas stood back from the melee. When he saw Kwame he said that he relied on him to retrieve his suitcases and Kwame assured him with a smile that he would guarantee their safety. Then he stopped the professor pulling sterling banknotes from his wallet and heading for the foreign exchange counter with a few words about far better rates on the high street.

Some cases that had arrived early had been removed from the carousel by airport staff and now stood waiting for collection a short way off. Kwame retrieved the professor's two matched valises and led the way to the customs benches where with a few words of Twi the luggage was marked with chalk and passed through unopened. The professor marched proudly on past the line of less-fortunate passengers with their exposed belongings undergoing a thorough rummaging by customs officials.

Professor Thomas had regained his composure in the air-conditioned confines of the arrivals hall but Kwame knew that the real challenge would be faced when they emerged into the hot stagnant air of the Accra night and the dense mass of excited welcomers. The secret of ameliorating this culture-shock-inducing experience lay in planning for self-sufficiency.

If the professor emerged carrying his own suitcases he would be overwhelmed by an army of would-be porters clutching at his luggage. So Kwame took one bag and asked Kwaku to carry the other. The second assault wave would be mounted by taxi drivers. So Kwame asked Akos Mary to go ahead and find the TCC driver who was there to meet them and bring him as close to the exit as possible. Kwame knew from experience that the assault of the taxi drivers was quickly abandoned once the chosen driver had been clearly identified.

Even though he had made these preparations, Kwame realised that the dash from the arrivals hall to the car could still be traumatic for the virgin visitor. They would be required to force their way through a dense crowd, made up not only of porters, taxi drivers and persons of less-honourable intent, but also of extended families of excited relatives and friends all intent on attracting the attention of their arriving travellers and blind to the presence of everyone else.

Kwame was relieved to find that the TCC driver had brought a mate to help with the luggage so he quickly organised a bodyguard around Professor Thomas and led his cohort into battle, hoping that he had done enough to frustrate any would-be bag snatcher or pick-pocket. Reaching the faithful Land Rover they carefully inserted the heavily perspiring professor into the sole upholstered passenger seat next to the driver, piled the luggage in the back, and scrambled onto the remaining seats. Then they took a short break to draw breath, calm the spirits and audit the luggage, before plunging into the chariot race to their hotel in downtown Accra.

'Well done, Kwame,' said Tom, using one of his few useful Twi phrases, and Akos Mary added her congratulations. 'How is he?' she asked.

'I can't say,' Kwame replied. 'I'm just hoping that he likes his cool room at the hotel.' The professor sat in silence with his seatbelt tightly fastened across his damp shirt, staring wide-eyed at the semi-structured chaos of the traffic. Thinking of the long uncomfortable drive to Kumasi the next day, Kwame asked the driver about the condition of the road. The answer was not reassuring. 'It's normal,' he said.

Having eaten on the plane, none of them felt hungry and so as soon as they reached the hotel they dispersed to their rooms for showers and bed. Kwame asked them to assemble at 06.00 in the dining room for breakfast so that they could make an early start to Kumasi. He would have liked to start even earlier but the dining room would not have been open and he doubted if Professor Thomas would agree to travel on an empty stomach.

Setting out at about 07.00 Kwame anticipated about one hour's comfortable driving followed by three hours that would feel almost unbearable to anyone unaccustomed to tropical heat. Kwame remembered Sandra's distress on this journey and worried about the professor who was much older and less fit. He discussed the issue with Tom who said, 'We must have a stop on the way for a cold drink.'

'Then I'll tell the driver to pull into the SOS Children's Village rest stop after Kibi.'

They assembled in the dining room as planned but it was past 06.30 before a waiter appeared and they were able to order food and drink. The food was slow in coming and Kwame had to sit and watch most of his comfortable hour disappear before they were crammed into the vehicle and battling with the rush hour traffic to escape from Accra. Another hour passed before they emerged through Achimota police barrier and they could feel that they were out of the big city and on the road to Kumasi. By then the cool of the morning was a rapidly fading memory.

A long stretch of road was under reconstruction and they were forced to run on a red rutted laterite surface in a cloud of orange-red dust. Occasionally they passed a small tanker truck spraying water on the surface of the road and trailing a few hundred metres of dust-free road that provided the travellers with a few seconds of respite. It wasn't long before Professor Thomas was showing visible signs of distress. Sitting bravely in his lonely front passenger seat, his once white shirt was orange-red with darker damper patches. He struggled to protect his face behind wrap-around dark glasses, an ex-army wide-brimmed soft hat pulled well down at the front and a handkerchief tied over his nose and mouth.

It was with considerable relief that the dust cloud vanished abruptly and they found the vehicle running on a smooth tarmac surface. Through universal sighs of relief Kwame imagined he could hear prayers that the tarmac would last all the way to Kumasi, but as suddenly as it had stopped the dust cloud started again and Kwame listened to the laughter of the spirits of the forest.

Tom was growing increasingly alarmed. 'When are we stopping for that cold drink?' he asked.

'Not long,' replied the driver, but Tom had been to Ghana enough times to know that 'not long' was always 'too long' for most Europeans.

It is a curious phenomenon that even 'too long' can come to an end, and the vehicle turned off the road to the right and into the designated parking space of the SOS Children's Village rest stop. Here were some seats in the shade and a chance to buy locally made meat pies and at least one variety of internationally marketed soft drink. Kwame and Tom helped Prof Thomas down from his high perch in the vehicle and over to what appeared to be the most comfortable chair on offer. There he slumped, idly beating the dust from his hat, while the others gathered a variety of goodies to tempt his refreshment.

'I'm sorry that the journey is so hot and tiring,' Kwame said to his slowly recovering inquisitor.

'Please don't concern yourself, young man,' replied the professor. 'If one is to trek into the bowels of the Dark Continent in the footsteps of Mungo Park, one must be prepared to accept some discomfort.'

Tom looked anxiously at Kwame who limited his reply to, 'Er, quite!'

Kwame had had ample opportunity over the years to observe the remarkable powers of ice-cold soft drinks to suppress the more obvious symptoms of heat stroke and on this occasion he was not disappointed. Much to his surprise it was Professor Thomas who suggested that the journey should be resumed. 'Mungo Park didn't have the advantage of a cold Coke, eh?' Tom whispered in Kwame's ear as they watched Greg and Kwaku reload the professor into the Land Rover.

The spirits of the forest accepted their defeat graciously and the rest of the journey was on metalled road that soon began its undulating path into Ashanti Region and to its famous city of the Golden Stool, Kumasi. Kwame hoped that even Professor Thomas could not be entirely insensitive to the historical and cultural significance of the city as they passed under the great concrete stool at the entrance to the Kwame Nkrumah University of Science and Technology and gazed across its extensive parkland at its flowering trees and fine modern buildings. He was sure that after a cold shower and a good lunch the professor would be ready to meet his partner university in a spirit of mutual respect and understanding.

Professor Thomas's academic reputation had preceded him and Kwame had no difficulty in arranging a meeting with the vice chancellor. The professor was warmly welcomed and asked to sign the visitors' book, a record of the passage of the academically and politically distinguished personages of the past half century. Similar, though lower-key, welcomes were extended by the dean of the School of Engineering and the director of the Technology Consultancy Centre. A business meeting was arranged for the following day.

That evening Kwame had arranged a special event. He had asked Comfort to prepare dinner for Professor Thomas, Tom, Akos Mary and himself at her house at Nhyiasu. He drove the party there shortly after 5 pm, in time to appreciate and enjoy the setting in daylight. They ascended the hill and turned into Nhyiasu, with its wide tree-lined roads, elegant colonial residences and extensive bougainvillea-bedecked gardens. As he turned into the driveway and approached the house, Kwame glanced to his right and was gratified to see a suitably impressed expression on the professor's round red face.

Comfort welcomed her guests at her front door, attired in the full splendour of a traditional dress that was liable to induce arrhythmia in the sternest of male breasts. Akos Mary, who was also spectacularly adorned, was visibly shaken by the impact her hostess made on the men in her company. Comfort invited the party to take drinks in the garden in the cooler evening air as the sun went down. Paying particular attention to Professor Thomas's partialities, she flattered her principal guest by her solicitude.

Much to Kwame's delight, Comfort did not rely solely on her own feminine charm to establish a decorous setting. The drinks and delicacies were served by young ladies who had obviously been chosen with great care. Seeing both the appreciation and the question in Kwame's expression, Comfort whispered in Twi, 'I chose girls that Mrs Dodoo trained.' So these comely and attentive waitresses had been instructed at the university swimming pool restaurant by the Nigerian catering guru! Guessing that some of their sisters were employed in the kitchen, Kwame looked forward to the dinner with even greater anticipation.

Comfort had prepared both Ghanaian and international dishes, so there was something to suit all tastes. Professor Thomas was persuaded to try small samples of local dishes but gained more sustenance from more familiar fare. Akos Mary could not resist her favourite snails with fufu

240

and Tom and Kwame tried to do justice to almost everything presented to them. Comfort excused her modest intake on the grounds of watching her figure, a pastime shared by her three male guests.

After the meal, relaxing with more drinks, Comfort asked Professor Thomas how he liked Ghana. 'So far,' he said, 'apart from the road from Accra, I've been impressed by all I have seen and heard. My welcome has been most gratifying and I find all the people friendly and cheerful. I must admit that Ghana is much different from how I imagined it to be and I am delighted that my colleagues assented to my request to come and see for myself.'

Kwame looked across at Tom who was beaming back at him in Comfort-induced euphoria. Kwame realised anew how appropriately his ex-wife had been named.

The business meeting took place in the dean's office next morning, Wednesday 16 July. The TCC director was present with Tom, Kwame and Professor Thomas. The dean took the chair and repeated his welcome of the guests from Warwick. Then he briefly reviewed the visitors' programme. It began, he recalled, with Miss Peggy Osei-Wusu and Kwaku Darko, continued with Stephen Okunor, Nelson Evans-Agyei and Yaa Williams and came up to date with Kwabena Addai and Kwaku Duah. He very much regretted that Miss Osei-Wusu and Mr Evans-Agyei had failed to return to Ghana but the other five academics had returned to post and all had expressed satisfaction with the training and experience gained at Warwick.

The TCC director said that his people were especially pleased with the experience of Stephen Okunor who had returned to his Suame workshop and started to produce and sell a gear-generating attachment for shaping machines. The TCC was also active in promoting the local manufacture of school science equipment in collaboration with Miss Yaa Williams of the physics department and they were now seeking to exploit the new glassblowing skills of Kwabena Addai.

The dean then invited Professor Thomas to speak. 'I am very happy to be here,' he began, 'and to hear of some successful impact of the visitors' programme, but what concerns me more is the fact that out of seven of your emissaries, two failed to return home. Not only that, but one person was convicted of having carried narcotics into the UK and another is suspected to have done so. My colleagues, Professor Arthur and Mr Mainu, look after the technical aspects of the programme. My mission is to satisfy myself that everything is being done to prevent the programme from being exploited by undesirables and criminals. Only in this way can we protect the reputations of our two institutions.'

In response, the dean outlined the process by which visitors were selected with the final approval resting with a committee composed of himself, the TCC director and Mr Mainu. 'In the past,' he said, 'someone inside the university was passing the approved list to drugs traffickers who then approached the visitors offering money in exchange for carrying packages. The informer has now been identified and has ceased his activity. Security has been tightened to prevent any other future informer gaining access to the information. In addition I am informed that the group of Ghanaians who were formerly involved in trafficking has been broken up and is no longer active.' He asked the TCC director and Kwame to confirm what he had said.

The professor had flown three thousand miles to settle this issue and he wasn't going to be easily satisfied, 'Is there any guarantee that the old situation will not revive?' he asked.

'Long-term guarantees can never be given,' Kwame said, 'but the Kumasi-based group of drugs traffickers has been disbanded after two of its senior people died, another was persuaded to stop and two more were forced to stop by order of the *Asantehene*, the King of Ashanti.'

'This is what you told us in Warwick,' Professor Thomas said. 'Can anyone else confirm these facts?'

There was silence until the dean said, 'Mr Mainu worked on the problem here during his last two visits to Kumasi. What we know is what he told us but we have no independent confirmation of the details. For the university, I can say that we are now well aware of the problem and will be vigilant in trying to prevent a repetition.'

The professor looked directly at Kwame. 'What can you do to confirm the facts of what you have told us?'

'Can I use your telephone?' Kwame asked the dean, and following a nod of approval he called Comfort.

'Can I bring the professor back again tonight?'

'Did I make that big an impression?'

'Even bigger, but I want you to set up a meeting.'

'For what purpose?'

'To confirm the break-up of the Kumasi cartel.'

'Then you want to see Kofi Adjare, Bra Yaw and Kofi Boateng?'

'Exactly, can you do it?'

'I think so; what time will you come?'

'Shall we say 6 pm?'

Kwame had agreed with Tom that they would give priority to the needs of Professor Thomas. When that task was finished the professor would depart and they would be free to attend to other matters. So they both welcomed the opportunity to return to Comfort's house in a serious attempt to establish the facts of the changed situation.

Comfort had moved swiftly to gather her party and they were ready to greet the visitors from Warwick. Kwame introduced the two Kofis and Bra Yaw to the English professors. Professor Thomas remarked on two men bearing the same name and asked if 'Kofi' had a special meaning.

'It means born on Friday,' Kofi Boateng told him. 'Which day of the week were you born on?'

'I must be a Kofi too,' the professor replied. 'My parents always told me I arrived just in time for the weekend.'

Kwame laughed. 'I knew a boatbuilding company in Accra that was owned by three Kofis so they called if Kofifo; now we have a new Kofifo.'

Following the technique he had learned from Leon, Kwame let the small talk run on while they attempted to exhaust the liquid contents of Comfort's refrigerator. He observed that Professor Thomas was growing more and more relaxed under the twin influences of the convivial atmosphere and locally brewed Star beer. This is good but I mustn't let it go too far, he told himself, so he decided to introduce the purpose of the meeting.

'Professor Thomas has come to visit us from the University of Warwick in England,' Kwame said. 'Some of our young men and women from KNUST have been visiting Warwick to gain new skills and experience to help their work in Ghana. Unfortunately, some of them have been asked to carry drugs to England and have got into trouble with the police. Professor Thomas is very concerned about this situation and wants to be sure that when we send people in the future they will not be carrying drugs.' He repeated what he had said in Twi to make sure that his compatriots had understood.

Then Kwame asked Kofi Boateng to explain to the professor the part he had played in arranging the transport of drugs. 'I am a student at KNUST,' he began, 'and I knew someone working in the dean's office who would sell me the names of the people selected to travel to Warwick.'

'What did you do with the names?' asked the professor.

'I gave them to Bra Yaw.'

'Yes,' said Bra Yaw, 'and I would talk to the people and try to persuade them to carry a package to London.'

'Did you tell them what was in the package?'

'No.'

'Did you give them money?'

'Yes, of course.'

'Did they all agree?'

'No, only two of them agreed.'

'What part in all this was played by the other Kofi?' asked Professor Thomas looking at Kofi Adjare. Kwame quickly repeated the question in Twi, and anxiously waited for the albino linguist to reply. Would he mumble an obscure proverb in Twi? You could never be sure with Kofi Adjare. 'My role was in communication,' he began, much to Kwame's relief, 'I would inform our people in the UK of the details of the delivery.'

Now the professor reached the nub of his inquiry, 'Can you all assure me that you have stopped this activity?'

It was Bra Yaw who replied. 'Some years ago we were led by two big Kumasi traders but an Englishman persuaded them to link up with a Lebanese company. We small boys never liked this but were forced to go along with it. The Englishman was sent to prison in England and our two big people were sent to prison in Ghana. Now both the elders have died and *oboroni* is still in prison, so the connection to the Lebanese is broken. Our senior, Kofi Adjare, decided to stop the drugs work and we agreed with him. Now we have all stopped.'

The professor seemed to be satisfied. 'Do I have your word that you will never again try to send drugs with the KNUST people coming to Warwick?' The three men rose and solemnly offered their right hands to be firmly gripped in turn.

'This calls for a celebration!' Comfort cried and fetched a bottle of gin which Kofi Adjare used for pouring a modest libation to the ancestors before dispensing more generous portions to the living. Then Kofi Adjare and Bra Yaw 'begged for the road' and took their leave, and Kofi Boateng asked Kwame for a lift back to the campus.

Comfort insisted they did not need to rush off and they settled down for more drinks and conversation. Although Professor Thomas was satisfied with the outcome he still had many questions about how it had all happened. He first turned to Tom, 'I suppose you knew about all this?'

'Kwame kept me well informed about important developments but I hadn't met the people before,' he replied, 'and I've picked up more details here tonight.'

Then the professor asked Comfort about her role in winding up the cartel. 'Oh, I just helped Kwame,' she said with befitting modesty but Kwame leapt to her defence.

'Without Comfort we could never have succeeded.'

'What I still don't understand,' persisted Professor Thomas, 'is what motivated these three men to stop their lucrative involvement with hard drugs?'

'First of all,' Kwame said, 'Kofi Adjare was never in it for money. He had cultural reasons for wanting to get back at the British. What persuaded them all to stop was the realisation that hard drugs were being pushed to the young people of Ghana. The country was no longer merely a transit stop between producing countries and markets in Europe, but was also becoming a market in its own right. They suspected that Lebanese in Ghana and traders from South America were selling drugs here, and they wanted to take a stand against Ghanaians corrupting the youth of their own country.'

'From the passion with which you speak,' said Prof Thomas, 'I deduce that you have joined the crusade to rid your country of this scourge.'

'My aim,' Kwame said, 'is to promote cooperation between Ghana and the UK in sharing information and proven methods of detection to combat the drugs trade in both countries.'

'Then I wish you every success,' replied the professor, 'and if I can be of assistance in any way do not hesitate to give me a call.' He turned to Tom to emphasise his point, 'I hope that you have taken due note of what I have said, Professor Arthur.'

'Oh, absolutely!'

On the drive back to the campus the professor said that in two days he had completed his primary mission in Kumasi. He would now like to spend one more day looking around the university and getting to know more people. Then the next day, Friday, he would return to Accra and London. Kwame and Tom promised to make the necessary arrangements and suggested that his journey would be easier if he flew to Accra. Much to their surprise he replied that he preferred to travel by road in order to feel that he had really penetrated deep into the heart of the continent. Kwame was gratified at the professor's anatomical promotion of Kumasi.

17

Okomfo

After dropping Professor Thomas at his guest chalet Kwame asked Tom how he proposed to spend the rest of his stay in Ghana. 'I'll follow Prof around until he leaves,' he said, 'and then I want to take Akos Mary off on holiday for a week or two. We're planning to visit the Mole National Park then spend some time relaxing on a beach. I've been to Elmina so I would like to spend some time at Busua and Dixcove.'

'Then I'll work with you and Prof Thomas this week,' Kwame said, 'and delay my other duties until after you leave.'

Next morning Tom and Prof Thomas were keen to see the arrangements being made for the computer-aided drawing course so Kwame took them to the computer laboratory where Greg was busy setting up the machines. They counted twenty-one computers, most of them ready with the appropriate software installed, but Greg was not satisfied. 'We have twenty-eight people signed up and we would like to be ready for a full house of thirty,' he told them. 'Kwaku is scouring the campus trying to borrow more machines. Mick has stressed that the participants coming on these courses vary widely in ability and education, so I think it's very important for each student to have his or her own computer. That way, everyone can progress at their own pace.'

Kwaku came back with good news. 'Yaa has found us three machines from the physics department, and Kojo Doe and one other engineering lecturer have promised to lend us their personal computers for the duration of the course. Kojo already has the software installed on his machine, but we will need to work on the other computer.' Greg observed that they were still four short but Kwaku told him not to worry, he would find the rest.

'The lady you mentioned, Yaa,' Tom said, 'is she the Miss Williams who came to Warwick?'

'That's right,' Kwaku said, 'and Kojo was unsuccessful but still hoping to come.' 'Then we must remember to thank Yaa when we visit her later,' said Tom. 'As for Kojo, maybe he could be considered again.' Kwame was happy; it seemed that Tom was assured about the future of the partnership.

'Come and see this,' Greg said, turning one of the computers to show the screen to his visitors.

'Has Stephen Okunor seen this?' Kwame asked, recognising the drawing of the gear-generating attachment. 'He'll be pleased that you're using his project on the course.' Tom explained to Prof Thomas how Greg had helped Stephen Okunor to produce the drawings in Coventry.

'There's the prototype machine on that bench,' Greg said. 'Stephen brought it in this morning for us to demonstrate on the course.'

'It also demonstrates perfectly what we are trying to achieve through the partnership project,' said Kwame proudly.

On Monday 22 July Kwame saw Tom and Akos Mary off on their trip to the north and returned to his chalet. He wanted to telephone Comfort and arrange the meeting with Kofi Adjare but it was still too early to disturb a late riser. So he settled down to a lonely breakfast of *gari*, groundnuts and evaporated milk, a favourite since his childhood.

He was not alone for long; someone was knocking on his chalet door. Wiping his mouth, he rose to find an attractive young woman on the doorstep. Her face and figure were indelibly imprinted on his memory but he searched in vain for an identity. 'Do you remember me? Janet Dery?' said the visitor. 'Comfort sent me to you last year. You asked me about the Lebanese parties and drugs and you gave me twenty pounds.'

'Of course,' Kwame said, 'it's good to see you again; come in.'

Kwame asked if she would like to share his breakfast, an offer that was eagerly accepted. So they sat in silence broken only by the inevitable slurping sounds until both were satisfied. 'Shall I prepare some hot chocolate?' Kwame asked, but Janet said that she preferred water, and so did he.

As so often happens, Kwame wasn't sure how to discover the reason for the visit. It wasn't polite to ask too directly.

'Do you want to hear more about the drugs?' Janet asked abruptly.

'Yes,' he replied, 'what more can you tell me?'

'I told you that I stopped going to the Lebanese parties when I had enough money to start trading.'

'I remember. Comfort helped you to start selling shoes.'

'That's right.'

'So how have you got on?'

'Comfort showed me how not to spoil the trading money. She's a good woman.'

'You're right, but what did you come to tell me?'

'The Hanabis people asked me to go to a special party. They offered me a lot of money.'

'How was the party special?'

'Cecilia Obeng-Mensah, she's Suleiman Hannah's girlfriend, said that some of their Lebanese brothers were coming from a country in South America.'

'Venezuela?'

'I think that was the name.'

'Did you go?'

'Yes, I wanted the money for my business.'

'Do you want to tell me what happened?'

'Only about the drugs, they wanted to give us the new ones you asked me about.'

'Did they call it cocaine or coke?'

'That might have been the name.'

'Did you take any?'

'No, I remembered what you said, so I refused.'

'You did the right thing, well done!'

Kwame realised that Janet had brought him confirmation of what they had long suspected: the Lebanese in Kumasi were linking up with compatriots from South America and they were introducing cocaine to Ghanaians. He needed to know more, both to meet the needs of Leon in preventing exports to the UK and to fight the scourge in Ghana. He asked Janet if any of the girls had continued to use the new drug.

'Yes, a few of them have.'

'How do they get money to pay for the drugs.'

'Some use the money from the parties and some sell the drugs on the street and at schools.'

Kwame groaned; the problem had started sooner than he expected. Perhaps it had been going on for years but only now come to his notice. He wondered if the Lebanese were also reviving the traffic to the UK, 'Are any of the girls being asked to carry parcels to *aborokyiri*?' he asked.

'Yes, but not by the Lebanese.'

'By a Ghanaian?'

'Yes.'

'Do you know his name?'

'It's the same as the archbishop, Peter Sarpong.'

Now Kwame groaned aloud. 'Do you know him?' Janet asked.

'Yes, I'm afraid I do,' Kwame replied, swallowing hard and remembering his breakfast. It was a while before he stilled the whirlpool in his head and in his stomach. His companion waited patiently. She refilled his glass and took a sip of her own water.

As he regained control of his thoughts Kwame began to wonder if Peter Sarpong was acting alone or as an agent of the Lebanese. He remembered that last year Comfort had told him that Oboroni had not been the only link between the Ghanaians and the Lebanese; Uncle George had also played a part. Peter Sarpong was Uncle George's nephew and had been very close to his uncle. Was he also close to the Lebanese? He asked Janet if she thought Peter was working for the Lebanese. 'He could be but we only see him on his own; I can't be sure.'

Kwame was tempted to ask Janet to try to find out more but he realised he could be putting her in danger. He told her that he was grateful for her call and pressed four ten-pound notes into her hand. Her big smile signalled that her hopes had been realised. He strongly advised her to keep to shoe trading and to avoid contact with both the Lebanese and drugs. If she had any problems she should consult Comfort. Janet replied that she always did that.

After Janet had departed, Kwame sat trying to digest what he had learned. The reappearance of Peter Sarpong seemed to completely change the outlook. Happy thoughts of progress were replaced by dark fears of regression; feelings of satisfaction had dissolved into apprehension. Peter Sarpong free and returned to Ghana posed a threat to Kwame himself and to Akos Mary. It might also threaten to reverse all that had been achieved in disbanding the Ghanaian faction of the cartel. Would Bra Yaw and Kofi Boateng be able to resist the blandishments and threats that might be deployed to restore their participation?

Kwame felt that he had been forced to take several steps backwards. Problems he thought were solved seemed to have been re-energised and actions he was about to take appeared to have been put on hold. For nearly two years in Coventry Peter Sarpong had cast a dark shadow on his life. Even in prison he had been a cloud on the horizon. Now, restored to freedom, Peter Sarpong had become a great black cumulo-nimbus threatening thunder and lightning.

Kwame decided it was late enough to risk telephoning Comfort. He was in luck and she replied immediately. 'I wanted to call you to try to arrange a meeting with Kofi Adjare,' he said, 'but something else has come up. I need to see you urgently; could I come there tonight?'

'Not tonight, maybe tomorrow.'

'Why not tonight?'

'I have a date.'

'A date!'

'Yes, your old friend, Peter Sarpong, has invited me out for dinner.'

Now Kwame really was ready to part company with his breakfast and he reached the toilet only in the nick of time. During the short period that they had been conjoined his world had fallen apart. He remembered how Peter Sarpong had always admired Comfort, commenting on her good dress sense and telling Kwame what a lucky man he was. Was he now seizing his chance to move in and gain revenge at the same time? His dismay was further intensified as he recalled Tom's mother saying that Peter Sarpong was 'almost as handsome as Kwame'.

The telephone call was still open and a concerned Comfort was asking if Kwame was all right. 'Yes, fine,' he blurted out. 'Can we make it tomorrow?'

'Don't you want to ask about Peter?'

'Isn't that your private business?'

'No, Kwame Mainu, I want to find what he's up to. I'm worried he will undo all our good work by recruiting Bra Yaw and Kofi back into his gang.'

'Be careful! Janet was here this morning and she told me Peter is trying to recruit couriers, so he's definitely back to his old ways.

'Trust me.'

That's what he must do: trust Comfort. He was pleased that she had used that expression. Separated from him for many years, Comfort was an independent person and could do as she pleased. No doubt she had experimented with new relationships over the years that they had been apart. He had accepted the situation and chosen to live with Afriyie. Why did he now feel jealous if Comfort made a date with another man? His feelings were irrational, but they were still his feelings and he could not escape from them.

He realised that he should be grateful to Comfort. Faced with a surprising new problem, she had bravely chosen a course that might lead to a solution. It was more his problem than Comfort's, so he should be grateful that she was willing to help. During his recent visits to Kumasi they had begun to work as a team again with some success. He should regard Comfort's meeting with Peter Sarpong as a continuation of that process. He should – but it was difficult.

Kwame felt that he wanted a change of scene to clear his head so he jumped into the Land Rover and headed for his old battleground, Suame Magazine. He would immerse himself in its familiar sights, sounds and smells and recall selling market trolleys in his teens and promoting iron foundries in his twenties.

He had seen the magazine expand from a population of about seven thousand in 1973 to about seventy thousand in 1996; a remarkable ten-fold increase that did almost nothing to change its essential nature. Second only to the Ghana government as an employer, the magazine continued to suck in energetic and enterprising youths from rural villages all over the country and provide them with the basic skills to earn a livelihood as independent craftsmen and small-scale employers. He was proud to have been part of that evolutionary process and, with his colleagues at the TCC, to have been responsible for introducing much of the technology that made it possible. Here was where he felt at home; where real work was done and where he could exercise his professional skills.

Kwame went straight to the ITTU and to the GAMATCO workshop where Stephen Okunor was producing the new product that he had developed on his visit to Warwick. Kwame congratulated the master craftsman and thanked him for his support for the computer-aided drawing course. Stephen said that he was glad to return the help and hospitality he had received on his visit to Coventry.

When Kwame asked about the progress of his work Stephen said that the collapse of Yugoslavia had robbed him of his best customer, the Tomos motorcycle assembly plant. It was the Tomos plant in Kumasi that had provided GAMATCO with regular orders for hundreds of gear wheels and chain sprocket wheels for new production. Now GAMATCO was reduced to making replacement parts for imported Japanese motorcycles. It was for this reason that he was keen to introduce new products like the gear-generating attachment.

Kwame asked if any other assembly plant had shown interest in buying parts locally, but Stephen replied that none had approached him or anyone else he knew in the magazine. Kwame recalled that when the participants of the first engineering drawing course had visited the Neoplan bus assembly plant a year before, some collaboration with the magazine had been suggested. Stephen said that as far as he knew nothing had happened since. It seemed that multinational corporations had little interest in assisting grassroots industries. 'It's up to us to help ourselves,' added Stephen, and Kwame had to agree.

'What's new here?' Kwame asked.

'Have you seen the big casting Edward Opare has made?' replied

Stephen. The two engineers walked around the ITTU to where the little Akuapem chief technician had established his foundry. They found the proprietor and his assistant fettling a casting that appeared to be a replacement part for a large earth-moving machine.

'It was ordered by the British contractor on the Tamale road,' Edward explained.

'But it must weigh over a hundred kilograms,' said Kwame. 'How did you cast it with a furnace of only sixty kilograms capacity?'

'I fired up my furnace and the ITTU furnace in parallel,' Edward replied. 'Then we poured the cast iron from both furnaces together.'

'Well done!' Kwame said, impressed by his colleague's resourcefulness.

Kwame knew from his experience with GRID in Tema that such efforts can save months of delay in ordering spare parts from manufacturers overseas. When they needed a replacement part in a hurry, big foreign firms were eager enough to take advantage of local technical capability. He wondered aloud to his companions why foreign companies weren't more interested in helping to establish such capabilities.

That evening, back in his chalet, Kwame couldn't stop his mind constantly drifting to thoughts of Comfort alone with Peter Sarpong. She had told him that she wanted to find out what Peter was doing and he shared her curiosity with a personal intensity. He couldn't help hoping that the ravages of nearly a decade in prison had diminished Peter's masculine allure. He knew that Peter was clever and unlikely to give anything away, even to someone as astute and intuitive as Comfort. The whole mission seemed to Kwame too dangerous to justify the possible benefit. In an attempt to hasten sleep he told himself that tomorrow all would be clear. He told himself many times before dreams replaced his fears.

The next evening, after work, Kwame again drove up the hill to Nhyiasu. In his anxious state he had come too early and Comfort had not yet returned from the market. With a grimace he opened a shoe catalogue, the only reading material in view. It will be a long wait, he told himself.

In order to pass the time he set himself the task of discovering which style of shoe could conceal the greatest quantity of contraband. He soon decided that those with a sole and heel combined in a thick wedge shape would be ideal. He was about to dismiss the whole exercise as useless because the shoe trade flowed from Britain to Ghana, not the other way, when he remembered that few people entered the aircraft with bare feet.

252

Comfort would probably know which styles were popular with female couriers commuting to London.

'Which pair are you planning to buy me?' Comfort must have come in the back way and entered silently. Now she was leaning over his shoulder, enveloping him in her perfumed aura. She leaned further forward to point to her preferred shoe and Kwame felt electrified as her hair brushed his cheek and her soft breast pressed on the back of his neck. 'I like that style,' she said.

'And no man could refuse you!' he whispered in her ear.

'Steady, Kwame Mainu, or you'll be asking me to come back.'

'I never wanted you to leave.'

'It was a big mistake and I'm sorry.'

'So you'll not be hitching up with Peter Sarpong.'

'Certainly not! But I'll tell you about our intimate dinner at Rose's Tavern.'

Comfort told Kwame what she had learned from Peter Sarpong. Peter had told her that he had returned to Kumasi and immediately contacted his old friends, Bra Yaw and Kofi Boateng. When he asked them about Kofi Adjare, they told him that since Mama Kate died Kofi had returned to working for Comfort as her driver.

'So he learned that you were living here?'

'Yes, that's how I got a dinner date.'

'Did you tell him I was here again?'

'Oh no, he didn't want to talk about you.'

'What did he talk about?'

'Do you really want to know?'

'Yes, I do.'

'Well, he told me how much he had always admired me; how he used to regret that I was already married; how he felt that his luck had changed because he found me here living alone, and lots more stuff like that.'

'Do you think that he was being honest or trying to befriend you for another purpose?'

'You know Peter; he has at least two faces.'

Kwame felt little reassurance but struggled to keep his mind working objectively, 'I don't suppose he said anything about drugs or being imprisoned,' he said glumly.

'That's right, nothing about those things.'

'So he gave you no hint about starting his old work again?'

'No'

'But Janet told me that he was trying to recruit people to be couriers flying to London.'

'So what's this about you and Janet?'

'She knocked at my door yesterday morning. I hadn't seen her since last year when you sent her to me.'

'Lower your chest, Kwame Mainu; can't you see I'm only teasing?'

'About Peter too?'

'Especially about Peter.'

Kwame tried to analyse the situation. 'So it seems that Peter has returned to his old ways but he didn't want you to know. One question now is whether Bra Yaw and Kofi Boateng will be persuaded to join him. You told me last year that his uncle was close to the Lebanese; is Peter working with them now, trying to reorganise the traffic to the UK? How can we find out?' Kwame didn't really want to hear the answer to the last question.

'Do you want me to see him again?'

'No I don't.'

'Oh Kwame, I don't have any feelings for him! I just want to find out more about his criminal activities.'

'I think it's too dangerous. Leave it to professionals like Auntie Rose.'

'Auntie Rose isn't around just now.'

'Then just leave it alone.'

'What should I do if he asks to see me again?'

'Think of an excuse to put him off.'

Kwame remembered why he had arranged this meeting in the first place. 'Is Kofi Adjare around?' he asked.

'He's in his quarters,' replied Comfort. 'Shall I call him?'

In a few minutes Comfort and Kofi returned and Kwame rose to greet the albino *okyeame*. 'You are welcome as the rain that ends the drought,' Kofi said, and Kwame hastened to warn him that he might change his mind when he heard his mission. First, however, they discussed the return of Peter Sarpong.

'*Osofo* has returned to gather his flock,' Kofi intoned, reminding Kwame that Kofi always used the name *osofo* (priest) for Peter during the time that he was sending coded messages for the drugs cartel in the UK. 'He is finding that many have strayed during his absence,' Kofi continued. 'The sheep will not enter the folds of the camel herders.'

'So you think Peter is trying to recruit couriers for the Lebanese, do you?'

'So says the one who fears the worm.'

'You heard this from Bra Yaw?'

254

The old albino nodded slowly and Kwame was reminded that he was expected to take Bra Yaw with him when he returned to the UK. Could he be sure of Bra Yaw's cooperation now that Peter Sarpong was back on the scene? 'Do you think that Bra Yaw will keep his promise to stop the drugs work?' he asked.

'The one who fears the worm hates the camel herders.'

'Yes, he told me the small people in the cartel disliked working with the Lebanese.'

'They took his sister and made her a harlot.'

'That explains a lot.'

Kwame was worried about Kofi's own position. 'Do you feel threatened by Peter's return?' he asked.

'Trouble fears a beard,' replied Kofi.

'I doubt if the cartel respects grey hairs or Ashanti proverbs.'

'One should not fear joining the ancestors.'

'That's easier said than done, but I admire your courage.'

Kwame wanted to move on to the matter of trying to persuade the Ghana government to collaborate with Britain in controlling the drugs traffic between the two countries. 'Kofi, you are worried about the foreigners selling drugs to our children,' he began. 'Can you help us do something about it?'

'What can I do?'

'You know the *abrofo* have ways of finding drugs at the airport, even if they are well hidden.'

'Their juju is very powerful.'

'They will teach us this juju if our government agrees.'

'To help the government send more bad medicine to *aborokyiri*?'

'No! We need it to stop foreigners sending bad medicine to Ghana.'

'Will the *obanfo* have to stop sending it to *aborokyiri*?'

'Yes.'

'They will never stop, they like money.'

Kwame thought Kofi was right but he had promised Leon to try, so he pressed on. 'They say the small boy, Rawlings, always talks to *okomfo* before taking action.'

'It's good to follow the advice of the gods,' Kofi replied.

'Could we tell the *okomfo* about the *oboroni* juju?'

'The small boy talks to the Ewe *okomfo*. There is no way.'

'Would you try to go through the high priest of Ashanti; he may know a way?'

'Through the small boy's Ashanti wife, Nana Konadu Agyeman?'

'No, I was thinking of a body like the national council of fetish priests, if they have one,' Kwame said.

'We beg you, Kofi. Try to help,' said Comfort.

Kwame took the old man's indulgent smile as tacit agreement but he didn't feel he could press him any further. The return of Peter Sarpong had radically changed the situation and Kwame couldn't be sure how his mission should be adjusted or what Leon would want him to do.

Kofi rose to take his leave and Kwame said he must also depart. He would much have preferred to stay but he feared irreversible consequences. Always slow to make up his mind, he wanted longer to think things through before taking a step that would change his whole life.

The next few days were spent in making final preparations for the computer-aided drawing course. Most of the participants had attended the previous course and been motivated to return by Greg's one-day taster. So as they assembled once more on the campus on the afternoon of Sunday 28 July everyone knew everyone else. It was a friendly community of kindred spirits met together with a common purpose. Kwame was happy that the courses were now well established and popular with the artisans. In spite of the problems with the visitors' programme, it was clear that the partnership between the universities was yielding benefits.

Kwame reflected that it had taken Tom several years, two trips to Ghana and many meetings to make the partnership project a reality. He admired his friend's tenacity and was happy that there was now something to show in the way of useful outputs. From his personal point of view he was glad of the opportunity to continue working for Ghana, and in Ghana, while enjoying a comfortable living outside. It was what he had always hoped for and what Comfort had doubted would ever come. Now, he thought, she saw things differently.

He looked forward to Tom's return to Kumasi and to showing him the computer-aided drawing course in progress. Tom had promised to take at least one day to work on the campus before he continued his holiday with Akos Mary.

Comfort had told Kwame that she would like them all to gather at her house again for a purely social evening before the Arthurs went on to the south and back to England. 'I want at least one drug-free evening with you all,' she had said, 'a chance to talk about shoes and fashion and hair styles.'

'I'm sure Akos Mary will enjoy that,' he had replied, 'but I hope you'll also find some topics to share with Tom and me.' So it had been agreed that the dinner party would take place on the evening of Tom's working day in Kumasi.

Kwaku Duah had been justified in his optimism and a computer was ready for each participant to use. Greg had anticipated that some students would progress much faster than others. After only a few days had passed, a few bright young artisans were completely hooked on the *oboroni* juju and were staying in the computer laboratory late into the night. 'Young people these days seem to be born hard-wired to use computers,' observed one of the older IT instructors.

Kwame was curious to know how many workshop owners had already invested in a personal computer. He asked the participants one evening after they had all taken dinner together. So far, he discovered, only Sam Quaye had purchased a used machine for his ENTESEL workshop in Tema. Sam said that his daughter was using the machine for correspondence and accounting, but he hoped that after the course he would begin using the computer to produce drawings. Greg said that as soon as they were free he and Kwaku would be happy to travel to Tema to install the necessary software on Sam's machine. Kwaku added that he would continue to provide this service after Greg had returned to England and he urged those proprietors intending to buy computers to keep in touch with him.

Some of the older participants had already concluded that if they needed to prepare drawings on a computer they would hire one of the younger men or women to do it for them. All agreed, however, that it was useful to know what was possible in a rapidly changing world. Several said that they would follow Mr Quaye in using a computer for secretarial and accounting work, and others thought that email and the Internet could help them with marketing and sourcing equipment and materials. Kwame realised that introducing computers to these grassroots industrialists had served a much wider purpose than helping them to prepare engineering drawings.

Kwame shared this insight with Tom when he returned from his tour of the north on Tuesday 30 July.

'Unexpected side effects are welcome as long as they are useful,' Tom replied. Then he added in a more serious tone, 'Can our people get hold of affordable machines to buy?'

'Mr Quaye found a used computer but he seems to have been lucky.'

'Should we be trying to bring used computers for resale, like the TCC used to bring used machine tools?'

'I'm sure if we could, it would be appreciated.'

'Maybe Prof Thomas could be persuaded to donate some of his old machines when his computer laboratory is re-equipped next year.'

'We could ask him; he said he wanted to help.'

'Then add it to your list of things to do, Kwame.'

The next day was spent by Kwame and Tom at the computer-aided drawing course and Tom was impressed by the enthusiasm and attentiveness of the participants. This was Tom's first experience of the courses he had initiated and he was very pleased with all he saw and heard. After the close of work they drove to Nhyiasu in anticipation of a pleasant social evening with Comfort. Akos Mary was particularly excited. 'Wild animals are interesting,' she said, 'but I missed ladies' chat and wearing pretty clothes.'

'Well you're certainly making up for it tonight,' said Kwame appreciatively.

'Oh, I can never compete with Comfort,' she replied, and when their hostess answered her door bell Akos Mary was proved to be right.

Tom and Kwame had agreed that it should be a ladies' night. They let the ladies dominate the conversation, with the men making their observations and voicing their opinions only on request. Carefully avoiding all comparisons and criticisms, they helped maintain the peace through the heated discussion of a range of topics of which they had little knowledge and only a passing interest. For a few hours, engineering and drugs trafficking were forgotten while they watched the butterflies flit from flower to flower in the garden that men are permitted to overlook but only women may enter.

After a late dinner they relaxed, replete with food, drink and conversation. Eyelids were drooping and thoughts of bed began to intrude as the clock moved inexorably towards midnight. Then a sharp knock on the front door returned the party to full consciousness. Comfort rose in response, and bearing in mind the lateness of the hour, Kwame went with her. 'Oh, it's you Kofi, what do you want?' Comfort asked.

'I've come with *okomfo*,' Kofi Adjare replied.

'It's rather late to discuss business,' Kwame said. 'Couldn't you come back tomorrow?'

'*Okomfo* demands the presence of Akos Mary Konadu!'

Hearing her name, Akos Mary began to tremble and Tom put a protective arm around her shoulders. 'What do they want her for?' Tom asked.

'She must come outside,' Kofi said in a strangely hollow voice.

258

Akos Mary rose and walked slowly out of the house, still trembling and closely followed by Tom.

They emerged from the bright lights of the house into the half light of a half moon. As they peered around with dilating pupils Kofi directed their gaze towards a part of the driveway overhung by trees. There in the shadows dully glowed three white faces. The central figure stood head and shoulders above the others with the white glow extending down to the waist. Light glinted from what appeared to be a short steel blade held upwards in the left hand.

The apparition took one step towards them and they could just discern the outline of a bare-chested male body of athletic proportions, dressed in a grass skirt and long chains of office crossing below the breast bone. Two other men, with similar white faces but wearing dark cloths, were crouching in the shadows, one on each side. One of the crouchers called out that Akos Mary Konadu should step forward. Akos Mary, still trembling, took two paces, and Tom followed.

The fetish priest began to speak slowly and loudly; slowly enough for Kwame to translate for Tom, phrase by phrase.

'Akos Mary Konadu, you are condemned as a witch and devil worshipper. You gave your soul in exchange for satanic favours and this is the hour of reckoning.'

A dark object flew through the air to land at Akos Mary's feet. Kwame noticed at once that it was a dead crow.

Comfort screamed. Akos Mary gave a gasp and slumped against Tom who only just managed to prevent her falling to the ground. Kwame turned to help Tom and together they carried the unconscious woman back into the house and lay her gently on a sofa.

'What the hell is happening, Kwame?' Tom shouted.

'Look after Akos Mary,' he shouted back. 'I'm going after them.'

Kwame dashed back outside but found only Kofi Adjare who told him that the visitors had departed in a car. 'Why did you bring them here?' Kwame asked, still shouting.

'I didn't bring them,' Kofi replied, 'but I did go to see *okomfo* as you asked. He told me that he already had business at this house.'

'What can we do now?'

'There is nothing we can do,' said the old man sadly. 'The gods have spoken!'

Kwame returned to Tom and Comfort who were trying to revive Akos Mary, still lying inert where they had laid her. 'Can we get her to a hospital?' asked Tom.

Tom could bear it no more and demanded attention. He asked a second time. The young man slowly raised his head and asked Tom what he wanted. He was told that there was an unconscious woman needing attention. 'Have you registered with the nurse?' the young man asked.

'No, but this is an emergency,' Tom almost shouted.

'You must see the nurse first,' said the young man returning to his papers.

'Have you seen a nurse?' Tom asked Kwame, and Kwame asked the patients on the bench.

'They say they're all waiting for the nurse,' Kwame told Tom.

'Can you help me?' Comfort called. 'I can't manage Akos Mary on my own.'

The two men moved to her aid. They struggled to make the comatose woman a little more comfortable but it was not easy on a simple wooden bench with no backrest other than the wall behind. The other waiting patients tried to make a little more room available. 'There she is!' said one of the patients, as a nurse in a faded green uniform dress with once-white collar and cuffs sauntered over to the desk and began to talk to the young man.

Tom was back at the desk, towering over the medical staff engrossed in their intimate discussion. He waited patiently for a few moments and then demanded loudly if they were going to attend to the patients. Kwame groaned again, he knew that this sort of behaviour would further delay any medical attention. Tom's presence was ignored but the conversation had ended and the nurse called the first person on the bench.

An old lady rose with difficulty, helped by a younger woman, and moved slowly over to the table where the nurse, leaning over the desk beside the young man, took down the patient's name and personal details. At length the nurse handed the two women a slip of paper and they stood in supplication before the young man, whom Tom realised with a shock was the duty doctor. Looking up from his papers, the doctor took the slip of paper from the women and told them to follow him. They entered a room near the desk and the door closed behind them. The nurse called the next patient and the pregnant woman waddled over to the desk. A few minutes later, clutching her precious slip, she returned to the bench and resettled herself with a sigh.

'This is going to take all night!' shouted Tom in anger.

'You may be right,' Kwame said, 'but trying to speed things up will only make them slower.'

'Kwame's right,' said Comfort, 'the doctors and nurses feel insulted when people expect them to work faster. They are kings and queens in their palace and demand humble respect from their patients.'

Now it was the turn of the old gentleman who had given up his seat. Kwame helped him over to the nurse. When he returned there was a place for him on the bench. One by one the patients were admitted to the doctor's inner sanctum. The nurse escorted the pregnant woman to the maternity ward and the old man was given a prescription and told to take it to the pharmacy when it opened. He turned to go, muttering to Kwame that now he must look for a loan to pay for the medicine. Kwame slipped him a fifty thousand cedis note and said that he hoped it would reach.

Akos Mary's turn came at last. They were told to bring the patient to the doctor's consulting room. With difficulty, Tom and Kwame carried Akos Mary into the small room and the doctor indicated a waist-high couch where she should be laid.

'Has this lady, Mrs Arthur, been ill for long?' the doctor asked.

'No, she collapsed just this evening, or rather yesterday evening,' said Tom, looking at his watch. The young man scowled as though he thought Tom was making a joke at his expense. This isn't going at all well, thought Kwame. 'How did it come about?' asked the doctor. Kwame knew that it was best not to disclose the source of the problem but before he could warn Tom he had blurted out, 'She was cursed by some juju man.'

'I am normally reluctant to treat such cases,' the doctor said, 'but we can admit her to the women's ward and keep her under observation.' He called the nurse to show them the way and the nurse brought a trolley to transport the patient. Tom recoiled at laying his dormant wife on its bare aluminium surface but Kwame pointed out that it was the only way she would be admitted to the ward. Comfort had brought a nightdress which she now folded and placed under her sister's head. They pushed the trolley gently along a corridor to a lift and the nurse pressed the buttons for an ascent of several floors. Kwame caught Comfort's eye, marvelling that the lift was working and the power was on. He wondered how they would have fared otherwise.

The women's ward was large and contained two rows of narrow beds. Every bed seemed to be occupied by a sleeping woman but an empty berth was found at the far end. Comfort said that with Tom's help she would undress Akos Mary and put on the nightdress. Kwame waited in the corridor outside while this was done. Then they laid Akos Mary on the thin mattress and covered her with a single bed sheet.

Tom asked the nurse when his wife would be examined by a consultant.

He was told that Professor Andoh usually did his ward round at 10 am. Tom asked about visiting times and was told he could come at any time during the day but he would need to come at meal times to bring food for the patient. Comfort quickly assured him that she would arrange for the food to be brought.

Tom was reluctant to leave his wife's side but he was told that he couldn't stay through the night and Kwame persuaded him to follow the nurse back to her desk on the ground floor. Here he was presented with a bill and asked to pay a deposit for the daily cost of ward care. Then they returned to Comfort's house for what remained of the night.

None of them had much sleep and nobody had much appetite for breakfast. Long before the appointed time for the consultant's round, they were back at the hospital. This time the women's ward was filled with visitors who had brought food to their sick relatives. They made their way through the throng to the bed at the end of the row. It was empty.

They searched frantically for a nurse but none was in sight. Some patients and visitors said that the nurses had gone for breakfast. Others said that the night nurses had gone off duty and the day nurses hadn't yet arrived. Ten minutes later a large lady came into the ward and gazed imperiously around. She wore a stained white uniform dress that threatened to burst apart at the buttons down the front. An upside-down watch was pinned to her bulging chest. Visitors clustered round to enquire of their relatives' condition. 'That's the ward sister,' someone said, and Kwame translated before realising that Tom had understood. They joined the queue and waited with rapidly reducing patience until their turn came.

'Where is my wife, Mrs Arthur?' Tom asked, but he got only a blank stare in return. Kwame explained in Twi how they had come in during the night with an unconscious woman and pointed at the empty bed.

'I don't know anything about that patient,' the sister said. 'I've only just come on duty, but we can check the records.' She led the way to a small office where a file lay open on a small table. After a quick perusal she said in Twi, 'She has died.'

Comfort burst into tears and Tom knew at once what had been said. He showed every sign of collapsing and Kwame struggled to support both of his companions. 'Where is she? I want to see her,' Tom cried, and Kwame asked the sister.

'She will have been taken to the mortuary,' the big lady told him. 'I will let one of my nurses lead you there.'

They descended into the basement and walked along dark corridors until they came to a door which their guide opened, signalling that they had reached their destination. They entered a long room where the instant chill told them the dead bodies were stored at low temperature by a refrigeration system. The man in charge said that he needed the visitors to establish the identity of the corpse and led them to long rows of drawers set in the wall. Leaning low, he drew out the appropriate drawer and lifted a cloth to reveal what had once been regarded by many as the most beautiful face in Kumasi.

Tom sank to the floor and both Comfort and Kwame knelt down to share his grief. 'She's Akos Mary Arthur *nee* Konadu,' Kwame said. The attendant noted the name and silently left his visitors to their mourning. Kwame watched him go, wondering how anyone could live with this scene every day.

They remained on their knees for a long time until their shivering reminded them how unsuitably dressed they were for this arctic tomb. Helping Tom to his feet, Kwame called the attendant who replaced the cloth and gently slid in the drawer. From the corridor outside they found a flight of steps and a door opening to the dazzling sunlight of a tropical morning. It took only a few minutes to forget the cold, but the memory of Akos Mary, lying frozen like an ice queen, would remain with them for the rest of their lives.

Kwame drove them the short distance back to Comfort's house in Nhyiasu. In their misery nobody had much to say. Tom said something about burying Akos Mary in her homeland and Comfort assured him that she would arrange a suitable funeral. There ensued another long silence.

At length, Tom's red eyes begged his companions for an explanation, 'How did this happen?' he asked.

'It was the curse,' said Kwame.

'How can anyone be killed by that mumbo-jumbo?'

'Only by believing it,' Kwame replied.

'Did Akos Mary believe it?'

'Yes, she did,' said Comfort gently.

Kwame felt that Tom was not satisfied but he sat again frozen in the mortuary of his mind. After some time he muttered something about the dreadful reality of Hume's Law and Comfort asked him if he would like to lie down. With Kwame's help Tom was persuaded to move to an upstairs bedroom and onto a comfortable bed. As the house was air-conditioned, they covered him with a light blanket. Then they drew the window curtains in the hope that he might catch up on the lost sleep of the previous night.

Downstairs Kwame told Comfort that back in Coventry Akos Mary had left the Pentecostal church because she feared being accused of being a witch. 'But why are you so certain that Akos Mary was killed by her fetish beliefs?' he asked. 'Was she so much affected by what she did to Peter Sarpong?'

'No I don't think that it was that,' Comfort replied.

'Then what was it?'

'It was the guilt she felt about what she did to Afriyie.'

'What was that?'

'She used a fetish spell to steal Tom.'

'So, Peter was right about that!'

'He knew of the spell from the fetish priest.'

'When was that?'

'When Akos Mary was acting as a courier for the cartel and Peter was coming home for the university vacations.'

'How do you know?'

'Peter told me.'

'It seems that Peter told you many things,' Kwame said.

'I was trying to find out what the old cartel members were up to,' replied Comfort.

'Well, you won't want to see him any more, will you?'

'Kwame Mainu, I do believe you are just a little bit jealous.'

'I don't want you to get involved in Peter's affairs.'

'Or to have an affair with Peter?'

'Or to have an affair with Peter.'

They sat looking at each other but the messages that passed between them remained unspoken. Neither felt that this was the time for surveying the future. There was a funeral to arrange. Kwame said, 'Tom won't want a long delay.'

'No, I can arrange everything for next Saturday.'

'Will Akos Mary be content to be buried in Kumasi?'

'Oh yes, her parents have broken ties with the family, her father is dead and her mother is lost in America. Her friends are all here.'

On Saturday 3 August 1996 the funeral service for Akos Mary Arthur nee Konadu was conducted by the chaplain at the Protestant chapel on the KNUST campus. This was the most convenient location, both for Akos Mary's many friends who were traders at Ayigya junction and for Tom's friends working at the university. After the burial at Kumasi cemetery the guests gathered at Comfort's house for the social part of the event. The gathering was well attended, especially considering the short notice and the absence of blood relations.

Comfort asked Tom if he was content with the arrangements and he assured her that he would always be grateful for her support at this time. 'But I don't know how I can face going home without Akos Mary,' he said.

'Would it help if I travelled with you and Kwame?' Comfort asked. 'I need to negotiate for more shoes and I promised Akosua that I would visit her in England.'

'That would help a lot,' Tom replied. 'With both you and Kwame at my side I think that I can face the journey.'

The next day Tom told Kwame that he would stay in Kumasi until the computer-aided drawing course was over and then accompany him back to the UK. He mentioned that Comfort was planning to come with them. 'Yes, she's spreading her wings as the new shoe queen,' Kwame replied. 'We will be a big party again, travelling together with Greg and Bra Yaw.' Then he told Tom how Leon Thornet was arranging for Bra Yaw to travel to London in connection with the investigation of the reviving drugs cartel.

'I need to get back to work to keep sane,' Tom confided to Kwame. 'I hope you will let me attend all your meetings connected to our partnership agreement.'

'You don't need my permission to attend meetings,' Kwame told him, 'but as your friend I must advise you if I think you're doing too much. Comfort has said you can rest in her house as much as you like and I will be happy to report to you there most evenings.'

'I'm very grateful to Comfort for all her kindnesses,' Tom said, 'but I still think that work is the best therapy for my condition.'

Kwame invited Tom to join him at lunch with the participants; he knew that their enthusiasm would help assuage his friend's great pain. Almost all of the artisans had attended one of the earlier courses, and they were eager to express their thanks to the man who had inspired and led the link between the universities that made the courses possible. After the meal, someone proposed a toast in Tom's honour and this was conducted with all due ceremony. The professor struggled to stay dry-eyed as he uttered a few words of thanks. 'These guys really appreciate what we are doing for them!' Tom whispered to Kwame.

'They certainly do!' Kwame replied, happy to see his friend's spirits lifted, if only for a few moments.

Tom was anxious to sit in on a meeting of the committee approving visits to Warwick so Kwame arranged for them to meet the TCC director and the dean of the School of Engineering. The dean again brought forward the name of Kojo Doe with a recommendation from Greg Anderson and Kwaku Duah. Tom and Kwame had seen Kojo's contribution to the computer-aided drawing course but Kwame remembered Mick's initial assessment which had led to his earlier rejection. Mick had judged that Kojo had no practical research interest but an expressed interest in working overseas. It was only after a lengthy discussion that Kojo's visit was approved, based largely on his participation in the training programme.

So far, although Sosthenes Battah, the TCC director, had attended all the meetings of the selection committee, he had made no proposals. He saw his role as supporting the work of the participants and helping to ensure that their achievements were tested in the field. Today, however, he wanted to bring forward one of his own people. He turned to Kwame. 'Do you remember when your young lady, Sandra Garg, was here, she went to Tema with Ophelia Darko.'

'Yes,' Kwame said. 'They wrote a good report on foundry developments.'

'Ophelia was spending her year of national service with us,' Sosthenes explained, 'but we kept her on because we were pleased with her work. In Tema she developed a special interest in the new aluminium spinning industry and has started a project aimed at designing and developing new products. We want to offer some alternatives to the usual domestic pots, pans and bowls that the Tema workshops make at present. I'm hoping to find some industrial products like, for example, reflectors for lamps. We think that Ophelia could benefit from exposure to the industry in the UK.'

'This would be a task for Sandra to coordinate,' Kwame said, 'but she has taken maternity leave, so we would have to delay Ophelia's visit until after Sandra's return early next year.'

'Then I think we can approve the visit and schedule it for, say, February or March 1997,' said Tom. There were nods all round.

Kwame wanted to spend some time while he was in Kumasi trying to move forward his plan to build a diesel engine. Dan Nyarko had arranged to come from Tema for the last few days of the training course and so Kwame arranged to meet with Dan and Sam Sanders in Sam's office in the School of Engineering. He wanted to try out his idea to build not only one prototype engine but to build two engines in parallel, one in Tema and one in Kumasi.

Kwame began by giving Dan and Sam each a portfolio of all the information they had collected in Warwick and Ghana. These included a full set of drawings and material specifications together with Kwame and Mick's preliminary assessment of which manufacturing capabilities already existed at each location. He explained that he wanted to undertake the actual engineering work during a six-month visit to Ghana by Mick and himself, but Tom had not yet approved the budgetary allocation. Nevertheless, he wanted Dan and Sam to start making the preliminary arrangements for this mission.

'You should discuss with the workshop owners how they would be expected to collaborate in the work,' Kwame said. 'The cost of the work will be paid by the project but we must try to convince the participants that they will also gain in other ways. In other words we want enthusiastic participation such as we have often enjoyed in the past.'

'Do you intend that if the project succeeds the workshops might be asked to participate in a larger production programme?' asked Sam.

'Yes,' replied Kwame, 'but first they would share in the benefits of publicity; that should bring more work to their enterprises, and they will extend their range of skills and services.'

'My foundry will be one of the participating companies in Tema,' said Dan. 'How will that affect my role as coordinator?'

'I can't see any problems,' replied Kwame, 'as long as you don't handle the money. It will be part of my responsibilities to control expenditure because the funds will come from Warwick.'

'Should we get the companies to sign up for the project?' asked Dan.

'Yes,' Kwame said. 'Those companies that agree to participate in the project should be asked to sign letters of intent and that will include your Danco Foundry. These are not intended to be legally binding documents but they could help us to raise funds to support the project by showing that we have a serious commitment from local industries.'

'When will we know that funds are available?' asked Sam.

'That depends upon Professor Arthur,' Kwame replied. 'I will remind him of my request but not now while he's grieving over the loss of his wife.'

Kwame realised that he had made little progress in working with Kofi Adjare to gain the support of the fetish priests. He decided to meet once more with Kofi and Comfort before his return to England. Kofi had not yet reported on his meeting with the high priest. They met at Comfort's house on the day after the closing of the computer-aided drawing course.

Kwame began by observing that the tragic death of Akos Mary had completely overshadowed the original purpose of Kofi's visit to the fetish priest. Now, before Kwame's return to *aborokyiri*, they would like to hear what had passed between them.

Kofi explained that at their first meeting *okomfo* had told Kofi of the business he had with Peter Sarpong and said that he was unable to discuss any other matter relating to Kofi's friends. At a subsequent meeting, however, *okomfo* told Kofi that the national circle of traditional spiritual counsellors was concerned about the growing drugs trade in Ghana and the effect it was having on the youth. While he was in no position to advise the priests of the Volta Region on how they should influence the government, he knew that his colleagues were aware of the situation and shared the concern of the whole circle.

As for possible collaboration with *aborokyiri*, no doubt their juju was as powerful as ever but it was outside of the remit of *okomfo* and his colleagues. He doubted if those traditional practitioners advising the government would ever favour such collaboration; they would prefer to deal with the situation by their own methods. Kofi did not feel that he could take the matter any further, either with his contact or by any other route.

Kwame asked Kofi if he had seen Bra Yaw recently and Kofi said that Bra Yaw was just now visiting him in his quarters and he would call him. After the usual greetings Kwame asked Bra Yaw if he was ready to travel to London. 'I'm all packed and ready to go,' he replied, 'and this time I can use my own passport!'

Kwame wanted to know what Peter Sarpong was doing and, in particular, what was his relationship to the Lebanese. 'I think Peter would like to renew the link but it seems the Lebanese want to leave him out,' Bra Yaw said.

'They want to keep it all to the camel herders, do they?' asked Kwame, catching Kofi's eye.

'That's the way it seems,' said Bra Yaw.

'Do you think that Peter wants to continue in the drugs trade or could he be persuaded to stop like you and Kofi Boateng?' Kwame asked.

'Boat and I told Peter we have stopped and we tried to persuade him to stop too. So far, I think, he wants to go on,' said Bra Yaw.

* * *

270

It was another large party that assembled to return to the UK in August 1996. In addition to Kwame, Tom and Greg, who had travelled out together and were returning to Warwick, there were Comfort and Bra Yaw, who were travelling on other missions. Of the companions on the outward journey, Professor Thomas had returned in advance, Kwaku Duah was staying at his post in Kumasi and Akos Mary had made her last journey. Spirits were low and there was little conversation as most members of the party tried to formulate suitable explanations to meet the demands that they knew awaited them on arrival.

Afriyie and Akosua were waiting at London airport together with Little Tom. They were in the usual state of excitement and impatience and Akosua ran forward in joy at the sight of her mother. Afriyie, however, reacted immediately to the distress on the faces of Tom, Kwame and Comfort and the absence of Akos Mary. She solemnly embraced them all in turn while Akosua, realising that something dreadful had happened, hugged Little Tom in his pushchair and told him that whatever had happened to his mother she would always be his friend.

Reading the question on Afriyie's face Kwame said quietly that Akos Mary would not be coming home. They made their way in silence out of the terminal building and across to the car park where the six adults, Akosua and Little Tom squeezed into Kwame's Discovery. Kwame took the wheel with Tom by his side. As he drove out of the airport Kwame heard Comfort begin to explain the situation to Afriyie and Akosua, sitting three abreast in the seats behind and struggling in turn to restrain the energetic toddler. He was relieved that Comfort spoke quietly and in Twi to minimise any distress that her words might cause to Tom.

Kwame had not been told by Leon where to send Bra Yaw so he decided to take him home and await instructions. Bra Yaw was lodged in one of the two rear seats of the vehicle with Greg Anderson. Having only just met, the two young men might have had much to say to each other but each was aware of the professor's shock bereavement and so they spoke only briefly and in subdued tones. In this solemn mode Kwame drove resolutely to Coventry, dropping Greg at his lodgings and pressing on to his own house, wondering what to do next.

Much to Kwame's relief, Comfort and Afriyie took over. 'We've decided it'll be best if we all sleep here tonight,' said Afriyie. 'That will give us time to discuss how we will manage after that.' Then, leaving the men with the luggage, and Akosua with Little Tom and Takoradi, the two women set about arranging the sleeping accommodation and the evening meal for the expanded household. Tom made no protest. Still emotionally disabled, he was content for the moment to leave all arrangements in the hands of his friends.

Kwame decided to telephone David Barney to find out what Leon proposed to do with Bra Yaw. He was told that David would come to collect Bra Yaw the following morning. Bra Yaw was no stranger to England, which he had visited many times, but he had spent eighteen months in prison and earned the sobriquet 'the one who fears the worm' from Kofi Adjare. So Kwame was not surprised that Bra Yaw viewed his coming assignment with some apprehension. Kwame tried to reassure his countryman but as he had only a vague outline of Leon's plan, he was less effective than he otherwise might have been. 'They want to learn all you know about the Lebanese drugs traders,' Kwame told Bra Yaw. 'I would advise you to tell them all that you have seen or heard with your own eyes and ears but make it very clear if what you say goes beyond that and is only rumour.'

'Do you think I will be safe?'

'Oh yes, they will look after you very well.'

'Will I see you again?'

'I expect so.'

After Bra Yaw had departed with David Barney, Kwame called his people together to discuss how they could support Tom in readjusting to his new life. Afriyie and Akosua said they had enjoyed looking after Little Tom and they would be happy to continue to help in any way that was convenient. Comfort said that she had decided to come to England at this time to help Tom and she would be happy to keep house for him for two or three weeks until he and Little Tom could be settled in a new routine. She could devote some time each day to her shoe purchases so that her own business would not be neglected.

Tom looked gratified by his friends' generous offers and muttered his thanks. Kwame was surprised that the Englishman did not counter politely with the usual remarks about not wanting to be a burden and being able to manage all right. This increased Kwame's awareness that the wound his friend had suffered would take a long time to heal. The help that had been offered might provide adequate support in the short term but Kwame was filled with concern for the longer term.

Comfort moved into the guestroom at Tom's house. She prepared breakfast and an evening meal for the two Toms during the week and full board at the weekends. To provide Comfort with time for her own business, Afriyie took care of Little Tom for a few hours while his father was at work, and Akosua took Little Tom for a walk with Takoradi in the evenings and at weekends if Big Tom was otherwise engaged. This gave Tom an opportunity to get back into his work routine free of domestic worries. He was able to reassure his parents when they came to express their condolences that, in spite of the loss of his wife, he and their grandson were being well cared for.

At his office Tom seemed to be working as quietly and efficiently as ever. He called his team together to review the work programme in the light of the recent trip to Kumasi and congratulated Greg on the success of the computer-aided drawing course. Then he thanked the whole team for their efforts in achieving tangible results in Kumasi. He had been gratified to see these outputs for himself and to hear from grassroots artisans the sincere expressions of their appreciation of all the two universities were doing to help upgrade their operations.

Tom asked his team to press forward with arrangements for the visit of Kojo Doe to Warwick in the autumn, and the visit of Ophelia Darko in the spring of 1997. Greg was assigned responsibility for Kojo's visit and Mick was asked to prepare for Ophelia's visit until he could hand over to Sandra when she rejoined the team in January.

Mick told his colleagues that Sandra's twins had arrived on schedule. He had visited Sandra at her parent's home and could assure them that mother and daughters were doing well. He was sure that Sandra would be pleased to hear that Ophelia was coming to Warwick as they had enjoyed working together in Ghana. However, the assignment to study the metal spinning industry would be difficult because the manufacturing technique had largely been replaced by an alternative called deep drawing. Mick doubted if he could find examples of metal spinning in big manufacturing companies and might have to search in craft industries and art colleges. It was an interesting challenge and he would do his best to get everything ready for the two ladies.

Since his return to Coventry Kwame had been expecting a call from one of Leon's people but he had not expected it to be from Auntie Rose. They met once again at the hairdressers' salon. Auntie Rose was distressed to hear of Akos Mary's sudden death, and memories of this being Akos Mary's place of work made it difficult for both of them to retain their composure. 'Let's not meet here again,' Kwame said.

At first, Kwame thought that Auntie Rose had called the meeting to hear his first-hand account of events in Kumasi but he soon realised that the little lady had news of her own to impart, 'I stopped Akosua going to the Pentecostal church; did she tell you?'

'No, with looking after Professor Arthur and the little boy we've not had time for a proper chat.'

'The teenagers had decided she was a *dadaba* and she was getting nowhere.'

'Then I must thank you for being her guardian angel.'

'Akosua stayed out of trouble but I was less successful with Elsie Ntim.'

'Have you found Elsie? That's wonderful!'

'Not so wonderful, I'm afraid.'

'Why? What's wrong?'

'She's been badly beaten; she wants to see you.'

'Where is she?'

'In Walsgrave Hospital.'

'I must tell Afriyie.'

'No, she asked to see you first.'

19

Stalemate

Auntie Rose explained how she had pursued her own enquiries and had traced Elsie to a house in Birmingham that was known to be a brothel. Through Leon she had learned that the police were planning to raid the place to make arrests of suspected people traffickers. Auntie Rose had pleaded for the raid to be brought forward and Elsie had been released, but not before she had sustained a severe beating. 'She wants to come back when she is well but she is shy to face Afriyie,' said Auntie Rose. 'So I persuaded her to see you first.'

They drove to the hospital and found Elsie in a comfortable single room that Kwame guessed was private. He suspected that Leon had something to do with these arrangements. He couldn't help wondering whether if Akos Mary could have been brought to such a place she might have survived. From the look he exchanged with Auntie Rose he guessed the thought was shared.

Elsie lay sleeping with her head bandaged. Her arms, also wrapped in bandages, lay above the white sheets. A nurse who had been sitting by the bed offered her seat to Auntie Rose and told them, 'She will soon wake up. She was anaesthetised to reset some bones in her arm. Why don't you go to the restaurant for a cup of tea? I'll let you know when she's conscious.'

Kwame was only half way through his Danish pastry when the call came. Quickly wrapping the residue in a paper napkin he followed his little companion back to Elsie's room. The bandaged patient seemed both pleased and startled to see him. 'Please, I want to come back?' she asked quietly.

'Yes, you can,' Kwame replied and wanted to hug the redeemed absconder, but fearing causing further harm to her frail frame he contented himself with a kiss on her cheek.

'Afriyie will be very angry.'

'No, she won't be angry, I'll explain everything. Try to get well quickly.'

They left Elsie to sleep some more, promising to come back soon. 'How do you think she came to be beaten so badly?' he asked Auntie Rose.

'She hasn't told us yet but we suspect that she refused to do what they wanted,' Auntie Rose replied. 'Will they need her to give evidence?'

'Yes, I expect so, but later when she is healed.'

A few days later Kwame was back at the hospital with Afriyie and Akosua. This time Elsie was wide awake and sitting up in bed. Afriyie told her that they would all welcome her back home. 'As soon as you left, all we wanted was to have you back,' Afriyie told her. 'Akosua tried to trace you through the Pentecostal church and Auntie Rose found you had gone to Birmingham. Now we have to wait for you to get well and we can all be together again.'

That night in bed Kwame thanked Afriyie for her understanding of Elsie's plight. 'I should be thanking you and Auntie Rose,' Afriyie replied. 'Elsie's my sister's child and came here to help me do my work.'

'You owe thanks to Auntie Rose, but I did nothing except assure Elsie that you would have her back,' said Kwame.

'Thank you for that anyway,' Afriyie said.

They lay quiet for a while and Kwame wondered if Afriyie was sleeping. He was about to turn over and let go when he heard a tiny voice say, 'I know why she died.'

'Why did she die?'

'Because of the spell she put on Tom.'

'What spell?'

'The spell to turn away from me and love her instead.'

'How did that kill her?'

'When she was accused of using juju she knew it was true.'

'Did Comfort tell you this?'

'No, but I know it's true.'

There was another long pause. This time it was broken by Kwame, 'Are you sad that she took Tom away from you?'

'I'm jealous of Comfort.'

'Why are you jealous of Comfort?'

'She's staying in Tom's house.'

'Would you rather be in Tom's house?'

'I'm not sure.'

Comfort had been staying in Tom's house for more than two weeks and no more permanent arrangement was in sight. Afriyie told Kwame that

Comfort was wondering how much longer she might be needed because she couldn't afford to neglect her business indefinitely. Kwame suggested they should all meet again to discuss future plans. 'I've been thinking the same,' she replied. 'This evening, when I take Little Tom back, why don't we all go?'

They found Comfort sitting in the lounge with a pile of shoe catalogues. 'Ah, Afriyie, just the girl I need, which of these new styles will be popular in Ghana?'

Afriyie studied the glossy photographs with obvious enthusiasm. 'These look good and comfortable,' she said, pointing to an illustration on the open page, 'but I don't think the colours are right for us.'

'That's what I was thinking,' Comfort said. 'I may need to ask the makers to produce them in brighter shades; what do you suggest?'

'Oh Mum, you always choose shoes for old ladies,' said Akosua. 'Don't you want to sell to teenagers?'

Kwame realised that his discussion of future plans would have to wait until Tom came home and so he settled down to read the *Telegraph*. Much to his delight he found an article on British trade with West Africa and learned that Ghanaian entrepreneurs were exploiting opportunities to increase the export of tropical fruits and vegetables. One young man who had a contract to supply pineapples to Marks and Spencer was prominently featured. By a rare violation of Mainu's law, Kwame had enough time to finish reading before he heard the diesel engine of Tom's Range Rover rattling in the drive outside the window.

There was a delay before Tom came in, largely caused by Takoradi jumping into the vehicle to deliver his usual boisterous greeting. 'His muddy footprints are all over the seats and carpets as well as all over me!' Tom complained, but his wide grin was the first his friends had seen in several weeks. Akosua said she was sorry and hurried out to the car to clean up after her pet. Tom asked Comfort if she had arranged an impromptu dinner party. 'I didn't know you were all coming but you're welcome to stay,' she said.

Tom had always been a conscientious father, often taking over bath and bedtime duties, and since returning home from Ghana he had made it his permanent routine. So Kwame waited until Tom returned from a peaceful nursery before broaching his concern. 'We've been wondering how much longer the Kejetia shoe queen can continue to neglect her duties in Kumasi and whether we can help with longer-term support for the two Toms,' he said.

Comfort looked relieved that Kwame had raised the matter. 'Yes, I should be getting back before someone takes over my stool,' she said with a laugh.

Tom said that he was grateful for all Comfort had done to help him settle back into a regular routine. He felt that now he could manage on his own if he could arrange day care for Little Tom. Afriyie said that she would be happy to arrange the day care. Elsie was coming home again soon, and with Akosua's help at the weekends, they could manage for six months or so, and then Little Tom would be old enough to start at a nursery school. Akosua said that she loved having Little Tom and would help whenever she was free.

After thanking everyone for their kind offers, Tom recalled that Elsie had run away because she needed more pocket money. 'If I pay her a few pounds each week for her help,' he said, 'maybe it will help to stop her absconding a second time.'

Kwame said that he thought they had found a win-win solution. Comfort said that she would book her return flight in a few days time. She had enjoyed her stay and she would certainly come again.

The next call that came from Leon's people was the one Kwame had been expecting. David Barney summoned him to a meeting at the hotel in Oxford. This time Kwame had to drive himself, but he located the hotel on the road map and succeeded in finding his way there. He had expected a large gathering but only Leon and David were there with Bra Yaw.

Leon began by recalling the last meeting at this venue. They had briefed a Crown Prosecution Service lawyer on their objections to the early release from custody of Mr Peter Sarpong. Kwame had stressed the danger that a freed Peter Sarpong could pose to Mrs Arthur, especially in Ghana, and this had been included in the objections presented in court. They now knew that in spite of their objections Mr Sarpong had been released from prison and deported to Ghana, where he was suspected to have had a hand in the death of Mrs Arthur. They had failed to prevent the release, with dire consequences. He felt that the system had let down Professor Arthur and his family and friends. Leon said that he had written to the professor to express his apology and condolences.

Mr Sarpong was now back in Kumasi and suspected of trying to reactivate the drugs cartel. However, due to the good work of Kwame and his helpers it seemed that all the other leading Ghanaians had been persuaded to abandon the cartel. This had been confirmed by Mr Aidoo who was present at the meeting. It also seemed that Mr Sarpong's approaches to his former Lebanese partners had been rebuffed and that the Lebanese were engaging in an alliance with compatriots from South America.

Kwame and Bra Yaw were asked to confirm these facts and impressions. Kwame said that what Janet Dery had told him supported the impression that the Lebanese in Kumasi were joining in partnership with others from Venezuela and that they were beginning to introduce hard drugs to Ghanaians. Some young people had become addicts and these were being used to sell drugs to others on the street and in schools. He had also been told that Peter Sarpong was trying to recruit young people to be air couriers but he didn't know if Peter was acting alone or with the Lebanese.

Bra Yaw confirmed that Peter Sarpong had tried to encourage his former Ghanaian colleagues to revive the cartel, but Kofi Adjare, Kofi Boateng and Bra Yaw himself had all refused. He didn't think that Peter could succeed on his own, nor did he think that Peter was working with the Lebanese. 'Peter might have tried to recruit some couriers to have something to offer the Lebanese,' Bra Yaw said. 'If so, I believe the plan has failed.'

Leon tried to summarise the discussion so far, 'It seems that we have Peter Sarpong back in Kumasi, an energetic and dangerous man with much experience of the drugs trade but isolated for the moment and not an immediate threat. We also have the Hanabis people in Kumasi linking up with Venezuelans and beginning to promote drugs sales in Ghana. They seem to be laying plans to resume trafficking to the UK but for the moment they lack a UK sales network. We must hope that the Lebanese continue to rebuff Mr Sarpong. Then we have a breathing space to prepare ourselves for the next onslaught.'

Leon turned to Kwame. 'How did you fare with your plan to influence government policy through the fetish priests?'

'Very badly,' Kwame said. 'Our contact, Kofi Adjare, saw a fetish priest but only to be told he had work to do for Peter Sarpong at the same address. Kofi did try once more, and learned that the fetish priests share the general concern about local sales of hard drugs to children, but they refused to intercede with Rawlings' advisers from the Volta Region.'

'No, they won't want to work with the Ewe *okomfo*,' added Bra Yaw.

'Why is that?' asked David Barney.

'The Ewes are feared by all the other tribes for their powerful juju,' Bra Yaw said.

'So it seems that this route is closed to us,' Leon said.

'Yes,' said Kwame, 'none of us wants anything more to do with fetish priests.'

'Finally,' Leon said, 'can we do anything to trap one of the Lebanese directors of Hanabis?' He turned to Bra Yaw, 'You provided evidence that got two of them convicted and imprisoned in Ghana, didn't you?'

'Yes, and I've given you a written statement of all I know about what they were doing.'

'Are you sure you've told us everything?'

'Everything I can remember.'

'Our lawyers feel that it's insufficient to secure a conviction in England, and in any case it could be argued that they've already served a sentence for their crimes in Ghana.'

'Only two of them,' Kwame interjected. 'Bachir Abizaid has never been imprisoned in England or Ghana.'

'No, he fled Ghana in June 1979, didn't he?' said Leon reflectively. 'We only have an outline of where he's been until he returned to Ghana recently.'

Kwame remembered that Leon had said that he would talk to Oboroni, 'Could Crispin Russell tell you anything useful?'

'It might be useful,' Leon replied. 'Russell is anxious to help us, in the hope of shortening his sentence, but what he can supply is limited to the time Abizaid spent in England.'

'Abizaid flew to Britain with Russell in 1979 and stayed for a few years,' Leon continued. 'During that time the cartel was still in process of setting up its operating system. The first Rawlings coup in Ghana came at an awkward time for the cartel. It was not yet ready to start its activities in England and it couldn't do much in Ghana until Rawlings handed over at the end of the year. Russell can tell us about what he and Abizaid were doing in the early 1980s but Abizaid planned to travel to Venezuela to strengthen the cartel's links with their cocaine suppliers. Russell assumes that is what happened after he lost contact with Abizaid in 1983, but he has no definite knowledge. Now the situation reported in Kumasi by Kwame suggests that Abizaid was successful and is back in Kumasi with colleagues from Venezuela who are joining up with the three directors of Hanabis.

'We need to know what they are plotting in Kumasi,' Leon said. 'We know about Kwame's engine pistons and wooden coat hangers but we don't know how they intend to use them. I suppose the pistons could come by sea or by airfreight but the coat hangers might be brought here by air travellers. If they're not going to use Ghanaian couriers as before, how will they do it?'

Leon looked at his three companions in turn, appealing for some spark of inspiration: for a new idea to reactivate his mission. He has fought his enemy to a standstill but failed to defeat him, thought Kwame. For the moment it seemed that the cartel in Kumasi could do nothing in Britain, but neither could Leon do anything more to destroy the cartel in Kumasi, or lure one of its protagonists from their West African lair. Kwame felt sorry for his long-time employer and a little embarrassed that his weakness was exposed before Bra Yaw, so recently converted to the path of righteousness.

It was Bra Yaw who ended the silence, 'Could I carry a letter from Mr Russell back to Bachir Abizaid?' he asked.

Leon looked doubtful. 'You told Peter Sarpong that you are no longer working with the cartel,' he said, 'so there is a risk that the Lebanese will know this and you will not be trusted. We cannot allow you to put yourself in danger. In the past the Kumasi people have not used much violence and guns have not been a factor, but Konadu was killed by shooting. If Venezuelans are getting involved they will certainly bring guns with them and they will not hesitate to use them.'

'For us, the situation in Kumasi is like a volcano,' David Barney said. 'It has become inactive for a while, but when it erupts again it could be much more violent than before.'

'And it is a danger to Ghana as well as to the UK,' added Kwame.

'Then I hope you will all rack your brains to try to find a way to stop the eruption,' said Leon. No more progress could be made and the meeting broke up without proposing any further course of action.

A week later, Elsie was released from hospital and driven home by Afriyie. She was welcomed in turn by Kwame and Akosua on their arrival back at the house. Still with an arm in plaster, Elsie was restricted in what she could do but she was soon taking a share in looking after Little Tom. She was delighted that Professor Arthur was paying her a weekly allowance and that she would now be able to afford more of the clothes and accessories that her contemporaries from the Pentecostal church were classifying as essential. She spent much time debating this issue with Akosua who had a somewhat different perspective based on peer pressure from her classmates at King's High School.

Kwame was concerned that these conversations between the girls were always in Twi. Elsie was still slow in learning English. She spoke mostly Twi to Little Tom and at first Kwame feared that Big Tom would not be happy. 'Don't worry, my friend,' Tom told him, 'I want him to know his mother's language. I would be happy if he becomes as bilingual as Akosua.' Kwame relaxed on that issue but he still wanted Elsie to make a bigger effort to improve her English.

'Are you trying to help Elsie with her English?' Kwame asked Akosua one evening while Elsie was resting.

'I did try for a while but I got frustrated,' Akosua replied. 'I got lazy and found it easier to chat to her in Twi.'

'I understand,' Kwame said, 'but let's give it one more try, shall we? She'll be happier here, as well as safer, if she can talk to more people and have a wider circle of friends.'

'OK Dad, we'll give it one more shot,' Akosua assured her father.

Afriyie had listened to the conversation but refrained from making any comment until Akosua had gone to her room to do her homework. 'You're right about Elsie learning English,' she said to Kwame. 'They took advantage of her only knowing Twi. They knew she would be shy to ask for help in English.'

'Has she been telling you about her experiences in Birmingham?' Kwame asked.

'She's told me a few things.'

'She was brave to stand up to them.'

'Yes, she was.'

'Did they try to force her to work in the brothel?'

'No, that's the strange thing.'

'How do you mean?'

'They wanted her to fetch packages from Ghana.'

Afriyie's remark sent questions flooding through Kwame's mind. Was this the new tactic to be tried by the drugs traders? Did the drugs traders think that UK-based travellers returning from a short trip to Ghana would be less likely to be suspected of being drugs couriers than Ghana-based people? Were the Ghanaians who held Elsie in Birmingham connected to the Kumasi cartel or an independent group? If they were connected, were they working for the Lebanese or for a new Ghanaian faction seeking to rejoin the Lebanese? Above all, were they linked to Peter Sarpong who had lived in Coventry for several years and had contacts with compatriots in Birmingham? Peter had sent Akos Mary to Birmingham in 1988 to stay with Ghanaians a week or two before they were both arrested.

Had Peter Sarpong, or someone else, found a new way to use the Ghanaian diaspora? In addition to using its members as a sales network in the UK, they could be sent to Ghana to fetch the merchandise. At first sight it seemed quite a good idea. It might draw in a few Ghanaians who were naturalised and held British passports. They wouldn't need a visa either way, using their original passport to enter Ghana and the British passport to re-enter the UK.

Then an urgent thought struck Kwame. He remembered that the police had made some arrests at the time of Elsie's release. Were these people still being held? Did the police know that they might be connected to drugs trading? Did Leon's people know? As far as he knew Elsie had not yet been interviewed. He decided to telephone David Barney right away. 'You take the lead,' he said to Afriyie. 'I'll be up shortly but first I must make a telephone call.'

'I'm sorry to be calling so late,' Kwame said, 'but something has come up that might require immediate action.'

David gave a yawn, 'Go ahead,' he said.

'Elsie Ntim told Afriyie that the Birmingham people who were holding her wanted her to travel to Ghana to bring back packages.'

'So the people arrested might be drugs traders; I wonder if the police are still holding them?'

'That's what I'm wondering.'

'We must try to make sure they hang onto them. Thanks Kwame.'

'Always glad to be of service.'

'Have the police questioned Miss Ntim yet?' David asked.

'I don't think so.'

'Then I'll try to arrange to come there with a police officer as soon as possible.'

'I guess you'll also question the people in police custody.'

'If they're still holding them or if they can be re-arrested.'

'What are the chances?'

'Well, it's two weeks since the raid and the police thought they were dealing with people smuggling and forced prostitution. If they found no evidence other than Miss Ntim, some of the people they arrested might have been released.'

'Then I'll let you get onto it.'

Kwame had promised Tom that he would ask Professor Thomas if he would donate some of his used computers to the partnership project to help grassroots industrialists in Ghana obtain affordable equipment. He rang the professor's secretary, Mrs Gupta, to arrange a meeting, and at the appointed time in the afternoon he walked to the IT department with Greg Anderson.

They were a few minutes early so Kwame had an opportunity to ask Mrs Gupta if she had any recent news of Sandra Garg. He was told that mother and daughters were all doing well and the twin baby girls were quite delightful. Kwame asked if Sandra had been able to visit Nelson in prison and Mrs Gupta said that Sandra had been to see Nelson once and next time she was planning to take the twins. 'Do you think Sandra will be able to resume duties in the New Year?' Kwame asked.

'Oh I think so,' Mrs Gupta replied. 'She seems to have enough help with the little ones.'

The professor was seeing off a visitor, and noticing Kwame and Greg he beckoned them to follow him back into his office and waved towards two comfortable chairs. He called Mrs Gupta. 'These young men are doing splendid work in Kumasi,' he said. 'Can we reward them with some tea and biscuits?' The departure of the electric blue sari seemed to remind the professor that the autumn nights were drawing in and he switched on the light before returning to his well-upholstered seat behind his expansive desk.

He beamed at his visitors through his bifocals. 'How nice to see you both,' he said. 'I've been wanting to thank you for looking after me so well on our expedition. I hope everything continued to go well after my departure – except for that dreadful business of Professor Arthur's wife, of course,' he added, remembering just in time what must be overshadowing Kwame's thoughts of those last days in Kumasi.

'Our training course went very well,' Greg said, coming to Kwame's rescue. 'Now most of our trainees want to buy computers to use in their businesses.'

Mrs Gupta returned with a tray of refreshments and the next few minutes were occupied in adjusting the beverage to individual specifications. The professor bit into a shortcake biscuit and brushed the crumbs from the dark-green leather surface of his desk. Kwame and Greg waited patiently for the discussion to resume. The professor repeated his ritual and sipped his tea. 'So your people are ready for the electronic age,' he said, as much to himself as to his guests.

'If they can afford it,' Kwame said.

'What you must do now is supply computers to your participants at affordable cost,' said Professor Thomas. 'Not new ones of course – much too expensive! No, you must seek donations from firms and institutions or buy them cheaply in the used machine market. I've given it some thought since I left you in Kumasi and I'm ready to provide an initial boost for this next phase of the work. We're about to re-equip our main computer laboratory and I want to donate the old machines to your project. They're not too bad really, upgraded last year to MS Windows 95 and the latest AutoCad. They should meet your chaps' needs for several years. Do you want them?'

Kwame and Greg were rather taken aback by the professor's rapid conversion to their cause. 'We will be very pleased to accept your donation,' Kwame said. 'I must thank you on behalf of the project and all our friends in Ghana. It's a most generous contribution to our efforts to boost grassroots industries.'

The professor turned his beam onto Greg. 'When can you start collecting the machines, young man?'

'As soon as you're ready, Professor,' Greg said.

'Then go and talk to Jim Proctor, he's in charge of the lab. We'll be starting very soon but the change-over will take two or three months.'

'That's fine,' Greg said. 'I'll liaise with Jim and arrange to collect the computers in small batches. That will make it easier to carry out checks and prepare for shipment.'

'When you've finished your tea I'll take you along to meet Jim,' Professor Thomas said. Greg grabbed the last of the biscuits and followed the others out of the office. The professor paused to tell Mrs Gupta where he could be found and led the way down a corridor to the laboratory. A tall slim technician in a white coat uncoiled himself from a computer on a desk in the middle of the room and greeted his boss. 'Are these the gents we're expecting from Microsoft?' he asked.

'No, they're from Professor Arthur's partnership project with Kumasi University in Ghana,' Professor Thomas replied. 'They're going to send these old machines to Ghana for use by small enterprises.'

Formal introductions were made and Jim was told to liaise with Greg on the hand-over of machines in small batches as he was ready. 'Ghana,' Jim said. 'I bet it's hot, but I wouldn't mind a trip to see, if I got a chance.'

'There could be a chance,' said Kwame, 'if we need any help with installations or teething troubles.'

Greg stayed with Jim to discuss details of the hand-over and Kwame walked back with Professor Thomas. They stopped at the door to Mrs Gupta's office. The professor took Kwame's hand, 'I meant what I told you in Kumasi,' he said, 'I'm ready to help in any way I can.'

'You've already shown that!'

'But is there anything else?'

'Well, we have a young man, Kojo Doe, coming here next week. You

285

may remember we spoke of him in Kumasi. He will be helping with future IT activities in Ghana. It would be useful if he could spend some time with Jim Proctor.'

'Send him over, my dear chap, send him over!'

Kwame was pleased with his morning's work and hurried back to his own office. He looked forward to telling Tom the good news of Professor Thomas's donation and help with the training of Kojo Doe. Much to his surprise he found all the staff crowded into Tom's office. The centre of attention was Sandra Garg and her twin baby daughters. 'Come on in, Kwame,' called Tom, 'if you can find any space!'

'Push the pram outside,' Sandra said. 'It's taking up too much room.' She was holding one of the babies, now about three months old, and Alice, Tom's secretary, was holding the other.'

'Which one is the older?' asked Kwame.

'They're twins, born at the same time,' Sandra laughed.

'One must have been born first.'

'Oh, that's the one Alice is holding, Shita.'

'We call her in Ghana *panin* or elder.'

'And what do you call her sister, Sylvia?'

'She's *kakra*, little one or junior,' Kwame said.

'Whatever you call them, I think they're lovely,' Alice said.

'Be careful, or Prof might find a reason to send *you* to Ghana!' Mick said with a wink. From the look on Alice's face it seemed she wasn't sure whether Mick was joking.

'Don't worry, it will be OK as long as you don't bring back any fertility dolls,' Tom said in an attempt to confirm the humour. Then he said to Sandra, 'Can we invite you home after work? The ladies would love to see *panin* and *kakra* and we'll invite Alice as well to help with the little ones.'

Later, at Tom's house, mother and twins were surrounded by Comfort, Afriyie, Akosua, Elsie and Alice. Little Tom was playing a supporting role but Takoradi was exiled to the garden. It was Comfort's last evening in England and she was happy that it was a ladies' night. Kwame and Tom felt that their role as catalysts had achieved its objective and they retired to Tom's study to review the work situation.

'Did you see Professor Thomas today?' Tom asked.

'Yes, I went over with Greg to talk about computers for Ghana,' Kwame replied.

'Any luck?'

'Yes, Prof said we can have all the machines he's replacing. He introduced us to Jim Proctor, the technician in charge of the computer lab, and Greg will collect small batches from Jim as they are replaced over the next three months.'

'What about Kojo Doe?'

'Prof said he would be happy for Kojo to spend time with Jim.'

'So your idea to invite Prof to Ghana worked out very well!'

'Yes, he thanked me for arranging the trip and told me he wanted to help the project in any way he could.'

'Well done, Kwame!'

'So the expense was worthwhile,' Kwame prompted.

'It was, but our budget is still very tight,' Tom replied.

'Not much hope for my diesel engine then?'

'I'm afraid not, Kwame, unless we can raise more funds.'

'Any hope of that?'

'Not at the moment but we'll try again later.'

Next morning, Comfort said goodbye to a tearful Akosua and an anxious Afriyie, wondering if they could reach school in Warwick on time. Then Kwame drove Comfort to the airport. Comfort had stayed in England much longer than she intended: from late August to mid October. Added to Kwame's several weeks in Ghana in July and August, they had lived in daily contact for about three months, by far the longest period since their separation in June 1988. Kwame had enjoyed getting to know the mature Comfort and he sensed the feeling was reciprocated. Had it not been for the death of Akos Mary, it would have been Kwame's happiest interlude for several years. So it was with some sadness that he steered his Discovery towards Heathrow.

They remained in silence as the miles sped by. Kwame recalled his first visit to England in March 1984 and his first ride with Robert Earl on a British motorway. He had wondered then if he would ever drive in the fast lane, and now it had become his everyday experience. To this extent he had achieved the ambition of his youth: to escape the poverty of his homeland and enjoy the riches of *aborokyiri*. Comfort had despised his poverty and stated it as one of the reasons for leaving him. Did she still hold that view? He didn't think so. He sensed that she now regarded him with a renewed respect, much as he now looked at her, although in his case the respect had never died.

Few words passed between them on the journey. Kwame felt that there was much they each wanted to say but did not dare. On his side it was the wish not to hurt Afriyie that held him back but he wondered what restrained Comfort. Maybe she too had Afriyie in mind. Whatever her reasons, Comfort left Kwame feeling regret for a missed opportunity tinged with relief for a decision deferred.

The parting was not too painful because Kwame expected to be in Kumasi early in the New Year for the next training course. So he limited himself to thanking Comfort one last time for her great help to Tom, and to all of them, over the passing of Akos Mary, and for keeping her promise to visit Akosua. Comfort said that now she had friends to stay with in England she would come more often.

20

Computer Studies

The following week Greg drove to the airport to meet Kojo Doe, the junior academic from Kumasi with an interest in computer-aided design. Kojo was one of the candidates proposed earlier by the School of Engineering but rejected on the grounds that his research interest was superficial and he was judged to be an absconding risk. Later he had helped with the computer-aided drawing course. It was largely on the strength of recommendations from Greg and Kwaku Duah that Kwame and Tom had reluctantly agreed to his visit.

The two young men arrived back in the office in the afternoon to be greeted by Tom, Kwame and Mick. Together they went briefly through the programme arranged for Kojo, which included time with Greg, two weeks at the Land Rover apprentice school and a week at Professor Thomas's computer laboratory. After the briefing, Greg took Kojo to his lodgings.

'I hope you're not having second thoughts about Kojo,' Tom said to Kwame.

'It's difficult to be sure about anybody,' Kwame replied, 'but we felt Kojo had earned his chance by helping Greg and Kwaku Duah, and he now has a special interest in returning to Kumasi to help with the computer-aided drawing courses.'

'Please keep an eye on him, Kwame.'

'Yes, I will.'

'He's going to spend time with Prof Thomas's people; we don't want any more trouble. You've turned Prof around very well but another absconder or drugs incident could put us back to square one: fighting to keep our project funded.'

'We'll do all we can to ensure that Kojo is on his best behaviour.'

Kwame had made an undertaking with Tom but he wanted Greg to share the responsibility. 'We agreed to Kojo coming here largely on your recommendation with the support of Kwaku Duah,' Kwame said to Greg, 'but earlier Mick and I had judged him to be an absconding risk.'

'I appreciate that,' Greg replied.

'Then you must share in the effort to try to prevent Kojo absconding.'

'I'll keep him closely monitored but I can't be with him all the time.'

Kwame feared that they might have made a mistake in changing their minds about Kojo Doe. These fears were increased when Kojo started to receive telephone calls from relatives and friends in London and Birmingham. One morning, shortly after Kojo Doe had moved to the Land Rover apprentice school Tom's secretary, Alice, called Kwame on the telephone. 'There's a call for Mr Doe,' she said, 'somebody wants to know where he's working now?'

'Put them through to me.'

Kwame held the silent telephone for a few moments before Alice came back with 'The lady's rung off.'

'Did she give you a name?'

'She said her name was Peggy.'

Kwame groaned. Was it Peggy Osei-Wusu, their first absconder? If Kojo had already made contact with Peggy it would seem that staying in the UK was very much in his mind. It was not surprising that they knew each other; they had been together on the staff of the School of Engineering. What did surprise Kwame was the possibility that they had kept in touch after Peggy had gone underground. Maybe they had made a pact or joint escape plan. Kwame realised that he could have a serious problem on his hands.

Kwame called Mick and asked if he knew the whereabouts of Greg. 'He's over at the apprentice school with Kojo,' Mick replied.

'Then let's catch up with him there,' Kwame said, pulling his car keys from his trouser pocket. On the short drive Kwame briefed Mick on his new problem. 'We should have given more weight to your initial assessment,' he told Mick. 'Now we must deal with the consequences of allowing ourselves to be steamrollered.'

'Can I make a suggestion?' Mick asked.

'Go ahead,' said Kwame.

'These days all engineers need to be up to date with IT and computer applications. I've been looking for an opportunity to ask you and Prof if I could spend some time with Greg brushing up on all that stuff. How about me attending the apprentices' school and Prof Thomas's lab with Kojo? I could kill two birds with one stone.'

'You mean keep an eye on Kojo?' Kwame asked.

'Yes, I would have a reason to be with him throughout the working day. If we become chummy, I might even spend some off-duty hours with him.'

'Very good, and at the apprentices' school you could programme machines to make some of the diesel engine parts as a further justification for being there.'

'That's what I had in mind.'

'Thank you, Mick; that's a big help.'

On arrival at the apprentice school they went straight to see the manager, Mr Dawson, to make their request for Mick to join Kojo. 'No problem,' Mr Dawson said. 'It's as easy to cater for two men working together as for one working alone. Kojo's on the lathe section just now; let's see how he's progressing.'

They found a technical instructor wringing his hands. 'I've told you a hundred times,' he said angrily to Mr Dawson, 'don't send me people to train on these computer-controlled machines who don't already know how to operate a manual machine!'

'Oh don't worry,' Kwame said quickly. 'I've brought Mr Gould to work with Mr Doe. He's fully trained on all machine tool operations.'

'Then all I need to do is clear this jam and replace the broken tool bit,' the technician replied, adjusting the slope of his diminishing anger.

'I'll give you a hand,' said Mick.

'What's been happening here?' Kwame asked Greg.

'I've only just got here myself,' Greg replied, 'but it seems that Kojo's first solo run ended in a minor accident. Fortunately nobody was hurt and the damage was slight but these are costly and powerful machines and mistakes can have serious consequences.'

'Well I've brought Mick to train with Kojo,' Kwame told him. 'That should ensure things run more smoothly.'

'And keep a close watch on Kojo!' Greg said with a wink.

Before leaving the apprentice school Kwame took Mick and Greg aside and told them that Peggy Osei-Wusu might have tried to telephone Kojo. 'We must be extra vigilant,' he said, 'and try to foil any attempt Kojo might make to disappear. We must try to prevent Kojo meeting Peggy. I don't think Peggy will risk coming here. If Kojo asks to travel away from Coventry we cannot stop him, but one of you should say you're going with him. If the trip is to meet Peggy he will probably abandon it.'

Kwame thought of one more thing to do: he would alert Auntie Rose to Peggy's reappearance. He telephoned the little lady and invited her to lunch at home on Sunday. If he forwent his customary siesta they could expect a quiet hour for a business chat.

* * *

'So you think we might determine Peggy's location from her attempts to contact Kojo, do you?' Auntie Rose asked Kwame after he had explained the situation.

'Yes, but we are all Ghanaians; I don't want anything bad to happen to Peggy – or Kojo.'

'If we find Peggy, she'll be put on an aeroplane home,' Auntie Rose replied, 'and if Kojo overstays his visa, the same could happen to him.'

'How can we stop Kojo from overstaying?'

'By sending Peggy home first.'

'Do you think you can do that?'

'We'll try!'

'Do you know that Kojo is attending the Pentecostal church?' Auntie Rose asked.

'How do you know?'

'I became a church member when I was tracing Elsie.'

'Are you still a member?'

'I attend less often but I must drift away gradually to avoid rousing suspicion.'

'Well, it extends our surveillance of Kojo.'

Then Kwame remembered what he had reported to David Barney about Elsie having resisted becoming a drugs courier. 'Could Kojo come into contact with the people who kidnapped Elsie?' he asked.

'That's a danger,' confirmed Auntie Rose. 'The police have confirmed that the group in Birmingham is involved in recruiting people to fetch drugs from Ghana but I'm not at liberty to tell you anything more about their on-going investigation.'

'Kojo won't be much use to them as a courier; they need UK residents.'

'No, he can't help them by overstaying his visa.'

'They might persuade him to go home and return later with the goods.'

'So far Kojo's done nothing wrong,' Auntie Rose pointed out. 'He might be tempted to overstay but that does not mean he would involve himself in drugs trading. For the moment we must restrict our activities to trying to trace Peggy Osei-Wusu. Have you tried to restrict Kojo's movements?'

'Yes, I've asked my people to work with him full time and to go with him if he travels away from Coventry.'

'Don't let anyone go with him if he wants to travel. It will constrain him. Wherever he goes, he'll be followed.'

'More work for Tam, eh?'

'For Tam or someone else.'

'Tam would be good; he'll blend in well but hear what Kojo and Peggy say if they meet.'

'If they meet, Peggy will be on her way home!'

Afriyie came in, still looking sleepy and rubbing her eyes. 'Who's on their way home?' she asked.

'I must be,' said Auntie Rose, looking at her tiny wrist watch.

'Oh stay for a cup of tea,' Afriyie said. 'We haven't had any women's chat yet.' She called Elsie and asked her to boil some water.

Akosua came in with Takoradi, and Little Tom in the push chair. 'Are you coming with us for a walk on the common, Dad?'

'Yes,' Kwame said. 'We'll leave the ladies to solve the rest of the world's problems.'

It was a cold and windy autumn day and they hurried along to keep warm. Akosua made sure that Little Tom was well wrapped in his buggy but like Takoradi he seemed oblivious to the cold. Boy and dog shared an interest is trying to catch the swirling multi-coloured leaves that blew towards them. On the common Kwame kept them well away from the benches under which he had found the hypodermic syringe. The big dog chased his ball and the toddler tried to chase the big dog, with very little success. Akosua did her best to serve both their needs.

After the game of ball Takoradi decided to check out the benches but Kwame managed to head him off and re-attach his lead. 'Once a drug sniffer, always a drug sniffer, eh Dad?' Akosua joked.

'I don't want him finding any more syringes,' Kwame said. 'Last time I reported finding one to the police they politely told me that if they wanted a needle they already knew where to find one. It seems they don't want members of the public telling them what to do.'

'Don't they ever collect them up, Dad?'

'I guess they do, but they get replaced every night.'

'Do we have drug addicts like that in Ghana?'

'Not too many on hard drugs but the numbers are increasing.'

'Why do they do it?'

'It seems that most people start because of peer pressure. I hope there's nothing like that in your school.'

'We've had a police officer come in to warn us of the dangers but I've not heard of any girls getting involved.'

'So the drugs dealers don't come there any more.'

'Not since the police came.'

They were walking home more slowly in the failing light, with a sleeping child and an exhausted dog. With the weakening wind on their backs there was less incentive to hurry. 'You like looking after Little Tom, don't you,' Kwame said.

'Yes, Dad,' Akosua replied. 'I want to work with children.'

'I thought you wanted to study medicine at university.'

'Yes, if I pass my A-levels with good grades.'

'Then how will you work with children?'

'If I succeed in studying medicine, I'll specialise in paediatrics.'

'Well, I'm glad you've got it all worked out, Akosua Mainu.'

'Did I take a long time, Dad?'

'No longer than most young people.'

After dinner Kwame asked the three ladies how they were managing in helping Tom look after Little Tom. They all agreed that they were happy with the present routine but it would be easier for Afriyie and Elsie when Little Tom started nursery school in the New Year. 'We all feel sorry for Tom,' Afriyie said, 'alone in that big house with only the little boy for company. It wasn't too bad while Comfort was here but since she went back to Ghana he's looked so lonely.'

'I've told him many times that he's always welcome here any evening or weekend when he needs company,' Kwame said, 'but maybe he's shy to come too often and we should do more to call on him.'

First thing next morning Kwame remembered what Auntie Rose had told him and called Mick and Greg to his office before they left for the apprentice school. 'We have a change of plan,' he told them. 'Cancel my instructions to travel with Kojo if he plans a trip.'

'You've arranged for him to be followed, have you?' Mick said. 'Converted a problem into an opportunity! That's smart! Instead of another absconder, we recover the one and prevent the other.'

There had been such a long delay that Kwame had forgotten that David Barney planned to come back with a police officer to interview Elsie. One morning early in November he had been working for two or three hours when a call came for him to return home to act as interpreter. Afriyie had refused to interpret because she felt that she did not know enough of the official terms that the police might use. Kwame knew that in any case Afriyie would be nervous in the presence of a guardian of the law.

Elsie was also nervous and Kwame took time to calm the young apprentice. David and the plain-clothes policewoman were patient and relaxed, showing every sign of having met this situation many times before. Kwame asked if Afriyie could sit in on the interview to help reassure Elsie that this was to be a friendly chat. Coffee and biscuits served to complete the domestic setting.

David began by saying how pleased he was to see Elsie's arm was out of plaster and her bruises seemed to be healed. She assured him that her wounds didn't pain her any more. Then encouraged by her first fleeting smile he said, 'Can we begin by asking you about the Pentecostal church?'

'Tell us about the church people,' Kwame said in Twi.

After some explanation and further prompting Kwame was able to tell the officials that Elsie said she had started going to the church because many Ghanaians were there and she felt at home surrounded by people who spoke her mother tongue.

'What happened when you ran away?'

'Some people said they would help me.'

'Was this before you ran away?'

'Yes.'

'How did they say they would help you?'

'They said we would go to a big town where I could find work with good pay.'

'Birmingham?'

'I don't know.'

'How long did you stay with these friends?'

'About two months before the men came for me.'

It was slow work with two-way interpretation and the interrogators knew that a hurried approach would be counter-productive. So the interview progressed patiently.

'How did they come for you?'

'In a car.'

'Who travelled with you?'

'A woman and two men.'

'Do you know their names?'

'The woman told me to call her "Nana"; the men called each other "Bra" or "*m'adamfo*" – my friend.'

After another brief pause while everyone drew a deep breath and the police officer caught up with her notes, David asked, 'What happened after that?

'They took me to a house. They gave me food and then I went to sleep.'

'Ghanaian food?'

'Yes, jolof rice and chicken!'

'Where did you sleep?'

'In a room with four beds.'

'Were there other girls there?'

'Only one.'

The police officer quickly turned a page of her notebook and scribbled a few lines before nodding her head. David continued with, 'Did you talk to the other girl?'

'Not that night, I was tired.'

'Did you talk to her later?'

'Yes.'

'What did she say to you?'

'She said I should do whatever they told me and then I would get money.'

'Did she say what they would do if you refused?'

'She said they would beat me.'

David looked anxiously at his companion who scribbled rapidly for several minutes before asking if there was any more coffee. Afriyie got up to serve this request and they all relaxed until the officer signalled that she was suitably reinvigorated. 'What did they ask you to do?' David asked.

'I told you. They wanted me to go to Ghana to collect things but I refused.'

'Why did you refuse?'

'When I came here sister Afriyie told me that if anybody asked me to bring something I should say no.'

'Why did she tell you that?'

'She said it might be wee or another bad thing.'

'Did they beat you when you said no?'

'Not that time.'

Again there was a pause to allow the note-taking to catch up. Kwame thought he knew what the next question would be. 'When did they beat you?' David asked.

'After the big man came, he told the other man to do it.'

'Do you know the big man's name?'

'Yes, I played a trick.'

'What trick?'

'When they beat me I pretended to be dead.'

'I think she means unconscious,' explained Kwame.

'What did you hear?'

'The big man shouted that the beating was too much.'

'What else did you hear?'

'The other man shouted back, "You told me to do it, Kwesi Konadu".'

At the mention of the name David and Kwame gave a gasp in unison before Kwame had a chance to voice his translation.

'The Kwesi Konadu we know is dead,' David said.

'It's a common name in Ghana,' Kwame said. 'There must be dozens of Kwesi Konadus around.' He wished he was as confident as his words sounded.

'But what if it is the Konadu we know? Could he have faked his death?'

'To escape his enemies?'

'We know he was in trouble. Leon will want to go into this.'

David decided that as soon as they finished the interview he would report immediately to Leon Thornet. They returned to questioning Elsie who said that the big man had been angry with the other man for mentioning his name. She had little more to tell them because she had been rescued shortly after her beating.

The policewoman produced a photograph album and asked Elsie to tell her if she recognised any of the men. Kwame explained carefully what was required and Elsie looked at each of the photographs in turn. 'That's the man who beat me,' she said, 'but I don't know any of the others.'

'Did the police arrest anyone called Kwesi Konadu?' David asked the police officer. 'I don't recall that name,' she replied, 'but I'll check and let you know.' She went out to her car to make a call and Afriyie took Elsie to her room to rest. Kwame and David continued to speculate on whether Elsie's kidnapper had been Akos Mary's father or another person with the same name. If it was Akos Mary's father, and he had gone underground after faking his own death, did he know of the death of his daughter? The speculation raised a number of intriguing questions.

The policewoman returned to say that the police were still holding the man who beat Elsie. He had given the name Kwesi Robert Gyan and was known to his associates as Kwesi Bob. It was his photograph that Elsie had recognised. There was forensic evidence of the assault, as well as Elsie's testimony, and he was charged with causing grievous bodily harm. The other men arrested with Kwesi Bob had all been released for lack of evidence. None of them gave the name Kwesi Konadu.

'Was any search made at the premises?' David asked the policewoman.

'We had information that the premises were being used as a brothel,' she replied. 'Our ongoing investigation concerned people trafficking and we were planning a raid but it was brought forward to rescue Elsie. We expected to find drugs but not in large quantities so a detailed search was not undertaken.'

'There won't be any point in going back,' David said. 'If drugs were stored there in commercial quantities they will have been moved by now.'

They all left at the same time: the police officer to attend to her other duties, David to report to Leon, and Kwame to return to the university. He called in on Tom to explain his absence. 'I was called home to interpret for the officials who came to interview Elsie,' he said.

'Yes, Elsie,' Tom replied. 'How is she doing these days?'

'She says that the wounds are no longer painful.'

'How did she stand up to the interrogation?'

'Not an interrogation, more a friendly chat.'

'Is she happier these days?'

'Much happier; your wages are boosting her morale.'

'I'm grateful for her help with Little Tom.'

'What's happening with Kojo Doe?' Tom asked. 'Was there a mishap at the apprentice school?'

'He did have a minor accident and the instructor got rather angry but I've put Mick with Kojo full-time and it won't happen again.'

'Mick? Can we spare him from his other duties?'

'He asked if he could brush up his computer skills and keep an eye on Kojo at the same time. We can spare him for the moment and he will be more useful when he returns to his normal duties.'

'I hear that Peggy Osei-Wusu was trying to contact Kojo, what are you doing about that?'

'I've informed Leon's people and they have arranged for Kojo to be followed. They hope that he will lead them to Peggy so that she can be arrested and deported.'

'That will please Prof Thomas!'

'And deter Kojo from overstaying.'

'Did anything interesting come from Elsie?' Tom asked.

'She identified her attacker,' Kwame said, 'but as the raid was brought forward to secure her release, the police seem to have missed arresting the people they were after. They have Elsie's attacker and he'll be brought to court but he's the only one they're holding.'

Kwame couldn't say anything to Tom about Akos Mary's father. Nothing was certain, and as far as Kwame knew Tom still believed that his father-in-law had returned to Ghana after the wedding. In view of the circumstances of Mr Konadu's deportation and reported death, Kwame felt that it was unlikely that Akos Mary had said anything about these events to Tom.

He guessed that Tom still thought Mr Konadu was living back in Ghana, but guesses are not always right.

Kwame summoned Mick and Greg to discuss the next course to be held at KNUST in January 1997. They had decided that the topic would be chosen in consultation with the workshop proprietors and artisans who had attended the earlier courses. Some of these men had told Kwame that they needed to develop skills in business management and after the recent course on computer-aided drawing there had been requests for instruction on using the computer for accounting and record keeping. Kwame had been waiting for final recommendations to come from the TCC in Kumasi and these had now been received, confirming the earlier requests.

'Is the School of Engineering the best venue for this course?' asked Mick.

'It would be good to use their computer lab again,' Greg said. 'We know we will have enough machines and Kwaku is there to help.'

'I agree,' said Kwame. 'Our clients are still engineers and whatever we give them must still be related to their field of activity.'

'But don't we need some help with topics like accounting and human resources?'

'We do, Mick,' Kwame said. 'The TCC tell us they can recruit some instructors from the department of economics and industrial management.'

'Enterprise management, even for small workshops, is such a broad field that we must focus on one specific area,' Kwame said. 'We can cover other areas on future courses.'

'What are you proposing?' Mick asked.

'I know from experience that most small engineering enterprises have problems with job costing,' said Kwame. 'I propose that we give them a week on basic job costing followed by a week of keeping accounting records on the computer.'

'Will they need more expert support from us?' asked Greg.

'Our friends in Kumasi tell us that it would be useful if we could bring someone with us who has special expertise in the areas I've mentioned.'

'Can we get someone from the business school?'

'They might consider the course to be rather below the level of their standard short courses for business executives but I expect we can find someone who would be interested in a trip to Africa,' said Kwame. 'Prof Arthur has contacted the head of the school and a note has been circulated inviting suitably qualified people to apply.'

Kwame asked Greg if the first consignment of computers from Professor

Thomas's laboratory would be in Kumasi in time for the course. 'The first batch is tested and packed and ready to be air-freighted,' Greg said. 'Will you offer them for sale on the course?'

'I was thinking that you might use them on the course in place of the machines you borrowed last time and then we would offer them for sale on a first-come first-served basis.'

Mick was looking glum. 'It seems as though I'll not be needed again this time.'

'Sorry Mick,' said Kwame, 'we need Greg to look after the computers and Prof will only provide funding for one more person and that must be the expert from the business school. Don't be too disappointed; you will still have done as many trips as Greg, and I need you to continue the preparations for Ophelia Darko's visit here. We must be ready by the time that Sandra returns from maternity leave.'

'Yes,' said Mick. 'I'm having difficulty finding places where they still do metal spinning. It seems to be more used on the continent than in this country.'

'Please keep trying; I don't want to have to send her to Switzerland!'

Kwame asked his colleagues how Kojo was progressing at the apprentice school. 'We should have followed Mick's original assessment,' Greg said.

'That's what I feared,' said Kwame.

'They told me not to leave him on his own,' said Mick.

'Was it because of the accident?'

'Yes, and they were right. If he had been left alone on a machine he might well have caused a similar mishap.'

'Where is he now?'

'I stopped him attending the apprentice school,' said Greg. 'He wasn't learning much so I transferred him to Prof Thomas's workshop ahead of schedule.'

'What's he doing there?'

'He's helping Jim Proctor check and disconnect machines that are going to Kumasi.'

The thought of Kojo Doe working in Professor Thomas's laboratory filled Kwame with dismay. 'The last thing we want is trouble around Prof Thomas,' he said. 'I'd be happier if he was helping you get the computers ready for shipping, Greg.'

'OK,' Greg said, 'that should keep him out of trouble until he goes home next week.'

'That's another problem: making sure he gets on the aeroplane.'

'Perhaps both Greg and I should escort him to Heathrow,' said Mick.

'Didn't we expect him to make a trip to meet Peggy?' Greg asked.

'Yes,' said Mick, 'do you still expect that to happen, Kwame?'

'He only has one weekend left to him now,' Greg cut in.

'So if they are to meet it must be this weekend,' Kwame confirmed, wondering if Tam was still on Kojo's tail.

'Well, speak of the devil!' Kwame said as he entered his lounge at home that evening.

'Uncle Tam has come to see Takoradi,' cried Akosua, 'and Afriyie has invited him to stay for supper.'

'Well it's not the first time I've been assigned satanic attributes,' Tam said.

'I'm sorry,' said Kwame, 'it's just that I thought of you this afternoon at the office.'

'I've heard that the devil has recently been at work but I assure you I had no hand in his machinations.'

'Of course not, *Akwaaba*!'

'*Ya eson.*'

'How are you?'

'Well but busy; we'll talk after supper.'

Later that evening Afriyie and Elsie were tidying up and Akosua was absorbed in homework so the two men slipped off to Kwame's modest study where they could talk without being overheard.

'I think you know I've been assigned to trail your Mr Kojo Doe,' Tam began.

'I was aware of the trailing and assumed it was you.'

'The aim is to apprehend Miss Peggy Osei-Wusu.'

'So I gather.'

'Leon wants to ask the lady a few questions and our friends at immigration want to arrange her repatriation.'

'So why are you here, not hot on Kojo's tail?'

'They're planning to repeat Peggy's escape at the airport.'

'How do you know?'

'They have been indiscreet enough to give guarded hints on the telephone.'

Kwame knew that if he was being informed of action in advance it could only be because there was a role for him to play. 'Why are you telling me all this?' he asked.

'Leon wants you involved to provide positive identification.'

'Positive identification of whom? Mick Gould and Greg Anderson will be with Kojo and they both know Peggy.'

'What if Kojo gives your bodyguards the slip? I don't know Peggy except from photographs; but Leon is more concerned about Peggy's mysterious brother playing a part, you're the only one who has seen him.'

Kwame took a few moments to digest this information. 'I've accepted Mick and Greg's offer to escort Kojo to the airport,' he said, 'and they've been told to try to ensure that Kojo goes through passport control into the departures lounge. Should I now ask them to ease off and allow Kojo more opportunity to meet up with Peggy?'

'No, leave it as it stands; we don't want to risk Kojo getting any hint that could cause him to change his plans.'

'Why did Tam come here this evening?' Afriyie asked Kwame as they were preparing to go to bed.

'Akosua said it was to see Takoradi,' Kwame answered with a yawn, pulling up his pyjama trousers and buttoning the waistband.

'But what about the real reason; was it to do with Elsie?'

'Oh no, nothing to do with Elsie.'

'Then what?'

'It was about one of the KNUST people who is here on a visit.'

'Did he bring drugs?'

'No, but they want to stop him getting involved.'

'Elsie refused to be involved.'

'Yes, she did the right thing.'

Kwame sensed that Afriyie had more on her mind, so he lay on the bed and waited patiently.

'Do you like Elsie?' Afriyie asked, as the bed springs protested at her rapid descent.

'Of course I do, she's a very nice young lady.'

'Have you taken her as a girlfriend?'

'So that's what's troubling you.'

'Well have you? I wouldn't mind, I didn't mind about Gladys did I?'

'No you didn't mind about Gladys, but at that time I thought you were Tom's girl. Do you want to go back to Tom?'

'I'm not sure, it's too soon; but what about you and Elsie?'

'No, I haven't taken Elsie as a girlfriend.'

'Do you still love me?'

'Yes I do.'

'And you still love Comfort, don't you?'

'Yes I do.'

The weekend passed without incident. Kojo spent the time shopping and packing as Kwame had often done in the past before a return trip to Ghana. This reminded Kwame that his task had invariably been lightened by the expert help of Mrs Chichester. So he suggested to Akosua that their usual Sunday afternoon walk with Takoradi should be to visit his former landlady. It was a little further than they normally ventured but the inducement of Mrs Chichester's afternoon tea and cakes was enough to win the votes of both girl and dog.

As they walked home in the twilight under street lamps randomly igniting in red and shading to yellow, Akosua asked her father why he was so fond of Mrs Chichester.

'She looked after me so well when I came first to Coventry,' he said.

'Was she your English mother?'

'Yes, I suppose she was.'

'Then she's my English grandmother,' Akosua said, with a big smile that lit up the grey winter evening.

The following Wednesday morning was the time of Kojo's scheduled return to Ghana. Greg, Mick and Kojo set out in a university vehicle and Tam joined Kwame in his Discovery to travel independently with the aim of arriving at the airport a few minutes ahead of the traveller. In the terminal building Kwame and Tam positioned themselves with a good view of the British Airways check-in desks but effectively hidden by the bustling crowd of passing travellers.

They saw Kojo come in, flanked by his escort. The trio walked straight to join the shortest queue at the three active check-in desks. A black man from the back of an adjacent queue slid his bulging suitcase to reposition himself immediately behind Kojo. It was a natural move for someone anticipating faster service on the shorter line but it alerted Kwame. 'It doesn't look much like him but I think that's Peggy's brother,' he said.

'What do you mean?' whispered Tam.

'Last time he was dressed as a businessman with short, parted hair.'

'And now he's wearing jeans, a faded T-shirt and a Rasta hairstyle!'

'I know it sounds crazy, but my instinct tells me it's the same person.'

'Then let's move closer and watch carefully.'

Kojo reached the check-in desk and handed over his ticket and passport. Mick heaved Kojo's suitcase onto the conveyor and the digital read-out spun rapidly to settle several kilograms overweight. The bag was tagged without comment and Kojo was handed back his documents with a boarding pass. He listened attentively as the clerk explained the boarding procedures. At the press of a button the suitcase lurched forward on its journey to the aircraft.

Seeing the clear space on the conveyor, the next traveller made a great effort to swing his voluminous case onto the weighing station. Striking the metal edge of the desk the bag burst open scattering its contents on the tiled floor. Instinctively, Greg and Mick dived down to help retrieve the scattered socks and shirts and bottles of assorted toiletries that rolled away in all directions. 'Watch Kojo!' shouted Kwame, but it was too late; the reluctant traveller had seized his chance to slip away unobserved.

Kwame turned to warn Tam but he had also disappeared in the crowd. No doubt, thought Kwame, with trained professional reactions Tam had anticipated the diversion and kept his eye on the quarry. Greg and Mick saw Kwame for the first time and their faces reddened as they realised he had witnessed their failure. 'Where's the owner of this case?' asked the check-in clerk, pointing to the scattered belongings, and Kwame realised that they had also lost Peggy's brother.

They made their way to the exits, wondering what to do. Then Kwame saw that police had blocked all the doors except one, through which they were checking every person entering or leaving. With great relief he saw a smiling Tam with several police officers escorting Kojo, Peggy and a scowling brother. Kwame kept well away, he didn't want his compatriots to suspect that he had played any part in their arrest.

21

Homecomings

Kwame said goodbye to Greg and Mick and sent them back to Coventry, thanking them and promising to tell them more on his return. They were profuse in their apologies but Kwame told them, 'All's well that ends well!' Then he followed at a distance with Tam as the police led the absconders to the office of the chief customs officer. 'Wait here,' Tam said, indicating a small waiting room. 'I'll be back to update you as soon as we've completed the preliminary interviews.'

Leon's secretary brought water, coffee and the daily newspapers, and Kwame settled down to a good read. *The Times* crossword puzzle was only half completed when Tam came back. 'Your man, Kojo, caught his plane to Accra,' he said. 'It was soon clear that he knew nothing connected with drugs trading and was just hoping for help in avoiding flying back to Ghana. He was given the option of continuing on his journey or being held for further official investigations. He decided to follow his suitcase onto the aircraft and was escorted to the departures lounge.'

'What has happened to Peggy?' Kwame asked.

'She admitted overstaying her visa, saying that she wanted to stay with her relatives in London. When she was asked why she had agreed to help Kojo Doe commit the same offence she said that they had agreed to help one another before they left Ghana. Unfortunately for them, Kojo had not been nominated for the first visit and had been rejected by Warwick for the second. Peggy had been sent in the first group with Kwaku Darko, who was not in the scheme, so she had had to turn to her brother, Yaw, to help her stay in Britain. When at last Kojo succeeded in reaching the UK she felt obligated by their agreement to do what she could to help him extend his stay.'

'Peggy said it was Bra Yaw who asked her to carry a parcel to London and he told her to give it to Mr Konadu. When she was asked what was in the parcel she said that she wasn't told, but suspected that it was cocaine. After a few more questions, Leon decided to hand Peggy over to the police to be held in custody and charged with bringing a banned substance into the UK. He assured her that her guilty plea would shorten her sentence, at the end of which she would be repatriated to Ghana.'

'What about brother Yaw, was he interviewed?' Kwame asked.

Tam first confirmed that Yaw was not Peggy's true brother, just someone from the same village. 'When Yaw was brought in he presented Leon with a business card indicating that his full name was Alphonse Yaw Ankrah, Attorney at Law,' Tam said. 'Leon asked him if he was qualified to practise in England. He said that he was and he specialised in residence and naturalisation matters. He warned us that Miss Osei-Wusu's application for residence had reached an advanced stage and that he would vigorously contest any attempt to repatriate her.'

'How did Leon answer that?' Kwame asked.

'He said that if she's convicted of bringing narcotics into the UK even he, Lawyer Ankrah, would not be able to prevent her eventual deportation. He was advised to consider his own position. He had aided and abetted a self-confessed drugs trafficker to remain in the country illegally and he might well be suspected of attempting to commit the offence a second time today.'

'Then what did he say?'

'He said that he knew nothing about any drugs.'

'What will happen to him now?'

'He was handed over to the police for formal charging.'

Tam walked with Kwame to the Discovery. 'Are you coming back to Coventry with me?' Kwame asked.

'Yes, if you'll have me; I'm based there for the time being.'

'Then climb in and fix your seat belt.'

They reached Coventry mid-afternoon before Kwame realised they had not stopped to eat. 'If you're hungry,' he said to Tam, 'let's go to the senior staff club for a late lunch.' They served themselves at the buffet, chose a table that had been cleared of debris, and were still setting their places when Tom came in.

'Mick told me you were back,' he said, 'so I thought I might catch you here.' Assuming that Tom had already had lunch Kwame said, 'Grab a coffee and join us.'

Tom was soon back and took a seat across the table from Tam who glanced up from his cauliflower cheese to exclaim, 'My God, you look as though you've seen a ghost!'

'You may think that's true when you hear my story.'

'Why what's happened?' asked Kwame.

'You know Elsie has been helping to look after Little Tom,' he began, looking to Kwame for confirmation. 'Well, these days it's dark when she brings him home in the evenings. She's a nervous girl, especially since the kidnapping, and her English is so limited that the first time I didn't believe her.'

'What didn't you believe?'

'She said that a man was watching the house.'

'Not you, Tam?' said Kwame with a grin.

'Go on,' said Tam.

'I decided to go out to take a look around but I saw nothing. However, Elsie told me again and the next day I decided to take a more careful look. I went out by the back door and crept round in the shadows and, sure enough, there was a man standing in a dark patch under a tree.'

'Did you get a good look at him?'

'My road is very quiet, especially at night, and I waited a long time to get a better look at him in the headlights of a passing car. At the sound of an engine he realised that he would be exposed to view and moved quickly behind the tree trunk but not before I got a look at his face.'

'Did you recognise who it was?'

'I must be going crazy, but for a moment I was sure it was Akos Mary's father, Mr Konadu, but Akos Mary told me he was dead!'

Kwame knew that he could answer most of the questions raised by Tom's pseudo-paranormal experience. His problem was that there were a few things that he felt Tom would be distressed to hear about his late wife and her father. He was also concerned about what Tam might say or do. Tam would obviously be interested to know Konadu's whereabouts in order to apprehend him as soon as possible. It was with some relief that Kwame heard Tam gently trying to calm the distraught professor.

'It's all my fault,' Tam began. 'I was sent to Ghana to trail Mr Konadu but I failed to stay close enough to him. A brief press report suggested he had been shot and killed but I wasn't able to confirm his death. Recently we have been informed that he's still alive and in England. He was reported to have been involved in the assault on Elsie Ntim. So I suspect that you were not mistaken; you did see Mr Konadu. This information is of great value to the authorities.'

'Thank goodness for that,' said Tom, 'then I can still claim to be sane!'

'Yes,' said Kwame, 'and you did very well to recognise Konadu after all these years, having seen him for only a few days around your wedding.'

'I guess the wedding photos kept the memory alive but what do you

307

suppose Konadu wants at my house? If he's trying to abduct Elsie for a second time, the poor girl has every reason to be afraid.'

'If Elsie has seen him several times, he must also have seen Elsie. I'm sure he has no more interest in the young lady,' said Tam.

'No,' Kwame said gently. 'I'm afraid that it's more likely that he's trying to contact Akos Mary. We didn't tell you at the time, but Konadu came twice before to ask Akos Mary to help him.'

'What was he doing in England? I thought he went back to Ghana.'

'No, he didn't go back to Ghana after the wedding but we managed to get rid of him and he stayed away from Akos Mary for several years.'

'Then what did he do?'

'We don't have a complete picture,' said Tam, 'but it seems that he got mixed up in the drugs trade. Somebody he upset reported him to the immigration service and he was deported back to Ghana where, it now appears, he faked his own death'

'But he came back to the UK.'

'Yes, he must have used a false passport; many of the drugs traffickers do. We have various reports of Konadu getting involved with drugs, both before and after his expulsion. He seems to have started with trying to get your late wife to hand over Kwame's live snails stuffed with cocaine. Then he collected packages from couriers like Peggy Osei-Wusu and more recently attempted to recruit Elsie Ntim as a courier.'

'So why do you think he's come looking for Akos Mary again?'

'Poor Konadu is a born loser,' said Kwame. 'He told me himself that every business he tried in Ghana had gone wrong. He's probably failed with the drugs, quarrelled with the traffickers, run out of money, and come crying to his daughter to rescue him again.'

'Doesn't he know she's passed away?'

'Probably not,' said Tam.

'What can we do?' asked Tom.

'We need to apprehend Konadu,' said Tam, 'and if we do, it will solve your problem at the same time.'

'Can you let Little Tom sleep at my place for a few nights?' asked Kwame. 'Then we can ensure the safety of both Little Tom and Elsie.'

'Yes, of course,' said Tom. 'And will you arrange the arrest of Konadu, Tam?'

'I'll get on to it right away. Thanks for the lunch, Kwame,'

After Tam had gone Tom said to Kwame, 'Tam was unusually open in answering my questions. I guess much of what he told me would not usually be divulged.'

'I'm sure it was out of consideration for your family connection.'

'And my bereavement?'

'That too.'

Later that night a relieved Elsie was putting Little Tom to bed when the telephone rang. It was Tom reporting that Tam and two police officers were in his house with Mr Konadu in handcuffs. Could he come over and confirm that the prisoner understood the charges and his legal rights? Grabbing his overcoat and scarf, Kwame called to Afriyie that he wouldn't be long and stepped out on a dry cold night to walk the short distance to his friend's residence. Passing through the dark reaches between the street lamps he realised again that Elsie had every reason to fear any stranger she saw lurking in the shadows. If her English had been better she might have saved herself a few frightening journeys. The young lady from Kukurantumi was not lacking in pluck!

It seemed to Kwame that Elsie could not have recognised the 'big man' who had ordered her beating. If she had, she would surely have assumed that the man was seeking to recapture her and told Afriyie. She would certainly have refused to risk the journey a second time. No, Kwame assured himself, Konadu was looking for his daughter. He wondered if the news of Akos Mary's death had yet been told to the neglectful father.

Mr Konadu was on his knees weeping. 'He's just been told,' Tom whispered. Tam and the police officers greeted Kwame and indicated that they were waiting for the captive to regain his composure. Kwame tried not to think that Konadu's grief was more for his own plight than the fate of his daughter. He told himself that he was here in a strictly neutral capacity, a family friend, like a lawyer ensuring the prisoner understood his rights.

In due course Kwame was able to confirm the charges in Twi and ensure that Konadu fully understood his position. The charges included using a false identity to enter the UK, dealing in prohibited substances, kidnapping and physical assault.

'Why did you run off so quickly?' Afriyie asked Kwame on his return. Elsie and Akosua were watching a film on television with Akosua providing a soundtrack in Twi, so Kwame replied, 'Let's go to our room and I'll tell you.'

Afriyie closed the bedroom door and settled herself on her side of the double bed, giving Kwame time to gather his thoughts. He wasn't quite sure how Afriyie would respond to the news. 'They've caught the man who ordered Elsie's beating,' he said.

'Elsie says it was a man called Konadu; was it really Akos Mary's father?'

'Yes it was.'

Afriyie stared at Kwame with a look of incredulity and horror. 'Then the whole family are devil worshippers,' she cried. 'The daughter used witchcraft to steal my husband and the father beat my niece to turn her to evil ways!'

'It's not like that. Reach your chest down. The *abrofo* will punish him.'

'Will they? Will they? He'll use black magic to get away.'

'I don't think so.'

'He will; didn't he use black magic to return from the dead?'

'No he didn't; he just faked his death.'

'You don't understand. You think just like *oboroni*. They have cursed my family and we will be destroyed.'

'It's Akos Mary who was destroyed.'

With this brutal statement Afriyie calmed down. 'Akos Mary knew what she had done was bad,' Afriyie said. 'Do you think her father will do the same?'

'I don't think Konadu is very intelligent. He has tried many things but all have failed. I think he's bewildered about what has happened to him. I don't think that he knew that Elsie was your niece when he beat her. He wasn't trying to harm you or your family.'

'What will the *abrofo* do?'

'They will lock him up for a few years and then send him back to Ghana.'

'Do you think he will trouble us again?'

'No, I don't think so.'

Kwame was not surprised to be summoned when Leon interviewed Konadu, but this time they assembled at Coventry police headquarters where the prisoner had been held since his arrest. Kwame had made it clear to Leon that he did not want any of the drugs traffickers to know his part in their detection and so he would not be present at Konadu's formal interrogation. He had agreed to interpret at Tom's house as a family friend but any further direct involvement might eventually be dangerous for himself and his family.

Leon had also invited Tam Gordon, David Barney and Auntie Rose. He decided to conduct the interview himself with the help of Tam Gordon. The others watched through a one way glass. Leon was clearly expecting that his latest catch would fill in the gaps in their understanding of the situation of the Kumasi cartel. Knowing Konadu as he did, Kwame felt that Leon's hopes of getting Konadu talking would be fulfilled but Leon's expectation of understanding what was happening in Kumasi was over ambitious.

Konadu was willing to speak freely about his recent activities. He explained how he had stayed on in England in 1990 after the wedding, financed for some months by his daughter, Akos Mary. Then he had decided to try his luck in London where he met many Ghanaians who helped him in various ways. He struggled on for several years but, just as in Ghana, every business he tried ran into difficulties. So he consulted a fetish priest who told him that an enemy had put a curse upon him. He was advised to return to Coventry where the presence of his daughter offered a degree of protection.

Konadu related how he came back to Coventry early in 1994 and met a few Ghanaians who asked him to help revive the drugs trade. They did what they could for a few months with some help from Kumasi but not many packages reached them. In desperation he persuaded the Kumasi people to send a consignment of cocaine to his daughter, Akos Mary, concealed in the shells of live forest snails, but this too failed. He managed to collect one consignment from Peggy Osei-Wusu, but shortly after that he was betrayed by a colleague who wanted to take over in Coventry and the *abrofo* sent him back to Ghana.

'Where you faked your death,' said Leon.

'Yes, a friend who works for the *Ghanaian Times* put something in the newspaper for me.'

'Why did you do that?' asked Tam.

'I wanted to get back to *aborokyiri* as soon as possible to keep my position.'

'On a false passport?'

'Of course.'

'Did you succeed in keeping your position?'

'Yes I did.'

In answer to another question from Tam, Konadu said they had tried to recruit couriers from Kumasi University who were coming to Coventry to study and didn't need air tickets or living expenses. 'This saved us money when money was scarce,' he said, 'but soon the recruiting became more difficult and in the end our people in Kumasi stopped recruiting. So we started to look for couriers at this end.'

'Through the Pentecostal church?' asked Leon.

'That's right.'

'So Elsie Ntim was intended to become one of your couriers?'

'Yes, I'm sorry. I didn't know she was from Kwame Mainu's house.'

'A man who beats a woman is not a man,' Tam said in Twi.

Leon added, 'You made a big mistake turning to violence.'

'That was Kwesi's fault, he hit her too hard.'

'Kwesi Robert Gyan?'

'Yes'

'Did he know you before you changed your name?'

'Why do you ask that?'

'He called you by your real name after beating Elsie.'

'The man's a fool.'

At this point Leon suspended the interview and withdrew to his team in the other room, leaving Konadu with a minder from the local police force. He asked everyone how they felt about what they had learned so far. 'Everything fits in reasonably well with what we know already,' said David Barney.

'But he has spoken only of Ghanaians; he hasn't mentioned the Lebanese,' said Kwame.

'Exactly,' said Leon. 'What can we make of that?'

'Either the Lebanese have not been involved or he's shielding them,' said Tam.

'I think they're not involved, at least not at this end,' said Kwame. 'Konadu isn't clever enough to conceal anything, and he knows it.'

'Then let's go back and ask him,' said Leon.

As Kwame suspected, Konadu only looked confused when asked if there was any problem between Ghanaian and Lebanese factions of the cartel. 'I didn't meet any Lebanese in Coventry, only Ghanaians.'

'How would you describe the situation in Coventry when you started to work here?' Leon asked.

'The big men had all been arrested years before and only a few of the small people remained. The small people wanted to start again but they didn't know what to do.'

'So you thought that you could take over?'

'At first, they asked me to.'

'And later?'

'When things went badly they said I should hand over.'

'That's when you quarrelled with a rival?'

'Yes.'

'What's the name of your rival?'

'I don't want to say.'

'If you want a minimum sentence, you should tell us.'

'It's Pastor Arnold Obeng-Mensah.'

'Is he the pastor of the Pentecostal church?'

'He comes there sometimes but he's not the man in charge.'

'Are you a member of the church?'

'Yes, I am.'

Leon asked Tam if he had any more questions and in response to Tam's headshake he had Konadu returned to his cell. 'Where does all that leave us?' he asked, as soon as the team reassembled.

'It seems that what went on in Coventry was much as we surmised,' said David Barney, 'except that all the disruption appears to have been caused by Konadu and his rival and not by Lebanese factions.'

'Yes,' said Auntie Rose, 'it must have been Pastor Obeng-Mensah who betrayed Konadu's whereabouts to the police.'

'Do you know the pastor?' Leon asked.

'Oh yes,' replied the little lady. 'We suspect that he selects the young people to send to Birmingham to be trained as couriers.'

'Was he involved in Elsie's abduction?' asked Kwame.

'Yes, he was. I believe he sent Elsie to Konadu for initiation.'

Leon showed signs of wanting to bring the meeting to an end so he attempted to summarise the situation. 'Kwame has disbanded the Ghanaian cartel in Kumasi,' he began, 'and now we see that the attempt to revive activity here in Coventry is near to collapse. The removal of Konadu appears to have left Pastor Obeng-Mensah in charge but this gentleman may not be at large for much longer. He can be charged with involvement in the abduction of Elsie Ntim.

'We now have a clear picture of what the Ghanaian community has been doing but we have learned nothing new about the activities of the various Lebanese factions. Our one consolation is that there is no sign of any new Lebanese group attempting to take over what remains of the Ghanaian distribution and sales network. The split resulting from the removal of Uncle George and Mama Kate seems to have left the Lebanese in Kumasi completely cut off from their former market here and only Peter Sarpong seems to pose a threat of its reconnection.'

That year the Christmas festivities were much more subdued than in the two previous years. The absence of Akos Mary was felt by all and Tom was quite incapable of participating in any preparations. The grandparents made a brave effort to provide the usual diversions for Little Tom, and Kwame took his family along in support, but all failed to exorcise the ghosts of Christmases past. Tom and Kwame looked forward to getting back to the regular work routine as soon as the New Year dawned.

Kwame was aware that this year, 1997, was a special milestone in his life and in the life of his country. Both would turn forty, and he had heard it often repeated that life begins at forty. Would this year bring anything resembling a new life? Well, for one thing, his three-year contract with Warwick University would expire in July and he would need to decide whether to apply for an extension or return to his old role in Ghana.

Was it safe to return to Ghana? It certainly felt safer than when he left in 1994 but there was still the problem of Peter Sarpong. He had seen what Peter had done to Akos Mary but Kwame was sure that he and Akosua would not be susceptible to attack by juju. He was less sure about Afriyie; she had also abandoned the Pentecostal church when accusations of witchcraft had started. Could Peter be reformed, as the two Kofis and Bra Yaw had been? He had been abandoned by the Ghanaians and rejected by the Lebanese who formerly composed the Kumasi cartel. What other route was open to him?

Peter had shown an interest in Comfort. What did Kwame want to do about his rapidly improving relationship with his long-lost wife? He could envisage a sunlit future in which he settled back down in Ghana with Comfort and Akosua. There were no economic barriers; their life would be comfortable enough, but how long would it last? Akosua would be going on to university, maybe even this year; would she want to be in Ghana or in England? Then, in a few more years, she would be making an independent life of her own. He would miss her, but he did not think her absence would harm his relationship with Comfort.

The major consideration in a return to Comfort must be the fate of Afriyie. Did he want to maintain both relationships? It was certainly an option. Back in Kumasi he knew a number of academics and businessmen who happily maintained two households. At the university, some professors lived off-campus in houses constructed with a university loan while in their on-campus residences they maintained their second wife and family. Others, not so adept at working the system, lived on- or off-campus in Kumasi from Monday to Friday, slipping back to the village to tend the cocoa farm and their rural family at the weekends. 'No,' Kwame decided, 'that life would not suit me and I know that it wouldn't please Dad.'

In spite of much effort, Afriyie had produced no children. The chances of her providing him with a second family seemed remote. Kwame had no desire to condemn Afriyie to a lonely existence, waiting and wondering

314

each evening if he would come. Her own preference, he thought, would be to go back to Tom and help him raise Akos Mary's son. This was what in effect she was already doing. She had shown anger when her suspicions that Akos Mary had resorted to witchcraft to divert Tom's affection had seemed to be confirmed, and she had told Kwame that she envied Comfort staying in Tom's house. She said that she still loved Tom and he, Kwame, had told her that he still loved Comfort. Yes, the happiest outcome would be for Afriyie to marry Tom and leave him, Kwame, free to return to the wife he had never divorced.

Kwame knew that, as once before in his life, Tom was the key to his future happiness. How deep was Tom's wound, and how long would it take to heal? Six months had passed and there were some signs of recovery. Afriyie, Tom's old love, would be a natural choice when he next felt free to contemplate his domestic future. Immediately after Akos Mary's death Tom had turned to Comfort for tender care; now his reliance on Afriyie was constrained only by her attachment to Kwame. Should Kwame say or do something to loosen the ties? This issue required more thought. In the meantime he must attend to his professional duties.

Kwame needed to work on the final preparations for his next trip to Kumasi with Greg Anderson. Greg was in a buoyant mood. He was looking forward to being back in Kumasi in the warm weather that was nearer to what he remembered from his childhood in Australia. He was also happy to be working on another computer course. This time he would be using some of the machines donated by Professor Thomas that would be sold on cheaply to participating artisans at the end of two weeks' instruction. Greg had checked these computers and prepared them for shipment. He knew that they would update even some of the facilities they had borrowed for the last course from within Kumasi University. Introduced to small enterprises they would presage a new era in their development.

'Has Prof found us a job-costing expert from the business school to help us with this course?' Greg asked.

'Let's go to ask him,' Kwame replied, leading the way out of the office, but they met Tom coming towards them with a young white woman, smartly dressed in a light-grey business suit.

'This is Dr Sonya Carpenter who has volunteered to accompany you to Kumasi,' Tom said. After the usual introductions he said, 'You don't have long to prepare. I'll leave you to start the briefing.'

'I'm afraid this course will be well below the level at which you usually teach,' said Kwame, 'but we are running a series of courses for small engineering workshop proprietors in Kumasi who are being introduced to personal computers and have asked for some instruction in basic business skills.'

'I'm very interested to help,' Sonya replied. 'We have a training programme for small and medium enterprises, now known as SMEs, that we are developing for businesses in this country and overseas. I specialise in accounting and teach courses in costing and everything up to drafting full-scale business plans.'

'Then you should be able to give us exactly what we need,' said Kwame. 'Greg will give you a list of the companies who have applied to come on this course. You will see that they are mostly sole proprietorships with up to twenty-five employees.'

'Who won't grow any bigger until they delegate some functions,' said Sonya.

'Exactly.'

'And the first function to be delegated is accounting.'

'That's right – how do you know?'

'It's a common glass ceiling in SMEs everywhere.'

'Then I see you are the right person to help us,' said Kwame, and Greg was eager to agree.

Kwame wanted to be sure that Sonya would be ready to travel and start the course on time. 'The course starts in Kumasi on Monday 27 January,' he told her, 'and we must fly down on Sunday 19 January to give us time for final preparations with our colleagues down there.'

'No problem, I'll be ready.'

Kwame left Greg to work on detailing Sonya's assignment and turned to the concerns of his other assistant. Mick Gould was disappointed not to be travelling to Kumasi but he understood that he was needed to support Tom. He also had more to do before Sandra Garg would be able to take over the preparations for the visit of Ophelia Darko. Sandra had written to Tom expressing her intention to resume duty on schedule but no one could be sure that she would be able to sustain her work output with the additional commitment to her new family. Mick was prepared to support his colleague through what could be a difficult period of adjustment.

'We've found a couple of technical colleges that still teach metal spinning to craft students,' Mick told Kwame, 'but our suspicions that the technology is no longer used here in manufacturing seem to be justified.'

'The technology is well established in Tema,' Kwame said. 'What we need are ideas for new products; can we find some of these in your technical colleges?'

316

'I'm not sure.'

'Then you and Sandra had better visit them and see what they are doing before Ophelia arrives here in February.'

'What products are already being made?'

'They are listed in the report that Ophelia and Sandra wrote last year.'

Mick had seen Sonya come in with Tom and watched her accompany his colleague across to Greg's desk where the pair sat close together studying the documents relating to the forthcoming course. 'Who's the gorgeous girl?' Mick asked Kwame.

'Is she gorgeous?' said Kwame absent-mindedly. 'Oh, that's Dr Sonya Carpenter from the business school; she's helping us with the course in Kumasi.' Then, realising that he should have completed the introductions, he added, 'Come and meet her.'

They moved across to where Greg and Sonya were deep in conversation. 'I'm sorry to disturb your work but I want you to meet the last member of our team,' Kwame said to Sonya, who rose to take Mick's hand.

'Mick Gould,' said Mick. 'Please don't get up.'

'Sonya Carpenter,' Sonya replied.

'Mick is our most experienced expatriate in Kumasi,' Kwame added, 'a veteran of three trips to Ghana.'

'Then you must tell me all I need to know to minimise culture shock,' said Sonya.

'We can start with a chat over lunch,' said Mick.

'I'll look forward to it.'

Mick noticed the list of participants on Greg's desk. 'Do you mind if I take a look, Greg?' he asked.

'Go ahead,' Greg said. 'I expect you recognise most of the workshops; almost all are repeaters from our earlier courses.'

'That's what I'm thinking,' said Mick. 'I may be able to give you some useful background information.'

Kwame and Tom usually had lunch together whenever they were both in the office and free of visitors. Today they sat together in the senior staff club observing their two younger colleagues competing for the attention of the young lady from the business school. It reminded Kwame of the time when his contemporaries at the West Africa club were similarly engaged in a contest for the favours of Akos Mary, but Kwame could say nothing about this to Tom. 'Who do you think will win?' Kwame asked, recalling his question to Peter Sarpong.

'I expect a no score draw.'

'Why do you say that?'

'The young lady is being polite, but that's all.'

'Perhaps she'll meet someone she likes in Ghana.'

'That's very possible,' said Tom.

Kwame made his way back to his office thinking about all there was to do in the few days remaining before his next trip to Ghana. He considered the option of flying on to Kumasi from Accra. It would cost more than travelling by road but it would avoid a four-hour drive in heat and dust that *abrofo* found especially debilitating. Kwame recalled the distress felt by Sandra Garg and Professor Thomas, although the professor had insisted on returning the same way. He wondered how Sonya would stand up to the rigours of the road. Without further hesitation, he picked up the telephone and booked three return flights: London – Accra – Kumasi.

With a warning tap on the open door Mick came into the office and sat down facing Kwame across the desk. 'Did you have an entertaining lunch?' Kwame asked.

'She's certainly an interesting woman,' Mick said. 'She's been almost everywhere already but never to West Africa.'

'Then she'll enjoy her trip to Ghana.'

'Everybody does!'

'What can I do for you, Mick, is there something you need?'

'Yes, it's the list of participants coming to Greg's course; you heard me ask to see it.'

'I guess you know most of the workshops, even most of the people.'

'I do, but we usually have only engineers.'

'Are there any exceptions this time?'

'Yes, we have one spare parts store.'

'That's strange.'

'What's even stranger, it's the store you were looking for: *Sika Ye Na* enterprise!'

22

Contrasts

Kwame knew that, however much there was to do before his next trip to Ghana, Mick had added to the workload. If a *Sika Ye Na* enterprise had booked to come on the course it could be an attempt by the Hanabis directors to explore a new route to the UK for their contraband. Kwame, during his investigations in Kumasi, had discovered that there were numerous businesses with this same name, but the possibility of it being a Hanabis partner or subsidiary could not be ignored. He must alert Leon.

Told by David Barney that Leon Thornet couldn't leave his headquarters at such short notice, Kwame found himself driving once more to Heathrow with Tam Gordon as his companion. On arrival at the airport they hurried to Leon's office, helped by Tam's official security pass. Leon was curious to learn what had brought Kwame to him in such haste and uncharacteristically started questioning before Kwame had drained his glass of water.

'You will remember,' Kwame said with a splutter, 'that I found in Kumasi that the Lebanese company Hanabis is ordering artefacts that could be used for concealing drugs through a small company called *Sika Ye Na* enterprise.'

'I remember,' said Leon.

'Well, we have a participant on our next course at Kumasi University sponsored by *Sika Ye Na* enterprise!'

'Is it the same *Sika Ye Na* enterprise? You told us that there are several with that name in Kumasi.'

'That's true, but if it is the same company what do you want me to do?'

'When are you leaving?'

'This coming Sunday, 19 January.'

'When does the course start?'

'Monday 27 January.'

319

'Let me summarise the position,' Leon said, in his usual methodical manner. 'We know that the Ghanaian transport and distribution system that was employed by the Kumasi cartel has broken down, and the Lebanese faction is currently deprived of this facility.' In response to nods from his companions, he continued, 'We also know that the Lebanese have been innovating means for future drugs transfers, including Kwame's pistons and coat hangers. Purchases of these Kumasi-made artefacts are sub-contracted to a *Sika Ye Na* enterprise.

'We can assume that a high priority for the Lebanese is to find a way to replace the services formerly provided by their Ghanaian partners. In the dying days of their collaboration they might have come to know that couriers were being recruited through your university partnership programme. Now they could be exploring whether this programme offers any hope for re-activation. And what better means than to enrol someone on one of your training courses?'

'Can you cancel the participation?' Tam asked Kwame.

'I've thought about that,' Kwame replied, 'but it is our partner, Kumasi University, which controls participation. We would need strong grounds to recommend cancellation. In this case the company is listed as a spare parts store, not an engineering workshop, but they could still be accepted by our partners on the grounds that they place orders with the engineering workshops and could have a legitimate interest in job costing. Then, we cannot be sure that this *Sika Ye Na* enterprise is the one associated with Hanabis. If it isn't, it would be very unfair to recommend cancelling their participation.'

'As I see it,' Leon said, 'we have no choice other than to ask Kwame to keep a close watch on the *Sika Ye Na* representative. Kwame will try to discover if there is a Lebanese connection and, if so, he will report all he can learn about their motives and activities.'

'I'll do what I can,' Kwame said, 'but I can't be with the participants all of the time.'

'Then we'll ask Tam to help.'

'Can I ask you something?'

'Go ahead,' said Leon.

'How is your plan progressing to entice a Hanabis director to the UK?'

'We're not making much progress so far,' Leon admitted. 'Bra Yaw was not much help; what he knew wouldn't stand up in a British court. Your old friend Crispin Russell's information is long out of date and no viable way has yet been found to involve him in an enticement scheme.'

'So Bra Yaw is back in Kumasi?'

'He was put on a plane to Accra so he's presumed to be back in Kumasi.'

'That's good,' said Kwame, 'he might help me with *Sika Ye Na*.'

'Don't take any unnecessary risks, Kwame. Your job is to try to foil any renewed attempt to infiltrate your academic partnership programme and to prevent the recruitment of any more drugs couriers.'

'A task that's of interest to both my masters!'

'Precisely.'

'You were quiet during that meeting,' Kwame said to Tam as he threaded his way through the motorway traffic on the way back to Coventry.

'You know my role,' Tam replied, 'watching and listening.'

'Well, what does your watching and listening tell you?'

'That we are getting closer to the Lebanese.'

'How does that change things?'

'I'm not sure but it could be more dangerous.'

'Didn't we overestimate the danger before? We suspected the Lebanese were involved in the Konadu affair but we were wrong.'

'This *Sika Ye Na* business is much closer to them.'

'So you'll be around again this time?' Kwame prompted.

'Leon wants me to be there but this time I would like to play it rather differently.'

'How do you mean?'

'Could I be connected with your course – as a member of your team?'

'That's tricky,' Kwame said. 'There must be academic integrity. Professor Arthur would never agree to you doing any teaching without the appropriate qualifications.'

'I understand that, but don't you have any non-academic role I could perform?'

'Yes!' Kwame said, with sudden inspiration. 'You can help with selling Greg's computers.'

On arrival back in Warwick, Kwame and Tam headed for Professor Arthur's office. Tom had Sandra Garg with him but he beckoned to the newcomers to join them. 'Sandra's starting again next Monday,' he said.

'Welcome back,' said Kwame. 'I'm sorry I won't be here.'

'Say hello to Kumasi for me.'

'Sandra, this is Squadron Leader Tam Gordon,' Tom said.

'So you're the young lady with the twin daughters, congratulations!'

After Sandra had departed in search of Mick and Greg, Kwame briefed Tom on recent developments. 'Tam has asked to come along as part of our team,' Kwame explained, 'and I thought that he might help Greg with the allocation and sale of the used computers.'

'Those are the machines that came from Professor Thomas's lab?'
'Yes.'
'I can't see any problem with that, but you must work out the division of responsibilities with Greg.'
'I'm happy to do that,' Tam said. 'I'll just perform routine tasks and leave all the decisions to Greg and Kwame; I won't interfere with your work.'
Kwame took Tam to meet Greg. Sandra had gone, so Greg was called to join them in Kwame's office. 'I want you to meet Squadron Leader Gordon,' Kwame said.
'Pleased to meet you Squadron Leader.'
'Happy to meet you Greg; call me Tam.'
'That's fine with me, Tam.'
'The Prof and I have known Tam for some time,' Kwame explained. 'He's an old friend, now retired from active service. Tam would like to come with us to Kumasi as a volunteer on a working holiday and the Prof has agreed that he can help you with the allocation and sale of your used computers.'
'That sounds fine. I was wondering how I was going to support the teaching and handle the sales at the same time.'
'Yes, once you've explained the scheme you can ask interested participants to contact Tam for registration and full details. Please provide Tam with copies of the list of participants, the list of computers and any other documents that might help him.'
'What about the selling prices?' Greg asked. 'We want to recover the cost of transport, is that still the policy?'
'Yes, you can add, say, ten per cent to cover our handling costs.'
'Will all the machines be sold at the same price?'
'You're the best person to judge, Greg. If some are newer or better you can adjust the prices accordingly. Let me have your recommendations with copies for the Prof and Tam.'

Kwame flew to Accra with Greg and Sonya on Sunday afternoon. 'Where's Tam?' Greg asked, as he buckled himself into his tourist class seat. 'Does he prefer to travel business class like Prof Thomas?'
'Tam always makes his own way,' Kwame explained. 'He's not with us today.'
'He doesn't need you to guide him then?'
'He's an old Ghana hand and speaks Twi so don't be surprised if you

find him conversing with the participants in the vernacular. On the other hand he may hide his skill in the hope of hearing something he wasn't intended to hear.'

'Oh, I wish I could do that!'

'Then buy a teach-yourself book and take a few lessons while you're in Kumasi; that's what Mick has done.'

'Isn't there a quicker way?'

'You could take a Ghanaian girlfriend!'

After a night in the university guest house in Accra, they flew on to Kumasi. It had been comfortably cool in the plane but the sun was now well up and Sonya was experiencing its full effect for the first time. Kwame was glad he had not subjected her to the rigours of the road journey and she had escaped the ordeal of Sandra Garg. He couldn't help hoping Sonya would also escape Sandra's other ordeal, but that was an issue over which he felt he had little control.

A TCC vehicle was waiting for them and in ten minutes they were entering the university campus under the soaring stool gate, modelled on Ashanti's famous golden stool. 'Oh, what a beautiful campus,' Sonya cried. 'Are you sure the plane didn't crash and we've woken up in paradise?'

'It can't be paradise; Kwame and I are still with you,' quipped Greg.

'There was an Australian here once,' Kwame recalled, 'a born-again Christian, who on learning there was a fetish shrine on the campus assigned it to the estate of the devil!'

'I guess you see what you want to see,' said Sonya.

After settling themselves in their guest chalets they spent the rest of the morning meeting colleagues from the TCC and the school of engineering. In the afternoon they drove across Kumasi to Suame Magazine to visit the ITTU and some of the workshops that were sending participants on the course. Sonya was meeting people for the first time. Taking advantage of every patch of shade, she was making records in a damp, limp notebook and carefully checking the spelling of unfamiliar names. 'I'll never remember how all these names are pronounced,' she said.

'Don't worry,' said Kwame, 'with sixty languages spoken in Ghana, and people coming to the university from all parts of the country, there are some names that we all find difficult.'

When Kwame called Comfort to announce their safe arrival, he was invited to bring his companions to a welcoming dinner. So at the close of work Kwame took his party across town to meet Comfort. It was the customary visiting hour and the sun was still up. They drove from Suame down the hill to Kejetia, past the lorry park of the biggest market in

West Africa, then around a huge circle teaming with rush hour traffic and up Prempeh II Street, Kumasi's modern shopping centre. Turning left onto Harper Road they drifted down into the valley and then up the magic hill, past the great bulk of the City Hotel on the right to the garden suburb of Nhyiasu.

Sonya was first startled by the bustling vitality of the congested city centre then enchanted by the tranquillity and beauty of her post-colonial surroundings. 'What a city of contrasts is Kumasi!' she exclaimed. 'The whole spectrum of African life can be experienced within a few kilometres.'

'I like bringing new people to my city,' Kwame said. 'It lets me see familiar things through new eyes and I learn to understand and appreciate them anew.'

Comfort welcomed them warmly, and seeing that they had come straight from the heat and dust of Suame Magazine she invited them to freshen up before sitting in her bougainvillea-bedecked garden. Comfort asked Sonya if she would like to borrow a fresh dress and she reappeared in an elaborate local creation that had recently been sewn as a present for Akosua. This transformation provided an introductory topic of conversation, and they chatted and sipped cold beverages under a sun shade and in the draught of an oscillating table fan, until the falling sun sent mosquitoes on patrol to drive them indoors.

Thinking that it might be a little too soon to start Sonya on *fufu*, Comfort provided a dinner of chicken and jolof rice followed by pineapple and pawpaw. Sonya could contain her curiosity no longer, 'You have a beautiful house,' she said to Comfort, 'could I be taken on a guided tour?'

Abandoned by the two women, Greg and Kwame were left alone with their drinks in the lounge. 'How could you ever bear to leave a woman like Comfort?' Greg asked.

'I had no choice,' mumbled Kwame.

Sensing that he had touched on a raw nerve Greg hastened to add, 'Well, you seem to have patched things up very well. All of us on the project appreciate the generous hospitality Comfort provides.'

'Yes,' said Kwame, 'she even melted the heart of Professor Thomas!'

'Which greatly promoted my modest efforts,' said Greg.

When Kwame had first taken the house tour almost four years earlier it had lasted only ten minutes. Today the men waited for more than half an hour for Comfort and Sonya to return. It was not late, but Kwame suggested a return to the campus as they were all tired after their first day under the tropical sun. In a flurry of 'thanks', 'come again' and 'goodnight', they clambered into the Land Rover and drove quietly down the gravel drive.

As they descended the long hill and past the slaughterhouse, Kumasi brewery and silent sawmills, they found themselves on eroded dirt roads amid the broken-down mud-brick houses with rusty corrugated iron roofs. Fortunately for Sonya, save for the kaleidoscopic sweep of the headlights, the bulk of Kumasi's poverty was now shrouded in darkness and she could retain the image of Comfort's elegant residence. She had been duly impressed. 'I was only with Comfort for a few hours,' she said, 'yet I feel that I have known her for years. What an exciting life she leads in that lovely house with a thriving business and frequent trips overseas!'

'But isn't social life in Kumasi rather dull?' suggested Greg.

'Not according to Comfort,' Sonya insisted. 'She and her boyfriend, Peter, seem to find plenty to amuse them.'

Kwame felt Sonya's words like a bullet through his heart. Hadn't Comfort promised him that her relationship with Peter Sarpong was purely investigatory? How could she go back on her word to the extent of telling Sonya that Peter was her boyfriend? He had looked forward so much to seeing Comfort again and now all his hopes had crumbled to dust. He drove grimly on in the darkness, hardly caring to avoid the numerous potholes and gullies. 'Steady-on, Kwame!' Greg cried. 'We've all had a heavy dinner!'

Kwame dropped his friends at their chalets and then sat in the vehicle wondering what he should do. His first thought was to return immediately to Comfort's house. Oh yes, he realised, that's exactly what she wants me to do; the remark to Sonya was only the cheese in the mousetrap. Should he go? Should he allow himself to be enticed? One thing that the initial shock had done was to make him realise the strength of his revived feelings for his estranged wife. Should he be moved by those feelings? Pushing the heavy gear lever forward he let the ancient Land Rover retrace its path with ever ascending anticipation.

The week of preparation passed uneventfully and as usual on a Sunday afternoon before the beginning of a training course, Kwame and his colleagues assembled in the car park in front of the TCC office to await the arrival of the participants. Most of the expected visitors would be well known and greeted as old friends, but there were always a few new people from old client enterprises and a few newcomers from enterprises that were represented for the first time. Kwame was especially curious about their new client *Sika Ye Na* enterprise, the only non-engineering company yet to apply for training under the partnership programme.

Greg was concerned that although he had been a week in Kumasi, preparing for the course, he had yet to see his sales assistant, Squadron Leader Tam Gordon. Sonya was excited to be meeting her students and was hoping a few of them would be female. Kwame had warned her that only one or two women had attended the technical courses but he expected a few more female students to come on this course because he knew several workshop owners employed a wife or daughter to keep the accounts. Sure enough, as vehicle after vehicle disgorged its expectant passengers, six or eight women coalesced into a separate group and Sonya was able to assist Ophelia Darko of the TCC in leading them to their accommodation.

Greg had been ably assisted in preparing for the course by Kwaku Duah and Kojo Doe, and now the team of three shepherded a group of about twenty men slowly in the direction of the students' hall of residence that would be their home for the next two weeks. Their progress was delayed when Kwame was spotted, and he underwent the long process of shaking everyone's hand. Those who knew him already were eager to introduce him to the others and he heard 'Doctor Mainu' and Professor Mainu' too often to rebut.

'Have we got anyone from *Sika Ye Na* yet?' Kwame asked Greg.

'I don't think so, Professor,' Greg replied with a grin, 'but we can't be certain until we register them formally at the hall.'

That evening the whole community of instructors and participants assembled in the dining room for their first meal together. Greg confirmed to Kwame that nobody from *Sika Ye Na* had yet registered and they speculated on a late arrival the next morning. It was then that Kwame spotted Tam sitting quietly among the participants and apparently engaged in monitoring the friendly banter in the vernacular. Kwame wondered if Tam had changed his plan and was presenting himself as a participant, perhaps as an accountant in one of the larger engineering enterprises. A few Europeans were employed in this capacity. Was this a temporary or a permanent change of role?

Kwame pointed Tam out to Greg but restrained him from going to greet the older man. 'Leave him to plough his own furrow,' he whispered.

'What's he really doing here?' Greg asked, and Kwame realised that his assistant deserved at least a partial explanation. 'Come to my place after dinner,' he said to Greg, 'and I'll try to tell you what's going on.'

Later in Kwame's guest chalet, as he and Greg sipped mugs of Milo,

Kwame said, 'Before I begin I must stress that what I am going to tell you is strictly confidential. You must not repeat any of it to anyone else.'

'I understand,' said Greg, 'but does that include Tam?'

'Yes, it does, unless Tam broaches the matter with you.'

'You will have noticed,' Kwame continued, 'that some of our visitors to Warwick have been going astray. First Peggy avoided returning on schedule, then Nelson, and recently Kojo tried the same trick. We learned that a drugs cartel, based in Kumasi, was recruiting our academic visitors as couriers and both Peggy and Nelson were suspected of bringing cocaine into the UK. In Nelson's case the drugs were found and that is why he is now serving a prison sentence.'

'Wow! That's a lot to take in.'

'Well, we have made much progress in stopping the abuse of our programme, and we believe it is no longer happening at the moment. However a group is suspected of trying to revive the activity, possibly through *Sika Ye Na* enterprise.'

'So Tam is here to watch *Sika Ye Na*?'

'Exactly.'

'Thanks for telling me; I'll cooperate fully with Tam.'

'Just treat him as one of the team.'

'I understand.'

They sipped their Milo in silence. Kwame guessed that Greg was trying to digest what he had learned. It was getting late, and Kwame was contemplating a glance at his wristwatch or a stifled yawn when Greg asked, 'Which outfit does Tam really work for?'

'It's a mystery to me, but he's somehow connected to UK customs.'

'You say you've known him for some time?'

'Yes, more than two years.'

'Then you've been involved in this business that long?'

'It's been our problem that long.'

'Right,' said Greg, rising to return to his own chalet. 'See you in the morning.'

Next morning, after a brief opening ceremony attended by the vice-chancellor and a few other dignitaries, the course got under way. As soon as Greg mentioned that at the end of the course some of the computers would be sold at affordable prices, some participants started to clamour to be registered. Greg looked at Tam who gave a firm nod, so Greg was able to advise his flock to give their names to Mr Gordon at any time during the course. Tam started his task during the first coffee break, when a queue formed in front of his desk.

At the end of the morning's session the participants were leaving to walk to the dining room for lunch, but Kwame signalled to Greg and Tam to wait. When the room was cleared, he said, 'It looks as if our efforts are in vain; there's no sign of *Sika Ye Na* enterprise.'

'Don't give up yet,' Tam said. 'If they're who we think they are they won't be interested in job costing; they won't worry about missing a few lectures.'

'Who won't worry about missing a few lectures?' asked Sonya, emerging from a side office to join her colleagues in the computer laboratory.

'Teachers needn't attend lectures in which they're not directly involved,' Kwame said.

'I shall attend throughout,' Sonya said. 'I need to know exactly what others have taught before I start my lectures next week.'

'That's the best approach,' Kwame said. 'People don't always follow the agreed syllabus.'

'I've got a problem,' Tam said to Kwame as they sat taking lunch.

'Already?' Kwame replied, feigning surprise.

'Some of the participants are proprietors who can place firm orders for the computers, but some are employees who don't have this authority.'

'How is that a problem?'

'Well, several of the employees want me to reserve computers for their employers but it will take them several days to get written confirmation. They are worried that they might miss the boat.'

'Tell them all that we will need written orders by Wednesday week. All orders received by that day will be given equal consideration. Do you agree, Greg?'

'That sounds fair to me,' Greg said. 'They can telephone today and they will have more than a week for the post to reach them here, but what address should they use?'

'Here's the post box of the TCC,' Kwame said to Tam. 'Tell your people to get an order posted back to that address by Wednesday week.'

'That's 5 February?'

'Yes. We'll hold the allocation meeting the next day and announce the first allocation at the closing ceremony on Friday.'

'Then we leave the TCC to finalise the sale?'

'That's right.'

Something was now troubling Greg. 'Will those who are disappointed this time be considered for the next batch of machines?' he asked.

'Yes,' Kwame said. 'I suggest that we give them priority when the next consignment of Prof Thomas's computers reaches Kumasi. Ideally we want everyone who buys one of our computers to have been on our training course.'

'Should I tell them this when they sign up?' asked Tam.

'It will encourage them,' said Greg.

'Yes,' said Kwame, 'hopefully they will all be supplied eventually.'

'Eventually,' said Greg, 'we'll have more machines than candidates on this course.'

'Yes,' Kwame said, 'we will need to repeat this course in July.'

The training course went smoothly forward and the students expressed satisfaction with what they were learning, but day after day the vacant space reserved for *Sika Ye Na* enterprise remained unfilled. On Friday Kwame and Tam reviewed the situation. 'In one way,' Kwame said, 'I'm happy, because it means that the attempt to infiltrate our project seems to have been abandoned.'

'If they have abandoned their plan,' replied Tam, 'it would be useful to know why. Were they warned off in some way?'

'Perhaps the name of the intended participant will provide a clue.'

Kwame scanned the list of companies who had originally registered to attend the course. 'Look,' he said to Tam, '*Sika Ye Na* enterprise: Ms Cecilia Obeng-Mensah, proprietor.'

'Obeng-Mensah, Obeng-Mensah,' said Tam, 'where have we heard that name recently?'

'It's a fairly common name in Ghana.'

'Yes, but it came up recently – when we were talking to Konadu.'

'Do you mean Pastor Arnold Obeng-Mensah of the Pentecostal church?'

'That's it!' said Tam. 'Do you think there could be a connection?'

'The pastor would know of Elsie's release and the arrest of Konadu and Gyan.'

'So if there is a link Cecilia could have been warned to stay away.'

Kwame knew that if *Sika Ye Na* enterprise was connected to Hanabis, it was likely that the female proprietor was a former girlfriend of one of the Lebanese directors. In this case Cecilia might have been a contemporary of Comfort or otherwise known to Comfort through her numerous contacts in the trading community.

'There's a good chance that Comfort will know if Cecilia is connected to Hanabis,' Kwame told Tam. 'Let's pay her a visit when we close this afternoon.'

'Any excuse to see your ex-wife,' said Tam with a wink.

'It's a serious suggestion that will aid our investigation,' insisted Kwame with a grin.

'Combining business with pleasure,' Tam continued in the same vein. 'If you don't stop, I'll have your *fufu* rationed.'

'Oh, that'll stop me!'

Comfort welcomed them with, 'I'm glad you've come, Cook has prepared far too much *fufu* and I was going to throw most of it away.'

Kwame and Tam exchanged grins. 'Kwame threatened to have my *fufu* rationed earlier today,' Tam told her.

'Oh, don't do that, Kwame, we need his full capacity tonight.'

A fierce tropical storm, which often occurred at this time of day, prevented them conversing over a drink in the garden, and the drumming of rain on the roof, walls and windows prevented conversation indoors until the storm's initial fury was expended. 'Is this storm a freak or is the rainy season coming early this year?' Tam shouted in Kwame's ear.

'Whatever it is we'd better wait quietly until it passes,' Kwame shouted back, 'it won't last long.'

They sat in silence sipping their drinks, each lost in their own thoughts. Kwame felt that he and Comfort shared thoughts in common but what was Tam thinking? Was he narrowly focused on their present investigation, eager only for an early reduction in ambient acoustic pollution, or was he dwelling on past memories of tropical storms long ago, heralding cool passionate nights after long hot days? He looked across at Tam who stared back with an intensity that persuaded Kwame that telepathy might not be a myth. He decided to restrict his musing to his own affairs.

After twenty minutes or so normal conversation could be resumed. 'What can I do for you boys?' Comfort asked.

'First, please, can you give me another glass of this delicious Grunshie *pito*,' Tam said. 'It brings back so many fond memories,' he added with a pointed look at Kwame.

Comfort returned with Tam's glass filled to the brim and laughed as he struggled to lower the level without causing a spill. 'What reaches on two?' she asked in Twi.

'Second, we want to ask you if you know a woman called Cecilia Obeng-Mensah?'

'Cessie!' cried Comfort. 'I've known her for a long time.'

'Is she connected to the Lebanese?' Kwame asked.

'She was Suleiman Hannah's girlfriend for many years; she even hints the affair is not over. She's very beautiful.'

'Ah yes, Janet Dery mentioned her once,' said Kwame.

'What does she do?' asked Tam.

'She has her own business, I think.'

'What sort of business?'

'I'm not sure, I never asked her – she's not in shoes.'

For the next half hour the disposal of the *fufu* took precedence and conversation was limited to comments on the quality of the food and the hospitality of the hostess. It was when they were sitting and digesting with suitably stimulating beverages that Comfort's curiosity could no longer be constrained and she asked, 'What has Cessie done to excite so much interest?'

'She applied to come on our training course,' Kwame said.

'But she's not an engineer; as far as I know.'

'No this course is on computerised accounting and job costing.'

'So she's on your course – she must be popular with the men!'

'No, she didn't register on Sunday with the others and we haven't seen her yet.'

'Do you happen to know what Cecilia's father does?' Tam asked Comfort.

'Yes, he's a pastor,' she replied. 'We used to joke about a pastor's daughter being a Muslim man's mistress.'

'Is the father with the Pentecostal church?'

'Yes, I believe so; Afriyie told me she had met him once in Coventry.'

'Then it looks as if all our speculations are correct,' said Tam, taking another long pull on his beloved *pito*.

Driving back from Nhyiasu, Kwame and Tam felt that they had made some progress in spite of *Sika Ye Na* enterprise's failure to attend the training course. Using an ex-girlfriend and her father suggested that the Lebanese were being forced to extreme measures in their attempt to reconnect to a Ghanaian distribution network in the UK. 'They must have gained great benefits from the partnership in the past,' Kwame observed, 'to want to re-establish it so badly.'

'It looks like they've missed a chance to infiltrate your programme,' Tam replied, 'and with Konadu in gaol and Pastor Obeng-Mensah under observation, we seem to have blocked their efforts so far.'

'I can see why the Lebanese want a Ghanaian marketing organisation in the UK,' Kwame said, 'but I don't understand why they also need couriers. They have other means of sending drugs to the UK through the extensive export trade they control.'

'It's a case of smaller needles in bigger haystacks,' Tam explained. 'With so many millions of passengers passing through the major UK airports every year, it's impossible to check every person. Some air couriers are bound to get through.'

'Are cargo imports somewhat easier to monitor?'

'I think they must be,' said Tam. 'Drugs cartels use every means to transport their contraband by sea, including high-speed launches, specially constructed submarines and vehicles on sea ferries, but they still employ large numbers of air couriers. They wouldn't use them if they didn't show an advantage over other means.'

'So you think the Lebanese still need Ghanaian air couriers?'

'Isn't that clear from their continuing efforts to recruit your people?'

Kwame thanked Tam for explaining something that he had wondered about for a long time. 'So you don't think that what Leon calls "my pistons" have much chance of getting through as sea or air cargo?'

'No, Leon's much more concerned about your hollow wooden coat hangers and he's put out a special security alert on them.'

'Have any been picked up yet?'

'If they have, he hasn't told me.'

'Would you like to see where they are made?'

'Do you know the place?'

'No, but I believe I can find out.'

The next morning Kwame drove Tam in the old Land Rover to the informal industrial area known as Anloga, a place dominated by carpenters and woodworkers of all types. Behind the workshops charcoal-burning kilns were in perpetual operation, filling the air with gases that stung noses and caused eyes to redden and flood. 'I guess that if Sonya thinks the university campus is paradise, this must be the other place,' Tam quipped, as Kwame failed to find a path between piles of timber, stacks of wooden products and huge potholes filled with water from last evening's great storm.

'It's not far from here, we can walk,' Kwame said, 'but I'll have to get out on your side if I'm to keep my socks dry.'

Walking was almost as difficult as driving because a considerable pedestrian traffic dominated the least muddy tracks between the numerous obstacles. Competing with other human beings is one thing; competing with people carrying head-loads consisting of long wooden planks, chairs and tables, and huge sacks of wood shavings, is quite another. Those bearing burdens mostly wore shorts and went barefoot, they were practically mud-proof; they made no concessions to their visitors who were less-suitably dressed. 'I hope this will be worth it,' called Tam, as he slithered and cursed and watched Kwame draw ever further ahead.

Kwame was heading for SRS Engineering, the workshop where the coat hanger forming machines had been manufactured. He was about to turn off the road when he realised that Tam, trailing behind, might not see where he had gone. He waited for Tam to puff and perspire his way to where he was standing. 'It's right here,' Kwame said, leading the short distance to the SRS workshop and knocking on the open door of the manager's office. As always the welcome was cordial, and Coca Cola helped to dispel memories of the mud.

'What can we do for you?' Solomon Djokoto asked.

'First, we came to thank your brother, Ben, for giving his talk on keeping the books of a small enterprise.' Kwame said. 'It went down very well with the students, and they really appreciated getting copies of his book *Accounting for Beginners*. I was very happy when the TCC told us Ben was making a contribution.'

'I'm sorry Ben's not here,' Solomon said. 'It's his Saturday off this week, but I'll pass on your appreciation.'

'On our engineering drawing course,' Kwame said to Tam, 'we brought the participants here to see how drawings are used in practice.'

'Do you help with all the courses?' Tam asked Solomon.

'Only those mounted by the TCC,' Solomon replied.

Tam not being an engineer, his tour of the workshop was very brief. 'So you design all your new products, do you?' he asked Solomon.

'Yes, I like to be challenged by a new requirement.'

'What has challenged you recently?'

'A machine for making hollow wooden coat hangers,' Solomon said.

'Was that difficult?'

'The wood is formed in two identical halves, but they needed one machine to form the outside and another machine to form the inside.'

'That sounds like an impressive achievement; is there any chance of seeing the machines?'

'I doubt if they would show you. They regard them as industrial secrets.'

'Are they here in Anloga?'

'No, but not far away, near the Hanabis sawmill and the Shell filling station.'

'I know the place,' said Kwame.

As they were about to leave, a thought struck Kwame. 'Do you still have the original pattern?' he asked Solomon.

'No, they insisted on taking it away when the machines were collected, but I still have my sketches.'

'That's fine,' said Tam. 'Do you mind if I take a photograph?'

'Go ahead,' said Solomon.

23

Coat Hangers

They followed Solomon's directions and Kwame parked on the forecourt of the filling station.

'Before we go in,' Tam said, 'we must agree on our cover story.'

'What do you suggest?'

'I could pose as a foreign customer looking for a new line in wooden products and you can be my local guide.'

'And you don't speak Twi.'

'No, I don't speak Twi.'

It was a fifty-metre walk to the woodworking shop, which was wedged between residential houses and across the road from a large sawmill. Kwame asked what was being produced; he had a foreign customer looking for new ideas for exports. He was told to bring his client into a small showroom. Here was displayed the traditional range of wooden artefacts, including elephants and fertility dolls as well as stools of all sizes and hands holding eggs: the Akan symbol of good governance.

Seeing nothing he had not seen many times before in every store catering to the tourist trade, Tam said, 'These objects are all hand carved, so each one is different from the others. I'm looking for machine-made mass-produced goods that I can purchase by the hundreds.' Kwame carefully repeated in Twi what Tam had said.

'Yes, we make everything with our hands; that is their beauty. I don't know any machine that can do it,' Kwame was told by the salesman and he duly interpreted for Tam.

'I don't think we're going to get any further,' Kwame said, and Tam reluctantly followed him back out onto the street. They had only walked a few metres back towards the car when Kwame felt a tug on his sleeve. He turned to find a boy of ten or twelve years who whispered a few hurried words in his ear.

'What did he say?' asked Tam.

'He said, "Alhajji Hannah put the machine in his other house".'

'Which house?'

'He said we should follow him.'

The boy had walked quickly away back past the store they had just visited. The pair hurried to follow for a hundred metres or so, and then their guide turned into a narrow alley between two houses. He stopped beyond the houses where high walls continued to seclude back yards on both sides of the alleyway. 'The machine is in there,' said their helper, pointing to his left.

'Do you know what it makes?' Kwame asked.

'I don't know the name.'

'What's it like?'

'A stick you hang things on.'

'Good boy,' Kwame said, pressing a thousand cedi note into a small hand before their conspirator ran off to spend his windfall.

'We'd better run off too,' said Kwame. 'We don't want to be caught snooping round here. They walked briskly back to the vehicle trying not to seem to hurry. Kwame was glad that although Tam was a white man he had learned by long practice to be relatively inconspicuous, so no special curiosity could be detected on the faces of bystanders.

They agreed to drive back to the campus before analysing what they had learned. 'Let's have lunch at the swimming pool restaurant to celebrate,' Kwame said, and Tam nodded his approval. They found seats in the draught of a swinging table fan and placed their orders with one of Mrs Dodoo's attractive trainees. Tam waited until the drinks and food had been brought and took a few bites at a leg of roast chicken. 'Now let's see where we are,' he began.

'Well, I think we know where the SRS machines are installed,' Kwame said.

'And the whole operation is hidden from public view.'

'And the machines are not being used to produce for general sale, probably just for one customer.'

'Which strongly suggests that the purpose is illegitimate.'

Kwame pondered on what the boy had told him. 'Can we assume that Alhajji Hannah is the owner of the machines?' he asked.

'Not necessarily, he could be just the landlord,' Tam replied. 'I've noticed that small boys like to speak as though they are close to big men, and Alhajji Hannah appears to own two houses. That makes him a big man in that local area.'

'Yes, he could be a very big man. Suleiman Hannah is a director of Hanabis and according to Comfort he's also Cecilia's boyfriend.'

335

'Do you think that Alhajji Hannah and Suleiman Hannah are the same person?'

'The same person or a close relative.'

'And the house is close to the Hanabis sawmill.'

'It's all in the family then!'

It was Saturday afternoon, and Kwame had promised to spend the weekend with Comfort, so he dropped Tam at his guest chalet and drove on to Nhyiasu. He didn't expect to find Comfort in the house – she would be out on her weekly round of funerals – so he settled down for a good read of the British newspapers of the previous week and steeled himself for the inevitable rebuke about not keeping his word. Coming in from the heat of the afternoon, Kwame shivered in the air-conditioned room and asked the maid to bring him a pot of tea. 'Can we turn down the air-conditioning?' he asked the girl.

'Oh no, Madam sets the temperature; I'm not allowed to touch it.'

Kwame wondered if he dared raise this issue with his returning wife. Comfort had already made some concessions for his convenience. On a previous visit, he recalled, he had been reduced to reading a shoe catalogue. Now he had the pick of the London newspapers and weekly magazines. He had been given a set of keys to the house and could regard it as a second home. The big question now was, could he regard it as his first home and even share in the setting of the air-conditioning? He wondered if room temperature could be a decisive factor in making or breaking a marriage. He turned back to the *Economist* for guidance but it spoke only of *global* warming.

Kwame was only half way through his pile of reading material when the heat and exertions of the morning caught up with him and he drifted off to sleep. He had never become a dedicated siesta-taker but he had dabbled with the habit from time to time. As he grew older, however, he noticed that the practice became less a planned routine and more an involuntary imperative. For an hour he relaxed in the warm embrace of that other world.

Many years ago, when he had been working at the TCC in Kumasi, Kwame had met a young English lecturer who had asked him if he flew in his dreams. Being an engineer, Kwame had checked if flying in an aircraft was included. 'Oh no,' he was told. 'I mean flying like a bird without mechanical aid.' It was then that Kwame realised that he did fly in this way. He had heard of the English test of pinching oneself to check if one was dreaming. For him the criterion was fear of heights; the ability to fly eliminated vertigo in his dream world.

336

Kwame soared with the angels for an hour or so, and awoke gently when one of the most beautiful of the maids of paradise whispered it was he alone whom she loved. Comfort had kissed him gently on the lips.

'I've brought you more tea and some cakes,' she said. Then with a shiver, she added, 'Don't you think it's cold in here? Why didn't you adjust the air conditioning?'

'Welcome home,' he said, rubbing his eyes.

It seemed a good idea to get in the first word on his failure to attend the funerals. 'I'm sorry about this morning,' Kwame said. 'Something important came up and Tam needed my help.'

'Was it connected with Cessie's business?'

'Indirectly yes, we were checking on one of her suppliers.'

'I don't want you getting involved with Cecilia Obeng-Mensah.'

'It's very unlikely, but I don't want your imagination running wild again like it did with Akos Mary.'

'Or yours with Peter Sarpong.'

'It wasn't fair of you to use Peter to pull me back.'

'You can never make up your mind except under pressure, Kwame Mainu.'

'You're right as usual, Mrs Mainu.'

On the Wednesday of the second week of the course the application list for the supply of used computers was closed. As the team had expected, nearly every enterprise represented on the course had registered. The allocation committee met the following day. Kwame had invited the TCC director and the dean of the school of engineering, as well as Greg Anderson, Kwaku Duah, Kojo Doe and Sonya Carpenter, who had all worked closely with the course participants.

Kwame started by asking for the numbers to be confirmed. 'We've brought ten machines from Warwick so far,' Greg said.

'Yes, but one has developed a fault during the course,' Kwaku interjected. 'It can be fixed, but we shouldn't sell it yet. How many applications do we have?' Kwame asked.

'I've got Tam's list here,' said Greg with a grin. 'Twenty-seven participants registered but three companies hadn't confirmed their orders by yesterday's deadline.'

'So we have twenty-four applications for only nine computers.'

Kwame wanted to be clear on the criteria of selection. 'I suggest that the most important criterion should be the performance of the participants on the course,' he said. 'A selected company must have at least one promising operator. That's why we've invited the instructors to be with us. What other criteria should we use?'

'The size of the company should be considered,' Sonya said. 'A larger company has greater need.'

'I agree with that,' said the TCC director. 'A computer may help them break through the glass ceiling at about twenty-five employees.'

'On the other hand,' Kwaku said, 'a large company might be able to afford a new machine. Isn't the idea to help the poorest people?'

'I don't think any of our clients can afford new machines,' said the TCC director. 'I wouldn't want to judge who can afford what; we have no data to go on.'

'I think Mr Battah is right,' Kwame said. 'Let's not bring in what we cannot properly assess.'

At the end of two hours they had managed to reduce the approved list down to nine enterprises. The TCC director agreed to inform the chosen few and invite them to call to collect their machines. Kwaku Duah agreed to help with the installations. Kwame reminded Mr Battah to write to the disappointed companies, promising that their applications would be considered when more machines arrived from Warwick. The course had been over-subscribed, so it was agreed to repeat it in July. Greg gave his assurance that at least another fifteen machines would arrive by then. Kwame thanked everyone for their contributions and invited them to reconvene in six months' time.

That evening in his chalet Kwame received visits from two disappointed participants who had registered with Tam but whose companies had not responded in time. 'The best I can do,' he told them, 'is to ask you to send the written orders to the TCC director, and I will ask him to include your companies in the next allocation.'

After his visitors had gone, Kwame wondered how they knew so soon that they had not been included. Then he realised that they must have been told they were too late when they tried to hand in their confirmed orders. He made a note to advise Mr Battah to treat the third latecomer in the same way if a third confirmed order was brought in.

Later that evening there was another knock on Kwame's door. 'That's the third one,' he said to himself as he rose to answer it. As the door opened, a sweetly scented breeze alerted his nostrils a second before his eyes focused on a beautiful and elegantly dressed mature woman. 'Cecilia Obeng-Mensah, I presume,' he said, standing aside to admit his visitor.

Neither admitting nor denying her name, and avoiding his outstretched hand, she swept past him and settled herself on the most comfortable chair. Kwame hurried to provide a glass of water, which was graciously accepted.

Kwame was beginning to speculate that this woman, who seemed to be physically perfect, was actually devoid of a tongue, when she said abruptly, 'Why are you making enquiries about my business?'

'I'm an engineer,' Kwame said, 'helping workshops in the town to improve their products. One client showed me some engine pistons and said they were for *Sika Ye Na* enterprise. So I wanted to know more about the use of the pistons before advising on quality improvements.'

'The pistons are fine; they don't need any improvements.'

'Then there's nothing more for me to do.'

She stared at him for some time with doubt in her eyes. Kwame assumed that his visitor was trying to frame the next question in words that would give nothing away. With some relief he saw her give up the struggle. 'I want a computer,' she said.

'There are some on sale at Kingsway and UTC stores.'

'Not a new one, they're too expensive; I want one of your used ones.'

'I'm sorry, they've all been allocated.'

'All but one, I want that one.'

Alarm bells rang in Kwame's head but he tried not to show his surprise. How could Cecilia know about the one computer that had not been allocated? He thought that he could trust the members of the allocation committee. The members had not been sworn to secrecy; this necessity had not been considered, but he had assumed that their decisions would remain confidential until they were announced to the participants the next day.

It must be Kojo Doe who had passed on the information. He had maintained contact with Peggy Osei-Wusu, and perhaps through her with other members of the cartel in Kumasi. He might even have met Cecilia's father, Pastor Obeng-Mensah, in Coventry. If Cecilia knew what had been decided at the meeting he must stick to the facts. 'One machine has a fault,' he said, 'and must be repaired before it is sold.'

'I want it for *Sika Ye Na*,' she said.

'The allocation committee will not meet again until July. You can put in an order to the TCC but it won't be considered before the next meeting, and I must warn you that we favour enterprises which have sent their people for training.'

'You're a hard man.'

'I try to be a fair man who follows the system.'

'How can I persuade you to help me?'

'You can attend the course in July, or send one of your people,' Kwame said, still trying to be fair.

After Cecilia had gone Kwame felt a need to share what he had learned, so he walked across to Tam's guest chalet. Tam opened the door in his dressing gown and suggested it was rather late for a social call. 'This is your business,' said Kwame, 'and you will want to hear it while it's still fresh.'

'Come in then, and take a pew.'

'I've just had a visit from Cecilia Obeng-Mensah, the proprietor of the *Sika Ye Na* enterprise.'

'Is she as beautiful as Comfort said?'

'I'm telling you.'

Kwame quickly related what had transpired. 'First, she wanted to know why I had been making enquiries about her company, then she switched to demanding that we sell her the remaining used computer.'

'Nothing was said about coat hangers?'

'No, I mentioned only the pistons as the source of my interest in *Sika Ye Na*. I said that as an engineer advising client workshops I needed to learn more about the application. She couldn't mention coat hangers without revealing her own involvement.'

'And she knew what had been decided at your meeting?'

'Yes.'

'Do you think it was Kojo Doe who spilled the beans?'

'I do. I doubt if any of the others know the lady.'

Tam said he thought it was likely that their visit to the handicrafts store that morning had prompted the lady's visit. 'If that is so then she learned nothing new,' Kwame said, 'but we have learned that she has a contact inside our project and that contact is most likely Kojo.'

'And you think the link is either Peggy Osei-Wusu or Cecilia's father.'

'Probably both; if the Lebanese are using Cecilia and her father to revive a Ghanaian partnership, they might know of Peggy's past involvement and given her name to the pastor.'

'Then Peggy would have told them of Kojo.'

'It seems to make sense, but it's largely conjecture.'

'I'll let Leon know; he could ask Peggy about it. My impression is that the young lady will tell us all she knows to shorten her prison sentence.'

Kwame wondered how seriously Tam viewed these developments as a threat of renewed drugs traffic. 'It seems to me that the effort has already failed,' Tam said. 'Neither Kojo nor Peggy will be able to act as couriers, the pastor is under observation, and Leon will be forewarned about Cecilia if she attempts to enter the UK. They will probably continue their efforts, but in recent weeks they have gone backwards rather than forward.'

'I hope you're right,' said Kwame.

The next day they held the closing ceremony for the training course. Everyone was in high spirits, even those participants who had failed to be allocated a computer. They all went home with a certificate of attendance and a few proudly clutched documents bearing the words 'merit' or 'distinction'.

Kwame was looking forward to spending the whole weekend with Comfort before flying back to London during the following week. He had anticipated spending Saturday morning attending funerals but he learned from Sonya that the programme had been rearranged. 'Do you remember me wearing that beautiful dress Comfort has bought for your daughter?' she asked excitedly. 'Well, Comfort has agreed to help me find more like that tomorrow morning.' Then Kwame remembered the stock of half-read newspapers and journals in Comfort's lounge, and the past week's new arrivals, and decided the wait would not be unbearable.

Early on Saturday morning, Kwame drove Sonya to Comfort's house where Sonya was introduced to Ashanti breakfast of red bean stew, fried ripe plantain and gari. Kwame could never understand how women could rush out to the shops after such a meal but that is what Comfort and Sonya did, leaving him with the output of the London printing presses of the previous two weeks. He was quite content. Time moves slowly in Africa. If he wanted up-to-date news he could turn on Comfort's new satellite TV and watch CNN, but he preferred deeper analysis. He reached for the *Economist* and the *New Scientist*. Hadn't he been trying to get a grasp of the arguments for and against human activity being a cause of global warming?

Kwame had always been content with the temperature of his homeland. It was warm enough, sometimes even a bit too hot. England, on the other hand, was much too cold. As an engineer he hoped that the scientists would soon work out the mechanisms involved so that engineers could begin designing a means for transferring five or ten degrees Celsius from West Africa's atmosphere to the atmosphere over Western Europe. He speculated on the contribution this export of heat energy might make to the Ghanaian economy. Well, the macro climate might be temporarily beyond his control, but in the meantime he could enjoy his newly granted privilege of adjusting the micro-climate. He reached for the remote control of the air conditioner.

At almost the age of forty Kwame was well aware that there were many characteristics of the fair sex that the feeble male mind will never fathom. One of these was the female addiction to shopping. Once they set out on a trip there was no known means of predicting when it might end. Lunchtime came and Kwame realised that he must eat alone, so he called the maid and asked what was easy to prepare. After lunch he took the opportunity to indulge in a full-length siesta. This time he expected to awake naturally and he was not disappointed.

With the London publications fully digested, Kwame was about to turn on the TV when he heard the crunch of the car on the gravel drive. After a short interval Sonya burst in with, 'Look at the lovely dresses we found!' Comfort soon followed with, 'There are so many new stores opening these days, Kwame. Cessie has opened a new dress shop on Prempeh II Street and she's called it *Sika Ye Na* like her other business. We bought heaps of the latest styles. Every dress comes with a beautiful carved wooden hanger. Cessie says she's sending loads to Ghanaians in the UK. I'll give you the ones to take back for Akosua. I'm sure Afriyie will want to copy them.'

'I'll take the dresses,' Kwame said, 'but leave out the hangers.'

Kwame had looked forward to a quiet weekend with Comfort but it wasn't working out that way. Now, he realised, he still had work to do. He called Tam on his mobile telephone and asked him to come by taxi as soon as possible. When he arrived, Kwame showed him the pile of dresses and the coat hangers. 'All the dresses with wooden coat hangers came from Cecilia's new dress shop, *Sika Ye Na*,' Kwame told Tam.

'So that's how they planned to use them!' said Tam.

'Are you going to open one?' Kwame asked.

'Can we borrow a knife?' Tam asked Comfort.

'What are you going to do?'

'We want to split open one of the hangers to see what's inside.'

'You're not going to spoil one of these lovely hangers?' Comfort protested.

'If we find nothing inside, we'll glue it back together again.'

Tam and Kwame took one of the coat hangers to the kitchen where Tam selected a suitable knife from Comfort's considerable collection. 'Hold it steady, Kwame, while I press the blade into the join,' he said. With steady downward pressure the hanger split neatly into two identical halves.

'Just as I thought,' Tam said, 'there's nothing hidden inside these hangers for local sale.'

'Can we be sure all the others are the same?' Kwame asked.

'If we don't open them, I don't think Comfort ever will,' said Tam, 'and then it hardly matters what's inside.'

'How about Sonya's hangers?'

'We must advise her to leave her hangers behind.'

'Then Comfort can keep Sonya's hangers and you can take this one to show Leon,' Kwame said. 'It will alert his people what to watch out for.'

'Yes,' Tam said, 'now we have the pattern we were looking for last Saturday.'

Sonya was disappointed to be deprived of part of her bounty, but when she was shown how the hollow interior of the split hanger could conceal drugs, she decided she didn't want to risk carrying them into the UK. They couldn't guarantee that an export model had not accidentally got mixed up with the batch for local sale.

Kwame and Tam held a private discussion. 'I think Cecilia has missed the bus,' Tam said.

'How do you mean?'

'Well, you alerted us to hollow wooden coat hangers months ago, when the machines to make them were still under construction at SRS Engineering. As soon as we got your information Leon issued instructions for all wooden coat hangers showing up on X-ray scans at ports of entry to be further investigated. Now we have a pattern of the exact model and the system is already in place to detect them. It's unlikely that many of Cecilia's coat hangers will get through.'

'Prevention is better than cure, eh?'

Tam said that he thought they had stumbled on something quite fundamental in the war on drugs. Every device used by the traffickers to conceal their contraband needed something to be specially manufactured for that purpose. By being intimately involved in helping grassroots artisans and small workshops to develop their technology, projects like Kwame's were ideally positioned to detect trafficking innovations at an early stage. They had seen that this could enable the border agencies to be alerted in time to block innovations when they first came into use.

'I've learned more about your project on this trip,' Tam said, 'and I'm impressed with the work you are doing. The nature of the work requires keen observation and so your people are trained to spot anything unusual. Almost by accident you've spotted two devices being manufactured to aid the traffickers, but it was by accident only in the sense that it was not part of your project to report such matters to the authorities. You reported your observations because you were wearing two hats; working for the university and also for Leon. I'm going to suggest to Leon that a project like yours could be adapted to provide us with a structured early-warning system that would help us block future innovations, just like we're blocking the coat hangers.'

'How would you do that?'

'First, all your people on the ground could be trained to watch out for potential methods of concealment and report their suspicions.'

'Would you tell them this was part of the war on drugs?'

'They would need to know. It would motivate them, and we could provide cash bonuses for information leading to preventative action.'

'You would need to include all the people on the ground, including, for example, all the TCC people.'

'Of course, the more the merrier!'

'It might work,' said Kwame, 'but I fear that it might seriously interfere with our primary function.'

After dinner Tam took Sonya back to the campus in a taxi and Kwame was free to enjoy the company of his restored spouse. They relaxed watching *Osofo Dadzie* on the TV. 'I'm not sure I approve the way this programme has changed,' Kwame said.

'How do you mean?'

'Well, originally they used pure Twi, like Kofi Adjare speaks, but now they use modern street Twi, full of English words and American slang.'

'I suppose it makes it more realistic, especially for the younger people.'

'Yes, I suppose so, but my father wouldn't have liked it.'

'No, but he doesn't have to listen to it, does he?' Comfort said gently, putting a protective arm around his shoulders.

On the flight back to London, Kwame was accompanied not only by Greg and Sonya but also by the TCC's metal products designer, Ophelia Darko, looking forward to her long-delayed visit to her friend Sandra Garg. As usual on the night flight Kwame's companions were soon sleeping but Kwame knew that he had much to think through before he could join them. Now that his dreams had come true, and he was reunited with Comfort, he was forced to face reality in all other aspects of his life.

For the first time in many years Kwame felt that his future was clear before him. At the end of his three-year contract in July he would return to Ghana and live with Comfort in her house in Nhyiasu. They hoped that Akosua would join them, at least during her university vacations, wherever she was studying.

Kwame was determined to continue his technical work. He would build his diesel engine, either with KNUST or with a revived AT Ghana, perhaps with both. As long as the link with Warwick continued he would do all he could to support it; perhaps Tom could devise some new Ghana-based role for him to undertake for a few years. Whatever course he followed one thing was clear, he was no longer constrained by economic forces. He and Comfort together possessed all the resources they needed or would ever need.

Kwame realised that there were a few gaps in this vision of a golden future. Could he break the relationship with Leon, for example? In spite of Tam's vision of a long-term association, based on the idea of an early-warning system, Kwame had no desire to be involved. He felt that he had finished the tasks assigned to him. His people in Kumasi had stopped sending drugs to England and efforts to revive the trade had been foiled.

Kwame knew that although a few battles had been won, the war against drugs would go on, but it was time for younger warriors to take his place. He would do anything he could to stop hard drug use in Ghana but he was tired of helping the *abrofo* fight the influx to the UK. Ghana had been independent for forty years; it was time for Kwame Mainu to follow.

Just as he saw no place for Leon in his future working life, Kwame had come increasingly to realise there could be no place for Afriyie in his domestic affairs. At the same time he knew that he owed his long-time companion a great debt of gratitude. She had stood by him in difficult times and been his good friend and lover for almost nine years. She had been an affectionate surrogate mother to Akosua, through years when Akosua's real mother had neglected her.

Kwame knew that Afriyie would always remain his close friend. As a long-term partner, however, Afriyie had often spoken as though Comfort still had the first claim upon him, and since the death of Akos Mary she had shown signs of wishing to return to her first love. Tom's wounds might not yet be healed enough to reciprocate that love, and Afriyie would need gentle handling throughout a period of adjustment.

On arrival at Heathrow they were met by Mick and Sandra. 'Prof got us the faculty minibus,' said Mick, 'so we have plenty of room for all of you and your luggage.'

'Sonya's been telling me about all the dresses she bought in Kumasi,' Ophelia said to Sandra.

'Yes, I'll show you both when we reach Coventry,' Sonya said.

'Did she tell you about the coat hangers?' Kwame asked, grinning at Mick.

'Now *they* would be interesting to see,' Mick agreed.

'Kwame and that other old man made me leave them all behind,' Sonya said, with a pout.

'What other old man?' Mick asked.

'She must mean Squadron Leader Gordon, who helped us sell the computers,' said Greg.

'Should we wait for him?' asked Mick.

'No he's travelling independently,' Kwame replied. 'I'm your only geriatric passenger!'

Mick dropped Kwame at his house and drove on to the university with his other passengers. The house was quiet, nobody seemed to be at home, so Kwame let himself in with his front door key. Automatically he reached down to gather up a scattering of post and newspapers before realising that it made a rather large pile and must have accumulated over several days.

After bringing in his luggage and sorting the laundry from the rest, Kwame put his suitcase away and started the washing machine. Then he made himself some coffee and settled down with the post and newspapers. After an hour or so he picked up the telephone and called Tom's house; maybe Afriyie was tied up over there. The call was answered by Elsie who welcomed him home and told him Afriyie had gone to town to get medicine for Little Tom, who had not been well. Elsie said she was preparing lunch and would bring something for Kwame shortly.

After lunch Kwame, finding nothing requiring urgent attention in his personal post, decided to drive to the office. Mick and Sandra were there with Ophelia but Greg had gone home and Sonya had returned to the business school. Mick was telling Sandra and Ophelia what he had been able to plan for Ophelia's programme. 'We were under the impression that hand spinning in manufacturing was becoming rare in England,' he said, 'but I have found two firms in Birmingham which are still very active in this field. Both have agreed to take Ophelia for a week to expose her to the range of industrial products now being made.'

'Could I also go along with her?' Sandra asked.

'It should be possible, but you will need to get their agreement.'

'Oh, I'll take over now, Mick; can you give me contact details?'

Mick gave Sandra the addresses and telephone numbers of Spintex Metal Spinners Ltd of West Bromwich and Stockfield Metal Spinners Ltd of Balsall Heath. 'What are they making?' asked Ophelia.

'They both make a range of components that form part of other manufacturers' products.'

'What sort of products?'

'Food processing and pharmaceutical equipment, microwave antenna, sanitary ware, even musical instruments.'

'Wow, I can't wait to see some of that stuff!'

'Have you noticed anything that might be needed in Ghana?' Sandra asked.

'One company is making an elegant oil lamp with three or four spun parts fixed together,' Mick said

'Oh, we're not into that yet,' said Ophelia. 'That could be a good idea for a new product.'

Kwame smiled, he and Dan Nyarko had put some effort into trying to persuade metal spinners in Tema to produce new products incorporating two or more spun components. The efforts had failed because the existing spinners found enough business producing simple domestic pots and pans. However, the number of companies coming into the sector was still increasing and the resulting competition might force some proprietors to look for new products. This was where Ophelia's renewed effort might achieve success.

'When you go back to Ghana you should look out for graduate apprentices starting their own workshops,' Kwame said to Ophelia. 'They are the most likely to be receptive to your new ideas. Your input could help them find a market niche where there is no local competition for a while before the copiers come along.'

Kwame wondered why Tom was not in the office. 'He went off in a hurry yesterday,' Sandra said, 'and he hasn't been in today.'

'He said something about visiting his mother,' added Mick.

Greg had come in while they were talking and had stood listening to Mick's tales of the metal spinning industry in the English Midlands. 'Do your companies use CNC spinning machines?' he asked Mick.

'Yes, they do,' Mick replied, 'and more are coming in all the time. It's the same in all sectors; computer-controlled machine tools are becoming increasingly used.'

'Then could I be in on this one too?' Greg asked Kwame.

'These are commercial companies,' Mick said. 'They might not mind showing Ophelia their traditional hand-crafting methods but they won't

for Akosua. 'Comfort said these are the latest fashion in Accra,' Kwame told her, 'she thought you might like to copy them.'

Akosua couldn't wait to try on her presents and provide an impromptu fashion parade. Kwame told Afriyie that if she wanted to see some more, or to see how they looked on a white woman, he would ask Sonya to bring her new dresses to the house.

Afriyie noticed the time and called Elsie. 'We must take Little Tom home to bed,' she said, getting the toddler ready for the short walk to Tom's house. Soon they were gone, leaving Kwame alone with Akosua and Takoradi. 'Shall we play chess or Scrabble?' Akosua asked.

'You choose, you always win anyway,' said Kwame.

They sat at the table and the old dog came to sprawl under Akosua's feet. 'It's not fair, is it?' Akosua said, 'two against one!'

After they had been playing Scrabble for an hour, Kwame asked when Afriyie would be coming back. 'Oh, she doesn't come back these days, since Little Tom became ill,' Akosua said.

'Can't Elsie cope?' Kwame asked.

'Afriyie wants to be sure he's looked after properly.'

'He didn't seem too bad when he was here.'

'No, I think he's better now.'

'But Afriyie wants to be sure?'

'I guess so. Dad, I've told you, you can't use Twi words in Scrabble!'

'How else am I going to win?'

Kwame didn't mind sleeping alone that night; it gave him more time to think. Had Afriyie moved in with Tom or was it just a temporary measure while Little Tom was ill, as Akosua had implied? It would seem that Akosua had been left alone in the house at night while he was away and this thought did not please him. He was glad that Takoradi had also been there.

As for Afriyie, should he tell her that he would understand if she wanted to stay with Tom permanently? He could tell her about Comfort's return and they could all live happily ever after. It seemed too simple, and life was never simple. Kwame thought the problem might be Tom. Was Tom ready to start a new life? Would Tom's new life include Afriyie? He hadn't seen Tom yet, but he was sure to see him soon. What were they going to say to each other?

Kwame realised that he had exhausted his train of thought for that evening, and was about to retire for the night when the telephone rang. It was Afriyie. 'Has Akosua gone to bed?' she asked. When Kwame confirmed that he was alone, Afriyie continued, 'I wanted to explain the situation but not in front of Akosua. Tom's father is seriously ill and

Tom has gone to stay with his mother during the crisis. He didn't go to the office today and I expect that he will be away for some time. He told me that he'd left notes for you with Alice and that you would be in charge until he returns. He will try to ring you soon.'

'So that's why you're staying over there?'

'Why, what did you think?'

'We'll talk about that later.'

The next day Alice, Tom's secretary, brought Tom's handing-over notes and Kwame settled down to read them. He soon realised that he was required not only to manage the partnership project but also to present some of Tom's lectures. He asked Alice for the lecture notes and prepared to meet this new ordeal; he knew that he had grown rusty in some areas and was going to be stretched to the limit.

When Tom rang, Kwame was startled to hear his friend's voice so strained. 'I can't say much with Mum around,' Tom said, 'but it's serious and I'm needed here. Can you manage for a week or two?'

'Don't worry about work; concentrate on helping your mother.'

'Did Greg and Sonya's course go well?'

'Very well.'

'Has Ophelia come back with you?'

'Yes and they've all got off to a good start on the metal spinning.'

'You have no problems then?'

'Only with your lectures,' Kwame said with a chuckle.

'Ask Sandra for some help. She was one of my best metallurgy students and her memory is still fresh.'

Kwame called Sandra and asked her if she could spare some time to help him revise some of the material for Tom's lectures. 'It's ten years since I studied this stuff,' he told her, 'and Prof has added to the syllabus since those days. He says that you will remember it.'

'I hope I can,' Sandra said. 'Show me where you need help and I'll do my best.'

Then Kwame called Greg and asked him to be sure to send Professor Thomas and Jim Proctor copies of his report on the first computer sales. He suggested that Greg deliver the documents by hand, or make an early follow-up visit, to stress how much their donation was appreciated in Kumasi. 'Will you complete the delivery of the last fifteen machines before your next course in July?' he asked.

'That's certain now; Jim is a great help,' was Greg's cheerful reply.

* * *

It was more than two weeks before Tom moved back to Coventry and when he did he was preoccupied with family matters. In response to Kwame's enquiry he said that his father had been discharged from hospital but was still very frail. Tom had decided with his mother that it would be better for his parents to move in with him. That way he could continue to help them and still attend to his university duties. He was arranging for a nurse to help his mother care for his dad. He hoped that Elsie would continue to help care for Little Tom. Kwame assured him that he could see no problem with that.

Tom made no mention of Afriyie, and Kwame sensed that this was not a good time to raise an issue that might add to his friend's concerns. He promised to help Tom in any way he could. 'When are your parents moving in?' he asked.

'They'll be here in a day or two, as soon as an ambulance can be arranged.'

'What will happen to your dad's house?'

'Oh, we'll try to keep it safe for the time being; Mum's hoping they will go back when Dad is stronger.'

'The snowdrops and crocuses are up, and even a few daffodils; the spring weather should help the convalescence.'

'That's what we're hoping.'

Little Tom's illness was a distant memory but Afriyie decided that Tom now needed help with his parents. Together with Elsie, Afriyie still prepared most of Kwame's meals, and her part-time sewing business was located in his house, but she spent little time in Kwame's company. She made an attempt to help him celebrate his fortieth birthday by mounting a modest party to which a few friends were invited, but this produced no lasting effect. Kwame would have liked to invite Comfort to join him and Akosua in Coventry but he was held back by the lack of any sign from Tom that he laid claim to Afriyie.

For Akosua, now seventeen, this was a year of destiny during which she would take her GCSE advanced level examinations and move on to university. She had several offers of places in medical schools but all required success in the June examinations. Always a disciplined and hard-working student like her father, she redoubled her efforts at revision during the Easter holidays. Kwame helped her all he could with mathematics and science subjects but the teenager was far ahead of him in Spanish, her chosen foreign language.

Kwame would have enjoyed walking Takoradi while Akosua was studying but he insisted on his daughter taking a daily break from bookwork and getting at least half an hour of fresh air and exercise. That was how one afternoon early in April girl and dog returned home with Takoradi's old master, Tam Gordon. 'Look who was waiting for us in the park,' said Akosua.

Kwame welcomed Tam and said, 'I thought I might have seen the last of you.'

'Yes, it's more than two months since we were in Ghana,' Tam replied. 'Leon doesn't usually leave you undisturbed that long.'

Kwame asked Akosua to provide tea and biscuits and then she returned to her second-order differential equations. 'Let's leave her to her sums and have a quiet chat in the study,' Kwame said to Tam. Takoradi, bored with Akosua's inactivity, followed his old master. As soon as they were settled Kwame continued, 'I guess Leon was satisfied with your report and didn't need to see me.'

'He also realised how busy you were with Professor Arthur away.'

'Was he happy with what we achieved?'

'Leon? Oh yes, he feels things in Kumasi are pretty much cleared up for the moment.'

'Did Peggy confirm linking Kojo Doe to Pastor Obeng-Mensah, Cecilia's father?'

'Yes, she did.'

'He doesn't think that Cecilia and her father pose much of a threat then.'

'No, he agrees with me on that.'

'What doesn't he agree on?'

'I can't get him interested in my idea for an early-warning system.'

Kwame wanted to hear Leon's reasons for turning down Tam's idea before he expressed his own opinion. 'Why doesn't he like the idea?' he asked.

'He says that our methods of detecting hidden drugs are advancing quickly. Any early-warning system would become redundant before it could recover its start-up costs.'

'How do you reply to that argument?'

'Attached to a project like yours, I believe the costs could be affordable. It only needs some additional short-term training for the field workers and some funds for allowances and awards.'

'Does he have an answer to that?'

'He says that drugs do not come to the UK just from Ghana. To be really useful the system would need to be replicated in other countries, like Nigeria and Jamaica, where there are no projects like yours. That's where the high cost comes in.'

'What do you say then?'

'I say that Ghana is typical of other developing countries in Africa and the Caribbean, and traffickers everywhere copy each other's tricks. An early-warning system in one country is better that none at all.'

'I'm sure Leon has the last word?'

'Yes. He says you, Kwame, are a one-man detector; how do we know others could function as you do?'

Kwame suspected that Tam had not come on instructions from Leon. 'I get the impression, Tam,' he said, 'that this is not an official visit.'

'No, I was hoping for your support.'

'For your early-warning system?'

'Yes, it would put more funds into your project.'

'And distract our people from their main task.'

'How do you mean?'

'They would be seduced by your special awards and neglect their regular duties.'

'So you won't give me your support?'

'I'm sorry, Tam, but I want to separate my work completely from every aspect of drugs trafficking and that includes ceasing to play any role in detection.'

'You have benefited from helping us until now.'

'Yes, and I'm grateful, but I want to return to Ghana in July and devote the whole of my effort to the work I do best. Involvement in your activities broke up my marriage in 1988, and now it's repaired after nearly nine years I must avoid the same thing happening again.'

Tam reached down to pat Takoradi on the head. 'Old dogs don't like to let go of bones,' he said in Twi.

'I think it would be wise to let go of this one.'

'Have you told Leon of your plans?'

'No, but I intend to. I was waiting for the next meeting.'

'Will you take Takoradi with you to Ghana?'

'*Adjei!* I hadn't thought of that. He's rather old to adapt to a tropical climate.'

'Will Akosua go without him?'

'Perhaps not, but she will probably attend university here.'

'Then it's likely she'll opt to keep Takoradi here. Tell her I'll be happy to help if he needs a temporary home while she's away at any time.'

'Thank you Tam and whenever you're in Kumasi you'll be very welcome at our home in Nhyiasu.'

* * *

354

Since his last return from Ghana Kwame had kept in touch with Comfort by telephone and it was less usual than before for them to communicate by post. So when a letter came from Comfort, Kwame knew that it must be for a special reason. As soon as he read mention of Peter Sarpong he feared that Comfort was about to tell him something that he would not want to hear. He continued reading with a growing feeling of foreboding.

Peter had revived his attentions and seemed intent on establishing a romantic relationship. Once again Comfort claimed to have agreed to a few social engagements to try to find out what was happening towards the revival of the drugs cartel. This arrangement had continued for several weeks and she had come to the point where she realised that it must either go forward or be broken off.

Comfort said that her inclination was to make a clean break but she was reluctant to give up before she had learned something significant. She was about to tell Peter that their meetings must end when, much to her surprise and relief, his ardour started to cool and he began making excuses to avoid further commitments. This eased Comfort's concern but roused her curiosity. Was Peter once more getting drawn into his former occupation and seeking to distance himself from a situation in which he might give himself away?

Comfort continued in her letter that she suspected that Peter had a new romantic interest so she decided to play the role of the suspicious girlfriend. She made enquiries through her friends in the trading community, many of whom still had connections with the Lebanese. It wasn't long before she was told that Peter Sarpong was being seen around Kumasi's few sophisticated nightlife venues in the company of Cessie: Cecilia Obeng-Mensah. 'By all reports,' Comfort wrote, 'Peter is totally infatuated with Cessie.'

On reading this Kwame gave a sigh of relief. Why was he still so quick to let jealousy rear its ugly head where his restored wife was concerned? Deep down he knew he could trust Comfort but on the surface he still reacted emotionally like a teenager fearful of his first love. But then she was his first love! In spite of all the vicissitudes of the intervening years their relationship still preserved something of the pristine passion of their schooldays. It was a pleasant thought.

Kwame dragged himself from this romantic reverie to consider the significance of Comfort's story to his work for Leon. They knew that Cecilia was involved with the directors of Hanabis in trying to revive Ghanaian involvement in the work of the cartel. Bra Yaw and Kofi Boateng had refused to be reeled in again, but Peter was a much bigger fish. He had operated at a higher level and been privy to more of the cartel's secrets. The others had a dislike of the Lebanese but Peter's Uncle George had been close to them. Was Peter likely to be a more willing partner to the camel herders?

How much of a threat would Leon consider Peter to be? Peter had been imprisoned in the UK and was well known to the authorities. Would he risk trying to come back to Britain with a false passport? If Peter stayed in Kumasi, could he play any really significant role? One thing he might do is teach Cecilia's father much that would be useful to running a distribution network in Coventry. In this case a visit of the Revd Obeng-Mensah to Kumasi should be viewed with suspicion. Kwame decided to pass on this information to Leon; so the first thing he did after reaching his office was ring Jack Preece.

When Jack arrived, Kwame gave him a photocopy of Comfort's letter, with a few personal lines blanked out, but revealing all that he thought was of interest to Leon. As he handed it over he couldn't help smiling; no doubt Comfort had taken the trouble to write it all out for this very purpose. Jack took time to read through the letter and Kwame waited patiently.

'Thanks for passing this on so quickly, Kwame,' Jack said. 'I think Leon will take it seriously. I know he regards Sarpong as the most dangerous of the old gang presently at liberty, and now we have evidence of a direct link to his late uncle's Lebanese partners.'

After Jack had gone, Kwame called Mick and Sandra to ask about the arrangements for taking Ophelia back to the airport at the end of her assignment. She had been allowed to stay a few weeks longer than the other visitors because her visits to manufacturers had proved to be more fruitful than expected, and her serious intent had put her new knowledge to good use. The TCC's metal products designer would be flying home with a plethora of ideas for new spun metal products. Kwame advised Ophelia to work closely with Dan Nyarko and AT Ghana in Tema in persuading the more progressive metal spinners to adopt some of her innovations.

Kwame had no doubt that Ophelia would return safely to Ghana so he saw no problem when Sandra volunteered to drive her to Heathrow. Nevertheless, he took Sandra aside and reminded her that former visitors had avoided returning and she should watch out especially for relatives who might offer to take over at the airport. It was Sandra's duty to see Ophelia checked in and passed through emigration before returning to Coventry.

Kwame's next task was to check with Mick and Greg that all would be ready for the next training course in Kumasi in July. 'All the computers have been shipped,' Greg said. 'Kwaku has fixed the one that couldn't be sold last time so we should have sixteen available for sale at the end of the course.'

Kwame was happy. He now had complete confidence in his helpers and knew that they would keep the project going successfully after his departure. There were barely three months to go and he had much to do. He was glad that he would have a good portion of time to attend to his personal affairs.

Tom was not happy that Kwame was leaving and put much pressure on him to stay longer.

'You know I wanted to return to Ghana when it was safe to do so,' Kwame said. 'I'm lucky that I can return earlier than I could foresee when I came.'

'You have very bright prospects ahead of you here,' Tom insisted. 'All my colleagues are impressed with your work. In spite of the absconders and the drugs problems you have done a lot to establish an effective partnership with Kumasi.'

'I've promised to do all I can in Kumasi to continue to support our project.'

'We feel that you could do much more here.'

'How do you mean?'

'Well, Professor Thomas is retiring next year and I will apply for his post. If I succeed, my post will be vacant and the grapevine tells me that you have a good chance of taking over.'

'Wow! Professor Mainu! Please don't tell me things like that.'

Tom then turned to personal matters, 'Will Akosua move back to Ghana with you?'

'Probably not; if she gets into a university here I'm sure she will want to stay for the duration of the course.'

'Will she come out to you during the vacations?'

'Yes, she'll be able to spend almost half the year with us.'

'Well, she's welcome to stay at my place any time she's at a loose end.'

'Thank you; I'll tell her.'

'That leaves Afriyie and Takoradi.'

'Takoradi will stay with Akosua, and Tam has offered to take him back when Akosua is away.'

'And Afriyie?'

'She is free to do whatever she wishes.'

'Little Tom and Dad will benefit if she stays.'

Kwame was about to leave when Tom indicated that something else had come to mind. 'Wait a moment, Kwame,' he said. 'I've just remembered; we've had a complaint: someone says you should have given them a computer after the last course in Kumasi.' Tom sorted through the papers on his desk. 'Ah, here it is, *Sika Ye Na* enterprise: Ms Cecilia Obeng-Mensah.'

'Oh no!' Kwame exclaimed. 'She has no grounds for a complaint.'

It didn't take long for Kwame to explain to Tom what had happened in Kumasi: how Cecilia had come to demand a computer after neither attending the course nor putting in a request before the deadline.'

'Can she apply for one in July?'

'She can, but I explained we will favour people who attend the training.'

'Has she applied to come on the course?'

'She applied for the last one but didn't attend. I don't know about the July course; we haven't been sent the list yet.'

'We can ask her next week; she's asked to see me.'

Kwame suspected that if Cecilia was coming to Coventry it was probably to see her father and discuss resuming the drugs sales. He felt that he should warn Tom about these probabilities. 'I need to tell you a few things about Cecilia,' Kwame said. 'Please treat everything I say in confidence. I'm telling you because we need to be on guard against this drugs business again impacting on our project.'

'Go on,' said Tom, looking rather worried.

'Cecilia is the proprietor of *Sika Ye Na* enterprise, a company that is helping a Lebanese cartel in Kumasi to reactivate the drugs trade. Her father is Pastor Arnold Obeng-Mensah, a Pentecostal minister attached to the local church here in Coventry. Cecilia and her father are suspected of working together to recruit couriers, and Pastor Obeng-Mensah probably had something to do with Elsie's kidnapping. He is also suspected of being involved with Peggy Osei-Wusu and Kojo Doe, and to have put Kojo in touch with Cecilia in Kumasi. It was probably Kojo who alerted Cecilia to our project. That's how we think she came to apply to come on our course.'

'So her aim is to use us to further her drugs running?'

'That's what I think. We should try to have nothing to do with her.'

Kwame wondered if he should warn Tom about Cecilia's exceptionally beautiful appearance. It would have no particular importance unless the lady chose to use her charms in pursuit of her ends. She had certainly not taken this approach with him, Kwame, in Kumasi and it might not be in her nature to do so. On the other hand she was suspected by

Comfort of having started a relationship with Peter Sarpong. Was this just a means to gain information, a business arrangement, or a genuine romance? Kwame decided to remain silent and trust to Tom's recent bereavement to provide an effective defence.

Kwame thought that it might be possible to stop Cecilia entering the country, so after he left Tom's office he called Jack Preece again. This time he risked speaking openly on the telephone. He told Jack about Cecilia's intended visit to Professor Arthur and suggested that she might be denied entry at the airport. Jack said that he would pass on the suggestion but it was unlikely there would be grounds to refuse entry if Cecilia had the appropriate visa from the British High Commission in Accra and wasn't carrying any banned substances.

'I hope you'll check her luggage carefully.'

'Don't worry, we'll take a good look at her coat hangers.'

'And put Tam on her trail?'

'The lady's movements will be monitored.'

One afternoon during the following week Kwame was sitting at his desk when there was a soft tap on his door. In answer to his call two young people, one of each gender, came softly and diffidently into the office. 'Dr Carpenter said you might be able to help us,' the young lady said, and her companion grinned shyly and nodded his support. Kwame waved them to be seated and the spokeswoman chose the chair facing him across the desk. Her supporter settled himself with a sigh of relief in an easy chair behind and to her right. 'I'm happy to return Dr Carpenter's help in any way I can,' Kwame said, 'but first tell me your names.'

'This is Kevin Avis and I'm Helen Price,' said the young lady and Kevin nodded his confirmation.

'Now tell me how I can help you,' Kwame said.

'We are students at the business school and we've been given an assignment on labour productivity as a factor in economic development in developing countries. Dr Carpenter suggested that you might have some data from Ghana.'

Kwame knew that labour productivity in his country was very low but the amount of hard data was limited. 'The Technology Consultancy Centre (or TCC) of Kumasi University kept detailed records of its own production units over many years,' he said, 'but I don't know if they will help you much. Apart from that we have only anecdotal information gained from visiting various foreign-owned plants in Ghana.'

'I'm sure anything you can give us will be useful; we're particularly interested in comparisons between countries,' said his eager interrogator.

'Again we don't have much, but I can give you a report that the TCC director wrote after a six-month study leave in India. He gathered some data on the cottage textile industry in the two countries.' Kwame handed over a copy of a small booklet with a dark-pink cover. This was eagerly seized upon. 'You will find data for handloom weavers,' Kwame said. 'The TCC operated a handloom weaving production unit for several years and overall I remember the output was close to one metre of cloth per weaver per day.'

'And what was it in India?'

'Self-employed weavers using similar looms in Uttar Pradesh were found to be averaging about three metres per day.'

'Gosh, that's a big difference. Could you come up with an explanation?'

Kwame said that the first factors people mentioned were climate and the health of the weavers. 'Taken over the whole year the climate in Ghana is hotter and more humid than northern India and this probably had a small lowering effect on output. In terms of health, it was generally concluded that there was not much difference. Then it was thought that the critical factor might be that the Indian weavers were self-employed, but when some weavers were helped to become self-employed in Ghana their output only rose a little and this was mainly due to longer hours of working.'

'Have you found this difference in other industries?'

'Only anecdotally, I'm afraid,' said Kwame. 'I once took a party of students on a visit to a sugar mill at Komenda in the Central Region of Ghana. It was under Pakistani management. One student asked the manager if the plant was making a profit and when he was told "no" the student asked the reason why. The manager said that the problem was cutting the sugar cane in the fields where it grows. He couldn't get the cane into the plant quickly enough.'

'Did he quote any figures?' asked Kevin.

'Yes, he said that in Australia, where productivity was highest, each labourer averaged about five tons a day of cut cane. In India and Pakistan the comparable figure was about two tons a day, but in Ghana they had never been able to reach one ton a day.'

'Do you have any more stories like that?'

'Well, on another occasion I took students to visit the British Aluminium Company's bauxite mines at Awaso in the Western Region of Ghana. This is where they extract the ore to ship through the port of Takoradi to Britain, where it is processed into aluminium. We were lucky to meet the English managing director and one of the students again asked if the plant operated at a profit. Once again the answer was "no". Another student expressed his indignation by saying, "You can't make a profit with our cheap labour?" The managing director became quite angry at this remark and replied, "Don't tell me that Ghanaian labour is cheap. It's the most expensive in the world! With German labour at German wages I could make a profit." This brought home to us all that it is the labour cost per unit output that really matters, not low wages as such. I guess this is basic to you economists but it was an eye-opener for some of our engineers.'

The two earnest young undergraduates wanted to know if Kwame had any further explanation for these differences. 'I have puzzled over the issue from time to time,' Kwame told them. 'I think that our history holds the clue. Until the last fifty years or so life was relatively easy in my country. The population density was low, everyone was a farmer, food was plentiful and most people had enough to eat. In Asian countries, however, population density was high, food was often scarce and life was much harder. So the Asians developed a culture that honoured hard work. The Hindus have an adage: "work is worship". That level of veneration does not exist in my country.'

Kwame waited patiently while his two young visitors scribbled rapidly in their notebooks, their long hair veiling their faces as they hunched over their pens. It was only when they finished, coming upright with rapid sweeps of their forelocks, that their genders became clear again and the interrogation resumed.

As before, it was Helen who led off with, 'Do you agree that modern economic progress in Asian countries has begun with the exploitation of cheap labour: hard-working people willing to work for low wages?'

'Yes, that's what we've seen in countries like Malaysia and Singapore and recently it seems to be getting under way in China and India.'

'Do you think that it could happen in Ghana?'

'No, I must be honest with you, I don't think it can happen that way in Ghana.'

'Why not?'

'In the absence of a strong work ethic, and with an expectation of high wages, Ghanaian labour is almost exploitation proof, as the unfortunate foreigners found at Komenda and Awaso. Higher productivity must be based upon better means of production: new technology.'

'Are there any factors that might change this perception?'

'Well, our population is growing rapidly and there are more and more people living in poverty. In time, more people might be prepared to work hard for low wages, but personally I feel that this is a remote prospect. Most of us hope that we will be rescued by technology before a Victorian era of sweated labour becomes necessary.'

The young visitors seemed to be very pleased with what Kwame had told them but he felt it was his duty to remind them that this was a tutorial session. He had alerted them to a few key issues but they should do their own detailed research, gather more facts and seek more opinions before forming their own conclusions. He had tried to be brutally frank and present his country in a realistic light. At the same time he had reminded himself of Ghana's dire economic plight, and the need for him to redouble his efforts if he was to continue to influence the wellbeing of his countrymen. He was convinced that this work would be better done in Kumasi than in Coventry and he was reassured that he had taken the right decision to return home in July.

25

Last Gasps

It was nine months since the death of Akos Mary and Tom had still not regained the bright personality that his friends knew of old. His constant concern over the failing health of his father and the future wellbeing of his ageing mother further delayed the healing process. He managed to get into the office most days but his colleagues knew that he was repeating well-rehearsed actions rather than generating the ideas needed for new teaching and research programmes.

Early in May a general election had returned a Labour government to power in Britain with a large parliamentary majority. This did nothing to revive the spirits of Tom or his parents who were lifelong Tories. Kwame couldn't understand their concern as he could see little difference between the policies of the parties, but he was beginning to worry that his long-time teacher, friend and boss was failing in the role of project leader. He doubted if Tom was ready to be assailed by Cecilia Obeng-Mensah.

Inevitably, one afternoon later in the month, the formidable lady came to inform Alice that she had an appointment to see Professor Arthur. Tom's loyal secretary sensed trouble but could do nothing but announce the visitor's arrival and provide access to the inner sanctum. As soon as the door closed she alerted Kwame and he hurried to Alice's office to be on hand if needed.

Throughout the many years that he had known her, as friend, lover and wife, Tom had always believed that Akos Mary was the most beautiful woman he would ever meet. Now for the first time this belief was challenged. Yet he had been warned that before him stood a scheming siren intent upon promoting an illegal trade in narcotics and manipulating his project in pursuit of her illicit goal. In his weakened condition Tom felt at a considerable disadvantage and wished he could hand over Cecilia to be dealt with by Kwame. However the lady had already voiced her complaint to Kwame in Kumasi, so Tom felt obliged to hear her out before summoning reinforcements. He was much relieved when Alice slipped him a note to say that Kwame was close at hand.

Cecilia played the part of a damsel in distress. 'I've been unfairly treated,' she said, 'but I know that you, an English professor, will treat me fairly.'

'I'll do what I can,' Tom said.

'They tell me that it's the same with most aid projects.'

'What's the same?'

'The *abrofo* send out goods to help poor Africans but corruption prevents the goods reaching the people who really need them.'

'I can assure you that nothing like that happens in our project.'

'What about your Mr Mainu? He gives everything to his friends.'

'Are you referring to the computers?'

'Yes. I really needed one, but Mr Mainu said they had all been given out.'

'They were fairly distributed to qualified people.'

'Is that what he told you? Then why did he keep one back? Was it to give to his girlfriend?'

'One computer had a fault. It needed repair before it could be sold.'

'Mr Duah told me it has been repaired. You'll help me to have it, won't you?'

'I'm sorry, but it's out of my hands. The allocation committee in Kumasi decides which companies will be sold computers.'

The lady looked so downhearted that Tom feared she might burst into tears. 'Please don't get so upset over a computer,' he said. 'Why don't you buy one to take home with you? You can get one for less than you paid for your air ticket.'

'Oh, I didn't buy my ticket. My Dad bought it for me.'

'So you've come on holiday to visit your father.'

'Yes, it's only a short trip. I want you to help me come for a longer stay like you did for Mr Okunor.'

'Mr Okunor is a very old client of the TCC and a skilled engineer.'

'And a friend of Mr Mainu? You're the boss, why don't you bring one of *your* friends here?'

Cecilia's wide-eyed stare left no doubt in Tom's mind that he was being offered friendship of a very special kind. To bring her back with project funding was quite out of the question, but what if he funded her visit from his own resources? With a big effort he turned his wayward thoughts back to the lady's suspected ulterior motive and decided it was time to call for help. 'I don't think you understand what we are trying to do in our project,' he said. 'I will ask Mr Mainu and Mr Anderson to explain it all too you.' He buzzed Alice and asked for Kwame and Greg to be called.

Kwame waited for Greg to arrive and then they both went to Tom's rescue. After a few moments of small talk Kwame suggested that they should move to his office to let Tom get back to his regular work. Cecilia looked reluctant to leave but could think of no more ways to extend her stay so she followed Kwame, with Greg providing the rearguard. In Kwame's office Kwame and Greg took pains to explain how the computers were being allocated and how academic visitors to Warwick were chosen, but the lady was clearly bored and soon made an excuse to leave. She left empty handed but not empty headed. She had learned a good deal about how the project was run and the personalities involved. Kwame wondered whether she would be able to turn this new knowledge to her advantage.

When Kwame got back to his desk the telephone was ringing. He was asked to call at the hairdressing salon on the way home. It was several months since Kwame had seen Auntie Rose and he was intrigued to know what had caused the little lady to call him so urgently. This time they met in the comfortable first floor room which told Kwame that the matter had the full backing of Leon.

Auntie Rose had some tea ready and they sat chatting about all that had occurred since their last meeting. When asked how things stood between himself and Comfort, Kwame said that they were now fully reconciled and planning a future together. Auntie Rose said that this was the outcome she had expected but she was very pleased it had come about. Kwame took the opportunity to stress that he wanted to finish his work for Leon and return to Ghana to concentrate on his work in technology transfer.

When the time came to discuss business, Auntie Rose said that Leon was prepared to release Kwame from the work in July but wanted to appeal to him to help with just one more effort to defeat attempts being made in Kumasi to revive the partnership with Hanabis. When Kwame showed signs of reluctance the little lady hastened to add that the matter related to the good work Kwame had done on his most recent trip to Kumasi. 'You alerted us to the new danger and we want you to help us snuff it out before it can do any serious damage,' she said.

'Does it relate to Cecilia and coat hangers?'

'Exactly. But for you we would know nothing about it.'

'Tam helped a lot.'

'Yes, but his report makes it clear that it was your initiative and local knowledge that achieved the result.'

Kwame knew that Auntie Rose was using flattery to gain his cooperation, but he liked to be flattered as much as anyone else, and in any case she was only telling the truth about his activity in Kumasi. So he agreed to do what he could as long as his work would be finished by the middle of July. 'You know that Cecilia Obeng-Mensah has come to Coventry,' he began.

'Yes, that's what concerns us. She came to see Professor Arthur, didn't she?'

'She did, but don't worry. She made a groundless complaint and left empty handed.'

'No, that doesn't worry us, but Tam thinks she may go to see Dr Carpenter at the business school.'

'Why does he think that?'

'Dr Carpenter was impressed with Cecilia's dresses, wasn't she?'

'Yes, she was. She bought some to bring back with her.'

'Tam thinks Cecilia will seek Dr Carpenter's help in finding a UK agent for her dresses.'

'You mean, to bring coat hangers here as well?'

'That's what we fear.'

Kwame reflected on what had been said about dresses and coat hangers at Comfort's house in Kumasi. 'Dr Carpenter will be suspicious of Cecilia because we advised her to leave her coat hangers behind. I don't think she will want to help Cecilia. You don't have anything to worry about.'

'No, you don't understand; we want Dr Carpenter to help.'

'To set a trap?'

'Exactly.'

'So what do you want me to do?'

'We want you to see Dr Carpenter first and ask her if she will help us by agreeing to help Cecilia.'

Kwame wasn't sure that he liked this idea. 'What exactly would we ask Sonya Carpenter to do?' he asked. 'Should she recommend a specific person as an agent for the dresses?'

'At first we thought that Afriyie might be the agent. She already sells African dresses and has an established clientele. Then we decided that Afriyie's connection to you would make Cecilia suspicious.'

'So have you come up with a better plan?'

'Yes, I think so. In spite of our painful memories of this place, Leon has taken a lease on the building and wants to continue to use it for clandestine meetings and undercover projects. The plan is that I am now the proprietor of this hairdressing salon and I want to expand my business by selling made-in-Ghana dresses. I already have hundreds of potential customers who call regularly for hair care services.'

'That might work, but what do you want me to do?'

Auntie Rose explained to Kwame that she wanted him to introduce her to Dr Carpenter. She feared that if she made a direct approach she might be suspected of being an accomplice of Cecilia. Kwame had been with Sonya in Kumasi and had warned her about the coat hangers so it was obvious that he was not part of any trafficking cartel. She was sure that in this way Dr Carpenter was much more likely to cooperate.

Kwame said that he would try to see Sonya as soon as possible with a warning that Cecilia might come to see her. If she agreed to help them he would bring her to the salon after work. If Cecilia called before Sonya had met Auntie Rose, Sonya should offer help but arrange to meet Cecilia again later, after she had had time to think about the matter. Auntie Rose endorsed this plan but stressed the need for quick action to try to stay ahead of the pastor's daughter.

Kwame phoned Sonya early the next morning and asked if he could call at the business school for an urgent meeting. Sonya said that she would be free after the first two hours of lectures. He was waiting in her office when she returned carrying a bulging briefcase. 'Thanks for helping Helen and Kevin,' she said. 'You told them much that they wouldn't easily find elsewhere.'

'I was happy to meet them and pass on the little I knew; it set me thinking more broadly about the problems of my country.'

'And now you want some help from me; what can I do?'

'You have helped us a lot already with the course in Kumasi and our new request arises from that mission.'

'I'm intrigued, please go on.'

Kwame recalled how he had advised Sonya to leave the coat hangers behind when she brought her new dresses home from Kumasi. 'Oh yes, those lovely carved wooden hangers,' she recalled. 'I was so sorry to have to part with them.'

'Well, as we explained at the time, they are made hollow and are sometimes used to conceal drugs: cocaine or heroin.'

'I remember you telling me.'

'Do you remember the lady who sold you the dresses at *Sika Ye Na* enterprise?'

'The woman Comfort calls Cessie?'

367

'That's right, have you seen her since?'

'How could I? She's in Kumasi isn't she?'

'No she's here in Coventry.'

Kwame explained that they knew Cecilia was in Coventry because she came in yesterday to see Professor Arthur. 'She complained that she should have been given a computer,' he said.

'But she didn't attend the course!'

'No, we think that it was only an excuse to try to learn more about our partnership project with Kumasi University.'

'Why should she want to do that?'

'Why should she want to use hollow coat hangers? I'm afraid it's all to do with drugs.'

Kwame explained that since they started the partnership project three years ago a small group of people in Kumasi had been trying to persuade academics coming to Coventry to act as drugs couriers. 'Most people approached by the traffickers had refused to cooperate,' he said, 'but two or three had gone astray before we were able to break up the group and stop the traffic.'

'Who do you mean by we?'

'I am restricted in what I can divulge, but let's say staff of our project and UK customs.'

'You and Tam?'

'And a few others.'

Kwame then asked Sonya to recall any conversation that she had with Cessie when buying the dresses. 'Oh, I told her that her dresses were very beautiful,' Sonya said.

'Did you tell her you thought the dresses would sell well in England?'

'Yes, I believe I did, and they would.'

'Did you also mention being from the business school and being able to advise her on marketing in the UK?'

'Now you remind me, yes I did, although it was Comfort who told Cessie about the business school.'

'Well, we believe Cecilia will soon call on you to ask for your advice.'

'And you want me to refuse to help?'

'No, we want you to help in the way we direct.'

Kwame then asked Sonya if she was prepared to help them foil the drugs traffickers' latest move on the basis of what she had been told. Her first question was about the risk: did Cecilia have any collaborators in Coventry who might avenge her arrest, if that was how it ended? Kwame said that there had been a violent group which had recently been rounded up. The one member of the group still at large was Cecilia's father, Pastor Obeng-Mensah, who might soon be arrested for involvement in kidnapping.

'Then I must be brave,' Sonya said. 'As a single woman I have no dependants so I will seek adventure while I'm able.'

'I can't guarantee adventure.'

'Visiting Kumasi with you was already an adventure. Who knows, I might even get a chance for another trip.'

'We can start this evening after work. I want you to meet a little Ghanaian lady at a nearby hairdressing salon. She's anxious to start selling African dresses.'

'I'll come to your office when I close at 5 pm.'

'Oh, and if Cecilia should call on you today, please tell her you will help but she should come back later to discuss details.'

Kwame was waiting in his office when Sonya came in saying, 'She hasn't called in yet.' Kwame put a finger to his lips to indicate that it would be better not to voice the matter too openly. 'Oh, I'm sorry,' Sonya said, 'I'm not used to working in espionage.'

'It's not exactly espionage but we don't want any warning getting back to Cessie.'

'Shall I come with you in your car?'

'Yes, I'll show you the way and then next time you'll be able to drive yourself there.'

Kwame wound his way patiently through the rush hour traffic the mile or so to the hairdressing salon. 'The road should be quieter when I drop you back at the campus later,' he said reassuringly. When they reached the salon a few customers were still under dryers or settling their accounts. Kwame asked for Madam Akomwa and Auntie Rose came bustling out from an office at the rear looking every tiny inch as though she owned the place. She greeted Kwame warmly and thanked him for recommending the salon to a new customer. Then she shook Sonya's hand and asked them both to follow her to the lounge on the first floor.

They were invited to be seated and take tea and cakes. Then to Kwame's surprise they were joined by Jack Preece. 'I'm here to assure Dr Carpenter that anything we discuss has the blessing of the authorities and will not involve anyone in illegal activities,' he said. Jack showed Sonya his elaborate official credentials. Kwame asked why he had never been shown them before and Jack joked that he only used them to impress the ladies.

Sonya refused a third cake on the grounds of watching her waistline, then watched enviously as Auntie Rose finished the plate. 'How do you stay so petite?' she asked.

'Oh, we Akomwas never grow bigger, do we Kwame?'

'No, Auntie Rose has a niece in Tema who is just as small,' Kwame confirmed.

'If I ate any more I would never be able to get into my new Ghanaian dresses and that would be a disaster,' Sonya said.

'Yes, let's talk about dresses from Kumasi,' said Auntie Rose.

'As I understand it,' Sonya said, 'when Cecilia comes seeking my advice you want me to direct her to you, Madam Akomwa?'

Auntie Rose explained that she wanted to expand her business to include selling African dresses so she would be interested in being an agent for Cecilia's dresses in Coventry. Cecilia was expected to ask Sonya for her advice and, after due consideration and review of market opportunities, Sonya should suggest that Cecilia appoint Madam Akomwa as her agent. It was felt that finding an agent who was also a Ghanaian would be an added incentive.

'So will my task end once I have made the introduction?' Sonya asked.

'Yes,' Jack said, 'unless Cecilia asks for your help in negotiating the details of a contract or needs any other advice on doing business in the UK. You should drop out once Cecilia stops asking for your help.'

'After I've seen Cessie, should I ring Auntie Rose?'

'Yes, let Auntie Rose know anything she needs to know concerning Cecilia's forthcoming visit.'

Over the next two weeks Kwame enjoyed the quiet life that he liked so much but was so often denied. He was especially glad to have time to support Akosua as she began her GCSE A-level examinations. She was well prepared both by her school and by her own serious revision programme, so she approached this transitional ordeal with confidence. Nevertheless, Kwame knew that his close support and encouragement were both essential and much appreciated, and he did his best to perform this paternal duty in an exemplary manner.

In the office most of Kwame's time was used in supporting Greg's preparations for the repeat of his January course in July. One issue of pressing concern was whether they would again need Dr Carpenter or whether they could rely solely on the local academic who had understudied her role in January. Their colleagues in Kumasi wanted Sonya to come again but Kwame knew Tom was trying to cut costs and save money. When Sonya's two students, Helen and Kevin, called again to show him more data they had collected on labour productivity in Ghana,

Kwame was reminded that it might soon be too late to secure their tutor's services.

After the two business students had gone Kwame noticed that they had left a folded sheet of paper on his desk. He unfolded the paper to read a brief note from Sonya telling him that 'the visitor had called and been directed as instructed'. He wondered when the further visit to Auntie Rose would come.

Since Ophelia had returned to Kumasi, Kwame had noticed that Sandra's attendance had become increasingly erratic, so when he saw her one day in the office he asked how things were at home.

'Oh, the twins are teething and rather troublesome these days,' she said. 'I'm sorry to be out so much and I'll try to make up the time later.'

'Well, at least *one* of my assistants won't be wanting to go to Ghana this time.'

'No, not this time, but keep me on the list for the future.'

'How's Nelson, have you seen him lately?'

'Not lately, but we keep in touch. He's trying to keep out of trouble and get remission for good behaviour.'

'Is he succeeding?'

'It's difficult. He says the drug addicts in prison expect him to be able to keep them supplied and can be very rough when he says he can't meet their needs.'

'Don't the other West Africans help to protect him?'

'Some of them do, those that aren't addicts.'

Kwame told Sandra not to worry about not keeping up with her work schedule. 'Why not do more work at home?' he asked her. 'Prof has just taken delivery of some new laptop computers. Ask him for one; then you can finish the report on Ophelia's visit between picking up the dropped dummies!'

'Thank you Kwame; that will help a lot.'

Tom called Kwame to his office saying that he wanted to discuss his future activities. 'I've persuaded the board to give you a one-year extension of contract to work on our partnership project based in Kumasi,' he said. 'I'm afraid the salary will be reduced to reflect the lower cost of living.'

'That's wonderful news. Will we be able to build the diesel engine?'

'We can only afford a small amount to fund the purchase of a few parts and materials in the UK. Can you persuade your people to do the work as a private venture?'

'It might be possible; maybe the TCC could help. I'll give it a try.'

'We would expect you to run two more short courses.'

'Of course, and I assume Mick, Greg and Sandra will be available to help?'

'We will send one or two people as you need them. You will also be responsible for sending us drug-free non-absconding academics for training and work experience here at Warwick.'

'You have my personal guarantee.'

Tom had another important matter on his mind. 'Kwame, I'd like to have your opinion on who you would choose to be your successor here,' he said. 'Of course we must go through the formal stages of recruitment and this chat is off the record, but it would help me to have your assessment in mind when attending the appointments committee.'

'It's a difficult choice. All three have their strong points, but overall I would say that Mick is the most mature and the most innovative.'

'Yet he was the only one not to put himself forward last time.'

'Perhaps he's also the most unassuming. He told me that he didn't feel he was sufficiently experienced at the time I was appointed.'

'Then he also has good judgement.'

'I'd like Mick's help with the diesel engine.'

'If he comes to Kumasi for one of the training courses I'll try to let him stay on for a month or two.'

'That will be a big help.'

Kwame had not known how to raise the matter of Afriyie with Tom and so he was relieved when Tom broached the subject first.

'I think we've been avoiding talking about Afriyie,' Tom said. 'Is she planning to go to Ghana with you or stay here?'

'You've been seeing more of her than I have since I came back from my last trip.'

'Yes, she's been a big help with Little Tom and Dad. I'm grateful to you both and to Elsie.'

'It seems to me both Afriyie and Elsie would prefer to stay with you here.'

'That's also my impression,' Tom said.

'How would that suit you?'

'It would suit me very well.'

'Then will you tell her?'

'Yes, I will.'

Tom was also interested in the future of Akosua and Takoradi. 'You told me that Akosua may go to university in England,' he said. 'Is that still on?'

'If she passes her exams.'

'I don't think there's much doubt about that.'

'I hope not.'

'She wants to study medicine, doesn't she?'

'That's right.'

'Has she applied to the medical school here at Warwick?'

'Yes, she has, and about a dozen other places.'

'Why not let her come here, and then she can move into my place with Takoradi during term time and come to you in Kumasi during her vacations.'

'That sounds like an excellent scheme; thank you Tom. I'll put it to Akosua as soon as she finishes her exams.'

Kwame marvelled at his friend's generosity. 'Won't even your big house be bursting at the seams,' he said, 'with your mum and dad, Afriyie and Elsie, Little Tom, Akosua and Takoradi?'

'Oh Dad's much better. It's a miracle, or he's much tougher than he looks. He and Mum will be going home soon.'

'I'm very happy for you Tom, that's really good news.'

'And you're going home to Comfort.'

'Back to my first love. You know my dad knew Comfort?'

'The little man with broken legs and the courage to think for himself?'

'The one and only!'

Kwame left Tom's office and was surprised to find Sonya Carpenter talking to Alice. 'Don't go, Kwame,' she said. 'I want you involved in this,' and she dragged him back into Tom's inner sanctum.

'Ah, Dr Carpenter, what a pleasant surprise,' Tom said. 'What can I do for you?'

'Greg's just told me I won't be needed for the repeat of his course; I'm very disappointed.'

'What's the situation, Kwame?' Tom asked.

'Well, our friends in Kumasi want Sonya to help them again, but Greg and I were concerned about the cost.'

'Apart from the cost, would you and Greg like Dr Carpenter's help?'

'Most definitely.'

'Then let's send her just once more. It looks as though I'll be saving on your salary for a few months while we're recruiting a replacement.'

Kwame left Tom's office for a second time, and this time Sonya followed him back to his own office. 'Thank you for inviting me to come to Kumasi again,' she said.

'It was Prof Arthur's decision, he controls the money.'

'Yes, but you and Greg were also in favour.'

'Comfort will be happy to see you.'

'I can't wait to go shopping with her again.'

'But you can now buy the dresses here, can't you?'

'Not just yet, soon maybe.'

'How did you find Cecilia?'

'As beautiful as ever.'

'And you advised her to go to see Auntie Rose?'

'Yes, she insisted that her agent should be from Ghana.'

Kwame thought that one day he would hear what passed between Cecilia and Auntie Rose but he had no idea when that might be. So it came as a surprise to return home one evening and find Auntie Rose in conversation with Akosua.

'Auntie Rose has come to wish me luck with my examinations, Dad,' Akosua announced, as soon as she saw her father.

'That was very thoughtful of her,' said Kwame, adding his thanks to the little lady who was perched on the edge of a dining chair beside the robust teenager, with revision materials covering the table top before them.

Akosua collected her books and papers together and cleared the table for dinner. 'I've asked Auntie Rose to join us,' she said to Kwame. 'Elsie has brought our food and there's plenty for all of us.'

'Remember I've only a small appetite,' said Auntie Rose, grinning at Kwame.

They sat at table talking of school, examinations and future careers until the meal was over. Then Akosua announced that it was time for Takoradi's evening walk; the old dog was waiting in the garden. 'Will you come with us?' she asked Auntie Rose.

'Oh, you walk much too fast for me,' Auntie Rose said, 'and I've something to discuss with your dad.'

As soon as they were alone Kwame asked if Auntie Rose had met Cecilia.

'Oh yes, she got in touch shortly after her meeting with Dr Carpenter.'

'Did she ask you to sell her dresses here in Coventry?'

'She did, but there was a sinister condition attached.'

Auntie Rose then told Kwame that she and Jack Preece had both puzzled over one aspect of the trading partnership. If it was intended to conceal cocaine in the coat hangers, how were the traffickers going to collect the drugs? Kwame said that he had also wondered about that issue. 'Well, now we know,' Auntie Rose announced. 'The evil content is to be removed by Daddy before the goods are offered for sale.'

'Daddy being Pastor Arnold Obeng-Mensah of the Pentecostal church.'

'Precisely.'

'But why do they need Daddy's attention?'

The little lady beamed at Kwame, 'Cecilia explained everything very carefully. As a successful businesswoman she fears that many people in Kumasi are jealous of her wealth. She's afraid that there is a high risk of her products being cursed by her enemies and containing evil spirits. In Ghana her customers each have their own protection because everyone is aware of the danger and makes appropriate arrangements through their spiritual affiliations. In England the customers will be defenceless, so it is essential that the goods be cleansed of their evil influences before they are put on sale. Who could be better qualified to perform such an exorcism than a pastor of the Pentecostal church, the first Christian church in Ghana to offer such services?'

Kwame was impressed by this ingenious device. 'So that is why Cecilia wanted a Ghanaian agent for her dresses! She needed someone from the same cultural background to understand why the goods would need the attentions of a priest before being released onto the market.'

'Yes, it's a clever plan. Each consignment will be sent to Pastor Obeng-Mensah and he will pass them on to me to hang on the display racks in my store.'

Kwame thought that Leon would be very happy with this arrangement. 'Will the plan be to arrest the pastor with the drugs in his possession?' he asked.

'Even better than that, Cecilia will have a sample consignment sent before she goes back; there's a chance of catching them both.'

Akosua came back with Takoradi. 'You should have come with us Auntie Rose, it was a lovely evening.' Then they all noticed that the old dog had switched to his professional sniffing mode and Auntie Rose was the focus of his attention. He sat upright on his haunches beside her chair.

Kwame realised what had happened. 'Is your dress a new one from Cecilia?' he asked.

'Yes, do you like it?'

'It suits you very well,' said Akosua.

'Takoradi likes it too much,' said Kwame.

'Oh dear!' said Auntie Rose. 'Does that mean it's contaminated?'

'I'm afraid so,' said Kwame. 'I've not known Takoradi to make a mistake yet.'

Kwame's first thought was that the scent of drugs on the dress might have come from its hanger. There might have been a leak. Then he realised that it could easily have come from handling by Cecilia if she had brought drugs from Ghana in any form. He advised Auntie Rose to launder the dress before wearing it again. They would ask Takoradi to check that it wouldn't cause any embarrassment at airports. Auntie Rose said she thought the old dog's signal could only be taken as a suspicion, but she would mention it in her next report to Leon.

After Auntie Rose had left, Akosua wished her father goodnight and retired to her room. Kwame was left with Takoradi who was already curled up for the night in his basket. Feeling rather lonely, Kwame settled down for half an hour to read before bed.

Since helping Akosua with her English literature homework Kwame had developed an interest in English poetry, and he sometimes dabbled in trying a translation into Twi. He liked to find parallels with Asante proverbs. As he reached for a compendium of the works of Alfred Lord Tennyson he reflected ruefully on his failure to transpose "but the jingling of the guinea helps the hurt that Honour feels". The only jingling he could think of was the seductive sound of the talking beads worn around the waist next to the skin by Ghanaian women and girls. Could this jingling also help the hurt that honour feels?

The unexpected sound of a key in the front door lock, followed by the click of the hall light switch brought Kwame sharply back to the here and now. It could only be Afriyie, so he was prepared an instant before she appeared. She came in and sat facing him with, 'Oh good, I was hoping to catch you after Akosua had gone to bed.'

'Shall I make some hot chocolate?'

'Let me do it; I'll be quicker.'

Afriyie was soon back with steaming mugs and a plate of biscuits.

'This is just like old times,' Kwame said. 'Have you grown tired of Tom's place?'

'No, I like it there.'

'Do you want to stay there?'

'Tom says you want to go back to Ghana and stay with Comfort.'

'Did he also tell you he wanted you to stay with him?'

'Yes he did.'

They sat for a while in silence. He reached out and took her hand. 'I want to thank you for standing by me in good times and bad,' he said. 'I will always be grateful for what you have done for me and Akosua and I want us always to be friends. We are each returning to our first love but that does not mean that there cannot be a bond between us.'

She finished her drink, gave him a gentle kiss on the cheek, and without another word let herself out the way she had come. 'Then it's all settled,' Kwame said softly, but Takoradi did not respond.

26

Freedom Spurned

When Kwame told Comfort that they were free to resume their life together she decided immediately to fly to England to help Kwame and Akosua prepare for their transitions. Kwame was pleased that he would have help not only in winding up his own affairs but in preparing his daughter for life at university. Akosua was delighted that she would have her mother with her throughout that dreadful period of waiting between the end of the examinations and the publication of the results. Fortunately the exams had gone well and she could face the future with quiet confidence.

Kwame told Akosua of Tom's offer to provide her with a home if she chose to study at Warwick. 'It's very kind of Uncle Tom,' Akosua said, 'but I want to be a doctor in Ghana. I've been thinking that the best place to study would be at one of the London colleges. Then I could go on to post-graduate studies at the London School of Hygiene and Tropical Medicine. I'll do part of my clinical training at Korle Bu Hospital in Accra.'

Thinking of the traumatic end of Akos Mary, Kwame was glad that Akosua had not mentioned Komfo Anokye Hospital in Kumasi. He hoped that there would be many years of steady improvement to the hospital before Akosua, as a UK-trained doctor, might have to face practice in the domain of the fetish high priest of Ashanti. Then he remembered his forty years and his youth slipping away. The young liked to face a challenge; perhaps Akosua wanted to be a doctor in Ghana to tackle just such apparently intractable situations. 'I'm sure Uncle Tom will understand if you choose to go to London for your training,' he told his anxious daughter, 'but don't dismiss his offer out of hand, it would still be good to do your basic training at Warwick.'

Kwame asked Akosua if she wanted to come to Ghana with her parents for what would remain of the long vacation. She replied that, although that was what she would like to do, it would depend on how far advanced she was in arranging for her new life. If she was going to stay with Uncle Tom it was likely that she could come to Ghana for a few weeks. On the other hand, if she was searching for accommodation in London she might need to stay behind in England. Kwame pointed out that he would be giving up his rented house when he left for Ghana, and if Akosua stayed on she would need to move to Tom's house for at least the remainder of the vacation.

Akosua was concerned about the future of Takoradi. 'I want him with me wherever I am,' she told her father.

'He will present a problem if you're looking for a place to stay in London,' Kwame said. 'Most landlords will not want dogs in their houses, especially big dogs.'

'Oh dear, maybe I should accept Uncle Tom's offer and study at Warwick after all. I can still take a post-graduate degree at LSHTM.'

'You can defer your decision until the results are out, but Takoradi should move to Uncle Tom's when we leave this house.'

They next turned to discussing what to do with the furniture and personal possessions that had accumulated in the house they rented from the university. 'First,' Kwame said, 'I think Afriyie should take anything she needs to Uncle Tom's. You should do the same with your things, Akosua. You can move them on to your new place if and when needed.'

'Uncle Tom's place is fully furnished, there's little room for anything else.'

'Afriyie will decide if she wants to replace a few of Tom's things with her own stuff.'

'What about my things?'

'If you don't need them at Tom's you can store them until you need them somewhere else.'

'And the rest of the stuff that nobody wants?'

'That must be sold, donated to charity or scrapped.'

Kwame had been concerned about the complexity of his move back to Ghana but with Comfort's help, and after this discussion with Akosua, he felt more relaxed. Now everyone seemed to be satisfied with what lay ahead and agreed on what needed to be done. Only Elsie had not been consulted and Kwame assumed that she would be content to stay with Afriyie. Since the trauma of her abduction and beating the young lady had settled back into a routine life with her aunt, helping with the sewing business and with the care of Little Tom. It seemed that both her physical and mental scars had healed and Elsie was likely to stay with Afriyie and Tom until in the course of time she made for herself an independent life.

Kwame was sitting in his office with Greg and Sonya, making last-minute adjustments to the forthcoming training course in Kumasi, when his telephone rang.

'I've a lady with me who would like to meet you,' said Tom. 'She's from the Volunteer Service Overseas and would like to get your perspective on volunteers you worked with in Ghana.'

'I'll be free in about fifteen minutes,' Kwame replied.

'That's fine; I'll bring her over when we've finished here.'

Sonya had dashed back to the business school for another appointment and Kwame was winding up with Greg when Tom came in. He was accompanied by one of those slim, dark-suited, professional ladies who are forever thirty-two. 'This is Mrs Lockington-Smythe of VSO,' Tom said, 'and this is Kwame Mainu from Ghana and Greg Anderson.'

'From Australia,' added Greg.

After ritual handshakes and greetings, Greg excused himself and slipped away. 'Mrs Lockington-Smythe is interested to hear your impression of the volunteers you worked with at TCC and GRID,' Tom said.

'Yes,' said the visitor, 'we get routine reports from headmasters and project managers but we want to learn more from Ghanaian colleagues. We heard that Warwick had a partnership programme with Kumasi so we thought that Professor Arthur could find us a suitable contact. I understand that I'm lucky to catch you just before you go back to Ghana.'

'I'm just finishing a three-year contract here at Warwick,' Kwame replied, 'but I'm glad you caught me and I'm happy to help in any way I can. I must say straight away that our projects in Ghana have benefited greatly from VSO involvement.'

'Then I'll leave you to go into details,' Tom said, with a parting handshake for the visitor.

Kwame invited his guest to be seated and left his desk to take the other easy chair. 'Now, how far back do you want to go?' he asked.

'When did you join the TCC?'

'August 1980, just as we opened the Suame ITTU in Kumasi.'

'Did you have any VSOs at that time?'

'Only one, a mature lady who helped the director with publications. We had German, American and Canadian volunteers but only one British VSO.'

'Did you hear of any VSOs who served in the 1970s?'

'I heard of two, both engineers. One left after only a few months but the other did good work in preparing for the ITTUs.'

'Do you know why one of them left?'

'He was reputed to have said that he didn't come to Africa to work in a factory!'

'Did he expect his service to be one long safari?'

'Possibly.'

Mrs Lockington-Smythe excused herself for a pause while she jotted down a few notes. 'And after 1980, were there more?' she asked.

'I remember two who worked on our minimum tillage farm, one following on from the other.'

'How did they perform?'

'They worked very hard. The farm workers told us that the white men were not afraid to hoe and weed and join in the physical work. They were popular with their local colleagues.'

'How were the volunteers you met at GRID?'

'We had four and they were all very good.'

'What did they do?'

'I worked mostly with Jonathan Wilkinson, a highly skilled technician engineer.'

'And the others?'

'One established our publicity and public relations section, one set up a team to produce video films and one trained the secretaries and installed the office records system.'

'Those were all essential services.'

'Yes, and they all succeeded, thanks to VSO.'

There was another pause for note taking and Kwame waited patiently for the questions to resume. The lady couldn't fully suppress a smile as she asked Kwame if that was all he could tell her. 'You worked closely with one VSO in Tamale, didn't you?'

'Yes, Sally Green, she came to start a project in Yendi, but the tribal war forced her to spend much of her time with us in Tamale.'

The mention of Sally took Kwame back to their last tearful parting at Gatwick airport in June 1984. It brought back painful feelings of guilt for having used Sally as a possible means of escaping from Ghana to the gold-paved streets of *aborokyiri*. He had turned his back on her when he had found another way to pursue his ambition. It had been a folly of youth and a much regretted episode in his long struggle to leave his homeland. He wondered what had happened to Sally over the past thirteen years. Was she married? Did she have children? Did she remember him?

Kwame had become wrapped in his thoughts and only slowly became aware that his interrogator had ceased writing and was gazing at him intently with grey-blue eyes. She seemed to sense his discomfort and said quietly, 'Have I changed so much?'

A surge of shame flooded through Kwame's whole being. It was some time before he could reply. She waited patiently, with a look of sympathy combined with mild amusement as he struggled to control his feelings. 'Oh, I'm really sorry, I didn't recognise you! It's been so long. You've changed a lot,' he stammered.

'You've hardly changed at all.'

'You're still with VSO?'

'In a desk job, UK based.'

The lady took a deep breath and seemed to make an effort to control her own emotions. Were the memories of her time in Ghana so painful? With a different name, Kwame assumed that Sally was now married. Was she happy, did she have a family? He realised that these were questions to which he might never know the answers. It was Sally who was still asking the questions. 'Would you say that Sally Green did useful work in Ghana?'

'She was given a very tough assignment which she tackled with courage and determination. She probably accomplished all that could have been done in that situation.'

'I'm glad to hear it – for myself, as well as for VSO.'

'Will you be sending more VSOs to Ghana?'

'I'm not responsible for operations, only evaluations, but I believe we intend to attach one or two volunteers to Kumasi University to work with Professor Arthur's project.'

'Then I look forward to meeting them.'

Mrs Lockington-Smythe abruptly signalled the end of the interview by standing up and smoothing down the front of her jacket and skirt. 'Thank you, Mr Mainu,' she said, 'it was good of you to spare so much of your valuable time.'

Kwame struggled to say something to delay her departure but every sentence he composed seemed clumsy or naive. The lady turned to the door and was swiftly through it and away.

Kwame rushed to the door, 'Sally!' he cried, but she strode on without a backward glance, as he had done thirteen years earlier.

He sat for a long time, head in hands, deep in thought. Why hadn't he recognised Sally? Perhaps the first reason was a change in her hair. In Ghana it had been pale blonde; today she had light-brown hair. In Ghana she had an unkempt look; today she wore her hair permanently waved. In Ghana her skin was very pale; today it was concealed under a layer of make-up. Then she was thirteen years older and had risen in VSO to a senior position requiring the projection of a mature and responsible image. She had appeared at short notice and said nothing to reveal her identity. She even gave a completely different name, presumably her married surname. If she had planned to deceive she had succeeded.

The interview had taken him through a brief re-run of his career at the TCC and GRID from 1980 to 1992. It had provided an Ashanti road ride of emotions from pride in success to pain of failure. Above all, it had brought back feelings of remorse over his treatment of Sally. Such past mistakes cannot be undone, he reflected miserably, the future can be faced without pain only in the firm resolve never to repeat them. With such self-counsel Kwame slowly recovered his balance of mind and the power to look forward to life with his restored family.

A few days later, Kwame and Akosua drove to Heathrow to meet Comfort. It was a happy reunion of their nuclear family. They were all in high spirits on the drive back to Coventry. 'We are going to be very busy over the next few weeks,' Kwame said.

'That's why I came,' Comfort replied. 'I'm sure that with us all working together we can get everything ready.'

Akosua grinned and held her mother's hand even more tightly.

Later in the day they went through their plans once again. 'I know you have to go to Kumasi in July for your training course at the university, Kwame,' Comfort said, 'but don't you think I'd better stay on until Akosua has her results? Then I can help her make her next move before coming back to Ghana.'

'Oh yes, Mummy, that would be lovely,' said Akosua enthusiastically, and Kwame had to agree that this was an improvement on his original plan.

That evening they all accompanied Takoradi on his daily excursion. 'I've spent quite a lot of time in England,' Comfort reflected, 'but it still strikes me as strange for the sun to be shining at 9 pm.'

'At least it's still warm,' Akosua replied. 'In winter we come home from school in the dark and it's very cold.'

'It's only Takoradi who seems not to notice the difference,' added Kwame.

On their return they decided to call at Tom's house so that Comfort could greet her other friends. They were warmly welcomed and invited to share appropriate nightcaps. Kwame was relieved to find that there seemed to be no trace of tension between Comfort and Afriyie; their long-term friendship seemed to carry them above changing relationships. It created a bond which, Kwame remembered, could only be threatened by attachment to houses. He was thankful that each now had the house of her heart's desire.

Kwame was aware that Tom was doing his best to appear as detached as the ladies but he suspected that in the case of the Englishman it was an exercise in stiff upper lip. There were still signs that Tom had not yet recovered from the loss of Akos Mary, and Kwame wondered whether whatever Tom promised Afriyie was more in the future than in the present.

Elsie had not met Comfort until the previous year when she had come back with Tom. Now she seemed rather subdued. Kwame suspected that she regretted the coming reduction in her small circle of Twi speakers. The young woman had gained a few useful phrases but in spite of all their efforts she was still far from fluent in English. Kwame also remembered how Elsie had turned to him to re-establish contact after her absconding. Maybe she regretted losing a trusted intermediary with her aunt.

They had now stayed up later than the June sun and thoughts turned to home and bed. Takoradi was already slumbering in his favourite corner of Tom's lounge so Akosua decided to leave him undisturbed. They walked the few hundred metres hand-in-hand in the dark and Kwame wondered why life couldn't always be like this.

Later, Kwame lay beside a sleeping Comfort and set himself to counting his blessings. He had plenty to count. He recalled how nine years ago in Konongo Comfort had rejected him because of his poverty, lack of ambition for his family and divided loyalties. Now his situation was transformed. He wasn't rich but he had enough to maintain his nuclear family in comfort for the rest of their lives and to make a substantial contribution to the welfare of his extended family. His ambition was now to care for his family in their homeland while continuing his professional career in service to the local community. This future ensured that his loyalties were indivisibly focused on his own people. No longer could Comfort taunt him with, 'Who are your people, *oboroni?*' A mutual respect had grown up between them which on Kwame's side had never faltered, but which he now believed would sustain them to the end.

With the diesel engine development, the continuing partnership with Warwick and the revival of AT Ghana activity, Kwame looked forward to an exciting new phase of his professional career. Life with Comfort in her Garden City home would be beyond his sweetest dreams. With Akosua joining them for five months of the year, and anticipated visits from Tom, Afriyie and other Warwick friends and colleagues, he expected to maintain a rich family and international social life. He would encourage Akosua to bring friends on vacation visits and Tom had promised to bring Mrs Chichester, Kwame's long-term landlady.

One class of frequent visitor was inevitable. His mother and all his extended family members from Wenchi would make the pilgrimage to Nhyiasu in their quest for a cure for all their ills. Kwame planned to build a house for his mother in Wenchi, and with Comfort's help he would establish his half-sister Adjoa's shoe trading on a sounder and larger scale. Beyond that he was faced with a dilemma. Would it be better to provide various cousins, nephews and nieces with taxis and tipper trucks, which might stem the flow for a few years, or accept the endless queue of supplicants on a piecemeal basis from the outset? The latter course might save money at the expense of loss of leisure time.

He must consult Comfort on this one. He would be guided by how Comfort handled her own distant relatives, although he realised that they were far fewer in number. Kwame's mother, Amma, in her lifelong search for the perfect husband, had established numerous genetic routes to his exchequer. Even in the days of his modest success in Suame Magazine he had felt that half of the people of Brong-Ahafo Region had a claim on him. Now, returning with the spoils of *aborokyiri* he was sure he would become acquainted with the other half.

Kwame was confident that Akosua would pass her university entrance examinations. He hoped that she would choose to study at Warwick and live with Tom and Afriyie. He was proud of his daughter's progress. She had succeeded in excelling at a good secondary school in England in spite of having had what the headmistress of her Kumasi school described as an "unstable education" in earlier years. Kwame hoped that he had contributed to Akosua's education and personal development by supporting her through long years as a lone parent, just as he had been supported by his father. Akosua had inherited her progenitors' capacity for hard work and he expected that after three or four years at Warwick she would be ready to move on to complete her professional training in London and Accra.

When he had left Ghana three years before, fearing for the safety of his family, Kwame had not expected to return this soon. The danger to him personally had diminished greatly as a result of the deaths of Uncle George and Mama Kate and the break-up of the Ghanaian part of the Kumasi-based drugs cartel. The political climate of his micro-world had improved even if there had been no change in the political leadership of Ghana. The military dictator turned democratic president, Jerry Rawlings, remained in power with a legitimate term extending forward another two years.

Presidential and parliamentary elections were scheduled for late 1999 and Kwame shared the hopes of many Ghanaians that Rawlings would honour his constitution and stand down, having served two terms as elected president. In the best possible scenario the party of Kwame's father's hero, Kofi Busia, might be returned to power. The Rawlings administration had been associated with extensive corruption, including involvement in the international drugs trade. There was little hope of improved international cooperation in the war against the drugs barons as long as the present administration remained in power.

The new millennium offered hope of a new start in national governance which could include a radical change in attitude towards drugs trading. Kwame expected that a reformed administration would present an opportunity for negotiating an international treaty between Ghana and the UK in line with Leon's ideas. While he supported such a move in principle, Kwame had no interest in any direct involvement, and had made it clear to Leon that his aim was total retirement from the service. He had no intention of remaining a sleeping agent, or serving in any other reserve capacity.

Kwame had many blessings to count and his outlook appeared rosier than at any time in the past. Wherever his mind turned he could discern only one dark menace: Peter Sarpong.

After Peter Sarpong's early release from prison and repatriation to Ghana, Kwame had hoped that finding no compatriots left in the Kumasi cartel Peter would settle for a quiet life in retirement as Bra Yaw and Kofi Boateng had done. He had hoped that, like Kofi Adjare, Peter would have no interest in working with the camel herders. Much to Kwame's horror, Peter seemed intent on reviving the old cartel and rebuilding the Ghanaian involvement in the courier and distributive functions. He showed no aversion to continuing to work with the Hanabis directors. Even more sinister was Peter's lust for revenge as visited upon Akos Mary for her involvement in his conviction and imprisonment. By this action Peter had shown himself to be a real and present danger.

Kwame suspected that he and his family might be in danger of violent retribution if Peter ever became aware of Kwame's own involvement in Peter's detection and arrest, or the imprisonment and death of Peter's Uncle George. While Kwame's future prospects of a comfortable and fulfilling life in Ghana looked safe in almost every way, he knew that his mind could never be fully at rest as long as Peter Sarpong remained at liberty.

When the call came from Jack Preece, Kwame sensed a note of frustration in his voice. 'Leon needs you here, can you come?'

On arrival at the police station Kwame was informed that Cecilia Obeng-Mensah and her father had been arrested. Leon told Kwame that he thought it might help if part of the interrogations were in Twi. Cecilia's father, Pastor Arnold Obeng-Mensah, might be pretending that his English was limited, but a Twi interpreter could call his bluff.

Kwame was reluctant to expose himself in any way. He reminded Leon that he had been assured long ago that the drugs cartel would not know of his involvement in the investigations. 'We've thought of that,' said Leon. 'Tam here will do the direct questioning but you can view the interrogation from behind the one-way glass. Hopefully you might catch a chance remark that Tam missed or be able to suggest a better way to pose a question. Also your knowledge of the background might help you make useful suggestions.'

Kwame sensed that he wasn't being told the whole story. 'What's the real problem?' he asked.

'We've seized a consignment of dresses from Kumasi.'

'Have you looked at the coat hangers?'

'That's the problem.'

'What problem?'

'We've opened them all, but found no cocaine.'

Now Kwame understood the urgency of the situation. Without hard evidence of an offence the police would soon be forced to release the detainees. 'Where are the dresses now?' he asked.

'We brought them here to the station,' Jack replied.

'Have you checked them with a sniffer dog?'

'No.'

'Then I suggest you do so straight away.'

Leon left to summon canine assistance, and Kwame reminded his remaining collaborators how Takoradi had signalled a problem with a dress worn by Auntie Rose. The little lady had told him that she would report the incident.

'Yes, she did report it,' said Jack, 'but we put it down to possible leakage from a coat hanger or an accidental spill in handling the drug.'

Leon came back with a dog handler and a large bundle of dresses. The hangers had been removed for testing elsewhere. 'Can you ask your companion to conduct the test in front of these gentlemen?' he said. He took one dress from the heap and draped it over the back of a chair and the police sergeant drew it to the attention of his large Alsatian bitch.

Kwame recognised the instant reaction as the same as Takoradi's.

'She's indicating a banned substance,' said the dog handler. Leon had several other dresses tested and they all provoked a positive reaction.

'Thank you, Sergeant,' said Leon. 'Please give your lady friend an extra biscuit with her lunch.'

The mention of a dog biscuit seemed to remind Leon of his habitual hospitality. 'Let's all have some coffee and biscuits while we digest what we have just learned,' he said. They moved to a more comfortable room where the refreshments were waiting but they failed to lapse into social chatter.

'Do we have enough to have them remanded in custody as traffickers?' Tam asked.

'I would prefer to have evidence of how they intended to recover the cocaine for sale,' Leon replied.

'There was a large bowl of water on the kitchen table,' said Jack. 'Look, we even photographed it. Were they intending to soak the dresses?'

'That's not all,' said Kwame, perusing the photographs, 'there's a large saucepan on the stove. It looks as though they had already done some soaking and were about to boil off the water and recover the cocaine. Were any damp dresses found hanging in an airing cupboard or on a line in the garden?'

'You've missed your vocation, Kwame,' Leon said. 'We must return to the pastor's house and make a more thorough inspection.'

The house was still cordoned off by the police and they entered with an officer from the forensic branch. They briefly explained that they were looking for evidence of attempts to recover cocaine from dresses that might have been impregnated with it in aqueous solution. Samples of liquid from the bowl on the kitchen table and the saucepan on the stove were taken away for analysis. Some damp dresses were found hanging in an upstairs airing cupboard. The Obeng-Mensahs must have been busy extracting their contraband when the raid took place.

On the way back to the police station Kwame wondered aloud about the purpose of the hollow coat hangers. Were they a sort of decoy or had they been abandoned through suspicion that their purpose had been detected? Had Kwame and Tam raised suspicion by their actions in Kumasi in search of the location of the SRS machine?

388

'Even if you did raise suspicion I wouldn't worry,' Leon said. 'The result was a considerable reduction in the quantity of drugs shipped, and we have it all anyway.'

On arrival they found Auntie Rose waiting for them. 'You'd better let us have your new dress for thorough decontamination,' Leon said. 'Now we know it was probably intentionally impregnated, normal washing may not remove it all.'

The interrogation of the Obeng-Mensahs, father and daughter, was now reduced to a formality. The pair had been caught red-handed in the process of recovering their illicit merchandise from the fabric of legitimate commerce. For a while Cecilia tried to maintain that the goods needed washing and ironing to remove soiling and creasing caused by packaging and transport. She said that the trace of cocaine might have come from contact with other goods in transit.

Cecilia's story wavered when she was asked why they had not used her father's washing machine. Was it because it would have sent the cocaine down the drain? Her story broke down completely when chemical analysis revealed the strength of the cocaine solution and the considerable quantity that could be recovered from the full consignment. It might not have been nearly as much as could have been stored in the hollow coat hangers, but it was still enough to gain a substantial profit on the operation.

Pastor Obeng-Mensah was found to lack the spirit and intelligence of his daughter. He soon broke down under questioning, begging for forgiveness, and was advised by Leon to save his prayers for the prison chapel. 'He was Cecilia's accomplice,' Leon observed later to his companions, 'that will be taken into account by the court. He'll probably get a lighter sentence than his daughter.'

'Were they both searched?' asked Kwame.

'The police conducted full body searches,' said Jack.

'Then you have Cecilia's waist beads.'

'Yes, and we checked them for cocaine; no luck I'm afraid,' said Leon.

'She's been here several weeks; she will have got rid of any drugs she might have carried through on arrival,' said Auntie Rose.

'What a tragedy that such a beautiful woman should turn to crime,' Jack said.

'Yes,' said Tam, 'and her Lebanese boyfriend will have lost interest long before she is free again.'

'You don't think he might come to England to visit her then?' Leon asked hopefully.

'No chance,' said Kwame.

'Or Peter Sarpong?'

Kwame was surprised to hear Leon mention his long-time adversary and present dread. He remembered reporting Cecilia's relationship with Peter and giving Jack a photocopy of Comfort's letter, but he had not realised that Leon had taken it as a serious issue. 'What about Peter?' he asked.

'Do you think he will come to see Cecilia in prison?'

'I don't think he'll risk coming to the UK.'

'Fortunately, Kwame Mainu, for once in your life, you're wrong!'

'Why do you say that?'

'Because he's already here and we have him in custody!'

Leon's expression showed how much he relished the look of amazement and delight on Kwame's face. 'Let's call it our farewell present,' he said, 'and I'm so glad we're able to give it to you, Kwame. According to your own testimony, the only cartel member remaining in Kumasi who posed any danger to you personally was Peter Sarpong. Well, that danger is removed for a long time. You can retire with honour and go home in peace.'

These sweet words triggered a whirlpool in Kwame's mind that sucked in many questions. With grins all around his companions waited patiently for him to regain his composure.

'Did you pick him up at Pastor Obeng-Mensah's?' Kwame gasped at last.

'Yes,' Leon said. 'We don't think he travelled with Cecilia but he was there in the house when we called.'

'Why do you think he came?'

'He claims Cecilia begged him to come to teach her father how to organise drugs sales in this area.'

'So he's putting the blame on his girlfriend?'

'Love led him astray, as it does so many of us,' said Tam.

Kwame was still amazed that Peter would take such a big risk. 'I suppose he travelled on a false passport,' he said at length.

'Oh yes, we have his travel documents,' said Jack.

'What will he be charged with?'

'Apart from entering the UK on a false passport and breaking an exclusion order, he'll be considered an accomplice in Cecilia's cocaine importation as well as aiding and abetting the pastor's intended career in crime. With his past record, and having been granted an early release, he should be looking at enough years in prison to afford you long-term peace of mind,' said Leon.

Kwame couldn't believe his good fortune. 'Can I see with my own eyes through the one-way glass?' he asked. On a signal from Leon, Jack left the room. When he returned he said that the police were still questioning Peter and they could file in and observe for a few moments. The police interrogators took a short break, leaving a despondent Peter with a desperate-looking solicitor who had been called in at the last minute to safeguard the detainee's legal rights.

As he gazed upon his old friend, adversary and rival, Kwame's joy turned to sadness. This handsome and intelligent young man, born free in a newly independent country, had been helped by the love of a rich uncle to come to study in England. How had he managed to make so many mistakes that he would spend most of his adult life still a captive of Ghana's former colonial masters? Why had he cast away the freedom won for him by his ancestors, spurning their gift and staining their honour?

What was different about their lives that put them on opposite sides of this one-way glass? What had given him, Kwame Mainu, the right to walk a free man back into the sunshine of their homeland? Was it all down to luck?

Or to the love of a good woman and the wisdom of a little man with broken legs and the courage to think for himself?

Glossary

Acronyms

AT Ghana	Appropriate Technology Ghana (an NGO)
ENTESEL	A Tema-based engineering company
ETA	Estimated time of arrival
GAMATCO	A Suame Magazine-based gearwheel manufacturer
GRID	Ghana Regional Industrial Development (project)
KNUST	Kwame Nkrumah University of Science and Technology
LSHTM	London School of Hygiene and Tropical Medicine
NGO	Non-governmental organisation
NPP	New Patriotic Party
TCC	Technology Consultancy Centre (of KNUST)
UNIFEM	United Nations Programme for Women
VSO	British Voluntary Service Overseas

Twi Words and Phrases

Abibini	Black person, African
Aborokyiri	Western World (white people's land)
Abrofo	White People, Europeans (plural of *oboroni*)
Adamfo	Friend (*m'adamfo* my friend)
Akoko	Chicken(s)
Akoko Antwiwaa	*Nyankopon's* senior wife
Akpeteshie	A spirit distilled from palm wine
Akuaba	Fertility doll
Akwaaba	Welcome
Anansesem	Spider stories
Asantehene	King of Ashanti
Dabone	Day of evil (work is forbidden on this day)

Dadaba	Child of wealthy parents (a spoilt child)
Dokono	Kenke (fermented corn dough)
Esono	Elephant
Fufu	Boiled and pounded yam, plantain or cassava
Gari	Grated and roasted cassava
Kakra	Smaller/younger/junior: name given to second born twin
Kenke	Fermented corn dough
Kofi	Male name for a person born on Friday
Kofifo	A plurality of Kofis, name of an Accra boatbuilding company
Kraa	The youngest and most beautiful of *Nyankopon*'s three wives
Kuraseni	Bushman, villager, uneducated person
Me den de Takoradi	My name is Takoradi
Mmebusem	Proverbs
Mmoatia	Imaginary forest creatures: small humans with backward-pointing feet
Nana	Sir/Madam (title of respect)
Nee awo aka suro nsonon	He who the snake has bitten, fears the worm (He who fears the worm – Kofi Adjare's name for Bra Yaw)
Nyankopon	The chief god, the creator
Obanfo	The government
Oboroni	White person, European
Okisi mpow adjwe	The rat doesn't refuse palm nuts
Okomfo	Fetish priest
Okraman ani agyie	The dog is happy
Okyeame	Linguist, chief's spokesman
Osagyefo	Saviour (title given to Kwame Nkrumah)
Osofo	Priest
Osofo Dadzie	Reverent Dadzie (popular TV sitcom in Ghana in 1990s)
Otumfuo	The Powerful One (title of the Asantehene)
Panin	Elder/senior: name given to the first born twin
Pito	A beer made from Guinea corn
Sasabonsam	Imaginary forest monster personifying evil
Sika duro	Money medicine
Sika ne hene	Money is king
Sika ye na	Money is scarce (popular name for a small enterprise)

Takoradi dea, wo ho ye fe	As for you, Takoradi, you're beautiful
Twi	The language of the Akan tribes of Ghana
W'adi mfie sen?	How old are you? (You have eaten how many years?)
Wo dea nso saa ara	You are the same
Wo den de sen?	What is your name?
Wodi esono akyi bosu nkawo	If you walk behind an elephant the dew won't wet you
Ya agya	Yes Sir (polite response to a greeting from a senior male person)
Ya enua	Yes Brother/Sister (polite response to person of equal rank)
Ya eson	Response to greeting that can be used generally
Y'ahyiahyia	We have met (greeting on the road)
Yesu mogya nka w'anim	Let the blood of Jesus splash your face